CINCO BECKNELL

D0468816

CINCO
BECKNELL

A NOVEL

LEE MAYNARD

VANDALIA PRESS

MORGANTOWN 2015

© 2015 WVU Press/Vandalia Press,

an imprint of West Virginia University Press

All rights reserved

Printed in the United States of America

22 21 20 19 18 17 16 15   1 2 3 4 5 6 7 8 9

ISBN:

paper: 978-1-940425-45-0

epub: 978-1-940425-46-7

pdf: 978-1-940425-47-4

Cataloging-in-Publication Data is available

from the Library of Congress.

Cover design by Michel Vrana.

The Display typeface of "Cinco Becknell" is Luis Serra, digitized and distributed by
Homelessfonts. Homelessfonts is an initiative by the Arrels foundation to support,
raise awareness and bring some dignity to the life of homeless people in Barcelona
Spain. Each of the fonts was carefully digitized from the handwriting of different
homeless people who agreed to participate in this initiative. All proceeds will be
donated to the Arrels foundation in support of their mission to provide the homeless
people in Barcelona with a path to independence with accommodations, food, social
and health care.

I love this life, with all of its misery,
with all of its pain.
I lie in bed in my trailer house, suffering,
unable to sleep at night.
At first light showing in the east,
I lie listening to the coyotes howling
and the owls in the canyon hooting,
and I do nothing but listen.
Pretty soon, on the eaves of my house,
little birds begin to sing their morning song,
the waking song.
And in my pain I see all of that in my mind.
I see them half looking at me,
thankful that I have arrived at another day . . .

Pete Catches
Oglala

from *The Book of Elders*
by Sandy Johnson

ACKNOWLEDGMENTS

There are some debts that can never be paid. But attempts can be made. My deepest thanks to . . .

Bill the Painter, who furnished the vodka while I furnished the coffee, at daybreak on the Plaza; **Big Tuna**, whose bulk and strength kept us safe; **Coco Channel**, ("It's '*chann*-el' buster, like on a tee-vee. It's not 'shah-*nell*', just so you get it straight. I ain't that French broad."), she of the incredible hidden beauty—all of them homeless in Santa Fe, all of them now gone from the city, and possibly from life

Virginia Conner, for her wondrous knowledge about the mysteries of the brain, and for her friendship

To the most generous of linguists: **Senora Marcie Sypien & Ms. Valerie Irene Peyton** *and to William Becknell, the one, the only, the original. May he be on yet another journey to Santa Fe.*

Author's Note: In some places in this novel, for effect, I have collapsed time and I have put some things back in their locations of some years ago. To those longtime Santa Feans who notice this, well, damnit, it just seemed like a good idea at the time.

LOS GENERACiONES

1541 · From far to the south, Conquistador Francisco Vasquez de Coronado begins explorations north into unknown territory, part of which will become known as Nuevo Mexico.

1607 · The Spanish found the city of La Ciudad de San Francisco de Assisi de Santa Fe. The city comes to be known simply as "Santa Fe."

1616 · In Europe, two writers die. The passing of the writers is duly noted in Europe, but not in Santa Fe, a place where news penetrates slowly, if at all. It is doubtful that even the most educated Santa Feans will learn of the events for many years; it is doubtful that they will care. One of the writers is Cervantes; the other is Shakespeare.

1620 · Sailing ships arrive on the coast of what is now Massachusetts. Passengers debark. History will call them Pilgrims. They arrive thirteen years after the founding of Santa Fe.

1680 · The various Pueblo Indian tribes combine to drive the Spanish from Nuevo Mexico in what is known as the Pueblo Revolt.

1692 · Don Diego de Vargas begins the reconquest of Nuevo Mexico. Some historians call it the "bloodless reconquest", but before it is over several years have passed and thousand of natives, and hundreds of Spaniards, are dead.

1786 · Spanish authorities hire Pierre Vial, a Frenchman of inexhaustible courage and energy, to blaze trails from their territory of Nuevo Mexico to various American centers of commerce, including St. Louis. He is called "Pedro" Vial by his Spanish employers.

1791 · *The Magic Flute* premiers in Vienna, Austria.

1792 · Pedro Vial forges a trail from Santa Fe to St. Louis. On the way, he and his companions are captured by Kansa Indians and held captive, stark naked, for six weeks. Kept alive by a friendly Indian, and finally rescued by another Frenchman, Vial and party eventually arrive in St. Louis. He has blazed what came to be known as the Santa Fe Trail. In subsequent years, the Spanish make little or no use of Vial's new trail.

1806 · A naïve young American explorer, Zebulon Pike, enters the Spanish territory of Nuevo Mexico. Apparently set up for arrest by his own commanding officer, Pike is duly arrested by the Spanish governor, Facundo Melgares, who is leading a huge expeditionary force outside of his home territory. Some historians believe Melgares and his army actually are looking for American Captains Lewis and Clark. Others argue Melgares assembles such an imposing force to impress the Indians. In any case, Melgares finds Pike instead. Melgares takes Pike to El Paso and Chihuahua. The two men get along very well. Melgares becomes an enormously fat man, and is the last Spanish governor of the territory.

1820 · William Becknell is a 24-year-old salt maker in Franklin, Missouri. He is not very good at his job, or at anything else. He has trouble managing his own affairs, falls into debt and is hounded by creditors. But he is a dreamer.

1820 · Pedro Vial, a tired old man unrecognized for his contributions to the opening of the Southwest, dies. He never heard of William Becknell, and few will ever know that Vial was the man who really created the Santa Fe Trail.

1821 · Nuevo Mexico becomes a protectorate of Mexico.

1821 · In June, William Becknell's creditors are surprised to read an article by Becknell in the *Missouri Intelligencer.* Becknell claims he is *". . . destined to the westward for Horses & Mules; and catching Wild Animals of every description."*

He seeks seventy men to join him in the venture. At an organizational meeting in August, only seventeen men are in attendance to hear of the great westward expedition.

1821 · Mexico wins independence from Spain. The first Mexican governor of the northernmost Republic of Mexico territories is— Facundo Melgares.

1821 · In Franklin, Missouri, on September 1, the appointed day of departure for Becknell's trading expedition, only five men, including Becknell, show up. But Becknell departs anyway. (One thing is certain: Becknell is getting out of town.) He leads a pack train of mules out of Franklin, follows a route that takes him over rugged Raton Pass, and arrives in Santa Fe on November 16. On the way, he is seen and watched by Indians, who, had the concept been

There is no record of anyone ever making such a speech to the Indians of the area.

1880 · A writer named Lew Wallace completes work on a novel, *Ben Hur*, for which he becomes famous. Wallace's other claim to fame is that he is, at the time, governor of the Territory of New Mexico.

1887 · Only 1,091 buffalo are still alive in the entire landmass of Canada and the United States. In 27 years, some 28 million buffalo have been slaughtered, a rate of almost exactly one million per year.

1902 · A man named W. Melgares Becknell, twenty-six years of age, arrives in Santa Fe. He says he was born there on the family ranch. His father died when Melgares was a boy, and he spent the rest of his youth with Indians in the northern plains. He came back to the ranch, he says, "because all the People are dead or dying." Like his father, he raises cattle, but never seems at ease with life in a single place. In 1907 he marries a local woman of Spanish and Indian extraction. They have a son.

1912 · After 64 years as a United States Territory, New Mexico becomes a state.

1916 · Early in the year, Melgares Becknell tells his wife he is going to tiny Columbus, New Mexico, on the Mexican border, to buy some Mexican cattle. He arrives on March 8. That night, the village is raided by Pancho Villa. Seventeen people die, including nine civilians. Melgares Becknell is wounded, but follows the raiders out of town and attacks them in their own camp, killing three of Villa's men before he, himself, is killed. His wife and young son travel to Columbus and bring his body north by wagon. Crossing the Rio Grande River, the wagon upsets and the wooden casket floats away. The body is never recovered.

1930 • The Great Depression smothers America.

1933 • In Santa Fe, Bill Becknell, known as "Wild Bill" to his friends, buys an airplane from a bankrupt neighbor and learns to fly. He takes delight in buzzing his ranch and stampeding the cattle, telling his friends that the cattle need the exercise. He flies the plane into a stand of cottonwoods on his own ranch. Only two things escape the crash with only minor damage—the plane's wooden propeller, and Wild Bill. In 1939 he declares Canadian citizenship, joins the Royal Air Force, and flies fighter planes over France and Germany. He is twice shot down, escaping both times.

1942 • On the high mesas to the west of Santa Fe, the tiny community of Los Alamos becomes home to secretive, nervous men and women who will build the atomic bomb.

1945 • Wild Bill Becknell returns to America. He meets and marries a stunning eighteen-year-old blond named Harriet Preston. He calls her "Harry." For their honeymoon, they travel to Columbus, New Mexico, where Harry finds the exact spot where Bill's father, Melgares, had fallen, firing the last shots from his pistol before he died. She scrapes away the sticks and old evergreen needles and scoops up the rusty earth. She stores it in an old canning jar.

Wild Bill never really settles into ranching. He writes western adventure stories for pulp magazines. Money is tight, and eventually small parcels of the ranch are sold to other ranchers. In 1958, after thirteen years of marriage, Wild Bill and Harry have a son.

1964 · Wild Bill takes Harry and returns to Europe, to show her the very field on which he landed the last time he was shot down. Walking across the field hand in hand, Wild Bill steps on an unexploded bomb. It takes the French three days, using dogs, to find what's left of Bill and Harry. The American couple is buried in France in the same casket. The casket is the size of a shoebox.

1968 · M. Scott Momaday, a Native American, writes *House Made of Dawn*. Richard Bradford, an Anglo, writes *Red Sky at Morning*. Today, both books are still in print.

1983 · In June, a young man named William Becknell V, called "Cinco" by his friends, graduates from the University of New Mexico. Graduating with him are his life-long friends, Wendell Klah, a mostly-Taos Indian; and Alvarez Montoya, a direct descendant of early Spanish explorers. They all graduate with honors. All were born and raised in Santa Fe, went to the same schools, fought over the same girls. Now, they know that something has changed, that the young part of their lives is over, that there are things in front of them they will not understand. For once, they seem quiet, sober, reflective.

They visit Wendell's family in Taos and eat green chile stew while sitting on a low wall at the edge of the pueblo, under a sky full of light like no other place.

They visit the Montoya ranch east of Santa Fe and ride horses that are the direct descendents of those brought by the Spanish. The younger sister of Alvarez, a Spanish beauty even at the age of fifteen, kisses Cinco on the cheek. And then, impulsively, on the mouth. The girl wants to know when Cinco will be back.

"Hard tellin', not knowin'." He smiles at his own joke.

They take a last look at what remains of the Becknell ranch in a canyon that spills into the Rio Grande. The ranch, the birthplace of Cinco and his grandfathers, now whittled down to no more than 50 acres, seems shabby and forlorn. Only *Tio* Cecilio and *Tia* Maria, old in years and old beyond their years, are still on the ranch. They sit on the *portal*, tears in their eyes, asking him not to go.

He kisses them, and they know that he is saying goodbye.

And then they find themselves below the foothills of the Sangre de Cristo Mountains, walking in the distinct ghost-ruts of the Santa Fe Trail.

They camp near a huge rock, another large rock stacked on top, as though put there by a giant. And they talk. And they know things will never be the same.

Out of some sense of history, and things lost, and in the fading light of a long New Mexico day, in a wagon rut they bury symbols of their heritage . . .

Alvarez buries a set of spurs with huge Spanish rowels, spurs that were a gift from one of his grandfathers. The spurs seem to glow as Alvarez gently places them in the earth.

From his bedroll Wendell takes a single arrow and holds it in both hands, his arms reaching toward the sky. In spite of himself, Cinco's breath catches. He has seen such an arrow before, has seen the long, heavy, true shaft with the thin red stripe that runs its length, has seen the fletching—two black feathers and one red, the red stripe ending at the red feather. A blood line, Wendell says. But most of all he remembers the arrowhead, obsidian, black as midnight, sharper than the straight-razor that lies on the shelf at the ranch. No one makes arrowheads anymore, except Wendell, using the natural black glass that Wendell's grandfather brought back from the Northwest decades ago. But won't it break? Cinco had asked. Yes, of course, Wendell said; you only get to use it once. And once must be enough. You will not get a second chance.

And then Cinco, a man of jumbled heritage, who has no single ethnic symbol—and so he buries something of himself, one of the small notebooks in which he constantly scribbles.

They make their beds in the eternal wagon wheel ruts of the Santa Fe Trail, wrapped in heavy blankets, lying quietly, surrounded by the tall grass of the prairie floor. They stare at a sky close enough to touch. No more words come to them; there is no more talking to do.

Once, in the darkest hours, Wendell hears sounds in the night. He lies uneasily in the wheel rut, not sleeping. He sits up, and sees that the others are awake.

"What's going on," Cinco wants to know.

"Nothing a white boy would understand," Wendell says.

"I'm not a white boy," Cinco grunts.

"Hell, you're whiter than either of us," Alvarez says. "You damn near glow in the dark."

The young men laugh. It's a joke they have made often.

"Cinco, go back to sleep. Al and I will make sure nothing happens to you, just like we always do."

But Cinco does not go back to sleep.

The young men get up and draw closer to the fire.

"One day, I'm gonna come back here and write about all this," Cinco mumbles, "and I'll tell the truth about you two. Probably get you arrested."

But no one laughs.

Later, Wendell will say he heard the grunts of horses and the squeak of wheels on wooden axles. Cinco and Alvarez believe him.

1984 · In July, Cinco Becknell, Wendell Klah, and Alvarez Montoya leave Santa Fe together. Some say they joined the military. Others say they became merchant sailors. One woman is sure she saw Cinco tending bar in a hotel in Nepal. But no one knows for sure.

Years pass. The young men are simply gone.

TODAY · A homeless man, who will come to be known on the street as "Stick," steps off a bus in Santa Fe. He has no idea who he is or why he is there.

ONE

He awakened easily, almost softly, his body motionless on the sagging bed.

It was the first day of the third part of his life. But he didn't know that at the time.

His consciousness drifted gently upward from the darkness and he was fully awake before he opened his eyes. He thought he had slept for a long time, but as his mind explored his body he knew there had been nothing restful about the sleep.

He lay there, trying to remember where he was and why, but nothing came. He searched his mind for information, for images, but there was nothing.

He was perfectly calm. And he was totally empty.

He breathed deeply, smelling nothing but the musk of his own night sweat. His mouth was dry and sticky, his tongue almost glued to his teeth, a foul taste in the back of his throat that he seemed to be able to expel through his nose. He eased his eyes open and stared at the ceiling, some sort of cheap cracked fiber tile that showed scattered brown stain marks from random years of leaking roofs. One of the stains moved and he watched a beetle of some unknown species tick its way across the ceiling.

His knees were bent—the cheap bed was too short for his long, skinny frame. He sat up and straightened his legs, working at the

Hawaiian shirt failed to hide a lanky, angular frame—*like sticks in a sack*, he thought.

In the mirror, he stared at his arms. Then the left one only. He raised the arm and dropped his gaze to it. Crude scars, old, ugly, dozens of them, some from wounds torn into the flesh, some of them crude puncture wounds the size of . . . teeth . . . peppered the arm from elbow to wrist. Animal bites? He didn't know.

He lifted the tails of the shirt and realized he could count his ribs. He looked more closely. There were faint scars across his ribs and stomach, ugly streaks long since turned pale with age. He turned, and the scars continued around to his back. He dropped the shirt-tails and briefly closed his eyes, but no images came into his mind. Nothing told him about the scars.

He was not wearing a watch or any other jewelry.

His pants sagged on his slim hips, held there by a simple, worn leather belt that was too large for him. Extra holes had been punched in the belt to take up the slack and he thought maybe he had weighed more at some time. If these were his clothes.

He hitched up his pants and realized he was not wearing underwear. He let his arms dangle at his sides and turned slightly for another angle in the mirror. The view wasn't any better. He looked like an aging bum. He raised his arms and let his forearms dangle from the elbows, swinging slightly. *If there were strings tied to me*, he thought, *I'd be a marionette.*

He turned around. There was no real reason to inspect the room. He knew, somehow, there would be nothing there of interest. He sat in the chair again and looked at the shoes. They were badly worn, the laces broken many times and knotted crudely. He thought he never would have tied the laces like that, but he didn't know why he thought so. He didn't see any socks. He slipped his feet into the shoes, knowing they would fit.

He went back to the door with the mirror, pulled it open, stepped inside the bathroom, the acrid scent of old urine crimping into his nose. He urinated in the permanently stained toilet. He leaned over the cracked sink and splashed water on his face and then into his mouth, trying to rid himself of the taste of whatever had invaded his body, the sour taste of panic. He drank, the water leaving a flat, metallic taste in his mouth. When he straightened up his head spun slightly and he braced himself against the wall until it went away.

Under the sink he noticed a plastic trash can, a wide cut running down one side, the inside stained with damp substances of unknown origin. In the bottom was a piece of rubber tubing. He knew what it was, he thought. Tie it around your arm. Make injection easier. He got dizzy again and braced himself back against the wall. Carefully, in the dull yellow light of the bathroom—a man seeking an answer he didn't really want to get—he inspected the insides of his arms. There were discolorations there, maybe puncture marks, maybe not. He couldn't tell.

He left the bathroom and stood in the center of the room, inspected himself in the mirror again. As he looked he waited for some sort of craving, some anguished message from his body that told him he needed chemical help to keep him upright, keep him going.

There was nothing but hunger, ordinary enormous hunger.

It occurred to him that humans were nothing more than a collection of their memories, their experiences. What a man is, is where he has been, what he has done, what he thinks about it. He had none of those things. He stood quietly, willing some memory, some image, however fleeting, to flash across his mind. Nothing came. He felt an emptiness that was almost total, not the emptiness of hunger, but the emptiness of . . . nothing, as though he were looking into the dark well of his life and could not see the bottom.

"Who the hell are you?" he said to the mirror, flinching at the deep rasping of his own voice.

He turned and stood before the door to the outside, noticing a sign on the wall that said the room could be rented by the hour. He knew the door would be locked. He put his hand on the doorknob. He turned it slowly, carefully . . . and felt the fear twisting again in his gut. He waited, swallowing hard. But nothing came.

The door was not locked. He could leave the room. If he wanted, he could simply leave the room.

They left the heavy door unlocked, knowing he would try the latch, as he did every time he woke. They saw the latch come up slowly. They grabbed the door and pulled it violently outward, spilling him onto the rock-hard dirt outside. They laughed, and dumped him back inside the hut. They locked the door and left, still laughing.

If he grabbed the doorknob he knew the door would fly open, spilling him outside . . .

But this door opened to the inside. How could they whip it open?

He stepped to the side and let the door swing open. He waited for the rough hands, the laughter.

There was no one outside.

He left the door open behind him and stepped out onto a narrow walkway with a waist-high rusted metal railing. The light and the heat crashed into him as though he had run into a wall and he clung to the railing with one hand, the other across his eyes. *The heat. Where the hell had this heat come from?*

A few minutes, and he could see.

A motel, and he was on the second floor. The view was off into some dark hills just beyond a thin brown river. Tiny houses and shacks of every imaginable construction were flung confetti-like along the hills and gullies, a tangle of human jumble that seeped dogs and chickens and kids. He saw no adults. He squinted into the sun, low on the horizon. He didn't know which horizon, didn't know if it were early morning or just before sundown.

A door opened behind him. He spun around, his arms snapping up in front of him, fingers loosely cupped.

A large Hispanic woman stepped out on the walkway beside him, looking at him curiously. She had black, shiny hair, a full mouth and eyes the color of Apache tears. She wore a thin blouse, some sort of a wrap-around skirt and tattered, worn sandals. A large cloth purse hung from her shoulder. Her blouse almost wasn't there and it held her large breasts loosely and openly, her nipples large and dark against the light press of the cloth. He looked, and she let him.

"We ain't boxin', hon. You can put your hands down."

He said nothing, his arms slowly falling to his sides.

"Didn't hear you come in last night, hon," she said, her voice low and silky, like someone used to speaking softly, no trace of Spanish accent. "Usually hear my neighbors. Walls in this place ain't exactly thick, you know?"

His brain spun a little and he gripped the rusty rail.

"Well, hon, looks like you had yourself a real night." She glanced into the room behind him. "Anybody I know?"

He turned to face her. She was not bad looking, just . . . used. "I seem to be alone," he mumbled.

"Well, hon, we can fix that," she said, grinning. Her teeth were perfect. She moved closer.

"Where are we?"

"Hon, you really was in bad shape last night, wasn't you. You're in the Mexi-View Motel and Spa. That's the spa, down there." She pointed off into a far corner of the parking lot to what once had been a hot tub. It was filled with dirt, a large, dying *cholla* cactus leaning in the center, some beer cans scattered at the base.

She nodded across the river. "That's Mexico over there, but I suspect you found that out the hard way."

"Mexico?"

"You just get off the truck? You got a turnip in your pocket? You're in El Paso, hon, *El Pass-oh*, where you can see the worst fucking homes"—she pointed across the river—"and get the best home fucking in the U-S-of-A." She took his hand from the railing, slipped it inside her blouse, guiding his fingers over her breast, holding it firmly there, the soft flesh incredibly warm under his hand, as though there were fire within the woman.

She knew what he was thinking. "A bra? Never wear 'em, hon. No panties, neither. They just get in the way. You got any money? Shame for a nice looking *muchacho* like you to be alone this early in the morning." With her other hand she rubbed his chest. A rustling sound from his shirt pocket. She deftly slipped her fingers in his pocket and fished out a slip of paper. It wasn't money. She tucked the paper back into his pocket. She was still pulling his hand firmly onto her breast.

"I don't think I have any money. I don't think I have anything," he said, knowing it was true.

She reached between his legs and squeezed him gently. "You might be right, hon." She moved her hand slowly, massaging, pulling gently, her fingers constantly exploring. "Well, you ain't got no life in you, that's for sure. You just danglin' there, sort of dead like."

She slid her hand into his pants pocket, sliding it smoothly and quickly to the bottom. The pocket was empty. She reached across him and patted the other pocket.

"Well, hon. I don't think you've got a *peso* on you nowhere. Least, nowhere I can get my fingers into, you standin' up like this. And 'cause you got no money, but mostly 'cause your dick just hangin' there, sort of dead like . . . you got your hand where it don't belong. Sorry, hon, but this is strictly professional. No money, no honey."

She gave his hand a last slow rubbing motion against her breast and he could feel her hard nipple move across his palm. She let his hand drop away.

From somewhere—nearby, he thought—he heard a bell ring, a sort of telephone bell, but with a higher, tinny sound.

The woman shifted her big purse and dug into it. He watched as she pulled out something small and shiny and flipped open its cover, putting the thing to her ear, listening.

"No," she said. A pause. "You still owe me the twenty."

The woman closed the cover and dropped the device back into her purse. *A radio, or a telephone. It had to be a telephone. Goddamn,* he thought.

"Wrong number, hon," she said, the low silky voice again. She adjusted her blouse and swung away down the walkway, her hips rolling under her.

"Wait," he mumbled.

She turned.

"What time is it?"

"What?" She put her hands on her hips and tilted her head, chuckling. "What *time* is it? My God, hon, you really are out of it. It's six-thirty in the morning."

"No," he said. "I meant . . . what month . . . what year?"

She looked at him closely, no hint of humor in her face now. "It's June. Late June. It's . . ." Her mouth closed slowly and she never finished. She backed away a few steps, watching him carefully, then turned and moved quickly toward the far end of the walkway, disappearing around a corner. He watched her, wondering if he had ever had a woman like that.

He dug the piece of paper out of his shirt pocket. He read it. He didn't understand. It was a bus ticket to Santa Fe, New Mexico.

There was something else in his pocket—a pencil stub, shorter than his little finger, the eraser broken off, teeth marks punched deeply into the soft wood. He stared at the wood. The marks were broad and crude, the marks of molars. He put the stub into his mouth, aligning it with the set of his jaw. He turned the stub until his teeth slipped into the marks. A perfect fit. He knew it would be.

He had some strange feeling, some emotion, or *lack* of emotion, that he didn't recognize, as though he were watching a movie, the scenery stretching before him as he searched the screen for the actors, for something that filled in the story. But there was nothing.

He looked around him, not knowing how he got there, not recognizing anything. He tried to think about yesterday. He tried to think about other yesterdays, any yesterdays, but no thoughts would come. The dizziness returned and he gripped the railing, squeezing hard, his breathing rapid and shallow. He realized that the earliest memory he had was awakening in the room behind him and seeing a beetle click across the ceiling. That was less than a half hour ago.

The rest of his life was gone.

Two

Little Jimmy was sleeping in a tire track in the fragile high-desert floor south of Santa Fe.

When the car came softly through the heavy night it was some dark invisible color and coasted quietly down the grade with the motor off and no lights showing and it was almost on him before he knew it was there. A wheel broke a small stick and the tiny noise snapped into Little Jimmy's mind. He rolled over quickly, flipping his short, bony body out of the tire track and under a *pinon* tree and covering his head with his arms. The car ghosted by. The only way Little Jimmy knew it was past and gone was the thick shushing of the tires on the soft earth at the edge of the *arroyo*, fading.

He huddled under the tree and waited, heart beating wildly, breath coming in deep gasps. The night sky spread heavy and thick over him, black and pressing, massive clouds pushing back against a thin moon. The desert smelled spring-sweet and clear but the high-desert air forced a chill through his skinny body and for the first time that night he was cold.

"Lord ha' mercy," he muttered, "was damn near kil't dead." And then he realized he had pissed in his pants.

A flare of red light burst through the night and then instant darkness again; a ratcheting sound. Little Jimmy knew the car had eased to a stop somewhere along the edge of the *arroyo*. He knew the driver had touched the brakes, seen the glare of red fanning across the near desert in the rearview mirror and then stopped the car with the parking brake. It was what Little Jimmy used to do when he got up in the middle of the night, dropped out of the second story window to the soft earth at the edge of the old clapboard house, and stole his uncle's car. He had the ancient Buick permanently hot-wired so he could start it whenever he wanted. But he didn't start the car—he would let it drift silently down the rutted dirt road that ran in the middle of the holler between the ridges and when he came to the narrow paved highway he would haul hard on the hand brake of the Buick, driving his frail shoulders back against the heavy seat. Almost every time before he got to the pavement he could stop the car with no brake lights coming on at all. Then he would sit in the darkened car with the window down, moist night air flowing across his face, trying to control his breathing, listening for anybody who might be coming down the hollow in pursuit. No one ever came. Little Jimmy would release the brake and drift the big car out onto the highway and down around a curve before he started the engine, the car still rolling, and turned on the lights. Usually, he would cruise into Kermit and sometimes all the way to Williamson but he would always be back at the house before daylight. Except for the last time. The Buick drifted a little faster than usual and before he could get it stopped the car was sitting directly across the two-lane road. Some heavy-hauler in a coal truck rounded the curve and tore the Buick in half without touching Little Jimmy. Little Jimmy took it as a sign from heaven. He walked away down the highway, into the darkness. He had never gone back.

* * *

The day had been long and gray and warm and Little Jimmy had spent all of it working this deep *arroyo* south of Santa Fe. The *arroyo* was "available," meaning none of the other street guys had laid claim to it yet. All day he had stumbled along the sandy bottom and tried not to breathe when the wind brushed the desert floor above him and grit and dust came curling down, filling his ears and nose, mixing with his sweat to make a fine crust on his skin.

He had pawed through stinking junk piles, pulled up pieces of rusted tin roofing and rotting cardboard, poked into some dark puffy plastic bags, swelling in the heat, and almost fainted from the putrid gas that hissed out of one of them. Long ago he had learned to explore the *arroyos*, to lift carefully the flaking pieces of unknown material, to search out the molding treasures underneath, to walk cautiously around anything that was wet enough to glisten in the sun, to ignore the scuttling of the beetles, small snakes, scorpions and centipedes, to probe the swollen plastic bags with a long stick and not with his hands. Sometimes Little Jimmy forgot the part about the stick.

But after an entire day in the *arroyo* Little Jimmy had nothing to take back to his "hide," his safe, hidden sleeping place behind a Dumpster on the south side of Santa Fe. And then it got dark and he knew he wouldn't make it back to the Dumpster, anyway. Usually, he stayed up most of the night and slept most of the day, nestled under a bridge in the heart of the old city. He felt safer sleeping in the day. But now it was dark and he hadn't slept at all and if he couldn't get back to his Dumpster he would stay where he was. He crawled out of the *arroyo*. In the near distance to the north he could see the lights of Santa Fe and he wondered briefly about the people there who were sitting down under soft yellow light to eat food someone else had cooked and then would go to sleep in an actual bed in a real room with a lock on the door. And sleep. Maybe fuck. Maybe just hold onto each other.

Nah, they'd be fuckin', Jimmy thought, *fer sure.*

He found his own bedroom—some sort of wiry tree bent with age—and he nestled his runty little body next to it in an elongated depression in the dirt. It was late June. The air was crystal black and carried the slight scent of *piñons* and the night chilled quickly, but not much. Little Jimmy went to sleep. He didn't even need his blanket.

* * *

He knew the car was out there. He could smell the exhaust, a foreign stink on the night air, but he couldn't see the car. He slid toward it on his belly for a few feet, his too-big floppy pants almost dragging down off his ass, getting muddy from his own urine. And then a cactus stuck him through his thin shirt and he sat up, mumbling "she-it" under his breath and trying to pick the thorn out of his belly. If he were going to sneak up on the car, he would have to do it on his feet. He rose into a crouch and lifted his feet carefully, try-ing to control the oversize tennis shoes he always wore. He moved down the slight grade and off behind some small trees to his right, walking almost bowlegged to keep the wet pants off his crotch. The *arroyo* was there somewhere to his right but he was not concentrat-ing on that; he was trying to find the car. If the people in the car were out here for some late night drinking, or fucking, or both, he might be able to ferret something out of the car, some food maybe, before they knew what was happening. He had found people fuck-ing before, and he had stolen some things that way. When people were fucking, all they thought about was the fucking. Once, he had reached his bony arm right inside a car, the car rocking gently to the rhythm of the two people locked together fucking, and had taken a whole shopping bag. He could see the woman's feet pushing up against the roof of the car and the man's ass bouncing up and down. He had resisted the temptation to peek over the seat and let the woman see him. That would have been a good joke, he thought.

There was no food in the bag. It had been full of damp women's clothing and he had given it to Hale Mary. She had taken the bag and clutched it to her heavy chest, then walked backward for an entire block, watching Little Jimmy all the way. And then she turned and disappeared down a narrow street.

* * *

The car was there in the darkness in front of him and he could almost touch it. Pale moonlight seeped through a hole in the clouds and, even in the weak light, the car seemed to glow, the paint shimmering, chrome glistening. Little Jimmy could see a large, intricate spider web painted across the trunk lid. He backed off a few steps and moved to the side, crouching behind a small *pinon*. There was no movement from the car, no sound. Little Jimmy waited, feeling the excitement build inside him.

"What the fuck do we do now?"

The voice was a whining drool directly in Little Jimmy's ear and he rolled over backwards, in panic. He twisted to his knees and put his hands up in front of his face.

I didn't mean anything! I was jist 'a-settin' here when . . .! He shouted it in his mind but his survival reflexes stopped his throat and the words did not come out of his mouth. He hadn't made a sound.

There was no one there. The voice had come from the car, the sound moving solidly against his hearing through the layers of night air.

"We do what we have to do, asshole." A different voice. Darker. Angry.

"Asshole? Who's a fucking asshole, huh?" The whining voice. "Who wanted to take pitchers of her, huh? Who was it backed off to take pitchers and then she run? Huh? Who did that? We never took pitchers of them others!"

"How the fuck I know she'd jump and run? Hell, she was all naked and bloody! How the hell I know . . ."

"How you *know*? Jesus fuckin' Christ! What else you think she going to do?" The voice paused, Little Jimmy still sitting with his hands in front of his face. "And you didn't have to do all that other shit to her, her not even bein' dead yet. We never did that to them others! We just left 'em . . ."

"She was just a stupid street bitch, climbed on my car, man. Nobody fucks up my car. Bitch needed a lesson. Bitches need a lesson now and then. I mean, what the fuck, it ain't like she's the first street bitch we ever taught a lesson!"

"A *lesson*! Jesus H. Christ! You went and . . . and . . . how's she gonna make use of your 'lesson' now?" Jimmy thought the whiner was almost crying.

The voices were silent for a moment. "Let's just do it and get the hell out of here," the dark voice said.

The doors of the car swung open and the dull yellow dome light glowed like a sickly moon. Little Jimmy dropped his hands to the huge wooden cross that hung at his neck on a piece of dog chain, gripping it until the edges made deep seams inside his fingers. He prayed silently for salvation and protection, promising his God that he would never steal again. Through the gnarled limbs of the tree he saw two dark shapes leave the car, one large and one even larger, silhouettes against the dim light. They eased the doors closed and came directly at him. He stopped breathing.

If the wind was with me, he thought, *I could piss on the both of 'em.*

They were at the back of the car, a key fumbling in the trunk lock. The trunk lid swung up and they made grunting sounds deep in their throats as they hauled something long and thick and limber from the bowels of the car. It slung between them, a sagging black weight, connecting them and yet not belonging to them. Belonging to no one. Something swung below the weight and for a moment Little Jimmy thought it might be an arm. But it couldn't be an arm, he thought. Not an arm. No.

"Why we out here? We never left any of them others out here." The whiny voice.

"Time for a new place. Besides, that other'n gettin' to smell bad."

They struggled away from the car and melted into the darkness and Little Jimmy could hear muffled scrapings in the dirt and then a fractured second of silence and then a bumping sound in the earth.

The black shapes moved back to the car. They stood by the open trunk

"Okay. Let's do our ritual thing."

"Rich-u-all thing?" The whiner. "Jesus, let's just git the hell out'a here. We ain't got to do no . . ."

"We got to do it. Man's got to have a ritual. Makes ever thing close up all tidy, like."

Jimmy saw one of the shapes bend, reach into the trunk. He heard a clinking sound. A bottle. The man raised the bottle and drank.

"Here," the man said, handing the bottle to the other dark shape.

"Rich-u-all," the whiny voice muttered. But he took the bottle. Jimmy saw him start to raise it to his lips. Then, "*Motherfucker!*" The whiner was yelling now. "Blood! There's blood on the fuckin' bottle!"

"Why don't you just dial 911, you dumb shit! You keep yelling like that . . ."

Jimmy heard breaking glass, but not nearby.

"You dumb bastard! I paid more'n five dollars for that bottle! That was good stuff! You didn't have to bust it! We could'a washed it off! We could'a . . . Aww, fuck it. Let's get out'a here."

Little Jimmy heard the trunk lid slam shut, the other doors bang closed.

"Why don't you just fire off a flare? You make any more noise . . ."

Then the car was rolling forward, still silent, still black.

The voices faded out.

In the distance, Jimmy heard the car's engine start up. And then it was gone.

He stood up and walked—stood straight up and moved forward to where the car had been, his eyes flat against the night and his little hands dangling. His feet found the tracks the tires had made, slight depressions in the sandy earth. He thought he could smell the car, not the exhaust but the faint odor of something metallic, but the car was gone and there was nothing to make such a smell and he moved off to the side not really knowing where he was or what he was doing there.

When his right foot came down there was nothing under it. He had stepped over the side and into the black space above the *arroyo*, falling. He did not scream.

His right side hit first and he bounced, flopping over on his back and then rolling over face-down on something that stopped him but which moved slightly when he hit it. He lay there in blackness so thick he thought he might never see again. Wondering, breathing hard, he pulled the thin scent of perfume into his lungs. He drew one arm up and felt along the soft and rounded things under him until his hand came to an ear. It was not his ear. He moved his hand across the ear to the face and felt the thin nose and the lips and then down across the chin until his hand rested in a flat plate of near-coagulation and retch and then Little Jimmy screamed as he had never screamed before. He screamed into the thing beneath him and screamed out into the *arroyo* and screamed up into the night, a slicing sheet of sound layered in the blackness.

His scream died away.

He lifted his hands from the thing and rolled away and scrambled to his knees. He wrapped his arms tightly around his chest and rocked back and forth, making mewling noises in his throat and wiping his hands on his shirt.

A light came stabbing down from the night sky and lit the face on the ground in front of him. The round black hole in the forehead, the flat eyes that stared up from under half closed lids, the mouth that hung in a slack smile that was somehow sneering and below the smile another smile at the neck, an open black-red gash with tiny pieces of torn flesh. Everything shellacked with blood. Little Jimmy stared at the smile where it should not be and then he screamed again. The light jerked to Little Jimmy.

"Son-of-a-bitch!" the whiner said.

"I knew I heard something back there," the darker voice said, the beam of the flashlight still on Little Jimmy's face below them there in the slot of the *arroyo*.

"Hey, I know that little motherfucker. Seen him at the Plaza lots of times. One of them street guys."

"Then ain't nobody goin' to miss him," the dark voice growled.

THREE

Little Jimmy ran as fast as he could. Usually when he ran he was aware of the slapping sound his big shoes made against the pavement and the way they shucked around on his feet no matter how tightly he tied the laces. But he was not aware of his shoes now. There was no pavement and he did not hear the slapping sounds. His feet plunged and dug into the sandy earth and every few steps he hit something in the *arroyo*; a broken bottle, a can. The heavy wooden cross bounced on its chain and once flipped up and struck him in the mouth. He didn't notice. His hands gripped into fists, fingers still sticky from feeling the thing in the *arroyo*. His breath tore through his throat like sand, rasping. As he ran he realized that he could see where he was going and knew pale moonlight was filtering into the canyon through a hole in the clouds.

He pumped his short thin legs in frenzy. He tried to listen to his feet, but all he heard were the sounds of other feet running behind him. The other feet were quick and sure, feet running in those expensive sneakers with the streaky logos on them, feet running and making soft sounds faster than the sounds made by Little Jimmy, feet running with a sureness that closed the distance.

The cooling air whistled by his head and he tried to keep his mind on his running but the drumming of his heart kept leaping into his ears and he knew he was afraid. His heart always did that when he was afraid, and he was afraid a lot.

Little Jimmy came to a low place in the wall of the *arroyo* and he leaped for it, making the top easier than he thought. He scooted along the rim and then paused, listening. And it was a mistake. Out of the darkness a pair of arms shot over the rim and made a grab for him, fingers raking his ankle and tangling in the laces of his large shoe. He threw himself backward, twisting and thrashing. He grabbed a small bush and held it like an anchor. He tried to jerk his legs up but the hand held solidly at his ankle and Little Jimmy knew he could never tear it loose. He let go of the bush, doubled over, and grabbed at the hand, trying to pry away the fingers. He was sliding back toward the edge of the *arroyo*.

Other hands shot out of the darkness. One hand grabbed him by the hair and the other tangled in the dog chain around his neck. The hand twisted and Jimmy could feel the chain rip into his neck. He thought his neck would break and it wouldn't matter if he were pulled back into the ditch. But the chain broke first and the hands flashed away into the darkness as the man fell backward.

Jimmy's hands raked the thin soil at his sides and his left hand fell flush onto a prickly pear cactus and he screamed again, but his right hand found a piece of deadfall, a tree limb as rugged and heavy as a ball bat, dried and skinned and hardened in the desert. He grabbed the stick with both hands, screaming again from the pain of the cactus thorns driven more deeply into his hand as he gripped the limb. He swung the club over the edge of the *arroyo* with all the strength his wizened little body could pull up from his guts. There was a dull cracking sound and the hand let go of his ankle.

And then he heard the pistol shot. He did not know where the shot went, and he did not care, as long as it had not hit him.

The bastards were tying to kill him. He was not going to wait around for another shot. Little Jimmy dropped the club and scrambled to his feet.

And then he was running again.

FOUR

El Paso? What the hell am I doing in El Paso? he wondered. *For that matter, what the hell am I doing anywhere?*

He stood in the sun in front of the motel office, feeling as though he were going to be dizzy, maybe vomit, but never quite getting there. The sun seemed to flatten everything, even the air. But from somewhere among the tattered shelters across the river came the scent of human shit, mixed with the thin sheen of rotting cardboard.

He turned carefully in a complete circle, looking for them.

Where the hell are they?

But there was no "them." He was alone in the sun.

There were a few cars in the parking spaces in front of the battered doors of the rooms on the lower floor. He stared at the cars. There was something about them . . . and then he realized that he did not recognize any of them, their styles unfamiliar to him, as though the machines were dropped from some other futuristic world.

He stepped inside the motel office. The tiny foyer was hot and stuffy, a smell like mold on rotten cloth. He moved only a single step into the room and already he could reach out and touch the small window across from him, a tiny metal grill in the center of the thick glass, a fat man behind it, dozing in a chair with one arm missing. A tiny metal sign bolted to the grill said "J. Otis owner/manager."

He spoke through the grill, getting used to—interested in—the sound of his own voice.

"Mr. Otis. I was a little drunk when I came in last night. Guess my friends brought me in. Mind telling me who registered me? Room 22?"

The fat man sat up, looked at him through the glass.

"Nobody in room 22 last night." The fat man's voice wheezing. "You in room 22? How you get in room 22? You got a key?"

"I . . . must have left the key in the room. Maybe I got the number wrong. Second floor. Last room, down there on the end. Nice looking lady in the next room."

"Lady? That'd be Miranda. You sure you wasn't with Miranda? She had an all-nighter . . . but I thought the guy left before daylight."

He watched the fat man through the glass. "No. Wasn't with her. Was in the next room."

"I'm tellin' you, pal, wasn't nobody in room 22 last night." The man raised a ham-sized hand, reaching for something out of sight beside the glass.

"And here's why you don't have a key, smart ass. They's only two keys for each room, and I got 'em both, right here." He held the keys up behind the glass and jingled them. "Don't use them key cards. Use real keys, keys I can look at and know I got the right ones. No matter what kind'a keys I use, don't you be thinkin' you gonna get back in that room tonight. I be watchin' you, scarecrow."

The fat man turned away and picked up a magazine, dismissing him.

On the narrow shelf lay a small pad of paper. The thin man picked it up and put it in his pocket. It seemed a natural thing to do.

Key cards?

* * *

He stayed off the main drags, wandering the bright, littered side streets of El Paso, watching the traffic, not recognizing the vehicles, listening to the people. He tried to run his mind from side to side, searching for whatever it was that caused the panic, the fear, but no reasons would come. He looked at clothes, colors, dogs, wondering which were his favorites. But he had no favorites.

And he looked at women. Somehow he knew there were more women to be looked at than he had seen in a long time. Did he like blondes? There sure as hell weren't many in El Paso.

El Paso. Why the hell am I here?

Late in the evening he passed a tiny, crowded Mexican café tucked into the end of an alley. Through the sagging screen door he could see past a narrow counter and into a cramped steaming kitchen where leaning towers of dirty dishes were stacked next to an overflowing sink. He watched the cook dish up a plate of food, wash a few dishes, and then dish up another plate, handing the food to the one waitress who was trying to keep up with the room full of customers. She was not young, but not old, her face showing the passage of time in a Mexican café in El Paso. Her damp hair hung loosely over one eye and drops of sweat ran down her cheeks. But she smiled at every customer.

Over it all, the cacophony of voices—food orders, greetings, more orders, jokes. One large family.

If there was anything larger than the blankness of his mind, it was his hunger. And he thought he knew how to wash dishes.

He pushed quietly through the battered screen door and without pausing walked behind the counter and started washing the dishes. He spoke to no one. The waitress and the cook stared silently at him for a few seconds and then went back to the crush of their own work. The warm sounds of voices at ease rolled gently over him as he worked. Gradually, the mound of dirty dishes grew smaller.

There was nothing to eat and he was offered nothing. He cupped his hand under the faucet and sucked at his hand, his mouth and nose sunk into the cool water. He felt a touch on his shoulder and the waitress handed him an empty Mason jar.

"*No vaso,*" she said softly. "Use this. We all have one. Saves on washing glasses." He smiled at her and took the Mason jar . . .

The old woman held the jar up in front of his face. It was full of dirt.

"Your mama said there was blood in the dirt." She spoke English, but her voice had the lilt of Spanish. "She said to give this to you one day. One day, when maybe you would think you were going to leave."

His claw-like fingers were wrapped tightly around the jar, shaking. He brought the jar to his chest to stop the shaking, then jammed it under the running water. He sloshed water around inside the jar and dumped it into metal sink, watching it carefully. There was no dirt in the jar. There was nothing in the jar.

At closing time, midnight, the cook dished up a large bowl of beans and covered the top with thick red *chile* and cheese. He stuck a large spoon in the bowl and handed it to the thin man who still stood washing dishes at the sink. The thin man dried his hands, took the food, sat on the greasy floor with his back to the wall, and began to eat. The bowl in his hands felt comfortable and right. The chile burned his mouth and tears formed in his eyes. He had never tasted anything so good. Somewhere deep in his mind a brief flash of recognition flared and he knew that he had eaten this food before. A very long time ago.

The thin man finished his food, stood up and washed the bowl.

The cook rolled some *tortillas* in a paper napkin and tucked them into the thin man's pocket, handed him a gallon milk jug half full of water.

"*Manana noche?*" the cook asked.

"*Si*," he mumbled, and slipped out the door into the alley.

It wasn't until he was halfway back to the motel that he realized he had heard only Spanish in the café—and that he had understood nearly every word of it.

* * *

At the Mexi-View Motel and Spa he sat in the darkness, curled in a corner behind the dirt-filled spa with its dying *cholla* cactus, his back to a bare, crumbling cement-block wall. He pulled a scattering of trash—some newspapers, a scrap of cardboard—over him and disappeared into his own skin. He watched the office and as many of the rooms as he could see, including room 22. The whores came and went. He saw Miranda, holding onto the arm of a short, fat man. They went into a room on the second floor, but no lights came on. A few drunks staggered by, including one who pissed on the *cholla*, never seeing the thin man pressed back into the corner. Other than that, he saw nothing.

He huddled in his corner, watching, until the sky began to wash out pale, then let his chin drop to his chest. He slept until oven-temperature air seared his face and the sun burned directly down onto the top of his head.

The rest of the day was the same as before. He ate his *tortillas,* wandered the streets, and looked for . . . something. Anything. But he saw nothing that was familiar.

He went back to the café. This time, the cook nodded at him and the waitress smiled. At the sink, a clean, white apron hung on a hook. He put it on, tied the strings behind him and looked out over the small room. The faces he saw were chocolate and coffee and bronze, faces from the sun, men and women in their café, safe and secure after a day of survival in El Paso and Juarez. A couple with four kids crammed themselves around a table near the counter, talking easily with each other, the mother hand-feeding the smallest kid. An old man nursed a cup of coffee at the counter. At a tiny table in the far corner a slender black woman sat reading a newspaper. It was the only reading material he saw in the whole place.

He washed dishes until after midnight, and again sat on the floor, eating his bowl of *chile* and beans.

An Anglo man opened the back door and came inside. He was tall and heavy, his face hanging in a scowl, a white dress shirt tucked inside a pair of tailored slacks, expensive boots. He looked at the thin man sitting on the floor, took a step toward him, then stopped.

The thin man on the floor looked up at the Anglo, a tiny gout of fear twisting slowly behind his stomach. But this time, there was something else. Anger. He was on the ground—the floor—in front of a standing man and he hated being there.

The Anglo turned and spoke in whispers to the cook. He left without looking at, or speaking to, anyone else.

Plain, old fashioned anger. He didn't know where it came from. Anger at the Anglo, anger at his manner, his walk, his very face. But the thin man said nothing, did nothing. He quietly finished his food and left the café, again with the roll of *tortillas* in his pocket. He went back to the motel and took up his post at the back of the dirt-filled spa, behind the piss-stained *cholla* cactus.

* * *

The night passed as before, in darkness turning swiftly to light. Whores and drunks. And nothing that he recognized.

No one came to room 22.

At first light he eased around behind the building, stood carefully on a pile of rotten wooden pallets and peered through a tiny, grimy window into the office. The fat man still dozed in the broken chair, the remains of a pizza on the counter, one piece fallen to the floor.

At the end of a counter inside the office was a door that, he thought, probably led to the manager's room. But the door was closed.

He thought the fat man was snoring but he could not hear him. And he could see nothing in the room that told him anything.

That night, he went back to the café.

* * *

The stack of dishes seemed higher than before. He worked faster. Dirty water ran down his apron and dripped on his worn sneakers, soaking through to his feet. Gradually, the stream of customers thinned and the pile of dishes began to disappear. It was almost time to eat.

The big Anglo banged through the back door, stood in the middle of the tiny kitchen, his hands on his hips. The cook kept his head down over the grill; the waitress vanished into the dining room.

The big man glared at the cook. "I thought I told you what to do."

The cook shrugged. "No think you mean this *noche.*"

"You know damn well what I meant. If you can't do your job . . ."

The big man whipped around and stepped quickly behind the dishwasher, grabbing the apron strings, pulling hard. He drove his other hand into the dishwasher's back, bending him over the sink. "Take off my apron and get the hell out. I ain't havin' no street trash . . ."

He never got to finish. The dishwasher spun, windmilled his left arm over the arm of the big man, shot his right hand to the man's

43

throat and stepped forward, pulling on the arm and shoving on the throat, the dishwasher whipping his leg behind the Anglo's knees. The Anglo dropped hard to the greasy floor, the dishwasher on him, not letting up. The dull crack of the Anglo's head hitting the floor could be heard out into the dining area. The Anglo lay still, groaning deep in his throat.

Kill him!

He heard the words so clearly that he thought someone was standing over him, telling him, ordering him. But there was no one, only the cook pressed back against the far wall, holding his apron up in front of his face. The dishwasher slowly uncurled his fingers from the Anglo's throat, eased away, getting up, never taking his eyes from the big man. The cook moved closer, bent and looked into the Anglo's cloudy eyes. He turned to the dishwasher.

"This man," he said, nodding at the body on the floor, "he the owner. He a *bastardo*, but he the owner. He say you no work here. I never tell you. *Lo siento, señor.*"

The dishwasher edged around the counter, out into the dining area, silent now, diners with forks frozen in mid-air. He nodded back at the cook. "*Gracias.*"

"*Adios, amigo,*" the cook said softly. "*Buena suerte.*"

The thin man walked out the front door.

* * *

He spent another night hiding at the motel, but learned nothing.

Kill him!

He still heard the words that came clattering through his mind. He thought about the café, about how easy it had been to take down the Anglo.

Where the hell did that stuff come from?

FiVE

The sun was still low in the mountains to the east of Santa Fe, not yet spilling fully down into the Plaza.

Elena Montoya stood just inside one of the gallery's huge windows, near the wall, waiting for the light. The gallery, on the south side of the Plaza and under a *portal* that ran the length of the block, would never be touched directly by the sun. Instead, the light would bounce around the Plaza, be broken by the trees and the other buildings, fragments scattering like shards of glass, some of them finding their way to her windows. It was her favorite time of day.

It was much too soon to open the gallery but she liked to come early, make strong black coffee, wait for the light and watch the Plaza come alive, as it had been coming alive each morning for nearly four hundred years. At a certain point in the morning, a reflection from some unknown window somehow caught the gallery's hand-carved wooden sign hanging under the *portal*, and "Alvarez Montoya," the only words on the sign, were briefly golden. Elena had owned the gallery, and the building it was in, for ten years. She opened early and stayed late.

Elena Montoya was the last of the Montoya's, who had, over the centuries, owned and ranched most of the cattle country southeast of the city—thousands of acres. As the decades passed and ranching life eroded into some dream of the past, the land had been slowly sold off, bits and pieces of it going to outsiders who built air conditioned homes, installed hot tubs and kept fancy dogs and overvalued horses. Finally, the grand old ranch had been reduced to two hundred acres, the original *hacienda*, some outbuildings, no cattle, and a handful of Spanish Barb horses.

Both Elena and her brother, Alvarez, had been born late, their parents elderly by the time Alvarez was in college, Elena in high school. Alvarez, six years older than she, had left New Mexico when he had graduated from college. Always a little wild and with wild friends, he had simply disappeared. No one had heard from him in more than twenty years. She had worshipped him, and he had left her, left them all.

As bits and pieces of the ranch had fallen away, and with no word from Alvarez, Elena's parents had lost interest in ranching, cattle, horses and life in general. They had died ten years ago, never having seen their son again. In order to keep something, anything, of the ranch, Elena had had to sell another hundred acres. She still lived on what was left. And she had bought the gallery building.

As she sipped the coffee she glanced back into the huge, high-ceilinged room at the paintings and sculpture, almost all of them from Hispanic or Indian artists. She had not yet turned on the lights and the sun fragments flickered over bits of oil paint, stone and bronze, seeming to set small fires among the pieces, tiny imaginary flames springing from the art.

Sanctuary. The gallery was sanctuary, here, in the middle of the town. She felt so strongly about sanctuary that she had never hired anyone to work with her. She ran the gallery alone. When she had other things to do, she simply locked the door.

Sometimes the light glittered from a framed black-and-white photograph hanging at the back of the gallery, high on a wall over the door that led to Matt Klah's office. It was a picture of Alvarez, dressed in his ranching clothes, his arms around two of his friends. The young men stood in front of a small, ugly building, the end of a grime-covered bus sticking out into the background. Elena had taken the picture of Alvarez and his friends the day he left Santa Fe. She had brought it with her the day she bought the building. It was the only photograph in the gallery.

She turned back to the window. Tourists had started to stumble out of downtown hotels and wander along the sunny, nearly empty streets, looking into the still-closed galleries. On the northwest corner of the Plaza, a lowrider was parked in the first parking space across from the bank, facing away from the Plaza. The guys driving lowriders usually came out in the evenings—more tourists to see them—but Elena had seen this car in the early mornings, in the same spot, off and on for the past week. By noon, it was gone.

Across the Plaza, under the long *portal* in front of the Palace of the Governors, the Indian jewelry-makers were spreading their blankets, preparing for another day of dealing with tourists. She knew that Georgie Suina was over there—and, usually, that meant that Matt Klah would be arriving soon.

Sometimes, she saw two street guys sitting on a bench near the corner of the Plaza, one of them tall and angular, the other a thick, stumpy man. They seemed to be a team, scouting tourists, the heavy man keeping an eye on his tall partner. As she watched, the tall man picked out an elderly couple and nodded to the heavy man, who got up and began an almost simian-like approach, the old couple rooted in place, watching him come.

But the street guys were not there today.

* * *

Matt Klah strolled slowly down Lincoln Avenue toward the Plaza, in no hurry to get to his office. Tall and slender, he walked rod-straight and silently, his moccasins touching the sidewalks softly, his steps almost delicate. He wore expensive suit pants and a brilliant white shirt, tie draped around his shoulders, suit jacket over his arm, his long black hair bound up short in a strip of dark red cloth, what the men called a "Navajo wrap." A rough, worn, leather briefcase dangled from his hand, a pair of expensive shoes stuffed into a side pocket. It was the way he always dressed, sort of half put together in white man's clothes, as though, at any moment, he might have to drop them and run, have to be an Indian again.

He reached the corner of Lincoln and Palace Avenue, walked slowly across Palace and onto the grass of the Plaza. He stopped, listening, waiting, clenching his toes and feeling the earth under his moccasins. Centuries ago, his grandfathers had run screaming across this Plaza, had sunk heavy clubs into the skulls of Spaniards, had cut their throats and burned their crude buildings. And had been slaughtered in return. As it always has been, between men, Klah thought. Crossing the Plaza, for Matt Klah, was like visiting an honored field of battle, now healing under a merciful sun. He waited, controlling his breathing, tuning out the modern noise. When all things were right, he could hear the sounds of the dying.

Somewhere in the downtown area, a street vendor already was firing up his *fajita* stand and the cool morning air carried the faint aroma of roasting meat. It broke Matt out of his stillness. He was hungry. He knew what to do about that. He turned and started back across Palace Avenue toward the Indian vendors setting up for the day's business under the *portal* of the Palace of the Governors.

Georgie Suina watched him come.

Oh, God, she thought, *what will he do this morning?*

Georgie fussed with her day's collection of jewelry, her blanket, her stool, her tiny workbench. And she watched him come.

Georgie was from Cochiti Pueblo, in her late twenties, slender, taller than most of the women of her tribe, her black hair hanging down to her waist, her face radiating an angular beauty that was stunning, even in a white world. Often, she noticed photographers using telephoto lenses taking her picture from across the Plaza.

She was the latest in a long line of Suina potters, jewelers and sculptors. She worked in silver and native stones, her jewelry finely done, delicate, each piece shining with a personality of its own. She brought to the *portal* only pieces she personally had made, and only a few pieces each day, never piling work on the blanket to make it look full. Sometimes she brought a few pieces-in-progress, finishing them carefully on the small workbench, working only when no tourists stood in front of her blanket.

Already, even before the galleries opened, a constant flow of tourists eased along the line of vendors under the *portal*, picking up pieces of jewelry and holding them out in the sun, as though the brilliance of the light would reveal hidden flaws. The vendors sat quietly behind their selling blankets, most of them speaking only when spoken to, and then with as few words as possible, playing the role of Indians for the tourists.

Georgie liked coming to the Plaza . . . because Matt Klah would be there. And now she watched him come, the man walking with grace, fluidity. A movement in the company of ancient animals.

He was there before she knew it. He stood stiffly in front of her blanket, his face pulled into a frown.

"I come for food, woman. I ride out today to attack the fort that houses white man's law. I must be strong."

Georgie looked quickly around, hoping that none of the tourists had heard him.

"Dammit, Matt, could you please, just *one* morning, not start a fight . . ."

A large woman, wearing at least two thousand dollars of neo-Santa Fe style, stepped in front of Matt, ignoring him, ignoring Georgie. She bent properly at the knees, smoothed her long skirt as she lowered herself, picked up a small bracelet from Georgie's blanket. She rose, holding the bracelet away from her with two fingers, as though it were a scorpion.

"How much?" Her voice had ice in it, a voice white people used when they were going to haggle over price, something Georgie always found interesting.

"One-ninety-five." Georgie's voice had a quality that seemed to evoke warm honey.

"Oh, really," the woman sniffed. "Seems a bit much for this trinket."

"I'll give you two-twenty-five," Matt Klah said over her shoulder.

The woman spun on her heel, indignant.

"Sir, I'm discussing price with this young woman . . ."

"Yeah, I know, so am I." He looked at Georgie. "How about two-fifty?"

The woman tucked the bracelet against her chest, protectively. "You are *bidding* on a bracelet that isn't even up for bid?"

"Everything's up for bid. That bracelet you're holding, this city, your land, my land . . . even my blood."

Matt bent to look at the bracelet, staring directly into the woman's chest. She took a small step backward.

"Look," Matt said to Georgie, "I can't go a dime over three hundred."

The woman daintily held the bracelet out to Matt, dropped it into his hand. She turned and stepped out into Palace Avenue, crossed to the Plaza. She stopped and looked back. Matt was still holding the bracelet. She disappeared into the early sun, heading west as rapidly as she could walk.

Georgie dropped her head into her hands. "*Lawyer* Klah, would it ruin your day to let me make a good sale, just once?" she asked into her palms. She tried to sound exasperated, but didn't quite pull it off.

"She wasn't going to buy anything. Not right now. Too early in the day. Just testing. She'll look at her watch all day—white people do that—and be back before five. Save the bracelet for her. Charge her two-fifty."

"You're early."

He grinned. "How do you know? How do you know what time I get to work?"

She felt the blood surge into her face. Matt leaned closer.

"Hey, I didn't know In-dins could blush. Did you know that? Hell, learn something every day . . ."

"Oh, *shut up!*" she hissed, glancing quickly down the line of vendors. "If you're going to stand around, would

you like some coffee?"

"Nope. Got to get to the office. Prepare for court this afternoon." He leaned across her, flipped open a small cooler, and took out a small package wrapped in foil. "What's in the *burrito* this morning?"

"The usual, just for you. Rattlesnake and prairie dog."

He grinned and stepped out into the street, striding off toward the Alvarez Montoya Gallery, across the Plaza, raising his arm and waving the *burrito* at her, without looking back.

God, she thought, *he looks so damned . . . Indian.*

* * *

Across the Plaza, inside the window of her gallery, Elena Montoya watched him come.

Six

Through the thin upper layers of his sleep Little Jimmy heard the shot but he tried not to pay any attention to it. The shot was only a dim echo, the shooter too far away in some other city in Jimmy's past to cause him any trouble. But he listened carefully anyway, waiting for the second shot, which almost always came. And sometimes a third. Maybe a fourth.

For years he had been sleeping in places where there were shots, sleeping where doors were cracked and warped and padlocked and windows broken, sleeping on the tiny slicing edges of shards of glass scattered in shallow entryways and out onto the streets, sleeping in any place where it might be dry and likely to stay dry and where he might not be found, sleeping fully clothed and ready to run and always in need of taking a piss.

He woke up, safe behind his Dumpster in Santa Fe. He sat up and rubbed his face with his hands, trying to scrub the dream from his mind—and jerked his hands away and sat bolt upright as a hundred tiny stabs of cactus-needle pain lit up his left hand. The pain helped clear his mind.

He had been sleeping in his most secret hide, a tiny space behind a Dumpster at the far end of a narrow alley behind a supermarket on Cerrillos Road. Only two other People in Santa Fe knew where the hide was. The big metal box was in an alcove, a space that might have been built for it, angled in against the wall, usually jammed, the lid open and leaning. The Dumpster and the lid and the alcove formed a sort of cave and Little Jimmy had crawled back in there as far as he could go, shoving back against the grimy trash and burrowing under the pieces of cardboard and old blankets he had stuffed into the space. He had found a few wooden pallets and had dragged them in behind him, jamming them between the Dumpster and the wall—the pallets kept the dogs out—and if a garbage truck backed into the Dumpster before he awoke, the pallets would keep him from being crushed. Maybe. Nobody ever seemed to clean out the trash from behind the Dumpster. His cardboard and blanket scraps were always there.

He had gotten back to the Dumpster at daybreak. He stayed hunkered down, curled into a tight ball, hiding all that day, all night, and all the next day. Only on the second night did he try to sleep, and then the dream came in the middle of the night, shots and terror from some other city warping across his mind. And so he sat up and rubbed his face, knowing there would be no more sleep.

Except, this time, he had been shot at here, in Santa Fe.

He thought he was safe, but still he felt the cold knot behind his stomach that he knew was solid fear. He let the fear lie there, inside him, not trying to deal with it, knowing it might keep him alive. He lay silently and nursed the fear, letting his fingers trace lightly around his aching, tender neck, so swollen that he could hardly swallow, which was okay, he thought, since he didn't have anything to eat, anyway. But maybe that would change. Sometimes the stock boys from the night shift at the market dumped stuff he could eat into the Dumpster. He would check it out when it got daylight.

There was another Dumpster in the alley, closer to the parking lot, but Little Jimmy didn't like that one. Too exposed. He liked *his* Dumpster, all the way at the end where a chain link fence blocked off the cluttered alley. The nook behind the Dumpster was the only place where Little Jimmy could sleep during the night and still feel fairly safe. And if they emptied the Dumpster at least once a week, the smell was not too bad.

But Little Jimmy knew that wouldn't matter now, knew he would hardly sleep at all, waiting to hear the shush of near-silent tires rolling toward his sleeping place, waiting to hear car doors open softly, waiting to peek out of his hide and see the expensive sneakers with the silly logos.

The dream cleared from his mind. No other shots came. He crawled silently to the corner of the Dumpster and peered through the thin darkness. He saw nothing.

He lay in the stinking, cramped darkness of his hide, thinking about the car with the fancy paint job, the guy with the expensive sneakers. The other guy; the whiny voice.

Thinking about the girl. He knew he should tell the cops, but, in his entire life, Little Jimmy had never talked to a cop and none of the People in Santa Fe would talk to one unless they were lying on the ground with the cop standing over them, holding a gun. He couldn't talk to the cops. He just couldn't. He knew they would blame him, just like the sheriff back in West Virginia always blamed his uncle whenever some bad shit had to be put on somebody.

And if Little Jimmy didn't talk, he couldn't tell them in any other way. Little Jimmy could not read or write.

When daylight came he sat picking the cactus spines from his hand, content to stay in his hide. When he had to urinate he just stood up and poked his tiny penis around the corner of the Dumpster and let fly. Later on that day he had to have a bowel movement and he did what he usually did—climbed into the Dumpster, pulled the lids closed and made himself comfortable on whatever trash he found there. Only this time some stock guys came out of the market, whipped open the lid—they never bothered to look inside—and threw three cases of rotten lettuce into the box. The lettuce knocked Little Jimmy into his own shit. But there was plenty of damp lettuce he could use to clean himself. He even found some lettuce he could eat. He didn't mind eating the lettuce. He would eat anything. Back home, sometimes his uncle wouldn't show up for days and there would be nothing to eat in the house. Little Jimmy found his uncle's old shotgun but he couldn't find any shotgun shells. He made a crude bow and arrow out of some stuff he found in the barn, but it didn't shoot straight. *Well*, he thought at the time, *maybe it was me that didn't shoot straight.* Anyway, he could not go hunting. In the old slat-sided corn crib he found a few kernels of stone-hard feed corn that the barn rats had not eaten. He carried the kernels in his mouth until they softened enough to chew. Once, he had broken a tooth trying to chew the corn and when the stump rotted and shot pain along his jaw and into his brain, his uncle had made him drink one of those little half-pints of cheap whiskey and then pulled the tooth with a pair of needle-nose pliers. The whiskey was the best part of the whole thing.

* * *

Jimmy knew, sooner or later, he would have to leave his hide, have to go back out into the town, have to find some better food.

Either that, or he would have to leave town.

Leave town. He had left every town he had ever been in. In the years since he had walked away from his uncle's house, he had been in towns he couldn't even name, had no idea where they were or how he had gotten there. He didn't want to leave Santa Fe. When he thought about it, there was no place else to go.

* * *

Now and then he would creep along the fence toward the market's parking lot, climb carefully onto a pile of pallets and scan the cars. By noon the air was searing, the heavy scent of hot pavement full on his face, but he still clutched his arms across his chest, as though he couldn't get warm. He was looking for the dark car with the spider web on the trunk. He hoped he would see it: he wanted to know where it was.

He was terrified that he *would* see it.

Santa Fe was a small town—sooner or later he would spot the car.

One thing he knew for sure. If he didn't see the car before it saw him, he was probably dead.

"Where you at, you fuckers?" he mumbled to himself.

* * *

Little Jimmy stood under the end of the portal at the Palace of the Governors. He scanned all the streets carefully—Palace Avenue, Washington, across the Plaza to San Francisco Street. He did not see what he was looking for, and that made him feel better.

Waiting until the streets packed with tourists, Jimmy moved carefully across the street and onto the Plaza, crossed diagonally until he was on the far corner. Mulligan was there. Mulligan was always there.

Mulligan was a tall black man with a lined face and a brilliant smile who stood on the sidewalk in front of a jewelry store. He wore jeans, an ancient pinstriped suit coat and a white shirt, sandals. Dark sunglasses fit tightly over his eyes and he kept his chin up, accentuating his height and seeming to stare across the street into nothingness, doing his Ray Charles pose. The tourists thought he was blind, but he wasn't. Mulligan saw everything that went down on the Plaza.

There was a battered tenor saxophone on a stand beside him, a hat turned upside down between his feet on the sidewalk. The sax had no reed, but no one ever seemed to notice that.

Little Jimmy leaned on a trash bin and watched.

"Any jazz tune," Mulligan said to the people passing, his voice smoky and rich, molasses, never looking at the Citizens, always looking straight ahead in his fake-blind act, hand resting on the saxophone. "Any jazz tune."

Jimmy saw a heavy guy in Bermuda shorts and high white socks stop and look closely at Mulligan, Mulligan pretending he didn't see the guy. The guy seemed to be thinking, trying to come up with obscure tune that would make him look knowledgeable, maybe stump the street guy with the saxophone.

"Midnight Sun," the tourist said.

Some other tourists stopped to watch.

Mulligan turned his head, as though he had just realized there was someone standing there. He carefully raised his foot and nudged the hat.

The tourist dug into his pocket and pulled out some change and some bills. He dropped a few coins in the hat. Mulligan didn't move. Reluctantly, the tourist plucked one of the bills from his hand and dropped it into the hat.

Mulligan leaned toward the sax—but then straightened and pulled a battered kazoo out of his pocket. And began to play "Laura," humming-breathing the notes out of the old kazoo with precision.

"Hey," the heavy guy said, "I said 'Midnight Sun,' and on that . . ." He pointed at the sax.

"Never said I could play the sax," Mulligan said, in that voice of his. "Just said, 'Any jazz tune' and, friend, 'Laura' is any jazz tune."

The guy's face got red. He'd been had. The tourist stalked away, some of the onlookers laughing.

Mulligan pocketed the kazoo, ready to start the whole scam all over again.

Little Jimmy grinned, watching the Bermuda shorts guy stomp away. He knew Mulligan would work the corner all day, and he would always play "Laura."

Jimmy eased up beside Mulligan, fished a quarter out of his pocket and dropped it into the hat.

"Laura," Jimmy said, trying to disguise his tinny voice.

Below his sunglasses, Mulligan's smile flashed broadly. He didn't look around. He reached into his pocket for the kazoo and breathed out the first notes of . . . "Midnight Sun."

Mulligan put the kazoo away. "Mornin', little brother," he said, in that voice of his.

"Mornin'," Jimmy said. "Hey, you think them tourists ever wonder how you know when that dollar bill hits yer hat? After all, yew cain't hear it hit, and yew supposed to be blind, and all."

Mulligan chuckled. "It's a good thing tourists ain't too smart, little man, we all be out of business."

Jimmy stood silently beside Mulligan, thinking, trying to figure out what to ask.

"You hearin' anything . . . goin' on?"

"What you talkin' about, little man?"

"You know—goin' on. Like maybe somebody . . . maybe somebody lookin' fer me?"

The smile left Mulligan's face. "Yeah, I seen 'em. Both of 'em big. One of 'em works tag-team on the Plaza now and then. Works with that crazy fucker, wears that long coat. Fat guy tried to take some bills out'a my hat one day, him thinkin' I was blind. Had to plant a foot in his big white ass. Don't know 'em, though. Don't want to know 'em. Just know they been askin' around."

"What they askin' about?"

"Askin?" Mulligan dropped his voice even lower. "They ain't askin' nothing but . . . where you is, little man, where you is?"

SEVEN

He spent another night behind the *cholla* at the Mexi-View Motel and Spa, then swore to himself that he would never do that again.

A little after first light the sun was already bleeding the colors out of everything it touched and the pitted asphalt of the motel parking lot was beginning to reek of the years of bodily fluids that had dripped onto its surface. The thin man spat onto the ground beside the *cholla*. It was time to leave this place.

But he knew there was one last thing he had to do—even though he didn't know how he knew it.

He went to the end of the motel where a single room seemed tacked onto the end of the structure, extending out from the office. The room had a door but no windows and no room number.

The manager's room, he thought.

He eased around the end of the building to the back of the motel, keeping an eye on the street as he moved, and looked through the window into the office. The fat man was not there. The door at the end of the counter was slightly ajar. He could not see into the room beyond, but he knew the fat man was in there.

He went back to the door of the windowless room. He picked up a pinch of dirt and spat on it, working it with his finger until he had mud. He stuck the mud over the tiny glass eye in the middle of the door. And then he knocked, softly at first, then hard.

"Yeah? What you want?" The voice from inside the room was thick with old sleep, or perhaps whiskey. He could not tell.

"You know what I want. I got money." The thin man mumbled the sounds, making them up as he went, his hand partially covering his mouth. He knocked hard on the door again.

"What? Why the hell you bangin' on my door? Git the hell away from here!" The fat man's voice was clearer now, and he was standing just inside the door.

The thin man knew he was trying to look through the little glass eye.

"I got money. I want a woman. You got a woman in there, I know you do. Seen lots of 'em here ever night." He tried to put authority into the sounds, but he didn't think he made it.

There was silence from inside the room. *He's thinking about the money.*

"Go around to the office! Talk to me through the glass!"

"No! Goddammit, I got the money here and I ain't talkin' through no goddamn glass!"

"Shit! Goddamn winos . . ." The thin man heard a bolt slide inside the door. He saw the knob turn. He gathered himself, bent his knees and drove himself against the door, the effort almost making him dizzy. The door flew backward, smacking into the fat man. Light stabbed into the room from the open door and the thin man saw Otis staggering heavily backward. The thin man stepped quickly inside. The air stank of body odor and putrid food. Across the room weak light came from the door to the office. There was no one else in the room.

He rushed the fat man. Otis put up his arms but the thin man stepped forward and to the right, sliding his left arm across the fat man's neck and whipping his left leg into the back of his knees. The fat man's body seemed to elevate, levering backward, then down hard into the floor. The room shook. The thin man was on him, wrenching his arm just short of tearing it from its socket. Otis screamed.

"Tell me about room 22," the thin man rasped.

Otis drew in a lung full of air. "I don't know nothin'! There ain't been nobody in room 22 in a week!" He made a jerking movement with his body but the thin man slightly twisted his arm and Otis screamed again.

"Tell me about room 22," the thin man rasped.

"I don't know! I don't know! This is my place and I don't know how you got in that room! I'm tellin' the truth!"

"I've got a lot of time. We can stay here all day. I think I'm pretty good at this."

I think I'm pretty good at this? Why the hell do I think that?

"I'll ask you again—tell me about room 22." The thin man heard something in his own voice that he didn't like. But it was there. He *was* good at this.

"I don't know . . . !"

The thin man twisted hard on the arm, heard the shoulder joint pop loose with a sound like tearing apart a chicken. There was a high piercing sound, not really a scream, but something escaping from the fat man's throat. He went limp, his head falling backward and thudding into the floor. He did not move.

The thin man stood up and went quickly through the inner door and into the tiny office. There was only the narrow counter, the broken chair, a small television and a fan that was running on top of rusting file cabinet. He used the tail of his shirt like a glove and pulled open the file drawers—and found them full of old clothes, shaving gear, condoms, panties, porn magazines and other detritus left behind in the rooms by their hourly occupants. There were no registration cards, nothing that would provide a link to the whores and johns who used the motel, nothing related to room 22. Or to any other room. He could not even find the keys.

He kicked at some loose trash on the floor, tipped over the broken chair and looked under the bottom, dumped the overflowing cardboard box that served as a wastebasket. He knew it was useless. He went back into the other room.

The early sun was pushing hot air through the open door, the light falling on the fat man like a bright shroud. The fat man groaned heavily, holding his shoulder, his head moving slowly from side to side. The thin man started for the door, then saw a heavy folding knife on a table by the bed. He stopped, looking at the knife. He picked it up, opened it, hearing the blade lock into place, and stepped to the fat man. He grabbed the fat man's broken shoulder— a deep groan came from the man's bowels—and sharply rolled him over onto his stomach. He grabbed the fat man's hair, lifting his head, exposing his throat. He put the knife at the fat man's neck.

He held the knife in front of him, the blade flat to the ground, pointed at the other man's throat. The other man advanced a step, waved a baton he was carrying, a stupid grin on his face, the smell of sweat from his dark uniform floating out across the room . . .

He stopped.

A memory.

His hand and the knife were frozen, rasping sounds coming from the fat man. He searched hard in his mind, trying to find more of the memory. But it was gone. There was nothing left but an anger so deep that it made him grind his teeth.

I was going to kill him, he thought. *I was not going to hesitate, not going to think about it, I was just going to kill the son of a bitch.*

But I did hesitate.

64

He let go of the man and stood up, the knife dangling from his fingers.

Who the hell am I?

The fat man started to twitch, tiny mewling sounds coming from deep inside him.

And do I really want to know . . . ?

He folded the knife and put it in his pocket and went out into the bright, killing sunlight of El Paso.

* * *

He fished the bus ticket out of his pocket and stared at it, squinting in the hard light. The ticket was his only connection to some other life, some other time and place. He thought maybe the bus station was somewhere near downtown. He walked slowly off in that direction.

* * *

The bus was almost full and he worked his way to the back and into the last seat. He closed his eyes and waited for the bus to move and when it did a faint odor of diesel fumes came into the back of his throat and nearly made him ill. He fell asleep.

* * *

When he awoke he stared out the window but saw nothing. The light was weak and strange and he had no idea how much time had passed. It didn't matter.

The other seats around him had been full when he sat down but now they were empty, some passengers doubled up in seats farther toward the front of the bus. It took him a moment to realize he was the reason the passengers had moved away. He inspected himself. His clothing was out of a throw-away box; his shoes badly worn, stained, as though he had pissed on them. He apparently hadn't shaved in several days. He had no idea when he had last bathed; he could smell himself. He stared at the empty seats and knew that he was different. Whatever he had been before, *whoever* he had been before, he wasn't that man now. The empty seats told him it was true.

He was homeless and penniless. But that wasn't the hard part. The hard part was, he was nameless.

He half-slept in small bits of time as the bus moved north, his body engaging some sort of reflex that prevented him from going fully under, always on the verge of being fully awake, instantly, as though afraid some unseen danger might get close to him before he could react. A couple of times he jerked upright in his seat, his body tense, only to see that no one on the bus was paying any attention to him. He stared at the backs of their heads, looking for anything familiar. He got up, intending to walk to the front of the bus and back again, just so he could see their faces. *There must be someone on this bus who knows me.* But he stood there at his seat, weaving slightly from the motion of the bus, knowing he would find no one who knew him. He sat down.

He closed his eyes and tried to let his mind summon images, some familiar bit of recall that would open doors to other images, other times. But there was nothing. He took out the small pad of paper and the pencil stub and began to write whatever came to his mind, single words, phrases, a description of Miranda, the feel of the knife in his pocket . . .

He watched the man come, the stupid grin turning into a sneer, the baton moving faster now, twirling. He knew the other man expected him to back up, but he didn't. He took a quick step forward, seeing the slight surprise on the other man's face. The baton came down hard but he had stepped inside it, the man's wrist whipping into his shoulder. He stroked the knife downward at an angle, the blade slicing down across the other man's left shoulder and down across his chest, across the right side of his gut. A two-foot cut. The other man looked surprised, his eyes dropping to his belly, his blood running freely and down onto his legs.

His mind snapped back to the bus, the image gone. There was a sheen of sweat on his forehead and the backs of his hands. But whatever had happened, wherever he had been, he wasn't there any more. But he remembered it, and he wrote it down.

There was a buzz of conversation from the other seats, most of it in Spanish, and again he was interested to know that he could understand it, nearly every word.

Somewhere just south of Albuquerque he awoke to find a small girl standing in front of him. She had raven black hair and the delicate rounded features of Pueblo Indian children. She slowly raised her arm and held something out to him. A sandwich wrapped in waxed paper. He stared, wondering how long it had been since he had seen waxed paper. She pushed the sandwich a little closer. He took it, holding it reverently in both his hands. He unwrapped it. He had no idea what it was but he began to eat it—some sort of meat between thick slices of Pueblo bread. When he looked up again the girl was gone.

Pueblo bread. He remembered Pueblo bread.

* * *

The long, sloping hills north of Albuquerque were nearly barren and the high desert sunlight turned them a bright sand color that hurt his eyes. In every direction there were misty purple mountains parked on the horizons, guarding the limits of his vision. The country had a sameness to it that he found comforting, and yet, each time he looked, things changed.

His head rested against the window and he dozed.

* * *

The bus struggled up a sharp rise in the land and eased over the top where the Interstate dropped toward a long slope toward some mountains in the distance. He looked forward through the front windows of the bus and saw the low-slung disruption of a town piled up against the flank of the mountains like a jumble of broken *adobe* bricks.

The road made a miles-long descent, dropping onto a high plain, then rising slightly as it pushed into the edge of the city. He was watching carefully now, wondering. He saw a racetrack to the west, the dirt oval empty, weeds growing along the fences. Houses and commercial buildings were scattered haphazardly across the landscape, the late sun burnishing their upper edges until some of them glowed an odd golden color through the tinted glass of the bus windows. It didn't look familiar. It didn't look unfamiliar.

EIGHT

The big engine did not run smoothly but Angelo Marcuso didn't really care. The car was lowered and shiny, had fancy wheel covers, dark tinted windows, a paint job that probably was worth more than the car. Even in the evening's fading light the car's paint picked up lost pieces of glittering sunlight. It was the best paint job Angelo had ever owned. It looked *bad*, man, all that glittery paint on his cunt pick-up car, that bitchin' pin strippin' on the trunk, big spider like it was ready to jump right off a there. Didn't matter—well, it didn't matter much—that there was a tiny scratch back there where the bitch's shoe had raked across the paint.

He thought about his old pickup truck, the red paint faded to a dull rust, tailgate missing, one headlight punched out and dangling against the grill like an eye blown out of a cadaver. Piece of shit truck. Could never get a woman to get in, go for a ride. Woman just wouldn't get in a truck like that. He had parked it next to his shack on the edge of an *arroyo* south of town. Hadn't even started it up since he got this car. Yeah. This car. Best paint job he had ever owned. Didn't matter that the engine was a piece of shit.

Angelo eased the car up the slight grade of Old Santa Fe Trail and stopped at the traffic light at the corner of the Plaza, the heart of the old city.

But Angelo didn't care about that "heart of the city" shit, had never really wondered how long the Plaza had been there. He sat with his foot on the brake and leaned forward, his chest resting on the steering wheel. Dozens of tourists were crossing the intersection, going and coming from restaurants and galleries. Angelo was bored with tourists. Too many tourists covered up the locals, made it hard to keep looking. He thought he had to look at everybody, even the tourists, each and every one. Then he remembered he only had to look at short people, short skinny people, clothes about to fall off their backs.

"Too many fuckin' tourists, man. Ain't no room for us *nativos* no more. *Nativos*, man, born and raised here. We got rights, man."

Beano Clapper looked at Angelo. Beano was an Anglo. He didn't know what Angelo was, but he wasn't Hispanic. At least, he wasn't all Hispanic. Maybe he wasn't anything. Beano wondered what *nativos* meant.

"You wasn't born here, Ange. You wasn't even raised here. Come to think on it, you ain't been here but about a year or so. Where you from, anyway?"

"Fuck's it to you? I live here now, dickhead, and that gives me rights."

"What we doin' on the Plaza anyway, man?" Beano mumbled. "Ain't never gonna see that little street fucker, all these tourists flappin' around."

"Cause this is where he's gonna show up, dummy. 'Cause everybody comes to the Plaza, even them street fuckers—goddamn, the only thing I hate worse'n tourists is them street fuckers. Besides, I seen him down here lots'a times. It's just a matter 'a time 'till he shows up. Anyway, this is more fun than lookin' in them shit piles where all them guys hang out."

Beano knew what a shit pile was. He lived in one, his trailer-house, in the desert outside of town. They had put him in there long ago and simply gone away. "They." His family, Beano thought.

Maybe. He had never seen "they" again. Beano vaguely remembered a farm, or maybe a ranch, remembered a dog hanging from a rafter in a barn. Maybe that was it. He was pretty sure he had hanged the dog. It was one of his favorite memories. It was one of his few memories.

A shit pile. He thought maybe one day he'd stuff Angelo into a shit pile. He thought maybe Angelo *was* a shit pile.

"Ange, how come you hate them street people . . ."

A woman stepped in front of the car and Angelo blew the horn. The woman leaped, nearly falling. She whirled and glared at the car, saw Angelo's face leering through the windshield and quickly walked away.

Angelo laughed, and that made the pain shoot through his head again. His head had ached every hour, every day, for the past week. He shifted his bloated body in his seat and looked at himself in the rear-view mirror. The bandage on top of his head had started to come loose and he tried to stick the soiled tape back to his thick, black hair, so loaded with oil that it made Angelo's hand shiny. The tape wouldn't stick. He reached forward and wrapped his fist around the big wooden cross that dangled from the mirror on a piece of chain. He squeezed as hard as he could.

Little son-of-a-bitch, he thought. *Little son-of-a-bitch.*

He rolled his head and looked to his right at big Beano slouched in the other seat, his belly rolling out over his belt.

No wonder Beano never got no women, Angelo thought, *belly like that.*

Through the window Angelo could see a tall black woman standing on the corner by the La Fonda. She was looking at the car. The woman was maybe six feet tall and stood straight, proud of her height. Her skin had the color and texture of mild chocolate and her midnight hair hung glistening below her shoulders. She was wearing a long, thin blouse and pants of some sort of soft, thin material, clothes that clung to every soft, rounded place on her body, clothes Angelo had seen only in the magazines his cousin kept strewn around her apartment, magazines he sometimes took into her bathroom and masturbated on, closing the pages on his own semen, knowing his cousin would find the stuck pages and know exactly what it was. Angelo thought he could see the mound of the woman's cunt rising through the thin pants.

She must be a whore, Angelo thought. *A high priced black whore.*

He punched Beano on the shoulder, hard. Beano jolted upright, staring at Angelo.

"Jesus, Ange . . ." Angelo was always punching Beano to get his attention, usually to tell Beano to kick the shit out of somebody Angelo had taken a dislike to.

One of these days, Beano thought, *I'm gonna to kick the shit out of Angelo.*

Now and then, Beano had flashes of . . . thinking, which was hard for him. He didn't know what caused the thinking, but he recognized it when it came. Usually, his thinking just confused him. Beano had a flash of thinking now.

But then who I got to hang with, I beat the shit out'a Angelo? he wondered. *I only know one other guy in this whole fuckin' town, and he's a street guy, just like that little fucker we lookin' for. And if Angelo finds out I know one of them street guys, he won't ever let me hang with him again.* And he knew it was why he always did what Angelo said. Damn. It was early in the morning, but Beano wished he had a beer.

Through Angelo's window, something down the street caught Beano's eye, a slight movement, a slight man, big feet on a small body.

"Ange! Ange!" Beano whispered, gripping Angelo's shoulder.

But Angelo wasn't paying attention. He was looking through Beano's window at the black woman. "Look at that. Ain't that fine, now," he muttered, more to himself than to Beano. "She lookin' at my car, man." Angelo ran his hand through his oily hair. He wiped his hand on the steering wheel.

Beano turned and looked out the window at the black woman, who noticed their stares. He whirled back to face Angelo.

"Ange! Ange, dammit, I'm tryin' to tell ya, I think I seen him! Seen that little fucker! Went into one of them art stores down there . . ."

Angelo leaned across Beano to get closer to the window. "Hey, bay-bee," he said. He tried to make his voice low and husky but it just sounded mean and scratchy. "You lookin' for a ride?"

The woman looked past Beano, directly at Angelo, expressionless, as though Beano were not there, then turned and walked across the street. Her walk was smooth and regal, her hips moving under silky material in the ultimate dance of barely concealed flesh. At the other side of the street she turned right and started east along the store-fronts.

"Ange, man, I tell ya I saw . . ."

"Shit, man," Angelo said. "Watch this."

He swung the car sharply to the right, through the red light and into the left lane of the one-way street, holding the big sedan back, keeping pace with the woman. A block away the street ended at St. Francis Cathedral, its cool stone face in the shadows thrown by the first honey-colored warmth of the sun.

"She ain't lookin' at us man, but she knows we're here. I know how these bitches operate. She's available, man, she's trollin', just tuggin' us along 'til she gets us to where we can talk."

"C'mon, Ange, she ain't no whore. She's a goddamn tourist. You keep messin' with her . . . Why you keep messin' with her when I saw him, man, I saw *him.*"

Angelo eased the car forward, passing the woman, then stopped, jamming the shift lever into Park. "If she keeps on walkin' you take the wheel and keep even with us." He was already opening the door.

"Hey, bay-bee," Angelo said, putting one leg out of the car. The woman stopped. Beano started to slide over under the wheel but Angelo was still there. Angelo wasn't getting out.

Angelo sat stock still, his eyes focused on the compact, angry snout of a stainless steel .380 automatic. The woman was standing against the door, keeping it from opening further, the pistol inches from Angelo's face.

"Look at the hammer," she whispered, rolling the barrel down, pointing the gun at Angelo's chest. He could see the hammer at full cock. Angelo's head suddenly ached even more.

"You're a heartbeat away from breathing through your forehead," the woman said, no emotion in her voice. "Put your fat, ugly leg back in the car and drive away from me."

Angelo slowly pulled his leg into the car. The woman whipped her hip into the door, slamming it, cracking it into Angelo's knee. Angelo clamped his mouth shut against the pain. Beano hadn't moved. He and Angelo were both jammed behind the wheel.

"You make a wonderful couple," the woman said, her voice still flat. "And one more thing . . ." she planted the butt of the pistol hard against the door and raked it slowly toward the back, paint flecks chipping and flying "if I ever see either one of you again, I'll kill you."

Angelo shoved Beano hard across the seat and gunned the car up the street to the Cathedral, slamming it to a stop at the corner. He tried to whip the door open and leap out but the latch caught and he banged his aching head into the doorframe. Growling, he leaned back and rammed his shoulder into the door. There was a metallic cracking sound and the door flew open. Angelo leaped from the car, shaking from anger, his stomach roiling from fear, his knee almost buckling. He turned and rammed his hand under the seat, coming out with a snubby little .38 and waving it toward the Plaza.

"I kill you, bitch, do that to my car!"

The woman was gone.

"Fuckin' bitch! Fuckin' bitch!" he screamed. *"I hate all you fuckin' bitches!"*

Two-dozen tourists quickly faded through the doors of nearby galleries.

Still shaking, Angelo got back into the car and whipped the door shut. It hit with a bang and bounced open again, the latch broken. Angelo threw the gun into Beano's lap and held the door shut as he jerked the big car around the corner to the right and down Cathedral Place.

Beano Clapper cradled the gun in his lap like a baby. "I'm tellin' you, Ange," he said calmly, "that skinny little bastard went into one 'a them art stores."

NINE

The bus station was a small, ugly masonry building that didn't belong where it was and there was nothing about it he found familiar. On the way into Santa Fe he kept waiting, watching, wanting to find something he recognized, something that said he should be here, belonged here. But there was nothing. For all he knew, the bus ticket the whore had found in his pocket was there by accident. Maybe the whore put it there. Maybe he had no connection to Santa Fe at all.

The bus pulled up by the small building and the people spilled out in a confusion of feet and legs and cheap luggage and relatives. Most of them had someone waiting, and even those who didn't seemed to have a place to go. He was the only one who went inside the building.

He was alone. He sat on a bench and waited, still smelling the diesel fumes that clogged the air. For some reason, he thought someone might be there. Maybe some cops. Maybe a middle-aged woman with a clipboard, a lumpy bureaucrat or two.

A lumpy guy in an ill-fitting suit, a stained gray shirt that once had been white, a wide tie that hung six inches above his belt. He wore a layer of cheap cologne that could not mask the odor of a man who had gone days, many days, without bathing. The lumpy guy had a file folder under his arm. He took the thin man by the arm and the thin man knew that they were going somewhere "official", somewhere he did not really want to go, somewhere that would produce pain.

The vision of the lumpy guy passed, and he sat there, quietly, feeling that slight tingle of fear behind his stomach. He expected the fear, but he did not know why.

He looked around for the cafe, but there wasn't one. He didn't even know why he looked. As far as he knew, he had never been in this building before.

"Eat at Joe's," he mumbled to himself. And a vision of a chess-board flashed across his mind.

Night was coming to the city and the ticket clerk was looking at him. The clerk nodded toward a sign. The top line of the sign said "No Loitering." The bottom line said "Por Favor, No Tiren Nada en el Suelo."

Outside the bus station the first thing he noticed was the air. It didn't carry the odd smell that he had noticed in El Paso, some sort of industrial thickness that had come at his face like a blanket. He pulled this new air deep inside him again and again until he felt dizzy and he sat on a curb at the edge of the small parking lot away from the few cars parked there and dropped his head and let the dizziness wash over him. He had found something familiar. The air.

He could see the steep flanks of forested mountains rising above some buildings across the street. The failing light painted the hills a golden color and then, while he watched, the color deepened into a blood red that seemed to flow down into the town like thick paint from an overturned can. There were no houses on the hills and he knew the town could not be too large if there were real trees and fine blood-red hills within walking distance.

He had the strange feeling again, the lack of emotion, as though he were carrying a bucket and it was empty and he didn't know why he was carrying it. He sat and waited and watched the traffic on the wide street and then he realized what the feeling was. He was a spectator, not a participant. Whatever was happening to him was not of his making and there was nothing he could do about it, nothing he wanted to do about it. He was completely passive. Waiting.

He took out his notebook.

* * *

Little Jimmy hunkered down at the worktable in the basement of the woman's art store. Bright lights in a low ceiling gave the long, narrow room a feeling of unreality, as though the sun had somehow been trapped down there. He looked at the piece of paper the woman had left on the table. Her handwriting was fluid, graceful, although Little Jimmy would never have thought of it in those terms. He looked at the paper, not understanding what the symbols said. But the woman always told him what the paper said. And Little Jimmy never forgot anything. Four shipping crates to build, the woman said, each measured precisely. Little Jimmy never forgot the measurements.

He went to work, carefully cutting, fitting, shaping, hammering. He liked working with the wood, liked holding the hammer, liked the feel of the saw ripping across the small planks. Lines of sweat ran through the dust on his face. Now and then he adjusted the faded bandana that he had knotted around his neck, pulling it out away from his skin, away from the torn places that still oozed some sort of cloudy fluid.

After about an hour the woman brought him some coffee. She never brought him food. She had tried more than once, but the little man never accepted it. He worked for money, not for anything else, he had said, not looking directly at her. She understood.

Jimmy wrapped the thick cup in his hands and stared at the rounded faces of the old stones that formed the walls of the basement. Even now, he could not bring himself to look directly at her; he could not make small talk with her. Until he got to Santa Fe he had never stood next to a woman like her and he was afraid. Afraid, if he looked at her, she would truly see him and be disgusted. Afraid, if he said more than a few words, she would be unable to bear the sound of his scratchy voice, the way he said his words. Afraid she would be amused.

She was smiling. He knew she was smiling, but still he could not look at her.

The woman walked back to the stairs at the end of the long room and climbed gracefully back up to the gallery, her long skirt swinging, her boots making soft sounds on the ancient wood of the steps.

It was the lawyer, the Indian, who had seen him outside the gallery window, gazing inside at sculpture and paintings, at the weavings, at the glittering jewelry, and who had asked him if he could handle a hammer and saw, if he could build crates. Little Jimmy had only nodded, speaking to the Indian only when necessary. He was afraid of Indians, too. But they had worked out a deal.

He sat on a crate and finished the hot, strong coffee, the best he had ever tasted. Not like the watery stuff he sometimes got from the fast food joints in town. He looked at the far end of the room, at the stairway, at the narrow door at the top. Normally, he would not like being down in a basement, but the stairway was not the only way out. There was a door at the end of the room, opening out into an alley behind the gallery, a full level below the Plaza. He had opened the door once, just to look out. It was always better to have another way out of anything, he thought. Just in case.

Two hours later Little Jimmy fastened the last piece of wood on the last crate, put away the tools and swept the basement floor, the dust rising into the bright lights suspended from the low ceiling.

He climbed the narrow stairs and found the envelope stuck into a crack at the upper end of the handrail. There was money in it, he knew. It was how the woman paid him. He didn't count it. He knew it was right, sometimes even more than he was owed for building the crates. She did that, now and then.

She was standing behind the counter talking with a tourist, the man's pants cut much too short for the stiff boots he was wearing, a new Western hat tilted back on his head. Little Jimmy walked quietly past them. He knew the woman was looking at him and he raised his hand in silent salute.

He paused just inside the door. His eyes swept what he could see of the Plaza and the streets, the soft light of early evening making deep shadows in the doorways. He stepped carefully outside, to the edge of the sidewalk, his body tense, ready. He always did this, now, especially at the gallery, checked everything he could see before he moved. He did not see anyone who looked familiar. He did not see a shiny, low car. The Plaza smelled sweet and old and was safe in the light. It was one of the things about Santa Fe that Jimmy liked most.

He took a deep breath. He felt the envelope in his pocket. He would head to the south end of town. There was a Chinese place down there. He could get a lot of food for the money he had in the envelope. A *lot* of food.

He started down San Francisco Street, his huge sneakers making flapping sounds on the sidewalk.

Behind him, Elena Montoya stepped out of her gallery, watching Little Jimmy plod quickly down the street. She smiled, knowing he was going after food, knowing he would be back.

* * *

On the far side of the Plaza a shiny car eased around the corner, two men slouched in the front seat.

"See, see, I told you he went into that art store," Beano said.

Angelo stared across the Plaza. "Yeah, you told me." But Angelo wasn't really watching Little Jimmy. He was watching the woman standing in the door of the gallery. "You think that little shit talks to that woman?"

"Sure he does, Ange. He goes in there, like I told you. Must talk to her a lot."

"I don't mean just talk, idiot. I mean *talk*, like about what he's seen . . . maybe out there in the dark."

Beano didn't like the word "idiot." One of these days, he would stuff Angelo's tongue down his throat. But Angelo had a good question. Beano thought hard, staring at the woman across the Plaza. Woman like that, hell, Beano would tell her anything. "Yeah, he prob'ly talks a lot. Prob'ly tells her . . . everthing."

"Yeah," Angelo said. "Too bad. She's a fine lookin' bitch. Too bad . . ." His voice trailed off.

* * *

Anthony Cordova's grandfather had been a police officer in Santa Fe. He had watched as *burro* carts loaded with vegetables came up the dusty road from the tiny village of Agua Fria. Brown-skinned men wearing straw *sombreros* led the *burros* and walked steadily toward the Plaza where they would trade their vegetables. Before they went home, some of them would drink cheap pale whiskey in the many ramshackle saloons of the town and Anthony's grandfather would spend his evenings wrestling drunks and breaking up knife fights.

Anthony Cordova's father had been a police officer in Santa Fe. He had watched as battered pickup trucks rolled in from Pojoaque, dodging the potholes in the narrow, two-lane blacktop, moving steadily toward the open markets on the street corners. Other trucks and cars, mostly newer and driven by white-skinned men wearing wide ties and sunglasses, rolled down from the mesa at Los Alamos and bought the *chiles*, beans, apples and corn from the old pick-up trucks. Money would change hands, whiskey would be drunk, and Anthony Cordova's father would spend his evenings wrestling drunks and breaking up knife fights.

Anthony Cordova was a police officer, a detective, in Santa Fe, had been a cop for nearly twenty years. He had watched as crime became more "modern"; as cocaine replaced whiskey and guns re-placed knives and fists; as windowless mini-vans cruised quietly through the town, dealing homegrown *marijuana* out of the van's back doors; as gangs had sprung up and turf wars broke out; as young women disappeared off the streets, homeless women, three in the past eighteen months that he knew of. Maybe more. Some-times they found the bodies. Sometimes they didn't.

Fruits and vegetables were now sold at a well-organized farmer's market in the center of the city, sold mostly to well-heeled Anglo women wearing prairie skirts and turquoise jewelry who drank espresso as they shopped, then carried their shopping bags back to their Land Rovers and drove sedately away.

There were no drunks or knife fights at the farmer's market.

Anthony Cordova, called "Cord" by his friends, called "bastard" or "son-of-a-bitch" by a lot of others, sat in his unmarked police car in a parking lot across the street from the bus station, the thick eve-ning light painting the city that spread out around him. He was in his early forties, his skin the color most men strive for when they go to the beach. His dark hair was cut short, with just a touch of style;

a well-trimmed mustache. His stomach was flat. But he had begun to notice, especially while sitting behind the wheel of his car, a tiny roll of flab just above his belt.

He came to the bus station frequently, just to see who came in. He watched them come out of the station, carrying their paper bags or pasteboard suitcases, wearing shirts that were too small or too worn or too faded, pants that were too short, skirts that their grandmothers had worn, boots that were supposed to be leather but which were some unknown plastic material that would never bend and never be comfortable. He knew that some of the people on the bus were illegal aliens, but he had no interest in them, or in any other specific individuals getting off the bus. Rather, he watched them as a group, as a tiny cluster of bewildered humanity spilling out into a small city that existed nearly two centuries before somebody cracked the Liberty Bell. He watched out of simple curiosity, another way to keep tabs on the flow of people who kept coming into his city.

For contrast, he sometimes would park his car at the La Fonda, or one of the other, smaller, pricier hotels in town. He would watch the people getting off the shuttle that ran directly to the hotels from the airport in Albuquerque. Cord was very aware of the difference between the bus people and the shuttle people. He preferred the bus people. He believed, all things considered, they did less damage to his town.

Cord leaned back in his seat. He had watched the people come out of the bus station and hadn't seen anyone even remotely interesting. He fumbled in his shirt pocket for a cigarette, then remembered he had quit smoking that morning, as he left for work throwing his last cigarettes into the *kiva* fireplace of his small house.

He was about to start the car when the bus station door opened slowly. A tall, skinny guy in nearly-ragged, too-large shirt and pants shuffled out into the light. The air was cooling rapidly, but the man had no jacket. He stood in the parking lot, his face turned up into the fading sun. Even at this distance, Cord could see the man breathe deeply, drawing air as far into his lungs as he could.

Probably another escapee from LA, Cord thought.

He watched as the man looked around the parking lot, then sat on a curb, making no particular effort to hide himself.

A good sign, Cord thought. *If he were on the run, there's no way the guy would sit out there like that, in plain sight, almost as though he wanted to be seen.*

TEN

The bus station was empty. No one would be coming for him. He knew he would have to leave before the counter guy came out and chased him from the parking lot.

He got up from the curb. Off to his left he saw a railroad track. He would follow it. Railroad tracks had to lead somewhere. He shuffled onto the dirt beside the tracks.

He never saw the other guy coming.

The ragged little man came thrashing out of the twilight, legs pumping, arms flailing, oversize sneakers slapping clown-like as he ran, his head turned almost all the way to the rear, more terrified of what was behind him than of anything he might run into. He slammed into the tall man's chest, knocking him backwards, grabbing him, arms locking around his waist, the two of them spinning down into the dirt.

"No! No!" the little man screamed. "You got to let me go!" He rolled over in the dirt, arms flailing, his legs coming up to protect his groin.

Vaguely, at the edge of his mind, the tall man thought he heard the squeal of tires on the street, felt the anger begin to rise in his throat.

I can kill this guy in three seconds. The thought flashed in his mind, neon-colored hate. And then it was gone.

"I'm not stopping you, *amigo*," the tall man said, gritting his teeth, pushing the squirming little man away, getting up out of the dirt. "You got someplace to go, now would be a good time to go there . . ."

The little man leaped up. "I ain't never done nothin' to you! You ain't got no right . . . !"

And then a hand grabbed the tall man's shoulder and spun him, a heavy fist coming down out of the sky toward his face.

He knew he was going to be hit; there was no way to avoid it. He turned with the punch, trying to absorb it, feeling the heavy knuckles thud into the side of his head, registering a fleeting image of the thick, square man who was hitting him, feeling the switches in his brain snapping off, feeling his knees buckle, feeling the warm blacktop against his face.

The thick, square man spun quickly and threw the punch, catching him waiting, not ready. The tall man saw the big fist coming but really did not care. He turned with the punch, knowing it would still catch him, put him down. In an instant, he felt the sun-warmed earth against his face. He lay there, wondering if he would be kicked. He rolled his head slightly, could see the big man out of one eye. He crawled slowly to his feet.

The big man took off his shirt, preparing to do this in workman fashion, leaving nothing to question about how it worked, how it would end. He stepped forward and raised his fists.

The tall man snapped his left foot forward, shooting a left jab at the big man's head, high, and followed with a straight right to the same place. The big man raised his arms and flicked the punches away, and seemed surprised when the tall man's right foot came up and caught him in the balls. The air left the big man's body and bile flew through his throat, choking him. He fell into the dirt, gagging and moaning, vomit running from his mouth and onto the ground.

The others laughed. They did not bother the tall man again for the rest of the day.

The tall man lay there, still wondering if he would be kicked. He rolled his head slightly, could see the big man out of one eye. He started to get up, saw the big man coming. The tall man put his weight on one hand, whipping his legs, catching the big man at the knee, the leg folding up, the big man on the pavement instantly, on his knees, eyes wide with the wonder of it all.

Still on the ground, the tall man spun again, all the way around, felt his foot drive into the big man's ribcage, felt the ribs give, heard the air blow out of the man's mouth, the man sinking backwards, on his ass now, eyes squinting nearly shut from the pain. And then the tall man raised his foot again and drove it into the center of the big man's face.

* * *

Anthony Cordova watched the thin man at the bus station shuffle off toward the railroad tracks, saw the little man come out of the shadows and plow into him, saw them tangled on the ground. He saw the shiny car screech to a stop and the driver leap out.

Cord knew the car, a shiny piece of shit with a spider web on the trunk. He knew the driver, Angelo, knew that the other guy in the car would be Beano, saw Beano slide behind the wheel. But he didn't know what business they had with the two bums wrestling in the dirt.

Saw Angelo hit the tall guy.

Cord put his hand on the door handle, thinking maybe he would trot across the street and flush Angelo and Beano, just for the hell of it, before they could bust up the skinny guy, maybe save the paramedics a run, save the St. Vincent emergency room the expense.

Before Cord could get the door open, he saw the tall guy take Angelo down, the tall guy's moves smooth, practiced, not the phony dance-like moves from the karate movies, but anger-filled. Deadly. Saw Angelo kneeling on the ground, swaying.

Saw the kick. Saw Angelo slam onto his back. Angelo's nose spurted blood, the blood flowing hard enough that Cord could see it from across the street.

Well, shit, Cord thought, *what do we have here?* He waited, his hand on the door handle. *If the skinny guy weighed another thirty pounds,* Cord thought, *Angelo might be dead.*

* * *

Angelo rolled over backwards and kept rolling. He raised his heavy body to his hands and knees, crawled a few feet, then got to his feet and ran limping toward the car, screaming over his shoulder . . .

"I don't care what that little fucker told you! It ain't true! He's just a lyin' little fuck!"

He was almost at the car—but Beano was already pulling away down the street.

Cord could hear Angelo screaming something at Beano as Angelo chased the car, thought he heard the word, "gun", but he wasn't sure. The shiny car turned south on a side street and disappeared, Angelo still running after it.

* * *

The tall man turned toward the little guy, the little guy's arms up, something burning behind his eyes that bordered on hysteria.

"Whoa, buddy," the little guy said, "I ain't gonna do nuthin'. And I'm plumb sorry you had to be standin' here when I . . . uh . . . come passin' through," the little man said. "And, by the way, yew settled that business purty damn quick."

The voice was calmer now, no longer screaming, but, still, it was the worst voice the tall man had ever heard. He backed up a few steps, looking closely at the little man. He was short, wiry, brittle, a rickety crate of a human, his body a bundle of twigs held together by strings of sinew and brown flaps of old leather. Piling up all of his bones and muscles still wouldn't feed a small dog, the tall man thought. He had a rag wrapped around his neck like a huge cowboy bandana and he seemed to look everywhere at once, scanning the parking lot, the street, anywhere his eyes could roam. He was tense, a rabbit ready to run. His eyes stopped briefly on a gray sedan parked in the lot across the street.

Then he stepped slowly toward the tall man, his hands held up, palms out.

The tall man backed up again, his knees almost buckling.

"Yeah, thet's what I thought," the tiny man said, a scratching hillbilly twang, a fingernail dragging across a blackboard. "Yew ain't got the strength to fight nothin'. Angelo come at yew again, he'd 'a kicked yore ass. Course, Angelo don't never come at anybody straight on, not if they be watchin' out, only yew got no way of knowin' thet. Well, c'mon. Cain't hang around here. These here bus station people got no sense of humor."

"You know those guys? In the car?"

"Yeah, I know 'em. Didn't, until a little bit ago. But I know 'em now. Don't really want to know 'em, but ain't got no choice."

"They seem to want you pretty bad, *amigo*. They catch you, your ass is going to be grease. Not much grease, I admit, but grease nonetheless. How come they're after you?"

The little man ignored the question. "You talk purty fer a guy can't hardly stand up." The little man stepped next to him, turned him, an arm slid around his waist and he was led out toward the street. He resisted slightly.

"Yeah, I know, we hardly know each other," the little man said. "But thet guy over there"—he nodded toward the gray sedan across the street, but the man Little Jimmy knew as 'Stick' could see no one in the car—"has already got your vitals stored in his big cop mind and if we hang around here any longer he's goin' to have yore skinny ass stored in the back seat of that po-leece car."

The little man chuckled and the chuckle was worse than his voice. "Let's git you over to the edge of town. Eat some of the food I got stored over there. Then we can figure out what the hell you're gonna do to stay alive here in adobe-fuckin'-gulch."

"What's your name, *amigo?*" the thin man asked, looking down at the top of the little man's head.

"Name's Little Jimmy. That's what I been called since I been here. Kind'a like it. Little Jimmy."

"Who the hell was that guy? What did he want with you. What did he mean, not to believe anything you tell me? You have something to tell me, *amigo?*

The little man ignored the questions.

"Okay, then let's try something else. Maybe you can tell me why the hell I'm tangled up with you. I don't know you. I don't even know why I'm here."

The little man paused, thinking. "Hell, boy, don't none of us know why we're here, why we're there, why we're anywhere. We jist are, that's all. And I don't know you, neither. But, hell, man, anybody punch around on that pig fucker, Angelo, like that, like you did, they got to be all right in my book. If'n I had a book, that is. Say, where you learn thet fancy fight'n, anyway?"

"Somewhere . . . I don't know."

"Yeah," Little Jimmy said, "lots of us do things, we don't know where we learned 'em." He grinned sideways at the thin man.

The thin man stopped, Little Jimmy's arm still around his waist. "Listen, pardner, was there ever a café in that bus station?"

"A café? In thet place. Nope. Not since I been here."

"Eat at Joe's" the tall man mumbled softly.

"Well," Jimmy said, "I think they's a café by the name of Joe's, but it ain't nowhere around here. And it ain't in no bus station."

The tall man stared off into the fading light, his mind a blank. He waited for something else to come, but there was nothing.

Jimmy carefully turned the thin man around, toward the street. Detective Anthony Cordova stood directly in front of them. Jimmy stopped, frozen. He could feel muscles tense up in the thin man's back.

"Howdy . . . officer," Jimmy mumbled.

Cordova said nothing.

"We was jist a-leavin' this here public property," Jimmy said, moving the thin man slightly to the side, away from Cordova.

Cordova stared hard into the face of the thin man, who stared back, but Cord said nothing. He reached into his pocket and pulled out a cell phone, flipped it open, passed it in front of his face, than pressed it briefly to his ear. He snapped the phone shut.

"Wrong number," he said, not smiling.

Jimmy pushed the thin man farther to the side, around Cordova and toward the street. He tried to keep going, but the thin man stopped, turned back toward Cordova.

"Do you know me?" the thin man asked.

"Do you know me?" Cord asked.

"No," the thin man answered.

"Good," Cord said. "You don't want to know me."

"In that case," the thin man said, "I'm not going to invite you to the inaugural ball."

Cord did not smile.

Jimmy turned the thin man and managed to get him farther away from the detective.

Cord did not move.

They crossed the street and back onto the railroad track, Little Jimmy's head moving constantly, searching the street, now and then glancing back at the detective, still standing at the edge of the parking lot. The thin man thought he knew where the tracks went. But he wasn't sure.

"That cop know you?" the thin man asked.

"Thet cop know ever thing and ever body," Jimmy said, glancing over his shoulder again. Cordova was gone. "One bad sumbitch. I jist don't want no truck with him. Name's Cordova." He pronounced it "Core-dove'-a.

"No 'truck'?"

Little Jimmy ignored the jab. "What do they call you?" Jimmy asked. "What'd your mama name you, you don't want nobody to know about?"

He had no idea.

ELEVEN

The massive mountain called Santa Fe Baldy hunkers into the sky-
line north of the city. From its treeless summit you can see history
in all directions, hundreds of miles of New Mexico that stretch into
gentle blue images of other places and other times, dancing quietly
at the limits of your vision. If you stand on the summit at daybreak
and look east, the first soft light of new day hits you full in the face
before it touches ground.

You are alive before the earth is.

The sunrise lights up the top of Baldy and then moves quickly
down across the ridge and into the city. The light is thinly golden.
you can watch the light paint the lower hills and flow down onto the
high desert, splashing across narrow hard ribbons of highways in
the distance, then moving into Santa Fe, nicking the edges of buildings and flickering on turquoise doorways.

You can taste the daybreak.

Beano Clapper had never watched the light spread from the top
of Baldy; he had never been to the summit, never even been up to
the ski area parking lot where the trail to Baldy began. Once, Beano
and Angelo had talked about driving Angelo's car up to the ski area,
but they had never done it. Angelo said he didn't want to waste the
gas, but Beano knew the real reason—Angelo was afraid the car
wouldn't make it to the top and back.

Sure, Beano had noticed the mountain a few times when he stood in front of his trailer house and looked up. He didn't even know the mountain's name. He did not care what its name was. He wasn't going up there and could not understand why anyone would want to. It was just some damned mountain, something for the trust-fund yuppies to make a big deal over while they sipped expensive coffee in trendy little cafes in the middle of weekday mornings when the working people like Beano were already hard at their jobs.

I got a job, Beano thought.

Beano had seen the mountain only a few times because he seldom looked up. But Beano didn't look up much; there was nothing up there. And, for the most part, in spite of his size, Beano was always scared, wary, waiting for someone to step in front of him, waiting for someone to say, *Tell me about Angelo, and those girls.* So he kept his head hunched into his burly shoulders as he scuttled his round body across streets and through the city's few alleys, always moving with a firm pace as though he had some place specific to go, as though he couldn't wait to get there. It was all part of his defense: move purposefully and never meet their eyes. It was easy to do. He had learned it from his only other friend, Willie the Hook.

Willie knew that most Citizens would never meet his eyes, anyway. "If you didn't look at street people, they're not there," he had told Beano.

Except for cops. Usually, when someone looked Willie straight in the eyes, it was a cop. And he didn't like cops.

Beano was walking in the pale wash of early morning light as he hustled north along Galisteo Street and onto the bridge across the meager stream called the Santa Fe River, a narrow trickle that flowed through the heart of the city. Beano had gone down into the river channel a couple of times, but he didn't like it, didn't like being down there where he couldn't see people, couldn't see who was coming up on him. To him, the "river" wasn't a river, it was just some water in an over-sized ditch.

Beano always considered himself one of the working people and he was going to his job. He wore what he always wore to work: old combat boots, baggy dark cotton pants, a heavy black sweater and a flat, English cap with a narrow bill.

Like those guys wear who drive sports cars, he thought.

When he touched the cap he thought he had once owned a sports car, maybe. He wasn't sure. It was hard to remember things, sometimes.

None of the other street guys dressed exactly like Beano. Most of the street people had their own particular "uniform." If you knew what to look for, you could tell who they were from blocks away.

It's good they don't look like me, Beano thought.

Beano thought he wasn't really a street guy. After all, he had a job. And he had an old trailer-house on the south side of town, and every month he got a check from somewhere—Beano wasn't really sure from where—and he could cash the check and buy beer. Only, Angelo drank most of it.

The air was cool and fresh but Beano knew the sun would be warming the Plaza soon. He had a few bucks in his pocket. He would buy a large, black coffee and take it to the Plaza. The coffee was his half of the breakfast that he and Willie the Hook liked to gulp down to start the day, before they started their work. This time of year tourists oozed out the door of every hotel in town and spilled into the streets, pale white bodies moving like huge Styrofoam peanuts drifting in the breeze. If he could find Willie quickly they probably could work their job on the Plaza for a while before the cop on the bicycle showed up.

As he crossed the bridge he glanced down and to his right, down into the river. There was not enough water in the river to catch the light, but wading in the middle of it was a woman, her heavy, wide body covered from head to foot in layers of heavy shirts and thick skirts, the skirts dragging in the shallow water. A floppy, wide-brimmed hat was jammed on her head, her hair stuffed up inside it. A long shawl was draped over her shoulders, a bulging gunny sack slung over her arm. She wore some sort of high-topped shoes. She sloshed upstream for a few steps, then stopped, tensing, seeming to know she was being watched. She turned slowly and stared up at Beano. She looked thick-bodied and strong, her arms wrapped in layers of cloth and hanging out from her body like the arms of a weight lifter. And then she turned and waded on up the stream.

Beano knew who the woman was. Hale Mary, they called her, only nobody knew for sure if that was her name because the woman never spoke. Never. And Beano hated her.

Once, Beano had seen the woman at a picnic table by the river on the west side of town, her bulk barely able to fit on the bench, her gunnysack on the ground in front of her. Beano had always wondered what was in the gunnysack.

He had sat beside her. She did not look at him; did not speak. Beano looked at her, her face thin and finely made, hardly lined from life on the streets. Her face didn't match her body, Beano thought. But he wondered about that only briefly: Beano wondered about many things, but only briefly.

Beano had said that it was a nice day, and the water in the river was cool, and maybe they could find something to eat and would she like to go down over the riverbank and into the bushes and fuck. The woman stood up, smiling at Beano. Beano thought he was going to get laid. A sock dangled from the waistband of the woman's skirt and she pulled it loose. Beano noticed the long taper of her fingers, sticking out of tattered gloves with no fingers. Something else to wonder about . . . by the time Beano realized there was something in the toe of the sock—a bar of soap, he thought later—it was too late. Hale Mary whipped the sock across Beano's face, the heavy soap snapping into his nose. He felt something crunch inside and both his hands flew up to his face, blood beginning to pour between his fingers. He went to his knees and then rolled on the ground, blood everywhere. By the time he got to his feet, Hale Mary was gone.

After that, every time Beano thought of Hale Mary his nose ached. Sooner or later he would get his chance, find the bitch, teach her a lesson. Maybe get Angelo in on it and the two of them would . . .

Nah, Angelo wouldn't be interested. Hale Mary was an old ugly bitch and Angelo only liked them young skinny ones.

But, anyway, every time Beano had seen Hale Mary since then she was out of reach, like now, like she knew, somehow, that he was around.

Wait a minute! The thought shot through his mind. *The hillbilly. That bitch knows the hillbilly!*

"Hey! Wait a minute!" Beano shouted down into the river. "I want to ast you somthin'!"

The woman down below kept sloshing away through the water. Without looking back she slowly raised her hand above her head, then raised her middle finger. She stabbed the finger at the sky.

"Shit," Beano muttered, watching the woman. *I can wait*, he thought. *I got all the time in the world. One of these days . . .*

* * *

Beano got his coffee in a huge foam cup with a white plastic top. The woman who sold it to him smiled and was nice. She always was, even with people like Beano. She was tall and thin and had skin the color of caramel. Beano thought she was beautiful but he had never talked to her, just put his money on the counter and pointed at the coffee cups.

He crossed Water Street and hurried up Galisteo. At San Francisco Street he turned toward the Plaza, then cut through a bank parking lot to Palace Avenue. He wanted to come up on the Plaza from the north side, as far away from the La Fonda as he could. A lot of the early tourists on the Plaza came from the La Fonda and he wanted them coming at him, wanted to be able to get a good look at them.

Beano eased along the bank building, both hands wrapped around his cup of coffee. At the corner, he leaned against the building and waited, watching.

Off to his left, under the *portal* of the Palace of the Governors, the Indians were setting up for the day, spreading blankets on the sidewalk and unpacking jewelry cases. Across from the Indians, in the center of the Plaza, some kids sat on the ledge at the base of the stone obelisk and passed an early morning joint back and forth. A city worker watered the sparse grass. A few tourists sat on scattered benches and gazed toward the still-closed galleries and shops. A tall Indian guy wearing a suit came down Lincoln Avenue, crossed Palace and sauntered east on the sidewalk. He stopped, then held his foot up, showing it to one of the other Indians under the *portal*, a woman. He waggled his foot.

Fuckin' guy's barefoot, Beano thought.

The woman under the *portal* covered her face with a shawl. The tall Indian guy grinned, turned and walked casually across the Plaza.

But none of what he saw really interested Beano. He was looking for Willie the Hook and a cop on a bicycle.

* * *

Most of the iron benches on the Plaza were empty. It was still too early for a lot of tourists, and the locals seldom came to the Plaza during the summer anymore. Beano saw the bicycle cop by the Museum of New Mexico. The cop wasn't watching him, but Beano shuffled off toward the La Fonda Hotel anyway, as far from the cop as he could get. Damn bicycles, he thought. Used to be you could just run away from the cops. Most of 'em around the Plaza were too fat to chase you, or they had to go get their cars. You could be gone before they could get their bellies behind the wheel. But there was this one bicycle cop looked like a body builder, could be on you and have your ass on the ground before you let go of your dick, got your hands out of your pockets and started running.

Beano sat on a bench on the corner near the La Fonda, one eye on the cop. He held the coffee between his legs to keep it warm.

A hand slid over Beano's shoulder. Beano froze, his eyes pinched shut, his bowels ready to erupt in gas. He waited for the cop to say something.

"Open your eyes, you chickenshit Citizen. You got your half of breakfast?"

Willie the Hook eased around the bench and slid in beside Beano. He had a half-pint of cheap vodka in a large foam cup. He was wearing stained painter's overalls, ragged sneakers, and a knee-length, ancient brown duster. Beano had never seen Willie when he wasn't wearing the duster. Willie the Hook was slender, rangy, built like a man who should be wearing a duster. His angular face was almost handsome, one of those chiseled faces that could change instantly, depending on what mood Willie was in or what he wanted you to think of him, or what he had been drinking. When he wanted to, he could make a good impression on people. When he wanted to, he could look like the angel of death.

"Holy Jesus, Willie, you damn near caused me to . . ." A thick gurgling sound rumbled from beneath Beano's wide ass.

Willie jumped up and moved away a couple of steps, waving his hand in front of his face. "Let me know when it's safe," he said.

"You shouldn't do that, Willie, sneak up on a man like that. Ain't good for the di-gestive track. And I ain't no Citizen."

"Well, you ain't one of the People neither. Matter of fact, I don't know what the hell you are, except you can fart bigger'n any elephant I ever did see. We gonna do tag-team, or are you just gonna sit there and fart all the tourists away?"

Beano took the coffee cup from between his legs and held it up.

"Goddamn, Beano," Willie said, moving back another step, "you had it between your legs? Jesus, man, let it air out before you take the top off it!"

Beano waved the cup in front of him, sniffed it carefully, then eased the top off and held it out to Willie, who took a small sip and then dumped vodka into the cup.

They took turns sipping at the cup, dumping in more vodka as they went. It took them a half-hour to drink all the coffee and by the time they got to the bottom of the cup they were sipping almost pure vodka.

"Say, Willie, you ever see that little screech owl hillbilly guy? Wears that big fuckin' wooden cross around his neck."

"Yeah, now and then. Hate the little bastard. Always jittery and shit like that. Thinks he's better'n everbody else. Wears that big cross like he's some sort of preacher." Willie spat on the sidewalk.

Beano looked at him carefully. "He's a street guy, like us . . . you. What'd he ever do . . . ?"

"Got himself a job workin' for that broad owns that gallery over there." Willie nodded toward the Montoya Gallery. "That was gonna be my job. Broad wouldn't hire me."

"You know his name?"

"Yeah. Calls himself Little Jimmy. One of these days I'll 'jimmy' his boney ass. I like that cross, though. Maybe I'll get my hands on it . . . one of these days.

"How come you're interested?"

"Nuthin'," Beano mumbled. "Just wonderin'."

They sat quietly, sipping, waiting for the Plaza to come alive.

"How come she wouldn't hire you?"

"What?"

"That art store woman. How come she wouldn't hire you?"

"Fuckin' crazy woman. She said . . . she said . . . she said I stared at her tits a little too long. A little while was okay, she said, but somewhere in there I had to look her in the face. I never did, she said."

The tourists started to arrive. Beano and Willie the Hook were ready for tag-team. Beano, thinking about tits, forgot about the little hillbilly guy.

TWELVE

"Stick."

He didn't have a name, so Little Jimmy named him.

He was rightly named. When he moved, his thin body parts were like dry sticks, his rickety arms dangling at his sides on sinewy strings, bobbing with each step. His legs seemed to move forward at the hips, but never to the side, as though his bony joints could only move ahead, never dodging anything that confronted him. Each time a leg moved forward, his chin dropped toward his chest, his head jerking at the end of some unseen string. Long ago, in some unknown place, his eyes had squeezed into a permanent squint that did not let in the sun. The squinting eyes moved constantly, sweeping everything in front of him, darting to the side. At unexpected times he would stop and turn, staring directly behind him, his arms coming up slightly, an anger growing in his throat.

There's a word for this, he thought. *Paranoia.*

He was weak and always tired, as though recovering from some long ordeal. His head ached frequently and he was sometimes dizzy. His hair, graying at the temples, was cut short and ragged—the result of Little Jimmy's non-skill with a pair of scissors—and the sun burned into his skull.

If Little Jimmy had been taller, they would have been a matched pair. Except for their voices. Stick's voice was smooth, dark, low. It came at you softly from some place that couldn't be reached.

And he was restless. No matter where Little Jimmy took him to spend the night, Stick wanted to move on the next day. He just hadn't found the place he was supposed to be, he told Jimmy.

Little Jimmy walked with him, sometimes holding onto his belt to keep him from falling or to straighten him up when they saw a cop.

It's good to have Little Jimmy around, Stick thought, *even if he did seem a little bit, well . . . Christ,* Stick thought, *he's as paranoid as I am.*

The tiny man was a small deer in a forest of predators, constantly wary, his eyes darting quickly across on-coming faces and passing cars. He carried nothing that he couldn't get in the pockets of his baggy pants, always ready to cut and run.

"Some of the other People, they got them big bags 'er them grocery carts," Jimmy said. "Thet's bullshit, man. Cain't move near fast enough, loaded down like thet."

* * *

"I need a change of clothes," Stick said.

"Yeah, I know. You startin' to smell purty ripe. Let's go to the store."

* * *

The Salvation Army drop box was a large metal box with a hinged shelf, like a bin, in its front side. When you pulled the bin out it formed a shelf, like the lid on a street corner mailbox, only bigger. People would come by and stuff their old clothes into the bin, closing it, the clothing dropping inside. There was a hasp on the bin, but there was never a lock.

It was the "store."

First light was barely showing behind the mountains to the east when they got to the drop box. They stood across the dark street for a while, watching the Salvation Army parking lot. Jimmy was sure that none of the other People knew how he worked the box, and he didn't want to risk showing them. When he was sure no one else was on the street, they moved quickly across to the drop box.

Little Jimmy had it all worked out. He opened the bin and Stick helped him climb up onto the shelf. Little Jimmy curled up tight and when Stick pushed the cover closed Little Jimmy tumbled inside the dark, tiny room and dropped onto a pile of clothes. He rummaged around in the dark.

"She-it, man, they's a ton of stuff in here." Jimmy kept up a running commentary from inside the box.

"Come on, L.J., just check it out and let's move on. I don't want to be here when it gets full light."

"Too much stuff piled up, man. Have to take a minute to figure out where to start. Gonna use my lighter . . ."

Stick could hear Jimmy flicking a Zippo.

"Man, that's better . . . She-it!"

Someone had dumped a cardboard box of old kitchen utensils and Jimmy picked out a huge metal cup and a large spoon. He found a cheap tattered daypack, a body-sized piece of canvas and an old, dark blue blanket, probably from the bed of a *rico*. The blanket had only a few stains on it. Jimmy found a shirt and a pair of pants he thought Stick could wear. He stuffed everything into the pack, put it back up on the shelf and held it there. Stick opened the cover and took the pack out.

Little Jimmy climbed back up, clung to the shelf, and Stick pulled the cover open again. And there was Jimmy, grinning into the morning air.

Stick strapped the blanket to the pack and changed clothes, stuffing his dirty rags back into the drop box. But he kept the Hawaiian shirt.

The pack became Stick's home.

* * *

Actually, Little Jimmy could get into the box by himself. He had done it many times before. He just grabbed the handle and swung himself up, his weight pulling down the bin. Then Jimmy swung himself up on the shelf and the bin closed of its own weight.

But he always had trouble opening the bin from the inside. He would cling to the shelf in the darkness, pulling as hard as he could on the edge of the box. Sometimes, the shelf just would not move and Jimmy thought he would have to stay inside the box until the Salvation Army man opened the metal door in the back and found him huddled there. Little Jimmy didn't know if the Salvation Army took prisoners, but he thought they might if they caught him stealing their clothes.

It was easier, now that he had Stick to help him.

They did not really need to get into the box. He knew that he and Stick could just wait until morning and go inside the big building and the Salvation Army man would give them whatever they needed. But Stick wouldn't go inside.

And no matter how many times they raided the box, Stick kept the Hawaiian shirt.

THIRTEEN

The tourists were thick on the Plaza. Beano thought it was like a scene from one of those horror movies he used to watch as a kid, zombie-like creatures materializing out of side streets and buildings and doorways and cars, moving in slow cadence to some unheard music as they angled in toward the center of the Plaza, their heads swiveling slowly toward the La Fonda Hotel, to the Palace of the Governors, the museum, and then back to the La Fonda. They floated past each other in some sort of tourist-fog that seemed to hang in front of their faces no matter where they were, fat women and skinny men wearing clothes they would never wear at home, flowing along the sidewalks and looking but not really seeing and wondering why their kids were bored. Beano was never sure what they were looking for.

All Beano was looking for was a bicycle cop. The cop was gone.

Willie the Hook was wandering around the edge of the Plaza, scouting. Beano waited on a bench. It shouldn't take long.

And then Beano looked over his shoulder and saw the long, shiny car turning the corner over by the bank.

Angelo.

Beano slid down off the bench, trying to make himself smaller, trying to hide. If Angelo saw him here at the Plaza, he'd wonder why. Sooner or later, he'd find out that Beano was hanging out with his only other friend, Willie.

* * *

Willie heard the car before he saw it, the engine making a clump-ing sound as though one cylinder wasn't firing, the heavy engine having a hard time turning over at slow speed. The car stopped at the curb beside Willie. Willie decided not to run. There were a lot of tourists around. Nobody was going to do anything to him with all these witnesses.

The driver's door opened. A bulldog-faced man with dark hair and a fat ass hauled himself out from behind the wheel. Willie had always thought these cars were bullshit, too low and too slow for any good getaway work. But he had never been in one, so he really didn't know.

The fat-assed man raised his hand.

"Hey, man. Talk to you a minute."

Willie edged away a couple of steps.

"Hey, man, you know a skinny little guy, 'bout this big?" The man made a height motion with his hand. "Wears floppy clothes?"

"Don't know anybody like that," Willie mumbled.

"What? You got to speak up, man." The guy took a step toward Willie. Willie edged farther away.

"Hey, man!" The other guy was yelling now. "Hold up for just a damn minute! I got to find this guy! Owe him some money!" The guy pulled some bills out of his pocket.

Willie hesitated.

The guy raised his other hand, dangling a big wooden cross on a piece of chain.

"Bought this from him. Cop come along and I didn't have a chance to pay."

Willie was ready to run, but he waited, staring at the cross dan-gling from the fat man's hand. He knew who the fat man was,

Angelo, the guy Beano sometimes hung out with. Beano wanted to know about the hillbilly. And so did Angelo.

What the hell is going on?

"I might know . . . something," Willie mumbled. He didn't know anything, didn't know where the hillbilly was. But, what the hell, he could make something up. Maybe get a buck or two out of the fat guy. Maybe cause the hillbilly some grief in the process. "You maybe want to trade that cross . . . ?"

"Sure. I don't really like the thing, anyway. Just bought it from the hillbilly as a favor. Here, take it." Angelo held out the cross.

In spite of himself, Willie felt his hand start to reach for the cross. Then something inside him clicked into place, some survival reflex, some nerve-tingling jolt that fed a message to his brain—*don't let him get his hands on you!*

Willie spun and walked quickly down the sidewalk.

"Fuck you, asshole!"

Willie heard it, fading behind him, but he still didn't turn back. Too big a risk. He would find some other way to fuck with the hillbilly. Willie scurried all the way across the Plaza before he dared look back. The fat-assed guy and the car were gone.

And so was Beano.

* * *

On the south side of the Plaza, Little Jimmy stood just inside the Alvarez Montoya Gallery, watching the Plaza through the shaded light that pooled under the *portal.* He seldom hung out inside the gallery. The art woman didn't mind, but sometimes her cousin, the big cop, would just suddenly appear, like out of nowhere, and Jimmy didn't like to be in the gallery when he did that. And the cop didn't like him there, either. But this morning Jimmy had been watching Beano and Willie the Hook, Little Jimmy standing frozen, motionless, inside the gallery, knowing that bad shit was only a few feet away. Jimmy wondered what Beano was doing there, without Angelo. Angelo was dangerous because he was crazy, but Beano was dangerous because he was stupid. And when stupid people got wound up, bad things could happen. Really bad things.

Maybe they split up. Look for me one at a time. Cover more ground.

And then he had seen the shiny car, had seen Angelo dangle something in front of Willie the Hook.

Dangle something.

Even across the Plaza, Jimmy knew what it was, what it could only be. His cross. His big wooden cross.

Jimmy wrapped his arms across his bony chest. It was warm today, but suddenly Jimmy was cold.

He faded back into the gallery and disappeared down the back stairs and into the basement.

FOURTEEN

He lived the street life.

Little Jimmy, finally realizing that Stick's mind was empty, took him through the town, showing him where he could go in relative safety and where he should not go at all. Trying to jog something loose in Stick's head.

They started in the center, at the Plaza.

"Them locals will tell you they don't come to this Plaza no more. Too many tourists, them locals say. Thet's bullshit, man. *Ever-body* come to this place sooner or later, even people you ain't never met yet, don't want to see."

But Stick wanted to see everybody. Standing on the grass of the Plaza, Stick thought he might be in the center of some universe not of his making, but which somehow controlled his life.

On a Plaza bench he saw a small, hardcover notebook with spiral wire binding, a pencil stuck through the wire. The little note pad he had stolen in El Paso was almost full, so he picked up the notebook and put it in the pocket of his baggy pants.

He turned and looked south at the row of shops and galleries under a long *portal*. A woman walked out from one of the galleries and stood in the shade, motionless, staring at him, a slight breeze moving the hem of her long skirt. At first he thought she was look-ing at someone else. But she was not.

"I wonder who that is," he said, out of the side of his mouth, not taking his eyes from the woman.

Jimmy looked sideways at Stick. "Man, thet's my boss. Don't you be doin' no thinkin' about her. You a street guy. She eat you fer lunch and not have enough left over to give to the dogs!" Jimmy laughed, the sound jangling in air.

Stick could not take his eyes from the woman. She turned and walked slowly back into the gallery. Even from a distance, Stick could see how her hips worked under the long skirt, feel the flutter in his chest, feel . . . something.

"Your boss? What . . ." But Jimmy was gone.

* * *

They went out into the town and walked the lanes and the narrow streets, Stick's weak legs and his lanky frame combining to give him a staggering silhouette against a sun that grew hotter by the day. He walked, drank a lot of water. Sweat ran constantly from his body.

And they were not alone.

As he gradually learned what to look for, Stick saw street people everywhere, dozens of them, most of them trying not to be seen. But there were some who didn't seem to care, women who could not resist showing the Citizens that they still had a touch of class, a tiny remaining flash of dignity, of belonging, or men with a touch of brass who had some scam playing that only worked with tourists.

Little Jimmy had stopped wearing the bandana around his neck, and Stick could see the weird markings, maybe old bruises, that showed on his wrinkled skin. He would not explain the bruises.

But Jimmy did explain his "rounds," those routes that he considered his own, the routes where shelter, food, water and other things of necessity or interest could be had. He showed Stick the standpipes at public buildings that dripped clean water, the small *arroyos* that were scattered through the town and along the railroad tracks, the bridges that provided shade, places to forage, places to hide. He took Stick to one of his favorite places, the parking lot behind the Zia Diner.

"Them tourist Citizens, they come out'a thet diner with them foamy cartons. Put 'em on top of their car. Iffen yew quick, yew kin grab 'em and disappear 'fore they even git their car unlocked."

They stood scouting the lot.

"There's one," Jimmy whispered, pointing to a fat man fumbling with his keys, his foam container on the top of his huge sedan.

Stick didn't like the looks of the fat man. He put his arm around Jimmy and gently held him back. The fat man drove away with his food still on the roof of his car.

Stick turned to watch him leave, and that's when he saw the woman. She was standing in the back door of the diner, watching silently, her red hair pulled tightly against the back of her head. She turned and disappeared inside.

Little Jimmy knew every market and restaurant where food could be had from the Dumpsters out back, or where people would leave food, maybe wrapped in newspaper, on the back railing, an invitation for street people. Because of Jimmy they never lacked for food and as the days went by Stick grew stronger, his gait steadier. He no longer hitched and jerked quite so much as he moved and he could walk whole blocks without Little Jimmy's help.

And then one day he tried running, and discovered that he didn't jangle when he ran. The loose arms and legs that sometimes seemed uncontrolled when he walked, flopping idly, his feet seeming undirected . . . when he ran the limbs came together in firmness and agility and flowed around and under, carrying his slatted body with grace, the loose-limbed gait of large cats. He could not run far but he ran well and he knew it was something he had done often in the dark part of his life he could not remember.

Little Jimmy kept checking the Salvation Army box and finally came out with a pair of exercise pants like those he had seen the *ricos* wearing when they ran through the streets of Santa Fe. And a tee-shirt. And a bandana. He gave them to Stick.

"Nobody in his right mind jist runs fer the hell'uv it," Jimmy had said. "See a street guy runnin', always think he runnin' away from somethin'. You ain't gonna see me runnin'," Jimmy paused, glancing around, "'less I'm runnin' fer my life.

"Wear this stuff when you run. They don't look too close, they think you're jist another Citizen out fer a jog."

Stick began running every day. Gradually, he ran longer. And he ran alone. And he always wore the clothing Little Jimmy had given him.

* * *

He was running now, more like jogging, just dragging a slow pace along the road that ran up into the hills to the north of the town. He knew there was a ski area up there somewhere, but he hadn't been there yet. At least, he didn't think so. He thought he could ski, somehow feeling right when he thought about the equipment, a familiarity, something humming in the back of his mind. Once, he had stopped briefly in a ski shop on Water Street. Ski season was long over, but there were a few pairs of skis and boots stacked along one wall. Stick stared. He knew they were skis, and ski boots, but they looked strange to him, equipment that was from another time. Maybe even another age. Science fiction.

He never went back to the store.

He jogged up the road toward a place called Hyde Park. It was as far up the road as he had been.

He liked Hyde Park. So far, it was perhaps his favorite place. He had tried jogging up there several times, but never quite made it. Always had to hitchhike to finally get there. Maybe today he would make it.

He was jogging on the left side of the narrow, winding two-lane, facing the traffic. It was early morning, the sun not yet on the road in the bottom of the canyon, the air still and cool, nothing much moving in the hills above the town. The road took him into the pines and the pine smell floating against his face always made him slow down to a walk for a few yards, long enough to make sure he pulled the scent deep inside him. A pine forest. The scent washed back and forth in his mind, looking for a place to rest, a picture to paint. A memory. But nothing came.

He jogged past a couple of side roads that led off into expensive housing developments. He knew better than to jog up those roads. He kept to the highway, feeling the sweat begin to soak his t-shirt and the daypack that bounced on his back. The embankments on the sides of the road grew steeper. Today, he thought, he might make it all the way to the park.

He heard the car coming behind him, the heavy engine laboring up the incline. But it was behind him, would pass him in the right lane, plenty of room.

The sound of the engine grew louder, revving up when it didn't need to. Stick turned his head. The car was picking up speed, veering into his lane, the left wheels beginning to drift onto the gravel, the engine climbing. In a split second he saw the face of the driver and he knew the man would try to kill him. Stick turned sharply to his left, took one step, and launched himself flat against the steep bank.

The car missed him by less than a foot.

Stick peeled himself up from the dirt, darted across the road and dived down into heavy brush. He crashed across a small stream and into some sort of thicket and then he flattened himself against the forest floor and lay absolutely still among some small rocks. So still, he could hear his own heartbeat.

So still, he heard everything the car did, heard it slam to a stop, the clang of gears in a bad transmission, the revving of the engine, the spinning of tires as the car shot backward along the road. Almost directly opposite him, it stopped.

Stick did not move. He could not see the car but he knew where it was. If he heard the engine die or a door open he would know the driver was coming after him on foot. He assumed the guy would only do that if he had a gun. Then, and only then, would Stick bolt through the woods.

He did not hear the engine die. Instead, he heard loud voices.

"Where the hell he go? Goddammit, Beano, you supposed to be watching him!"

Beano? What the fuck kind of name was Beano? stick almost laughed out loud.

"Yeah, and you supposed to be runnin' him over!"

"Take the fuckin' gun, go look. He can't be too far into them woods. The fuckin' bank's too steep."

"Aw, fuck, Ange, you always want me to do that part, take the gun and do that part." Beano's voice dropped into a sullen whine. "I ain't doin' that no more."

Stick heard a car door open. He tensed, ready to bolt. But he heard nothing else. He rose slowly, quietly, moving carefully farther up the hill. He found a small opening in the brush, could see the car on the road below.

The driver stood in front of the car, looking up the hill on the other side of the road, the other guy still in the car, his face pressed against the windshield, trying to see what Ange was looking at.

Ange. It's the guy from the bus station, the guy I put on the ground, Stick thought. *The bastardo's looking on the wrong side of the road.*

"Well, go on. Go in there and find him." Beano's whiny voice from inside the car.

Angelo didn't move. Thinking. "I ain't goin' into no woods," he said, barely loud enough for his voice to reach Stick.

A car door opened. Beano got slowly, carefully out of the car, stood by the rear fender and stared up into the woods. "He can't be too far in there. Go git him." Beano was enjoying himself.

And then Stick couldn't resist. He searched quietly until he found a rock the right size, about the size of a softball. He moved silently farther to his right, marveling at how easy it was for him to move soundlessly through a forest. He found the angle he wanted. He launched the rock.

At first he thought he had made a bad throw. The rock brushed some small limbs and he thought it would fall short. But it didn't. It landed almost in the center of the roof of the car, making a heavy crunching sound and bouncing lamely off against the bank.

Beano threw himself to the pavement beside the fender.

"GODDAMMIT! HE'S . . . !" Angelo's words ended in garble as Stick watched him begin to rant, arms flailing, his voice losing all meaning except anger, strangling.

The shot pounded against the side of the small canyon, a flat sound quickly absorbed by the forest. Then two more shots. And then another. Angelo was shooting blindly into the woods. On the wrong side of the road.

Beano stuck his head up. "Wait a goddamn minute!"

Angelo still had the gun pointed up the hill.

"You goddamn . . . you're shootin' the wrong way! I seen the rock bounce! It bounced off that way!" Beano pointed in the direction Angelo had been shooting. "It had to come from back there!"

Stick saw Angelo whirl and look directly at him. He thought Angelo did not see him but he couldn't be sure.

Angelo lumbered across the road and charged directly up the hill, the gun pushed out in front of him.

"Well, shit," Beano shouted after Angelo, "he whack your car and *now* you go runnin' off into the goddamn trees! Whoo-eeee!"

Angelo was struggling up the steep bank, breathing hard, the gun still out in front of him. Beano crossed the road and started up the bank, moving more easily than Angelo.

Stick had not moved. Angelo's path would take him within a few feet of Stick, but Stick stayed motionless in the heavy brush.

Angelo crashed by, and then Beano. They fought through some brush, Angelo falling over a rotting stump, Beano laughing. Angelo pointed the gun at Beano. The laughing stopped. Somewhere beyond them an animal fled, making a distinct noise—the snapping of a twig, the whip of a small branch. Angelo whirled and fired a shot in the general direction of the sound, then charged again through the woods. Beano did not move.

Stick raised slightly. He knew he could get to Beano before the fat man could move, could get to him, could put him on the ground, could kill him. Could kill both of them. They would never see him until it was too late, would never hear him. But he turned and slipped back toward the edge of the bank above the car. Behind him, he heard the two bumbling men move further into the woods. He moved easily down the bank and crossed the road to the car.

Ten minutes. Stick guessed it took Angelo and Beano ten minutes to give up and come thrashing their way back down the hill towards the car. Stick was on the other side of the road now, above the car. Two other cars passed, but their drivers paid no attention to the purple sedan, its two left wheels off the pavement.

Stick saw them come down the other hill, Angelo still using the gun to poke his way through the brush. At the edge of the bank, Angelo fell, his fat body rolling all the way to the ditch beside the road. Beano, plunging down the bank behind him, wisely did not laugh. After all, Angelo still had the gun.

Angelo exploded out of the ditch and charged across the road, throwing his chest across the hood of the car, his breath coming in angry bursts, a man so angry that foam bubbled at the corners of his mouth.

Beano walked carefully to the car and got in.

Stick eased farther away, out of sight of the car. He heard the car door slam, the banging of gears, tires spinning, more metal sounds from the gears jamming back and forth.

And then Stick heard the car stop as Angelo realized there was a flat tire. And the scream from Angelo. Stick marveled at the volume of it, the length, a scream for all time.

Stick waited for more shots, but they didn't come.

Stick grinned. The big folding knife had punctured the tire's sidewall with no effort, no effort at all.

Stick heard the car moving, the odd sound of a disintegrating tire mixed with the engine noise. The sounds faded in the distance. He waited for at least a half hour before he crawled out of the woods. But he would stay up here for a while. It was not a good time to be going back into town.

Angelo and Beano were hunting him, and he did not know why.

He walked up the winding, narrow highway for a mile or so, and then a pickup truck stopped for him. He climbed in the back and felt the air on his face as the truck crawled up the canyon. At Hyde Park, he got out.

He spent most of the day in the woods, enjoying being in a time and place where he was equal to any man. He knew that. He didn't know how he knew it, or why, but he knew that. He wrote about it, about the equality, in his notebook.

He ghosted through the forest as mist moves among trees, vaguely, and without sound. He didn't have to think about it. He just did it. And it always amazed him.

He eased down the slope passing quietly among the fragrant trees until he came to the stream that fell and slid and sounded among the rocks. Across the stream and through a gap in the trees beyond he could see the painted logs and cemented stones of a picnic shelter. A car was pulled up there, its doors standing open. In front of the picnic shelter a man lay on a folding aluminum chaise, a can of beer balanced on his chest, his weight causing the tired webbing to sag almost to the ground. He appeared to be sleeping. Two small boys played at the edge of the woods, throwing pinecones and running and hiding in some mock battle. Inside the shelter he could see a white foam cooler and some cardboard boxes and the aftermath of a picnic scattered around the heavy plank table. He could see no one else. He did not see a dog.

A good bet, that one, he thought. The guy will be lazy. He won't clean up, or not very much. He'll leave some good stuff.

Stick dangled a hand into the stream and moved some floating green scum aside and then cupped his hand into the water and drank. The water was cold and slid between his fingers and dropped and ran down his legs. He drank more. He tried to drink every chance he got, never really knowing when he would get water the next time, or what he would have to do to get it.

He stepped across the stream getting only one shoe wet and moved off and above the picnic shelter and into the thick trees on the hillside. He found a line of sight to the shelter and took off his pack and lay down using the pack as a pillow. He slept. When the car started it would awaken him.

*　*　*

But the car was gone when he woke up and shadows had covered him, the mountain air no longer warm to the touch.

He found that he always slept better in the woods. He didn't know why, knew only that there was something about sleeping in the woods, especially in the daylight, that made him feel comfortable. Safe. He had slept so soundly he had not heard the car leave. That was dangerous, he thought. He would have to try, even in the woods, to sleep more lightly.

And he had been wrong about the man—he had taken the food. There was nothing in the picnic shelter but trash.

Stick sat on the heavy plank table and watched the sun slip behind the far ridges and the light soften on the road and in through the darker open spaces between the trees. He loved this time of day. Almost everyone was gone from the mountain. He saw only one car drift lazily down the road, a black woman behind the wheel, looking straight ahead, intent on her driving.

He got up from the table and stretched and started to move away and that's when he saw the paper grocery bag sitting back beyond the edge of the trees.

The bag was almost full of the remains of the picnic. There were some uncooked hot dogs, some buns, a jar of mustard, pickles, a clear plastic container of baked beans, half a bag of potato chips, three cans of warm beer. There was a small roll of paper towels and some salt. They had meant to load the bag in the car, Stick thought, but left it here in the dirt. Good food, left here in the dirt.

Stick picked up the bag and held it carefully in front of him. He moved off into the trees and up the ridge until he came out on a small rise where the trees gave way to heavy brush and through the brush and out the other side where the soft sun was still warming the rocks. He nestled among the rocks and brush and opened the paper bag and took out a can of beer.

A can of beer. How long had it been since he had had a beer? He started to fumble in his pack for his knife to punch a hole in the can, when he realized it had a small metal ring on the top. He levered the ring up, and the can opened. He sat staring at the open can, small bubbles of foam pushing through the opening. He opened his shirt to the fading sun and let it warm his lungs through from the outside. He raised the can to his lips.

He raised the glass of icy vodka to his lips.

He knew the game.

They did this, every now and then. Put him on display. Sat others, usually official visitors, around the huge table. Fed him. Gave him liquor. Made him say things in Spanish and that other language they thought was Eskimo.

That's where he sat now, at the long table in the banquet room, the table laden with rounds of meat, boiled potatoes, boiled cabbage, loaves of dark, heavy bread, bottles of vodka. He ate with a heavy spoon: they would not give him a fork or knife.

They had put the thin blonde woman next to him. She pulled her chair closely, knowing her role, her shoulders bare in the overheated room, her lips painted a brilliant red, her dress hanging open in the front, her small breasts easily seen each time he reached forward to the table.

The sensation of her presence, her voice, her scent, the whisper of her breathing . . . they were interested in what effect she would have on him. He knew he could never have her. They would never allow that. She was there to remind him of the things he would never have again.

He sipped the vodka, openly watching the woman as she ate and drank—not vodka, but a chilled pale wine. She was the only person in the room drinking wine. And then she drank more. And then more.

As the people at the table ate, drank and laughed, he was careful to tear off small pieces of the dark bread and stuff them in his pockets.

The woman talked and laughed with the others, not even looking at him, but now and then brushing against his arm, pressing her leg against him, leaning forward until her breasts were inches from his hand.

But it didn't go right. Reaching again for her wine she flung out her silken arm and knocked his own glass into his lap and the cold vodka ran down into his crotch. For a moment, she stopped talking. And then she laughed again with her hands flying to her mouth and her shoulders shaking as though he had done something enormously funny. He watched her laugh and he looked around the table at the others also laughing, slapping each other on the shoulder, rocking back in their heavy chairs.

The blonde woman put her head back and laughed some more and pointed at him with the silken arm and then she fell from the chair, arms and legs in awkward, drunken descent, sprawling on the floor, her face into the hard, harsh planking.

They stopped laughing.

He got up. The men with the guns at the ends of the room walked toward him. They led him from the room.

His hand was still cupped around the can of beer, but it had tilted, beer running down between his fingers and spilling into his crotch. He stared into the last of the light at the edge of the mountains and pulled hard at his memory. The banquet and the woman—were they a memory, or just a dream. Would he remember them, whatever they were, tomorrow? He took out his notebook and began to write, describing the memory, the dream, in detail. He wrote until the darkness shut him down. From now on, he would write about every memory—or dream—that he had.

He opened another can of beer and spread the food out on the rock next to him. And he ate. He ate until he could hold no more and he drank the can of beer and then he got the stained blanket out of his pack and burrowed in among the sun-warmed rocks and spread the blanket over him and over as many rocks as he could and the heat from them baked him gently to sleep.

He did not awaken until morning.

It was a night all men should have. He knew that.

FiFTEEN

Little Jimmy liked riding the city buses. With just the change that he sometimes had in his pocket he could go anywhere in town, and if the bus driver recognized him, knew he wouldn't cause any trouble, he could sit in the back, keep his mouth shut, maybe take a nap, ride around for a long time. In an air conditioned bus. Not bad for pocket change.

Jimmy taught Stick to ride the busses, where to get on, where to get off, which driver would let him nap in the cool of the bus.

Now, in the early morning, they sat on the bus, riding south along Cerrillos Road, Stick marveling at the cars he didn't recognize.

Say," Jimmy said, "you never did tell me iffen yew got yerself a hide."

"Sure," Stick said, "I got a hide. In the La Fonda. When things get out of hand, I just go down there and rent a room. Guy that owns the place likes me. Makes me a special rate on the presidential suite."

"It ain't funny," Jimmy said. "Ever street guy I know's got himself a hide. Always need a safe place to go."

They sat quietly, Jimmy scanning the passing scene for anything he didn't want to see.

"Yew know I got a hide." Jimmy's scratchy voice was almost a whisper. "Not too far from here. It ain't much, but nobody'd ever guess it was a hide. Yew go down Cerrillos to the . . ."

"Wait a minute," Stick said, "maybe you shouldn't tell me."

"Nah, it's okay. And, besides, yew might need to use it sometime."

And Jimmy told Stick about the Dumpster behind the market, just off Cerrillos Road.

* * *

"Let's stop by and visit with the Socket Set. Them boys is always a good show. Always got somethin' workin'."

"Socket Set?"

"Yeah, well, iffen the shoe fits," Little Jimmy said, a smile playing across his face, "er maybe in this case, if the socket fits. Them boys is right tight with each other, if'n you know what I mean. One of 'em's tall, he's the Mechanic. The other un's short, more like me. He's Pablo. They sleep on the back seat of a little bitty car. Kind'a sleep spoon fashion, you know? Pablo, he fits into the Mechanic like a socket onto a wrench handle. Don't hardly ever see 'em apart, even when they ain't sleepin'. The Mechanic, he don't talk much. But Pablo, he's right friendly. Comes up town ever now and then. When he can git away from the Mechanic."

They got off when the bus pulled in to a stop at a car dealership across the street from an All-Nighter, a combination gas station and convenience store that never closed. Little Jimmy thought the store was convenient only for bad guys—convenient to get to, convenient to rob. It had been robbed twice in the past month, but not by anyone he knew.

They were early. They sat in the brilliant morning sunshine on a grassy rise in front of a line of new cars and leaned back against a light pole, watching the All-Nighter across the street.

Across a side street from the gas station an auto repair shop was tucked into a cluster of small warehouse-type buildings. A few auto carcasses, some almost skeletonized, were scattered in front of the shop. From behind the shop they saw two men pushing a small, rusted car out into the auto shop's parking lot. Oddly, one of the car's doors was painted bright yellow.

"Them's the Socket Set," Jimmy said. "Like I said, thet tall one, there, he's the Mechanic. Them boys has got a good game workin'."

The Mechanic was gangly, his legs and feet flopping forward with each step, as though he didn't really know where to put them. His skin was pale, almost chalky. His large hands spread against the back of the car, fingers splayed out like compass points. He was bald, his pate covered with something oily that shined in the early sun.

"I ain't too keen on the Mechanic. He's a surly sort. But the other guy's my buddy, Pablo."

Pablo was small, almost tiny, his thin, short body nearly hidden behind the Mechanic as they pushed the car. Pablo's full head of hair was black and thick, hung down his back like a mane. Like his body, his features were thin and sharp, delicate, black eyes set into fragile bones. Pablo and Little Jimmy could have been brothers.

Pablo and the Mechanic wore denim shirts, bib overalls and heavy, almost crude shoes. Stick looked at Pablo, and then at Little Jimmy. Except for the shoes, they were dressed alike. Jimmy noticed Stick looking.

"Yeah, we look alike, Pablo and me. But I ain't got no real likin' fer the Mechanic."

"You mentioned that," Stick said. "That why you don't wear the big shoes?"

"Them ain't shoes, them's *brogans*," Jimmy said, the word dripping off his tongue. "Brogans. Used to wear 'em. Back in West Virginia. Only shoes we ever had. Could buy 'em at the general store. Ain't never gonna wear 'em again. 'Sides, cain't run in 'em."

The Socket Set shoved the car out of the lot and across the street, pushing it backwards into a small space by the side of the All-Nighter, the Mechanic doing most of the pushing. The car looked as though it had come from a junkyard. It had. It was the car they lived in, shoving it from place to place when landlords or storeowners ran them out of wherever it was parked.

From the car, the Socket Set could see the gas pumps, but the people working inside the store could not see them. The Mechanic raised the hood, then took a huge crescent wrench from the seat of the car, the wrench as big as a large hammer. He tucked it into his belt, the weight of it making his pants sag.

They leaned on the front of the car, waiting. It was early. Not much traffic.

They waited patiently. Usually, they preferred working the locals in supermarket parking lots, content with a dollar or two now and then. They picked their Citizens carefully, usually women alone who were putting their groceries in their cars. Most of the women felt vulnerable—they were alone, they had their groceries exposed out there in the parking lot, and the car was usually standing open.

The Socket Set carried around an empty milk jug. One of them, usually Pablo, would approach a woman, waiting until she had unlocked her car. "Trying to get home to Taos," he would say, holding up the jug. "Ran out of gas. Just need a couple dollars . . ." It took less than ten seconds to say that. Almost always, the woman would give him a buck just to get rid of him, to get him away from her groceries, her car, her purse, her life.

The Mechanic and Pablo worked separately. They found out the hard way that when they approached a woman together it scared the hell out her. Twice, women had punched 911 into their cellular phones while the Socket Set had been standing there, blank looks on their faces. Both times, they had managed to disappear just before the cops showed up.

After a couple of months they started running into the same women getting into the same cars. The Socket Set seldom remembered the women, but the women almost always remembered them. The women stopped being afraid and started getting mad, grabbing for their phones. The scam wore out. But there were other scams.

* * *

A car pulled off Cerrillos Road and into the gas station, stopping at the pumps. The Socket Set watched as a man got out. He was well over six feet, burly, and had a full beard. He slammed the door of his car, then jammed a credit card into the pump, punching the buttons as though they were the enemy. He grabbed the nozzle like he was grabbing the head of a dangerous snake. The Socket Set didn't move from their car, the Mechanic putting his hand on Pablo's shoulder, massaging it slightly. Neither spoke, but both knew this was the wrong guy, too mad, too aggressive. No sense getting punched in the mouth this early in the morning. The man pumped his gas and left.

Stick watched the whole thing. The man pulled into the gas station; no one came out to pump his gas; he shoved some sort of a card directly into the pump and then pumped his own gas. Stick didn't recognize any of it.

Where the hell have I been, he thought, *where they don't use those cards.*

Another car pulled in, an expensive sedan of some sort. Stick didn't know the make of the car. It was another one of those things he still hadn't figured out, the makes and models of cars. Nothing was familiar. And they all looked alike.

The car's gas cover popped open, released from the inside. A slender man got out, casually brushing his hand back across his expensive haircut. He slipped his credit card into the slot on the pump, gingerly took down the nozzle and started pumping gas.

"Watch this," Jimmy said.

When the driver looked up, Pablo was standing right beside him, the huge, shiny wrench in his hand. Stick saw Pablo hold up the big wrench, saw the driver flinch involuntarily. Pablo said a few words, pointed back at the rusted car. The Mechanic had his head and shoulders under the hood, his ass sticking out into the sunshine, legs thrashing, apparently hard at work on the car. Stick knew the car had no engine in it.

"Pablo, he's done asked the Citizen for money to help fix the car. Thet big wrench, thet's just for effect. Ever one of them drivers thinks it's a weapon."

The driver looked at the Mechanic, then back at Pablo. He was smiling. He pulled some money from his pocket and handed it to Pablo, who walked quickly back to the rusted car and joined the Mechanic under the hood. They stayed that way until the Citizen got into his car and drove away. When he was gone, the Mechanic and Pablo again took up their positions in front of the old car, waiting.

From across the street, Little Jimmy and Stick watched them work the scam twice more.

"Jimmy, how long those guys been in Santa Fe?"

"Don't rightly know, Stick," Little Jimmy said. "They was here when I git here. Hear tell one of 'em, the Mechanic, he might of been borned here."

"They must see a lot of cars pull in here, or wherever they set up their game."

"Yeah, I reckon they do."

Stick got up and started across the street.

"Hey," Jimmy said, "where you goin'?"

"I'm going to ask them about a car."

Jimmy leaped to his feet. "Whut kind'a car?"

"Lowrider, or whatever you call those things. Purple. Fancy paint job. Come on, let's . . ." Stick looked over his shoulder. Little Jimmy was gone.

SIXTEEN

Once, the Santa Fe River had dropped out of the Sangre de Cristo Mountains and plunged uncontrolled out of the foothills and down a narrow canyon, cutting a shallow channel across a small, high plain at the base of the hills, a place the First People called the "Dancing Ground of the Sun." Once, it had been the main water supply for every living thing between the mountains and the Rio Grande River, its crystal, snowmelt waters sustaining thousands of years of humanity.

But that was then. Now, most of the river was caught in a reservoir in the foothills east of town, the remaining trickle dribbling along the bottom of an enlarged ditch through downtown Santa Fe. For much of its length through the main part of the city the river was channeled between concrete and rock walls, the channel so deep that a man walking in it could pass almost unseen through the heart of the city —safe passage for the street people. A narrow, green park ran along the top of the north wall where, in the long Santa Fe summer, tourists sat at picnic benches eating carry-out food from white foam containers.

There were bridges across the river at major streets and under the bridges there was shade and in the shade the street people found relief from a sun that burned easily and deeply through the thin, seven-thousand-foot atmosphere.

Stick moved cautiously up the shallow stream, the chilling water sloshing over his ankles and darkening the frayed lower legs of his pants. He seldom bothered lifting his feet from the water as he walked, just shoved each foot forward under the surface until he could set it down again. Sometimes his foot settled on a slick stone and slid off, grinding his ankle between the rocks. Stick didn't care. He was just a spectator to his own movement, letting his body take him where it wanted to go.

Most people would have walked beside the stream, not in it, walked in the heavy water-soaked grass that bent under the sun, walked beside one of the high concrete walls that trapped the stream and channeled it through the city. But Stick loved walking in the water, loved to feel it rush through the holes in his worn canvas shoes and caress his feet, loved the coldness of it against the heavy sun and heat that filled the little canyon caught there between the high sides of the concrete walls. The water brought him pleasure—and Stick could count the things that brought him pleasure on the fingers of one hand.

He dipped his cupped hand into the water and brought it to his mouth. Just in time he remembered he was downstream from the pipe and he let the water dribble through his fingers. He moved on upstream. He realized that he was moving easily, that his legs worked properly, that the dizziness that had once plagued him was coming at longer intervals.

At eye level a round black hole appeared in the south concrete wall, a hole that held the end of a pipe the size of Stick's wrist. From somewhere in the compacted sand and stone and fragments of clay pots and human bones and dried little hunks of ancient dung that formed the underbelly of the city a thick ooze formed and squeezed its way out of the pipe, a sluggish black-green muck sliding down the hard gray wall. A stench wafted from the muck and slid out over the stream. As Stick came to the pipe and the muck he held his breath to prevent the stench from invading his body.

A few feet above the pipe he again cupped his hand into the water. This time, he drank. He had been drinking the water for a couple of weeks. Once, something had made him very sick and he thought it might have been the water, but he didn't die, although at the time dying was not of particular concern to him. And then he had noticed the pipe. So he tried drinking the water again, upstream from the pipe, and he did not get sick and he just kept drinking it.

Farther upstream a concrete bridge crossed the gap between the stone walls and Stick knew there was cool shade under there, soft grass, back out of sight of the tourists. It was one of Little Jimmy's favorite places, a place where he slept during the heat of the day. And today, in the bright sunshine, Stick thought Jimmy would be here, under the bridge.

As he neared the bridge he saw a pair of feet sticking out into the sun. Stick moved closer.

"Hey," he said.

They were not Little Jimmy's feet. The feet drew back quickly and then a shape stood up and moved out of the shade. It took a few seconds for Stick to realize it was a woman. Stick had never seen her before. She was taller than Little Jimmy, every inch of her body covered in heavy skirts, loose blouses, scarves. Layers of them. He had no idea how old she was.

The woman backed away, never taking her eyes from Stick.

"Sorry," Stick said, "didn't mean to come up on you like that."

The woman said nothing, backing away another step.

"Was looking for Little Jimmy. You know him? Little Jimmy? Little shorter than you, voice like nails rattling in a tin bucket?"

They stood, looking at each other, not moving.

"Look, I'm not going to hurt you . . ."

The woman turned and plunged away from Stick, her heavy legs swishing through the tall grass, her gait almost a waddle. But she watched him over her shoulder.

And Stick watched her until she was out of sight.

* * *

He had not seen Little Jimmy for days, not since they had visited the Socket Set, but that wasn't unusual. Little Jimmy was one of the spookiest guys Stick had met on the street, his head on a swivel, always looking, always prepared to run. Once, when they had been crossing the Plaza, Stick stopped to pick up a newspaper out of a trash can. When he straightened up, Little Jimmy was gone. Disappeared. That time, Stick didn't see him for three days. And he would never say why he disappeared, or where he went. Hanging around with Little Jimmy was always some sort of warped adventure, a fragmented disappearing act.

And yet, hanging around with Jimmy was somehow familiar, as though being alert, being ready to run, being somehow . . . afraid . . . was the normal thing to do. The normal way to be. Stick thought about that now and then, about being afraid. The fear was there, but he could not make an image, a cause, come alive in his memory.

He sat on the grass in the shade, where the woman had been sleeping. He thought about Little Jimmy, why he had been gone so long. He knew that sometimes street guys went for a walk and never came back. Nobody looked for them. Nobody cared.

He cared for Little Jimmy. The little man had taught him almost everything he knew about living on the streets. There were some darker things Stick seemed to know instinctively, some sort of survival reflexes that kicked in when he least expected it, but most of the good street stuff, the stuff about restaurants, Dumpsters, the dry *arroyos*, the plain clothes cop with the flat eyes who drove a gray unmarked sedan . . . most of the good stuff he had learned from Little Jimmy in the time he had been in Santa Fe.

He settled back against the wall, stretching his feet out into the sun to dry. He heard voices from the street above and he knew the tourists were beginning to come out of the hotels and take over the city.

If Little Jimmy didn't show up, he would make his rounds alone, again. It was important to make his rounds. It added some sort of pattern, some stability, to his life. When he made his rounds, he knew that he had once had some sort of life pattern, some routine that meant stability. Perhaps meant safety.

He and Little Jimmy had several routes they covered at different times of the day, different days of the week, setting up the routes to get to certain places when there was more likelihood of food being left out, clothing deposited, small jobs to be done. Some of them— like the Plaza route—they did just because they liked to, liked to watch the people, see the sights . . . whatever. He would do the Plaza route today. Maybe the woman in the gallery would be there. Jimmy's "boss." Maybe he would see her.

And he would wait a couple of more days before he went looking for Little Jimmy.

He listened to the river bubble gently. Finally, his chin dropped to his chest and he dozed off, sitting in the shade by the Santa Fe River at the bottom of a tiny man-stone canyon in the center of the city, a thousand flag-colored tourists walking the street ten feet above him.

SEVENTEEN

Beano was glad to be away from Angelo for a while. They had spent the night in Angelo's car, Angelo bitching all night about the scratch on the car's door and the big dent in the roof. Angelo playing with the pistol all night. Beano thought that if Angelo could fuck the pistol, he would. After all, Beano thought, the barrel was just about the right size for Angelo's little dick. The very first time Angelo had talked a woman into going with them to park in an arroyo south of town, and Angelo had pulled out his little dick, the woman laughed so hard she squeezed her eyes shut, never saw Angelo come up with the pistol, never saw it coming, never saw anything until the butt of the pistol cracked into her forehead and Angelo shoved her out into the desert. Beano didn't know if the woman saw anything after that—they drove off and left her there.

* * *

Beano sat on his bench on the Plaza, waiting for the early morning wave of tourists to come out of the hotels. Waiting for the sign from Willie the Hook.

Willie caught Beano's eye. He nodded at a couple on the far side of the Plaza. They were old, and that was one of the requirements.

Old. The man's hair was white and the woman walked with a cane with little claw feet on the bottom.

Another requirement was fear. Beano watched as the couple moved slowly toward a bench, their heads tracking back and forth in a constant watch for danger, for things they didn't recognize or didn't understand. They were reticent. Doing nothing quickly or without careful consideration.

They were perfect.

Beano got up and ambled slowly toward the couple, checking constantly for the bike cop. As he got closer his walk became a swagger, his big arms swinging and his feet hitting the concrete with an aggressive slap. But they didn't see him coming. That wasn't the way it was supposed to work, so he angled off to the side, turned, put a little more space between himself and the couple, swung his arms more, said something loud to one of the kids at the obelisk.

Now they saw him. Couldn't take their eyes from him. He jerked his head around, looked them straight in the face, and carefully took one step at a time straight toward their bench. As he walked he increased his pace, his feet slapping, arms swinging, until they almost screeched to a halt in front of them.

They had seen him by the obelisk, behaving like a bully. Before they could leave he was there, right in front of them, his huge body blocking the sun, arms dangling. The odor from his body seeped out from his clothes and fell to the ground of its own weight, oozing across the sidewalk and onto their shoes. They thought they could taste the smell of him through their feet.

"Howdy," Beano said, trying to lower his whining voice, trying to sound rough. "Nice one of them Santa Fe mornin's, ain't it?" As he talked, he moved his arms slightly, almost in a muted punching manner. The couple stared and said nothing.

Beano leaned in toward the couple; they edged back against the bench. "You ain't much for talkin', are you? You two okay? Cat got your tongue?" He reached out and waved his hand in front of their faces, as though checking to see if they were awake. The old man looked around, panic growing in his throat.

"Well, you don't have to talk. All you have to do is give me a couple bucks, and you can go back to sleep . . ."

Wille the Hook was suddenly there. He grabbed Beano by the arm. "Benjamin, you know you aren't supposed to be down here bothering the people. The shelter don't like it when you go out so early in the morning. Now, be polite and apologize to these nice folks."

Beano's manner changed at once. He hung his head, his big arms clamped to his side. In almost slow motion he raised a hand and removed his cap, pulling it down to his chest and holding it over his heart.

"Didn't mean nothin'," Beano mumbled, head down, eyes on the sidewalk. "Was just hungry. Didn't get fed this mornin'. They done run out of food before . . ." His voice trailed off.

Wille looked at the couple. "Sorry, folks, but sometimes we don't get food for two or three days and Benjamin here gets a little out of sorts when that happens." He turned to Beano. "Benjamin, you go on, now, and I'll catch up with you. We'll get you something."

Beano shuffled off across the Plaza, still gripping his hat over his heart.

Willie heaved a sigh of relief. "I'll be going now, folks. Have to keep an eye on him to see he don't bother people. See if we can raise a little money to get him something to eat. It don't always turn out this easy. Sometimes he gets right nasty before I show up."

Willie turned slightly, about to walk off. The woman nudged the old man with her elbow. Without looking at her he pulled a five-dollar-bill from his pocket.

"Here," he said, his voice raspy. It was the only word either of them spoke. He held the bill out to Willie.

Willie took the bill, nodded, said, "I thank you kindly," and strolled off in the direction of Beano.

He glanced over his shoulder to see if anyone were following. No one was. The couple already had disappeared. He caught up to Beano.

"When do I get to be the good guy," Beano grumbled.

"Never," Willie said. "You ain't got the talent for it."

* * *

Stick wandered along Alameda to Cathedral Street, then up past St. Francis Cathedral with its truncated towers and on to Palace Avenue. He turned left on Palace and eased down to the corner of the Plaza, looking across the square to see if the lights were on in the Montoya gallery. They were not. He would wait until the lights came on before he crossed the Plaza and looked through the windows. The art in the gallery drew him each time he came to the Plaza—and he actually pretended to look at it. But he was looking past the art, looking for the woman. He never actually had gone inside. It didn't seem to be a place where he belonged.

He found a thick magazine in a trash can and sat on a bench, acting as though he belonged there. He didn't panhandle or mix with the tourists in any way and the Plaza cops had never bothered him. In fact, he felt safer on the Plaza than any place within the city. He kept the magazine up in front of his face.

Peeking over the top of the magazine he watched two street guys work an old couple who had just wandered out of the La Fonda Hotel and onto the Plaza. One guy was tall and rangy, the other thick, maybe fat, stomped around like he was mad.

Beano. The fat guy is Beano. Stick quickly looked around for Ange, *probably Angelo,* Stick thought, but Ange was not on the Plaza.

Stick watched the game they were running, the fat guy confronting the old couple, the tall guy butting in, sending the fat guy away. Stick watched the woman hand some money to the tall guy. Tag team. Little Jimmy had told him about the scam.

A woman was suddenly standing in front of him. She was tall and hard-lean, a woman familiar with work. Her hair was so black it glistened like polished coal and Stick thought he could see drops of light playing in the blackness. Her eyes were as dark as her hair and her face was carved from Spanish aristocracy five hundred years ago and improved with every generation until it reached perfection in her. She wore an expensive white silk blouse that did nothing to hide her full breasts. Her black skirt was long, coming all the way down to the tops of her polished, expensive Western boots, real boots, the kind you could actually wear to ride a horse, or to walk through cow shit in a corral. A tooled leather purse hung from her shoulder. Her left hand gripped the strap of the purse and he saw the rings on her fingers. The rings were old, polished and worn, far older than the woman.

There was no wedding ring.

His breath caught short and he swallowed, as though something were stuck in his throat, the magazine slowly falling into his lap. He had never seen her outside the gallery, and he made no attempt to hide the way he looked at her.

She looked back, directly. Her eyes locked onto him in a grip he thought he could feel, could actually sense the pressure of her gaze. She was looking completely through him, out the other side, and far into some faded history that he didn't even recognize.

What the hell is this? he thought. But he did not move.

For a moment he thought she was going to speak to him. But she did not. She unlocked her gaze, turned, and strolled slowly toward the center of the Plaza, in no particular hurry.

Stick watched her walk away—again, those hips working beneath the form-fitting skirt. He loved watching her, loved watching all women. It was the women who sustained him, made him know he was still alive, who, when they looked at him, looked at him directly, not sliding their eyes past him as they realized who he was. Who he was not.

But not the men. In his time in Santa Fe the men had never looked at him. Most men only look at competitors, and Stick was competition to no one.

As the woman passed the Plaza's obelisk the fat street guy stepped out directly in front of her and went into his act.

Well, now, Stick thought. *Well, now.*

* * *

Beano saw her coming, the bitch from the art store. She wasn't old enough to be a mark, and she was on the Plaza every day—maybe she had seen him, would recognize him. But Beano was thinking. He did that sometimes. Think. He would let her know that he was there. Shake her up a little, have something to tell Angelo. He stepped out in front of the woman.

* * *

Stick got up and rolled the magazine into a tight tube, tucking it under his arm as he walked slowly toward them. The fat guy had his back to him and Stick moved slightly to the side so he could see the woman's face. He could tell she was onto the scam, knew what the fat guy was doing, but she didn't back away a single step, just stood there, her hands gripping her purse. She glanced over the fat guy's shoulder, noticed Stick approaching, and Stick knew she thought he was part of it, part of the scam. If the thought bothered her, it didn't show on her face.

". . . just need a couple of bucks," the fat guy was saying, his arms moving slightly, a boxer loosening up.

The woman said nothing.

Stick glanced around, looking for the other guy, the tall one. He was gone.

"So, how 'bout it? You goin' to help out?" Beano looked off to the side, trying to find Willie, who was late with his entrance.

"Seems like the cowboy is gone, fat man. You'll have to do this one all alone," Stick said softly into the back of Beano's head.

Beano spun, glaring at Stick. And then his face began to pale. "What the hell you doin' here, you fuckin' spook?" Beano's voice was shrill, a combination of anger and fear.

"Just passing through."

"Well, go pass through som'ers else." Beano waved his arms, indicating the whole of the Plaza. "This place ain't on yer map." The woman had not moved. "Git on, I said!" He reached out to shove Stick.

Stick grabbed the magazine from under his arm and slapped it across the bridge of Beano's nose. The blow made a popping sound and several others on the Plaza turned to look at them. Beano stumbled backward, more embarrassed than hurt, hands over his nose.

"You fuckin' stick man! You always hittin' people in the nose! My nose already been . . . !" Beano gathered himself and rushed at Stick, arms pushed out in front of him.

Stick stepped to the side, jamming the end of the rolled magazine into Beano's stomach as he passed. Beano's arms came down, wrapped around his stomach as he staggered to a stop, bent at the waist. Stick whipped the hard roll of paper across Beano's big ass and Beano jerked upright, hands covering his ass now, only to see the roll coming at him again, sharply down across the bridge of his nose. Again. Beano clamped his hands to his face and stumbled backward, blood beginning to flood from between his fingers.

"You son-of-a-bitch! You done it again! Hit me in the nose! You gonna hit me in the nose one time too many, just like . . .!" Beano was yelling as tourists watched, frozen in place.

"How many is too many?"

"Huh?" Beano pulled is hands down and inspected his palms, looking at the blood and snot.

"How many is too many?" Stick asked softly. "Just want to know when I'm reaching the limit." And he smacked the roll again across Beano's nose.

Beano screamed, lost his balance, staggered backward and fell onto the grass. He rolled over, got to his knees, holding his nose again. "Fuck you, stick man," Beano gritted between his teeth. "Sooner or later, we gonna fuck you up! Yeah, all'a you, you and that little shit, and this bitch! You gonna get fucked up!" He hauled himself to his feet and turned—and found Stick in front of him.

"Didn't your momma tell you not to say things like that about women?" Stick asked softly.

Beano had no idea what Stick was talking about. He grunted between his fingers, "Huh . . . ?"

And Stick swung the rolled magazine again, aiming higher this time, the hard roll smacking across Beano's left eye.

Beano screamed, staggered backward, turned, running now, scurrying across the Plaza, a huge beetle disappearing down San Francisco Street.

Stick turned back toward his bench.

"Why did you do that?" Her voice was low register and tempered, a voice that came from long days of talking against the weather.

He turned back to her, noticed the set of her jaw, saw again the hair so black it must have been born in midnight, noticed that he couldn't see into the bottom of her eyes.

"I didn't want you to shoot him."

She still held the strap of the purse with her left hand, her right hand tucked into a slot at the back, touching the pistol hidden there.

"I wasn't going to shoot him. His name is Beano. He's a bully, and he's not too bright. I would only shoot him if he touched me. Anyway, shooting him would just ruin everybody's day. Especially his."

Stick smiled at her.

She slowly pulled her empty hand out of the purse.

"How did you know?" she asked softly.

"You mean, how did I know you have a gun in there? Me, a street guy, with no visible gray matter?" He kept smiling at her. "Tell the truth, ma'am, I haven't any idea."

"What's your name?"

"Haven't any idea about that, either. Some of the People call me Stick."

She put her hand into her skirt pocket and came out with a bill.

"Please take this." She held out a five.

He thought about it.

"You know, I really need that five . . . but I can't take it."

She turned her head slightly, an unspoken "why?"

"If I take the money," he said, "Beano's scam worked."

The woman smiled, turned and started across the Plaza.

"Excuse me," he said to her back.

She turned.

"Have you been here, in Santa Fe, for a long time?"

"Life," the woman said.

"I was just wondering . . . did you ever eat at Joe's?"

She stared at him for a long moment, then turned and walked slowly away.

* * *

Elena Montoya did not go directly to the front door of her gallery. Instead, she walked slowly around the block and came in through a small door in the back.

Inside, she went to the window and stood in the shadows and looked for Stick. She had seen him before, always on the Plaza. Little Jimmy had pointed him out. She would watch him cross the grass, walking casually, seeming to pay no attention to the tourists, but she thought he saw every one of them and could describe them in detail. This morning was the first time she had seen him up close.

Now she watched him, still standing by the obelisk. When he turned and went back to his bench his back was straight and his arms hung loosely at his sides and he walked across the Plaza as though he owned it.

Perhaps he did, she thought.

He sat with the magazine in front of his face, but she knew he wasn't reading. She could see his eyes above the paper, knew that he was watching the people on the Plaza. And, she knew, he was watching her gallery, waiting for the lights to come on.

The woman turned, staring at the photograph hanging high on the wall at the back of the gallery. Her brother. And his buddies. The back end of the grimy bus. The old building.

EiGHTEEN

In the beginning he thought about getting a job. Little Jimmy followed him around while he applied at some fast food joints, a janitorial service, talked with a couple of lot managers at auto dealerships about washing cars, checked out some restaurants to see if they needed after-hours cleaning help. But he had no social security number, no car, no address. Everyone made him immediately as a street guy. They shook their heads "no," sometimes before he was finished talking. He thought about trying the El Paso gag—just walk into a restaurant and start washing dishes. But this was Santa Fe, not El Paso. There were no restaurants like that.

"I don't know why yore havin' so much trouble gittin' a job. Hell, it didn't take no time at all fer me to git one," Jimmy said. "And I kin work whenever I want." They were sitting on a low wall across the street from a restaurant, watching well-fed tourists stroll out the door, belch, fart, and pick their teeth. It was one of Jimmy's favorite things to do.

Stick looked at him. "Yeah, I know. You work for the woman with the big tits."

"Well, she has. And there ain't nothin' wrong with big tits . . ."

"I met her the other day," Stick said.

Jimmy turned and looked at his friend, saying nothing for a long moment. Then, "You met her? You talked to her?"

"Yep, sure did."

Jimmy turned and stared off into the distance. "I ain't never really talked to her. I cain't seem to find nothin' to say when she's around. I jist go down into the basement and build them crates to put them art things in so's she can ship 'em. Sweep out. Scrub the floors. All that shit."

Stick still looked at him.

"I *do*, I tell ya. Used to do carpenterin' fer my uncle, helped him build chicken coops and such. Go down to that art store ever now and then, when I need a few bucks. Woman saves things fer me to do, mostly them crates." He waited, but Stick said nothing.

"You want to go down there with me, sometime?"

"No," Stick growled. "I'm not taking a charity job from some rich *chica*."

"Well, now, how you know she's a *chica*? And how come you all bent out'a shape?" He waited, but Stick said nothing. "Yew afraid, ain't yew? Yew as afraid of thet woman as I am."

Stick got up and walked away.

"Why don't yew write about thet in yer little bitty notebook?" Jimmy yelled after him.

*　*　*

In the clear early light that spilled down into San Francisco Street, Little Jimmy and Stick stood on the corner by the La Fonda and looked across at the Plaza. There was no traffic, but neither man made a move to cross the intersection, each staring at the empty Plaza, neither knowing what the other was looking for.

Finally, as though on some unknown signal, they turned and crossed the street, moving under the *portal* that fronted the galleries on the south side of the Plaza. As they walked, Little Jimmy looked over his shoulder one last time. The spider car was not there.

They stood in front of the Alvarez Montoya Gallery, looking through the glass at the cool deep room inside. Muted light
bounced off the Plaza and into the room and gave life to the edges
of things Stick saw in there. Stick sensed the presence of the woman, maybe standing motionless in the pale darkness, but he could
not see her.

"Thought you wasn't gonna come down here," Jimmy muttered
under his breath, a smile twitching at the corners of his mouth.

"Shut up," Stick growled.

"I'm goin' ter wait 'til she opens. Build a couple crates. Make a
buck. Look at them tits." Little Jimmy waited for Stick to say something, but Stick just kept looking through the windows. "I hate it
when you do that, jist git lost somewhere, lookin' at things . . . like
there ain't nobody home in yer head. Hell, boy, one of these days
I'm gonna hang a 'vacancy' sign around yer neck."

Stick grinned, but said nothing.

"Anyways, I bet she got somethin' you can do, sweep out, scrub
the win-ders, 'er somthin' like thet . . ."

Stick turned and started away from the gallery. "No," he said over
his shoulder. "I told you before, no charity jobs. Not even for *chicas*
with big tits. She can scrub her own 'win-ders' . . ."

"You are not interested in tits? Perhaps you have some abiding
interest in little boys?"

Stick had heard the voice before. He snapped around and saw
her framed in the doorway—the Hispanic woman from the Plaza.
He stared. At her tits. He couldn't help himself.

She broke his stare. "I thought you weren't interested in tits."

"I didn't mean to offend." He realized that he was almost mumbling. "It's just that . . . you filled up my vision when I wasn't expecting it."

"That's very poetic."

"For a street guy."

Little Jimmy stood with his back pressed against the window, trying hard not to be there. He's never heard anybody talk to the woman like this.

She smiled. "Okay . . . I wasn't expecting an articulate street guy. So, you're a poet, and you rescue damsels in distress. What else are you?"

"I don't know." He let it go at that. No sense trying to explain to a woman he didn't know, a woman who, at any moment, would tell him to move on.

"That's what Jimmy said. How did he put it? 'There ain't nobody home in yer head.' And you don't take charity jobs." She said it with a smile.

"I thought Jimmy didn't really talk to you."

"He's changed in the last few days. Talks a little, now. Mostly about you. Now, about that 'charity' job . . ."

"I could take it up with my talky manager," he nodded at Little Jimmy, "perhaps make an exception."

"Perhaps even do windows?"

"Perhaps."

"How much would you charge to do these?" She pointed to the huge windows at each side of her.

He stepped back and looked at the glass. It was spotless, glistening. "Maybe I can come back when they really need cleaning."

"Maybe you could."

He nodded and backed away, still looking at her.

"*Un hombre honesto. Como salio asi?*" she said, smiling.

"*Quien sabe, señora,*" he said quietly, "*quien sabe.*"

She did not seem surprised that he understood her. "*Hasta la vista, senor.*" And she walked away into the gallery, Little Jimmy following meekly at her heels.

The words came as she faded far back into the gallery. "And it is *señorita, hombre.*"

* * *

It was Stick's idea, but Little Jimmy was the guide. On days when the restaurant pickings were good and they were well fed, they would explore, working their way in ever widening circles out toward the edge of the city.

"What yew lookin' fer?"

"I don't know," Stick said. "Maybe I'll know it when I see it. Then again, maybe I'll never see it."

Jimmy took Stick cautiously through the west side *barrio*, with its tiny, immaculate houses, people standing by their front doors and watching as they passed, not asking to help, but not interfering. Taking him even more cautiously through the east side *barrio rico* with its mixture of old lanes just wide enough to allow the passage of two *burro* carts, and newer, wider streets that led past large houses now owned by Anglos who had bought the land from the old people, many of whom now lived on the west side. Or did not live in Santa Fe at all.

As they made their circles they always came, sooner or later, back to the narrow canyon of the Santa Fe River.

"Hell," Jimmy said, "back home this wouldn't be called a river. Wouldn't even make a good crik. We got a crik near to where my uncle lived, called it 'Twelvepole Crik'. Had way more water in it than this little pissant stream. These people out here, if'n it moves, they call it a river."

Stick looked at him. "Crik?"

Little Jimmy stood in front of him. "Crik. All right, yew kin call it c-r-e-e-e-e-k." He drew out the word, his face red.

"It's okay, L. J., it can be 'crik' if you want it to."

* * *

The days moved past their lives in the slow dance of time in the Southwest.

They ran out of streets so they widened their circle, roaming high on the east side of town, the hills starting to climb away from the back of large, expensive houses.

"Let's git back down into town. Bein' out here with these damn trees be too much like back home," Jimmy had said, looking cautiously into the woods behind him.

"C'mon, Jim, lighten up," Stick said, walking into the edge of the trees. "I want to see what's on the edge of this town—all the edges. Besides, I sometimes run up here."

"And thet's another thing," Jimmy said sharply, "all thet runnin' yew do. It ain't good fer a body."

* * *

Stick laid it out like a military campaign. They circled the town carefully, taking in the foothills on the east and north, even edging up into the higher mountains, Little Jimmy complaining that there was nothing to eat out there on the brink of wilderness, no restaurants, no grocery stores, nothing to scavenge or steal. Several times, when night fell, they were in the edge of the trees. They stayed there, sleeping under deadfalls or next to rocks that had gathered heat during the day, Stick comfortable, Little Jimmy complaining. Sometimes remembering.

"Used to sleep in the woods now and then, back home. Had to. Iffen folks was lookin' fer me, it was the best place to be. The higher on the ridge I could git, the safer I wuz."

Stick pulled his piece of tarp up under his chin. "Ever climb all the way to the top?"

"Top of what? Hell, they ain't no real spikey mountains back there, not like out here. Not like thet ski area, 'er Baldy."

"Which one is Baldy?"

"Thet big roundy-topped one, kin see it from some places out on the edge of town."

"Want to climb it??"

Jimmy sat up, staring up at stars that were beginning to burn in the heavy night sky. "I would like thet, I think. Yeah. I would like thet. I'd be up higher than anybody in the whole state of Wes' Virginia," he said, not knowing he was already up that high.

"Well, why haven't you done it?"

"Well, thet's an easy answer, there, Stickman. I'd be scared shitless."

* * *

They went back to the west side of the town and picked up the Santa Fe River again, following it into the high desert and *arroyos* farther to the west.

Once, they walked all the way to a canyon that spilled out into the Rio Grande. They worked their way north along the river until sheer bluffs cut them off and they had to scramble up steep banks of loose dirt, kicking down rocks the size of soccer balls, some of them rolling all the way into the water.

Now and then, Stick would stop, hold up his hand, maybe squat beside some brush. When he did that, Jimmy knew there would be something going on, something up ahead that Stick wanted to watch, see but not be seen. Something maybe dangerous. Maybe not. But Stick wanted to be sure.

Jimmy wondered how Stick knew all that stuff. It had not been that long since he had seen Stick get off the bus, and already the stickman seemed more at home on the streets and in the mountains and desert around the town than Little Jimmy had ever been. For a man who didn't remember much, hell, didn't remember anything, Stick just seemed to know how to do things.

Hell, thet boy jist pulls the knowin' and the doin' right out'a his ass, Jimmy thought.

They passed small side canyons, found the sun bleached remnants of line shacks, tripped over rusted strands of barbed wire, squatted beside the broken skeletons of long-dead cattle, the bones sucked dry and licked clean.

Stick kept looking across the river.

Jimmy's gaze followed Stick's eyes, but all he saw over there was more of the same country they were struggling through, except that it quickly rose higher and steeper, the whole thing becoming a mass of wilderness that Jimmy wanted no part of.

"Thet country over there looks worse than what we be thrashin' through. What's over there you so all-fired interested in? What is it you see?"

Stick stood in the shade of a canyon wall and stared silently across the river. "Sanctuary," he said.

* * *

It was when they got around to the flat plains on the south side of the city that Jimmy quit entirely.

"Nossir, ain't goin' down there," he said flatly, or as flatly as his tinny voice would allow. "Been down there once't. Ain't goin' back into that damn country. Nothin' down there but more *arroyos* and then you run into thet damn prison, you ain't careful. I'll see you back in town, man." And he was gone.

Stick sat on a gentle rise in a field south of the city and watched him go. He didn't follow. But neither did he go any farther south. Instead, he took out his notebook and pencil and started to write. Now and then he put the pencil into his mouth and clamped his teeth down on it.

Days went by before he saw Little Jimmy again.

NINETEEN

The little man was running too hard and he knew he wouldn't last long but the car was closing the gap between them and if he didn't find a place to hide pretty soon the two guys in the car would be on him and so he told himself it would be okay to turn down the alley behind the market. He hadn't really planned to turn down the alley and run toward the Dumpster, he told himself, it just worked out that way. He didn't want to let them follow him to the hide. Nobody was supposed to follow him to the hide. Nobody was supposed to know where it was. But he had to gamble that he could get there before they saw where he went.

But they saw him.

He didn't think about the car coming in the alley after him, never thought that it would come so fast, never thought about its lop-eyed headlights flooding the stacks of pallets, the piles of boxes, making the Dumpsters look like squat metal monsters in the last of the night's broken blackness. But the car did come into the narrow alley. He made it about halfway down the alley before he knew the lights were going to sweep across him and he threw himself at the bottom of a pile of crates, jamming in next to the wall of the market. His pants caught on a piece of wire and ripped jaggedly at the knee.

The sedan rammed into the first pile of boxes, backed up, rammed the next pile, the lights brightening everything. Two more piles, and then the sedan would ram the crates he was hiding behind. He peeked out and saw the huge Dumpster looming off to his right. The best hide in Santa Fe. And he lost all reason.

He broke in a panic toward the Dumpster, heard the car's engine revving behind him, felt the lights grow brighter, hotter, closer. He ripped aside the pallets that guarded the hide and leaped into the small space behind them, then twisted his body until he was behind the Dumpster. He squatted, making himself as small as possible, hands flailing, reaching for anything that might protect him but finding only scraps of blankets, pieces of canvas and slabs of cardboard. He pulled a piece of blanket up to his chin, hands trembling, his eyes peeking over the ragged top, waiting.

* * *

Stick ran along the front of the buildings—an office supply store, a market—their windows still dark, everything closed and silent. He was running well, the gray, sweet air flowing easily into his lungs, his feet hardly making a noise as they kissed the asphalt, running so quietly that he could hear his heart beat.

He had been across Cerrillos Road, checking out the little Chinese restaurant. Usually, at night, the kitchen man set out the last of the containers of rice that couldn't go back on the steam table, stashing three or four paper containers on a ledge jutting from the back of the building where the dogs couldn't get at them. Stick had picked up a box of the rice, cold and sticky. He had started back toward the corner, eating the rice with chopsticks he had whittled from cottonwood sticks. He would cross over, then go behind the shopping center and sit on the wall. And he would wait. At least until full light.

He had been keeping an eye on the entry to Little Jimmy's hide, knowing the little guy would eventually show up there. Jimmy had been gone for days. But Stick knew, sooner or later, he would come back to his hide.

* * *

Stick hadn't reached the corner when he saw the little man running, panicked, into the light of the intersection, streaking along St. Michael's Drive.

The bib overalls, so large it seemed the little man would run right out of them.

Little Jimmy. And a big, ugly sedan closing fast.

Stick dropped the rice, jogged across the street, tracked the runner on the other side, watched as the little man cut hard to his right, down the alley—toward his hide.

But nobody runs to his hide when he's being chased, Stick thought.

And then he saw the dark sedan curl into the alley, the car slung so low it scraped the curb, throwing sparks as it tore into the narrow lane behind the stores.

Stick charged across the street, running hard now. He ran toward the alley, changed his mind and cut down in front of the darkened stores, remembering a break between the buildings farther down, thinking he could cut them off, get in between them and Jimmy.

He cleared the front of a large store that sold hobby supplies and found an opening leading back to the alley. He cut hard into the opening and into a morass of foam cups, newspapers and food wrappers. He skidded and fell, sliding on his left side and feeling the pavement grind away layers of his skin, burning. He was up quickly, oblivious to the pain, running again. He could see car lights back in the alley. They seemed to be blinking.

* * *

The car nudged the front of the Dumpster. The little man could hear the motor revving. Small metal wheels kept the Dumpster off the ground a few inches and the car's lights flared underneath.

He tried not to breathe. He wished desperately for someone to be there, someone who would know what to do, someone who could help.

For a moment nothing changed, the flood of the lights and the sound of the engine flowing beneath the Dumpster. Seconds dropped on his head like small stones. He grew cold with anxiety, his spindly legs quivering beneath him. The car's lights seemed to grow dimmer as the night faded. Maybe the car would leave. But just when he felt he could stand it no longer he felt the Dumpster move toward him. Just a little.

He jumped to his feet, scraping his arm against the rough wall of the alcove. The Dumpster moved again, pressing against an old pallet that was under his feet. The car moved again, and the pallet splintered, sending sharp wooden stabs up into his legs. And moved again, touching his shoulder now, and moved again, the revving of the car engine in time with the movement of the heavy metal wall against him. He dropped the blanket and put his back to the wall, his frail arms pushing hard against the Dumpster. When the engine roared again the metal moved hard against him and caught his arms against the wall and he felt the bones crack in both of them at the same time. He was calm, idly wondering how he would ever be able to shove the Dumpster back from his compressed body, knowing that he would never get the chance.

"Aww, shit," he said quietly.

He heard the engine roar once more and somehow there wasn't room for his chest and breathing came hard and then not at all and then some more cracking sounds and he wondered if maybe he should have stayed home on that warm night years ago, just after his father had hit him with the cane again. The old man was crippled, but he could use the cane like a sword and when you're only twelve it's hard to hide from things like that. If he had stayed home maybe he'd be on the front porch, now, feeling the dawn air against his face, looking east at the gray edge of the world. Man could breathe while he was waiting for the dawn.

But he could not breathe now. Not even in the dawn. And his head hurt. Badly.

*   *   *

In the darkness, running as hard as he could, Stick hit the chain link fence face-first. The heavy wire sagged hardly at all, stiffened, and he felt the strands penetrate thin flesh, making patterned blood lines across his face. New wounds. He didn't even bounce backwards, just crumpled to the ground, groaning. He may as well have run into a wall.

He rolled onto his stomach, got up. His face was numb and he could feel the wetness of blood dripping, but his mind was clear. He felt for the fence, wrapping his fingers into the wire, pulling himself up, starting to climb. He could see the lights of the car from around the corner of the building, hear the engine, hear the grind of metal on metal. There was no barbed wire at the top of the fence and he swung himself over, landing cat-like on the other side, running for the corner of the building.

The sedan was nosed against the Dumpster, engine revving as the driver toyed with the accelerator, tiny chirps coming from the rear wheels as they lost their grip and slipped on the pavement, reflected light showing the broken windows, the dent in the top.

The car. *The* car. Angelo and Beano.

The driver. He wanted the driver.

In three or four strides Stick was at the side of the car, launching himself across the hood, sliding down into the alley, jerking open the driver's door, reaching inside, seeing the flash of fear on the big round-faced man, the man saying "Who the fuck . . . ?" before Stick's hands closed around his throat, pulling.

Angelo. Stick could feel things in Angelo's throat working under his hands, the man desperately trying to pull air past Stick's fingers. He dragged Angelo out of the car by his neck, feet flailing, and snapped him away from the car like cracking a heavy whip, Stick still gripping his throat.

The car jerked backwards and slid to a noisy stop, the driver's door slamming shut from the momentum, Beano behind the wheel.

The driver's door burst open and Beano leaped out, a dark shape almost hidden behind the headlights.

"Hey! Hey, you motherfucker, We been looking for you!"

Stick threw Angelo toward the door, Angelo slamming into it, the door slamming into Beano. Stick followed Angelo into the door, caught him on the rebound, spun him, drove a fist into the base of his throat, threw him backwards into the corner of the Dumpster, the man's head making a dull thunking sound when it hit.

"Okay, motherfucker, you just hold still for a second . . . !"

The gun! He has the gun!

Stick bent his knees and dropped quickly, rolling over backward. He came up fast, diving for a stack of pallets at the side of the alley, pieces of wood scattering in front of him.

The gun fired.

Because Stick heard the shot he thought it hadn't hit him. As he rolled back toward the building he felt time stretching out like a rubber band, slowing, Stick feeling oddly detached, wondering where that came from, that knowledge about gunshots.

TWENTY

He lay there as though death were upon him, and maybe it was.

There were two more shots. Stick heard the bullets rip into a stack of pallets across from him, heard heavy voices gurgling and screaming, heard heavy feet kicking piles of trash. Heard Beano whining, almost crying.

I didn't do it right, Stick thought. *I should have killed both of them. I knew how to kill them. I should have killed them.*

He flattened himself out on the thick tree limb, holding the knife gently but firmly, the blade tucked inside his coat sleeve to prevent reflections. He willed himself to be motionless, invisible.

At the edge of a clearing to his right he could see the outline of a man standing silently, bulky clothing hanging open as though he were hot, waiting to cool down, clouds of hot breath floating out above his head, trying to control his breathing before he came on into the trees.

He waited, feeling the knife.

The man edged forward, poking his rifle out in front of him, ready for anything he saw.

But not ready for things he didn't see. The man moved slowly toward, then under, then away from the tree limb.

And the moment was lost. The man in the tree watched the end of the rifle barrel poke through some brush and disappear.

I could have killed him. I should have killed him. I knew how, and I had the chance. I'm losing my edge . . .

He heard the heavy sound of the car's engine and the grinding of metal as the car made one last smashing shove against the Dumpster, one headlight exploding, a tiny star winking out in the black of the alley.

The engine roared again, backing away, fading in the distance. And then silence.

He crawled slowly from beneath the jumbled, broken wood. In the thin darkness he could see the outlines of piles of trash, smell rotting garbage and the exhaust of the car. He put his hand on the wall to steady himself and stood quietly, not wanting to move out into the open until he was sure they were gone.

He waited, listening.

The alley was empty.

Stick moved quickly to the back of the Dumpster, grabbed the corner and pulled. Nothing moved.

"Jimmy!" he said, half whispering, half shouting into the thin space behind the Dumpster. "Goddammit, Jimmy, give me a hand here!" There was no answer.

Stick put his feet against the wall and shoved, pulling at the Dumpster until his hands slipped from the metal. Nothing moved.

He whirled, kicking through piles of trash, looking for a bar, a piece of wood—anything he could use to lever the heavy metal bin away from the wall, and away from the little man behind it. But there was nothing in the alley but useless trash.

He threw himself back against the Dumpster, grabbing, lunging—and stepped into something slick and unspeakable, his feet shooting out, legs flailing, tangling. He landed on his side and slid. And he knew what it was. And he knew he was too late.

And then he heard the high whines of sirens floating in on the night.

* * *

In the early gray light of a cool Santa Fe dawn Stick sat on a broken plastic milk crate and leaned back against the wall and watched the cops work around the Dumpster, each man seeming to have a specific job, knowing what to do.

There were three patrol cars and an unmarked. A good looking Hispanic got out of the unmarked, a guy with a mustache and clothes that fit the way clothes should, his tie the right size and tied at the right length and his coat tailored to help conceal the 9mm pistol on his right hip. Stick had seen him before, in the parking lot of the bus station. The detective. Cordova.

They hadn't moved the Dumpster, were still doing things with tire marks, looking for bullet holes. The big metal container was so full of garbage that its hinged lids did not fit flush against the top, the heavy flaps of metal pushed up from the inside like enormous eyes half open to a hung-over day. The sides of the box were streaked with the juices of months of garbage and Stick knew the smell would be unbearable once the sun rose, even if the Dumpster were empty. No one would want to spend any time around this particular Dumpster. Which was why Little Jimmy had picked it as his safe hide.

As the light grew Stick could see that the Dumpster was jammed hard into the alcove. Scattered around the alley were stained wooden pallets, crushed and mangled as though run over by thick tread, shards of wood scattered like heavy confetti. There was no room to slip around the Dumpster and into any space that might be left behind it. One cop had grabbed the top of the Dumpster and swung up, his leg hooking into the garbage oozing from beneath the lid.

He hauled himself into the garbage and waited quietly, listening. He heard nothing. He worked himself over the lid and slid toward the back until he could see down into the tiny space that was left between the Dumpster and the wall, down into the shadowed cleft of what was left of Little Jimmy's private hiding space. He turned his head and stared at a plain-clothes detective until the detective noticed him. The cop shook his head slightly. The detective nodded. Stick caught both of the movements.

Stick's ass hurt from sitting on the broken plastic of the crate and his back ached from pushing against the wall. The gray light had given way to a soft gold that eased up behind the mountains, the light finally coming up strongly enough to glisten off the meandering flow of coagulated darkness that showed on the pavement beneath the Dumpster, something heavy, thick, terrible.

He left the crate and squatted in front of the dark pool and he knew it was blood.

"Don't touch that."

It was only the third thing anyone had said to him since the cops arrived. The first thing had been, "Lean on the car and spread your legs." And then, "Sit over there. And if you try to leave, I'll blow your fucking head off." Each time, it was the guy in charge. Cordova.

The cop stood directly in front of him, reached out and put a finger on Stick's chin, turning his head slightly.

"Face looks like you fell into a lawn mower," the cop said, looking at the thin hatch marks running across Stick's cheek. "How's the rest of you?"

"Doing well, thank you. I spent a few days at the Mayo Clinic and they fixed everything."

"You're a smartass. You get off a bus a few weeks ago, you . . . didn't take you long to end up with a dead guy." Cord paused, waiting. Stick said nothing. "You know the guy?"

"What guy?"

"Jesus, I hate a smartass." Cord jerked his thumb over his shoulder. "The guy back there, chest as flat as a *tortilla*. You know him?"

"I don't know. Maybe. I'll have to go look."

"You do that."

Stick swung himself onto the Dumpster and slid toward the back. The other cop was still there, a tiny camera in his hand. The cop moved aside and motioned him forward.

"Jimmy," Stick said. But he did not expect an answer, and somewhere inside him he knew something was lost. He looked down into the cleft. All he could see was a human head, flattened into an oval, hair matted with blood.

* * *

They had to use a patrol car and a tow cable to pull the Dumpster out of the alcove, the Dumpster's wheels jammed or broken, the thing making screaming noises as it came grinding out of its space. The ambulance arrived at the same time, its myriad lights glittering against everything they touched. Two medics jumped out of the ambulance and ran to the back of the Dumpster, squeezing in behind it before it had stopped moving.

Stick sat on the pavement, his back against the wall. Cord sat in the open door of the unmarked, facing out, the car blocking Stick's exit from the alley. The flashing strobes of the vehicles threw the alley into an unreal dimension, bursts of color against dark-uniformed cops standing motionless, staring where medics worked unseen behind the Dumpster.

They waited. No one spoke.

A medic squeezed from behind the Dumpster, walked slowly toward Cord. The medic shook his head slightly.

"He never had a chance. Probably broke half the bones in his body. Cracked his skull. Brain matter on the wall. It'll take a while to get him out."

Cord watched the medic go back to the ambulance, pick up some equipment, and go back to the Dumpster. A cop was taking pictures, another was writing on a clipboard. Other cops were staring at him. Cord did not move from his car, watching Stick, Stick sitting with his head in his hands, the side of him covered with blood.

"I see you at the bus station, you can hardly stand up. But stood up well enough to whack a fat guy, as I remember. Next time I see you, you're here, in an alley. Dead guy behind a trash bin." Cord waited. Stick said nothing. "How long you been here?"

Stick raised his head, his eyes glittering and focused on some place that no one could reach. "Got here just before you did."

"Just before? How did you know to come here?"

Stick looked at the Dumpster. He could hear the medics working back there, grunting sounds, the pool of blood still spreading. "Was picking up some food over behind the Chinese place. Heard what sounded like a car crash. Some shots. Two. Maybe three. I know a guy uses this place to sleep . . ."

"His hide?"

"Yeah," Stick said, glancing at Cord, "his hide. By the time I got over here, got across the fence, it was over. Car backing hard down the alley. Nobody here. Except him." Stick nodded toward the Dumpster. "I tried to pull the trash bin out. Couldn't move it."

"And the blood on you?"

"Slipped. Landed in it. Not my blood. Why? You want my blood type?"

"Type?" Cord wondered if the street guy were bullshitting him. "So you weren't involved?" Cord asked. "You didn't see anybody?"

"No."

"But you saw the car."

"Just a car. Didn't really see it. Too dark."

"A lowrider?"

Lowrider. Another word for Stick to roll around in his mind. *Lowrider.* He knew what a lowrider was.

"I don't have any idea. Too dark."

"That's not a lot of help."

Stick hesitated. "There was a huge cross, maybe wooden. Hanging from the rearview. Heavy chain."

Cord got out of the car. "Strange, you see that much detail when otherwise you 'didn't really see' the car."

"Yeah. Odd," Stick said.

"You don't seem to know much."

"Been too busy to notice. Lots of things on my mind. Have to close a deal to buy the La Fonda."

Cord smiled. Slightly. The quality of his voice changed: "That guy back there, he that bony little friend of yours?"

A medic was backing out from behind the Dumpster, another medic following, a plastic sheet sagging between them. They lay the body carefully, gently, on a stretcher and stood back, both medics breathing deeply, as though just coming up for air.

"Yes. I think so."

"That why you don't know anything? You figure to take care of this yourself? Some sort of street-guy justice?"

Stick said nothing, keeping his head turned toward the stretcher.

"You think you know how to do that? Take care of the people who did this?"

Stick raised his head, thinking. "Not sure. It might come to me. That is, if I were going to take care of something like this."

For a moment, no one moved. Stick stood looking at the plastic-wrapped shape on the stretcher, Cord and the medics hardly breathing, live men in the presence of death.

Cord broke the silence. "I doubt anyone will claim the body. Almost never do. You want to see him before they take him away?"

"Yes. Thank you."

Stick dragged himself up from the pavement, his back aching, his knees not working well. He shuffled heavily to the stretcher, his hand hesitating above the black sheet of plastic. He took a deep breath . . .

At first, they were not going to let him see the body. There was no hurry. The body lay in a badly-built wooden box on the back of a truck, parked just inside the fence. The body, the box and the truck were frozen solid. The truck sat there for two days.

And then they told him he had ten minutes—and they gave him a rusted pry bar. He would have to open the lid himself.

He sat on the bed of the truck, staring at his friend. He counted eight bullet holes, one just above the left eye, the eye still open, the face marred by the teeth of dogs.

He didn't use the ten minutes. He was freezing—to keep him from running they had taken his heavy coat and his thick cap. He reached into the box and tried to close the eye just below the bullet hole, but the flesh was frozen in place.

He used the pry bar to pound the lid back on the box. He jumped down from the truck, threw the pry bar over the fence, and went back to his hut. Inside, he waited until they were gone and then he pulled the tattered sheets of folded paper from between the planks, got his pencil stub from behind the leg of the stove, and started to write.

He would make them pay. He would make them pay.

They left the truck outside the hut for nine days. And then, one morning, it was gone. He had not heard it leave.

He pulled back the corner of the plastic sheet and looked at the ragged face, the flattened skull, the expression of ultimate terror that showed clearly, even on a face so distorted it looked like an image in a fun house mirror.

But it wasn't Jimmy.

Pablo was looking up at him but not seeing him, eyes wide with wonder and yet flat, a dark stain running from his nose and one of his ears.

Pablo. The name ran through Stick's mind, jamming behind his eyes and he felt the dry burn of tears that would not come. *Aw, damn, Pablo.*

Stick turned to find Cord standing behind him.

"It's not . . ." Cord said.

"No, it's not." Stick muttered. "But it's somebody." He paused, looking at what was left of Pablo. "What happens if no one claims him?"

Cord waited, his breathing shallow. "It's . . . a long process. This is a homicide. The body goes to OMI in Albuquerque. Autopsy. Then they try to find relatives. If that doesn't work, they usually turn the body over to the county."

"If they don't find a relative, can someone else claim him?"

"Someone else?" Cord paused. "Yeah, but who . . . ?"

"This one will be claimed. I know a guy. I'll tell him."

* * *

They were gone, all of them.

He had sat with one of the cops, answering questions, the cop taking notes, bored. He told the cop the truth, but not all the truth. The cop did not even bother threatening him.

He almost asked them to take him with them, to the police station, maybe to do whatever cops do to find out who he was. Maybe they would. Maybe not. Or maybe he did not want to find out when cops were around. Some small twitch happened in his brain, a warning. He would not take the chance. He kept his mouth shut.

Now he sat on the wall, where he had sat before. He looked down at the floor of the alley, at the dented Dumpster, the blood, the streaks in the gore made by the dragging wheels of the gurney.

The fat boys had tried to kill Little Jimmy, honest-to-God tried to kill him. Jimmy was being hunted, and Stick didn't know why.

Hunted. Inside him a darkness grew, grim, like the inside of a shroud.

Somewhere in the field across the wall a dog began to bark, the dog smelling the blood, racing back and forth and bouncing up and down, a civilian hyena waiting for his chance. Stick could tell it was a large dog, its voice heavy, coming in weighted bursts. Stick's breath seemed to hang in his chest. His ears rang with the voice of the dog. Dogs. Stick had paid no attention to dogs since he had been in Santa Fe; had no reason to. But this dog wanted across the wall. It wanted Stick. Somehow he knew that. He closed his eyes and listened . . .

They turned him loose again. They would give him a longer head start this time, maybe an hour, maybe a little more. At least, that's what they said.

An hour. If he went east, straight into the woods, the way he always went, he could get far enough away that he would not hear the baying of the dogs, the laughter of the men. But he knew that would be happening.

He had stood in the open gate, awaiting the signal. When one of the men had shouted "Byegi'!" he had started east from the camp, across the open ground at a slow trot. They knew about his running, had even encouraged it. It made the game better. The "game"—their lesson to him that he could not, would not, ever get away. They just turned him loose, and then they caught him, again and again. Sometimes when they caught him they gave him food and wine, even vodka. Sometimes they beat him. It just depended on their mood. It broke the monotony for them.

He entered the heavy woods, pushed forward for a few yards and then turned, hidden, to look back and make sure they had not yet followed. They were still at the gate, smoking, laughing, the dogs straining at their thick leashes.

He jogged farther into the woods, looking for the rotting tree stump that he had found the first time he had run, no more than a half-mile from the edge of the woods. He found the stump, lay down in front of it and reached inside, working his arm upward. Jammed up inside the stump was a heavy glass jar, the kind Maria used for canning. Except this jar was heavier, the crude glass almost too thick to see through, the screw-on top made of some metal that he couldn't identify. He pulled out the jar. It was empty. It was always empty when he found it, no matter what he had put into it the last time. He rolled over and dug down inside the front of his pants to the tiny pocket he had sewn inside. He pulled some small scraps of paper—pages ripped from some sort of manual—from the pocket. Around the edges of the pages he had written in tiny script a segment of his life, what was happening to him, what he saw, what he felt, and what they were doing there in the town next to the camp. And who they killed. He put the scrap of paper inside the jar, made sure the cap was screwed tightly, and put the jar back where he had found it. He knew, the next time he opened the jar, it would again be empty.

He got up and pissed on the ground next to the stump, knowing that the smell of his urine would overpower any other scent around the stump. The dogs always yowled, but the men never bothered with the stump—it was much too small to hide a man.

He found a small stream he knew was there and it was like finding an old friend. He splashed across and out the other side, then a hundred yards farther. He stopped, backtracked on his own trail, then began running crazily in circles and slants, cutting great arcs through the trees and grass that grew in thick bunches among the trees, always coming back and crossing his original trail. Sweat ran into his eyes. He was always surprised at how hot the summers were in country that had winters that could hammer a man into stone.

After a few minutes he was done, but he kept at it until he found a deadfall. He carefully picked up two pieces of dead bark, then followed his original trail back to the stream, waded in, turned north, and began to slog quickly with the flow of the water. When the men and dogs came to the stream he knew that they would first check the other side. It would take the dogs a while to figure out that he had come back to the stream. If he got out into country that was more open, kept up a hard jog, maybe double back a couple of times, he might add another half-day to his lead time. Last time, it had taken them four days to catch him.

The dogs. Maybe they would only use one dog, the wolf-dog, the big bastard that always caught him, always ripped off his clothing.

He kept going until his breath came hard in his throat and he thought he was not going to find any way out of the stream.

And then he saw the rocks, the low ridge of them coming down into the water. He placed a piece of bark on one of the stones, stepped out onto it, and then placed the other piece in front of the first one. He took another step on the bark, careful that his hands and feet did not touch the stone. He kept up his awkward bark walk until he was down off the *rocks, across a small open space, and at least a hundred yards away from the stream.*

He threw the pieces of bark in opposite directions through the trees and started at a hard jog to the west. Somewhere out there was an ocean.

Maria?

Vivid detail. He had had a memory in vivid detail. He held it, thinking about it, trying for more, getting nothing. He opened his eyes, listening to the dog. The dog's barking had the ring of forever in it. But it could not get across the wall. The dog would bark until someone drove it away.

TWENTY-ONE

Elena had wedged open the front door of the gallery, and the warm afternoon air drifted in from the Plaza. She could smell the meat cooking at the *fajita* stand and the perfume of smoke from an expensive cigar. She knew she probably shouldn't leave the door open, but the smells were the nectar of the Plaza, signs of life still going on. She loved it.

Anthony Cordova stepped through the open doorway and moved immediately to his left. There was a space between a large sculpture of a bear and the door frame, and he stood in the space, not moving. Looking.

He always does that, Elena thought. *Always checking the room before he actually comes in.*

Cord was satisfied with what he saw in the room. He walked slowly down the front of the counters, eyes scoping the jewelry and carvings in the cases. "Hey, kid," he said softly, a smile in his voice.

"Hey yourself, Cousin Detective," the woman said. "Business or pleasure?"

"Always a pleasure to see you, Cousin Elena. But, some business, as usual."

"Want some coffee?"

"Your coffee? Hell, not even cops can drink your coffee. Stuff takes the tarnish right off our badges."

Elena smiled, and poured him a cup of coffee anyway.

"Little guy downstairs?" Cord asked.

"No. I haven't seen him . . ." Elena couldn't get out any more words. She looked at Cord, no hint of humor on his face.

"Oh, God, Cord. I saw in the paper . . . the killing at the . . ." She stopped, breathing heavily. "Was that Little Jimmy?"

"No," Cord said softly, reaching out with his hand and touching her shoulder. "I would have told you before this. Was another guy, another street guy. Looked a lot like your Jimmy."

Elena felt the weight lift from her mind. She knew that it was only a matter of time until she heard such news about Jimmy, or until Jimmy simply didn't come back to the gallery, or until Jimmy . . . just was not Jimmy anymore.

"But the other guy was there," Cord said. "Tall, skinny guy. Hangs out with Jimmy. That is, whenever Jimmy can actually be found."

"I know who you're talking about. I've . . . met him."

"Met him?"

"Yes. On the Plaza."

"On the Plaza." Cord paused. "I 'met' him at the bus station. Got to see him in action, so to speak."

"So did I," Elena said, and she told Cord about Stick and Beano and the rolled-up magazine.

Cord pulled out his cell phone, flipped it open, punched a few buttons. A picture appeared on the small screen. He handed the phone to Elena.

"That the guy?"

Elena stared at the picture, Stick looking directly into the camera, Little Jimmy's image fading out of the frame. "Yes," she said, not taking her eyes from the picture. "It seems so . . . odd . . . seeing him in a picture. Almost as if he belongs there." She gave the phone back to Cord.

Cord looked at the picture again. "You know, in this whole gallery, you only have one photograph." His eyes raised to the old photograph on the back wall.

"I know. It's the only photo that will ever hang in here."

"Your brother looks happy there."

"Yes, he was. It was the day after Wendell and Cinco's birthday. They were born on the same day. Every year, since they were thirteen, they climbed Santa Fe Baldy on their birthday, and Alvarez always went with them. The sat up there, the three of them, like blood brothers or something. They watched the sun come up. And that's all they did."

"Interesting way to celebrate a birthday," Cord said, his mind drifting back to his last birthday, recently 'celebrated' while he was in the desert south of town, where a hiker had found the remains of a body.

"I think they thought they were Santa Fe's version of the Wild Bunch. Alvarez and Wendell were bad enough, but Cinco . . ." She paused, remembering.

"Before they left the summit, they would add a few stones to the cairn that's up there. They would never take me with them, the bastards." She said 'bastards' lightly. "Always made some excuse. I didn't really want to go. I just bugged them for the hell of it."

"They're in front of the old bus station. Were they going somewhere?"

"They had just sold their cars and were taking the bus to Los Angeles . . ." She paused. "Something about a 'great adventure.' Everything with those guys was a 'great adventure.'"

Cord stared at the photograph, the young men, the dirty bus, the building, in the window a sign that read, "Eat At Joe's." He had never really known the three young men in the picture. There was no reason for them to be familiar. And then, for no reason he could think of, he held up the cell phone, his eyes moving back and forth from the black and white photograph on the wall to the brightly colored image on the screen of the phone.

This is nuts, he thought.

TWENTY-TWO

Time was passing, slipping quickly out of his reach. For days, he had been trying to get his head clear. Pablo was dead and he didn't know why and there was nothing he could do about it. And Jimmy had picked this time to pull one of his disappearing acts.

* * *

He had stopped going up the road to the ski area in the daylight. The bastards in the shiny car had seen him there, and they would be watching, sure that he would not break his habit of running up the road in the liquid cool of morning. But he did.

He loved the mountains and he would go up there, but now he went only after sundown, running along the road in his dark, tattered shirt and pants, his shoes making only soft sounds on the pavement. Wherever he could, he ran off the pavement and onto the soft berm at the side of the road, his feet far more comfortable on the giving earth than on the pavement.

When a car came, he would move quickly off the road and stand motionless in the brush, his arms folded up across his face so the car's lights would not reflect from his skin.

Each time he went up the road, he rose farther and farther into the hills, knowing that one day—one night—he would come to the end of it. When he tired of running he eased off into the woods and waited for his body to cool and dry. Then he would take the piece of canvas from his pack, wrap himself in it, and spend the night under a tree, covered in the soft duff of the forest floor.

In the morning, he ghosted down the mountain, staying in the woods above the road until he could angle off onto one of the myriad paths that cut through the trees above the town.

*   *   *

Now, in the daylight, he went other places, places where the shiny car could not go, almost always to the west, out beyond the edge of the town and along the far, squat ridges that led to the canyon of the Rio Grande.

*   *   *

The water was the color of stale coffee heavy with old milk. He sat on a low ridge, looking down into the big river canyon, watching the thick water carve slowly through the bottom. Somewhere down there the water, struggling with some obstruction, made a rattled gurgling sound, much as an old man might make, clearing his throat on a pale hot morning. If he found the right spot, he thought he could cross the river easily . . .

He was sitting on the side of a small canyon, watching the river, this same river—he knew it was the same—and he had a rifle in his hands. He could feel the smooth coolness of the rifle's stock, feel the weight-tug of the barrel. He was looking across the river, scouting for a place to cross . . .

And that was all. He stared hard at the water, but no other memory, no vision, would come to him just because he watched the river. The brief memory fragment was gone. But he was a hunter. He knew he was a hunter.

But what did I hunt?

To the north and south of him smaller canyons opened into the river, their dry mouths seeming to gulp at the water.

He took a sip from his water bottle, smelling the scent of something soft floating on the dry air, feeling the sun on his shoulders. In the beginning, when he had first started coming out here, he thought he should try to explore them all, all the side canyons. But there didn't seem to be a reason; he had found nothing much in the few he did look into—the metal husks of long-abandoned cars, old trash, and, once, new blood. He never found out how the blood got there.

Now, he let his body and his blank mind lead him, moving up into canyons only when his feet seemed to point that way. And he always seemed to come back to this canyon.

Across the Rio Grande and slightly upstream a larger canyon, thick with trees and tangled brush, backed away from the river and ran jaggedly off toward dark mountains in the western distance. He dug in his pack and took out the torn topographic map he had found in an alley behind a store that sold camping supplies. He studied the map, realizing that, even without the map, he could tell north from south, east from west. On the map he found the mountains in front of him, the Jemez. The map showed nothing but mountains and deep canyons on that side of the river; no towns, no people, no roads. A total wilderness, less than fifteen miles from Santa Fe.

The canyon below him ran off to his right, to the east, and he could see an old trail that led back toward some sort of heavy building in the distance, and then a stand of gigantic old cottonwoods.

Through the cottonwoods and brush he thought he could see the faint lines of another building, maybe a house, but he wasn't sure.

He moved east along the top of the canyon wall, heading generally back toward town. He has seen nothing, found nothing. He didn't know what he had been expecting, but no images had come. No memories. Below him, he passed a barbed-wire fence, rusted and slack, with a sagging gate that, he thought, had not been opened in a long time; months, maybe years. He knew there was some sort of homestead in the canyon below, but he was too far back on the ridge to see. He would check it out another time.

The trail slowly curved toward the closed end of the canyon, rising slightly. Below, he could see the parallel tracks of a narrow dirt road cut into the hard-pack. A scraggly stand of cottonwood trees was tucked against the far wall and a small deer was taking shelter there. He saw the head of the deer move up and down, looking for food, but wary. There was little for the deer to eat. He wondered what the deer was doing there and thought maybe it had somehow crossed the river, moved up-canyon. He knew that if it didn't go back across the river, it would die.

He sat, leaning back into the base of a *pinon* tree, the spiny limbs embracing him, shading him, and watched the deer, now and then letting his eyes wander down the dirt lane toward the larger trees in the distance. He could see the tops of them, knew there were some buildings down there. Maybe next time he would get a little closer, see what he could see. He sat for more than an hour, watching the deer, thinking of the river. He wondered why he was there. He had no real reason. But whenever he wandered alone out of the city he always ended up in the mountains to the northeast, or here, to the west, next to the river, watching the water flow.

The sun was directly overhead. He snaked his body underneath a *piñon* tree and closed his eyes.

He didn't know why he woke. Maybe there was a small noise, a movement. Maybe there was nothing. Maybe his vacant mind was just trying to fill itself up. But there was something, he was sure. A tiny noise that didn't belong in the canyon.

He opened his eyes and waited. And waited.

The deer was still there, almost at the edge of the road, head still moving up and down, nose searching for food, eyes searching for anything. Stick watched the head move up and down, the eyes always coming back to the same point, staring for long seconds before the head would drop again towards the ground. Stick looked where the deer was looking.

And he saw the truck. It was off the road, tucked back into the brush, its dull rust color almost invisible in the heavy shadows, its nose pointed down canyon.

Pointed so the guy can watch the road, Stick thought.

The driver's door was fully open, but, from his angle, Stick could not see into the truck. He moved cautiously to his left, crouching, trying for a better angle. He could see a little more of the truck, now. Tailgate missing. The truck was abandoned, he thought, a rusting hulk left in the high desert, shrubby growth moving in to cover it.

He started to rise from his crouch. Maybe he could spook the deer back down-canyon, maybe back across the river.

The arm came slowly out of the truck, rested on the bottom of the open window, and Stick saw the stubby pistol held in a chunky hand.

In that tiny last second of thinking, that instant flash of recognition when some primeval bolt of panic cuts through the minds of animals, the deer knew it had to escape.

Too late. The pistol fired. It was an easy shot.

The tiny deer bucked, all four feet leaving the ground, body twisting in the air. It landed hard on its right side, dust billowing softly out from the impact. The deer tried to rise, tried to get its legs working. But the legs only pawed a few times and then stopped.

Silence came on the canyon. It was a silence in the presence of death, a silence, Stick realized, that he knew well. He recognized it, could taste it, knew it in the middle of his bones, knew that, in the presence of death, birds do not sing and insects somehow know to fall silent. It seemed to Stick that he could hear his heart beat, hear the rush of blood through his body.

The guy got out of the truck, a big guy, awkward, shuffling through the soft loam in what looked to be dirty white sneakers, getting dirtier with each step. He stood over the deer, pistol pointed at the animal's head. He seemed to be waiting. He squatted, pistol ready. The deer did not move. The man stood and tucked the pistol into his belt. He turned and walked back toward the truck. Stick thought the walk was . . . jaunty . . . as though he were pleased with something he had done, pleased with killing the deer, pleased with the event of death . . .

Angelo! The name hit Stick's brain and clung there. *It's Angelo! What the fuck is Angelo doing out here? He sure as hell isn't hunting deer. But Angelo is here.*

And I am here.

The big man got into the truck. The engine started and the truck pulled slowly out of the brush. And then the driver punched the gas, the truck jamming hard down the dirt track, the wheels spewing sand and rock. It slid violently around a shallow curve and fishtailed back on the track, the driver hidden behind dusty, tinted glass and fighting the grip of the dirt and the speed. The truck straightened and accelerated, slashing down-canyon, slamming to a stop, a cloud of fine powdery dust nearly obscuring it.

He's celebrating. The bastard's celebrating.

The truck's engine idled, sun glinting from its darkened windows. Stick could hear the clacking mash of gears and the truck slowly backed off the track, turned, then shot forward again and away toward the high end of the canyon and was gone across a low rise, back toward the city.

He realized he was still in a crouch. He rose stiffly, feeling the nagging ache in his hips and knees. The ache usually came the next day, after he had been running, but now he wondered if there were something hidden in the dark attic of his unknown past that made his bones ache. He picked up his pack and started awkwardly down the ridge.

Halfway down the ridge he realized his body was running on some unknown source of knowledge . . . and he was fascinated by it, letting it lead him. When he got to the deer he saw that it was a small doe, its tongue flopped out of the side of its mouth, one eye staring desperately, directly into the sun, breath blowing hard out through nostrils that bubbled with blood.

The deer's alive. It's alive. The son of a bitch just looked at it, left it lying here to die slowly.

He never hesitated, knowing exactly what to do. He opened the big folding knife that he had taken from the fat man in El Paso and stepped quickly to the side of the deer—he did not straddle the deer, knowing that the animal might make a last attempt to rise—and in a single swift motion he cut the deer's throat.

TWENTY-THREE

The sun was low and blood-golden light was washing the Sangre de Cristo Mountains but Little Jimmy did not notice. He sat on the wall behind the market and stared at the space where his hide used to be. Everything was gone. They had taken out the Dumpster and hauled it off somewhere, torn out the little alcove and cleared all the broken cinder blocks. The pallets were gone, his old scraps of blankets, the trash, everything. And then they had brought in high pressure hoses and washed the alley, the backs of the buildings, the wall on which he sat, the other Dumpsters that they had moved far down toward the street. Washed everything. They had tried to erase the blood, the violence, the death. But it was still there. Jimmy could feel it in his gut.

He had spent a few days on the east edge of town in a little camp he had out there. He had come back into town in the middle of the night, ghosted his way to his hide—and it wasn't there. Everything was changed. Jimmy panicked, sneaked back out of town and stayed there until he got hungry, very hungry. He had come back into town and found Stick, and Stick had told him about Pablo.

He looked down into the alley, everything seeming shiny and new. *I could sleep down there and not even get dirty*, he thought. *Well, not get any dirtier . . .*

And then another thought hit him. *Pablo ran to my hide. My hide. How did he know where it was?*

And then another thought: *It was supposed to be me. Me. They were really gonna do it. They were gonna kill ME!*

* * *

Little Jimmy sat on the grass across the street from the All-Nighter, his back pushed up against a fancy wire fence that surrounded a car lot. Jimmy hunched against the fence, his escape route between the cars already planned out, knowing exactly where he would run and where the shiny purple car would not be able to follow.

Dawn had not yet come to Santa Fe. There were few cars on Cerrillos Road, moving slowly, their lights raking the pavement. The lights in the All-Nighter washed weakly out through the windows. Jimmy tried to see past the All-Nighter and into the parking lot in front of the repair shop, but it was still too dark. He could not see the trashed cars clearly, could not tell which one belonged to the Socket Set. He would wait for the full light to come.

The Socket Set. They were not the Socket Set anymore. There was only the Mechanic. He would have to talk with the Mechanic, explain things, try to make things okay. He knew it wouldn't work, but he had to try.

It was supposed to be me, he thought. *How can I explain that to the Mechanic?*

Jimmy edged under the wire and slid his bony little body under the edge of a car. He closed his eyes.

* * *

Jimmy opened his eyes but did not move. He listened to the traffic on Cerrillos Road, saw the brilliant summer sunlight glistening from cars.

He reached down and unzipped his pants, then pissed into the gravel. Satisfied that no one had seen him, he eased carefully from beneath the car and sat down on the grass. It was still too early for the car lot to be open for business, but the rest of Santa Fe was up and running.

He looked at the space beside the All-Nighter where the Socket Set dragged their car. It wasn't there. Jimmy tried to see if the car was in the other lot in front of the repair shop, but the angle was not right. He darted across Cerrillos Road and moved quickly to the corner and down the side street, not wanting to be in the open any longer than necessary.

Cars were parked randomly in front of the repair shop, the shop not yet open, Jimmy stepping carefully around thick oil stains.

The car was not there.

He went cautiously around the building, but the car was not anywhere.

Jimmy sat on the trunk of an old car at the back of the lot, not moving, his head in his hands, trying to think this thing through. He glanced through a chain link fence and noticed a semi-trailer loaded with crushed, flattened, car bodies. He stared at the load, car bodies stacked four or five high on the trailer . . . and saw the bright yellow piece of metal shining from the bottom of the pile.

TWENTY-FOUR

He took off his belt, stooped, gathered the hind legs of the deer, wrapped the belt around them and raised the deer into a *pinon* tree, forcing the carcass through the thick, tough branches. He tied it there, its head hanging almost to the ground. He did all this in less than a minute.

He waited until the drainage of blood slowed to only a drop, falling black and silently from the deer's neck. He took the deer down, gathered its legs in his hands, lifting, swinging the small body up and across his shoulders.

He started down-canyon toward the river, then remembered the buildings down there. If there were people down there, and if they had heard the shot . . .

He turned toward the high ridge, climbing slowly and steadily, sweat soaking him. At the top, he moved back away from the rim, dropping down into a rift that ran toward the river, out of sight of anyone back in the other canyon.

He was at the river again. He looked at the small sand bars that broke the sluggish surface of the water like the backs of unearthly fish, and then, without hesitation, waded into the water. He knew exactly where he was going, but he did not know how he knew. Only once did the water come up to his hips. And then he was across and on the other side, still standing in the water, at the edge of wilderness.

He turned upstream, wading slowly and silently, until he was at the mouth of the large canyon he had seen earlier. Over the years, water rushing out of the canyon had formed a small alluvial fan at the mouth, a spread of earth, stone and sand that pushed the river off to one side. A small stream cut through the fan, crystal water trickling into the amber of the Rio Grande. He stopped just downstream from the fan. He stood motionless in the brown river, the small deer draped across his shoulders. He didn't like to be exposed and yet here he was, exposed, naked to view, the sun beating on his face. He knew he couldn't run, even if he had to. Here, motionless, in the middle of the river . . . it was not a good place to be caught.

He climbed out onto the sand and gravel of the fan and in less than a minute disappeared up into the western canyon, water dripping from his pants, the head of the deer dangling loosely against his back.

*　*　*

Somehow he knew it would be there and so he was not surprised when he found it, a dark spot on the steep north wall of the canyon, a spot which, at casual glance, seemed no more than a shadow among the faded pink columns of rock. A cave, its open mouth angled to the south and gathering heat as it had been doing for thousands of years.

He stopped in the cottonwoods below the cave, dumped the deer on the ground and took out the knife. He cut a long stick, sharpened its ends, and drove the stick beneath the tendons of the back legs of the deer. He worked automatically, jamming the stick into the limbs of a cottonwood tree, hanging the deer head-down, gutting it, the warm offal tumbling loosely to the ground. He climbed the tree, raised the deer higher into the branches, then covered it carefully with a layer of small limbs, long grass and weeds in an effort to keep away as many insects as possible. He built a small fire off to the side, careful to use very dry wood to keep smoke to a minimum. He took the liver from the offal, sliced it, spitted it on a long stick, and jammed the stick into the ground, leaning the meat out near the flames.

He took the remainder of the now-cold and slimy offal down-canyon and buried it in the sandy soil as deeply as he could. When he returned to the fire, the liver was properly done and he pulled the stick from the ground, sat against a tree, and ate the liver directly from the stick, holding it with his teeth and slicing it with the knife, never touching it with his hands. It was a trick he had learned. From somewhere.

* * *

The mouth of the cave was forty feet up from the canyon floor and the climb was difficult. When he sat in the narrow mouth of the cave and looked down, he realized that the entire climb could be seen from where he sat; anyone climbing up to the cave was totally exposed to anyone who was already there.

The cave was narrow and shallow, just large enough for a man to sleep away from the mouth, the roof covered by the carbon black of countless small fires burning beside the sleeper, some of the ancient ashes still on the floor. At the back, the cave compressed into a narrow slot that a man could stand in, if he wasn't a very large man. At the mouth of the cave a narrow shelf jutted out to the east, toward the river, and he saw the worn spots made by the feet and backs of people who had sat there, watching. He could see the river clearly.

An easy rifle shot, he thought, *or a very long pistol shot. Or, maybe, a nearly impossible bow shot.*

How do I know if a bow shot is nearly impossible? Or any other weapon, for that matter?

It took him two hours to collect enough wood and carry it, a few sticks at a time, up to the cave. He knew he should store water but there was nothing in the cave to keep it in. He took the large cup from his pack, filled it in the stream, and carefully carried it up. It would have to do.

When he was done with the cave he went back to the deer and cut thin slices of meat from the haunch. Back in the cave he built a small fire where thousands of other small fires had been built, and again spitted the meat. To give the meat a saltier taste, he sprinkled on it some of the fine ash of the old fires. He sat with his back to the wall, watching the light go pale, smelling the dripping meat, feeling the gentle scent of the smoke invade his lungs.

He sat with his back to the wall of the cave, watching the light from the fire flick among tiny cracks in the rock. The fire made some of the cracks in the far back of the cave appear to be lines and drawings. He took a firebrand and held it in front of him, easing himself into the narrow back of the cave. The wall was sculpted with the lines of ancient voices—stick men, animals, charts and symbols—messages singing out across millennia. The uneven light from the firebrand made the figures seem to move, the stick men running after the stick animals, some dancing in celebration of food and life.

Some of the scratches on the wall looked somehow different. He held the torch higher and looked more closely. The scratches were newer than the others, much newer, the still-bright bare rock showing through the lines, no soot filling the delicately carved art. And yet the new carvings matched the style of the old ones perfectly, the same style, the same feel for the ancient lines. In the narrow space the heat and smoke from the firebrand made his eyes water and he wasn't sure what he was seeing: in the middle of the new drawings there were some rounded scratches, one leading into the other, like a climbing thunderstorm of clouds. Next to the clouds there was a sort of square. Lines crossed the square, each line precise and never running off the square. Maybe a garden plot. Clouds over a garden. Rain. Food. A time of plenty.

He opened his notebook and began to copy the petroglyphs, in detail, exactly as he saw them. He finished just as the light from the firebrand faded into darkness.

He sat back at the fire and let his mind wander, reaching for something that he would recognize. Only one thing came to him— he had seen such drawings before.

* * *

By the time he finished eating, the sun had moved behind the Jemez Range and was throwing dark amber light into the canyons. He sat on the ledge outside the cave, sipped his water, and watched the light grow thicker. Back across the river he could see a canyon he hadn't noticed before, some broken fencing at the mouth, a trail leading away from the river toward a large stand of ancient cottonwood trees. He could see the corner of what must have been a barn, and from somewhere in the trees a piece of glass glittered in the dying sun. But he saw no signs of life.

And he felt a stirring deep within his mind.

TWENTY-FIVE

Willie the Hook lay in the tall grass just over the bank above the Santa Fe River, his duster wrapped around him. He rolled over, got to his knees and raised his head slightly above the bank, to street level, peering across, looking into the parking lot and the big metal box. He didn't know the best time try this, didn't know whether to try it in full dark—it was too late for that, now—or wait for even more light. He knew the little hillbilly could do it in the dark, was real slick about it, go in and out whenever he wanted. The hillbilly had bragged to Mulligan, Mulligan thinking it was funny, telling some other People about it. And somebody told Willie, but Willie could not remember who.

But Willie had never done it, never actually pulled open the bin and tried to climb inside. He wanted enough light to see what he was doing, at least this first time, at least to make sure he was not too big to fit in the bin.

It was almost time. If he waited any longer, people might start coming by and putting stuff in the drop box. And seeing Willie.

Willie got up and stayed in a crouch, shoulders hunched, starting quickly across the street, his duster trailing on the dark pavement.

When he heard the noise from inside the drop box, Willie did not even break stride. He simply reversed his course, raised slightly to get more speed, scurried back across the street and dropped silently over the bank. He eased down into the tall grass and waited.

Willie heard the bin fall open, a grunting sound, and then the bin being shut again—not banging shut, but being shut slowly, carefully, making as little noise as possible. Willie raised his head slightly. It was light enough, now. He could see the bin clearly, Little Jimmy standing in front of it, he head swiveling back and forth, a frightened bird ready for instant flight.

Well I'll be goddamned, Willie thought.

* * *

Stick found the cigar behind the tiny Sanbusco Market Center, a block off Guadalupe Street.

He was waiting for Little Jimmy. Seems as though he was always waiting for Jimmy. Since Pablo had died, the little man had been spookier than ever, appearing and disappearing at random, never in the same place for any length of time. Except the gallery. Jimmy always went back to the gallery.

Stick sat on a bench in the mid-morning sun just outside the rear door of the mall and the man walked right by him as though Stick were not there. The man crossed the hot black parking lot to his expensive car. He carried a large cup of steaming coffee and juggled several small packages, dropping a few as he fumbled for his car keys. He got the keys, picked up the packages and got in and drove away and when he was gone the cigar was there on the pavement, next to some drying thick liquid that Stick didn't recognize. The cigar was a Cohiba and it hadn't been smoked and Stick thought it might be expensive. Perhaps very expensive. He had smoked such cigars, he thought. Somewhere. Sometime.

He picked up the cigar and sat back down on the bench, sorted through his pack and found a small metal tube with a top that screwed on, something he had found behind a restaurant. The tube had once held one of those cheap cigars made expensive because they came in a metal tube. When you smoked one of those cigars you found out quickly that the tube was the best part. He had kept the tube against the day he had a real cigar to put in it. And now he had. He put the cigar in the tube, softly blew his breath into the tube and screwed the top down tight. He knew the moisture in his breath would be good for the cigar, but he didn't know how he knew that. He would save the cigar until evening . . .

He was in a small concrete room sitting on a metal, straight-back chair, a gray metal table in front of him, his hands chained to the table. There was a small window and outside he could see green trees, evergreens, he thought, standing in thick clusters. But the trees were beyond a high fence, heavy wire strung tightly between poles that were as heavy and tall as the trunks of the trees.

He was cold, and he was very hungry.

A man reached around from behind him and held a cigar in front of his face. He looked at the cigar with his eyes, but he did not move, did not turn his head. Now and then they did this, offered him something, loosened up a little, seemed almost friendly. But it was all bullshit.

He drew in his breath, sucking in the aroma of the cigar. "Who are you?" he asked.

"It doesn't matter. You have not met me before. But I am your friend. There, that is good. Just call me . . . Friend."

Friend waved the cigar under his nose. He kept his head still. "You don't want it? It is Cuban, the best there is. It is good that we have friends like this."

He could not see Friend, but the cigar moved closer to his nose. He could see the cuffs of Friend's heavy coat, new cuffs, without the ragged edges that he was used to. Friend's other hand came into view, holding a tiny pair of scissors. Very gently, Friend clipped the end from the cigar.

"There, that is much better." Friend placed the clipped end of the cigar between his lips and instantly he could taste the tobacco, feel the sense of it on his tongue. He knew he should spit the cigar out, but he could not. He held the end of it gently between his teeth.

From somewhere behind him he heard the scratch of a match and the minute roar of the flame. Friend touched the fire to the end of the cigar.

No. No goddammit. He would not smoke the fucking cigar.

He drew in the smoke.

The smoke filled his mouth, his nose and his senses. It curled up and burned his eyes and he squeezed them shut, all the better to concentrate on the smoke. Only a moment ago he had been cold and hungry but now the cigar seemed to take over his body, to warm him, to feed him, the hunger pangs immediately lessened by the sensations of the tobacco.

A metal door clanged open and two men rushed into the room, the sounds of their hobnailed boots slamming into his hearing. Both men carried large buckets—they heaved the freezing water directly into his face, soaking every part of his body.

"Oh," one of the bucket men said, "we are so very sorry. But we smelled smoke . . . !"

And they left him there, his body shaking, feeling his ragged clothes begin to stiffen in the thick cold of the concrete room.

He could hear their laughter down the hard hallway.

Stick had his arms wrapped around himself, squeezing, his whole body shaking from the cold. Only, he realized, blinking his eyes, he wasn't cold. Not really. He sat in the hot morning sun, rocking slightly. Not cold.

He tried to blink back the images, get them to return to his empty mind. But nothing came. And then he realized he had squeezed the metal tube and crushed the cigar. He would keep the twisted tube, the expensive cigar, anyway.

Smoking was not allowed inside Sanbusco and Stick knew that mall employees came out to the bench and sat and smoked. He also knew, when he was sitting there, the employees never shared the bench with him. They moved off, smoking somewhere else, standing. When they came out the door with their unlit cigarettes in their hands, their faces would fall when they saw him. He was always tempted to keep his seat, but he seldom did. He knew if he got pushy someone would report him and the security people would put him on their list. He didn't want to be on anyone's list.

The little mall was one of his favorite places. It had clean public restrooms and Stick knew he could walk inside almost any time, go straight to the restrooms, use them, wash, drink some water and be out of there without disturbing anyone. Or being disturbed. The secret was not to waste time, and not to look the Citizens in the eye.

* * *

It was almost noon before Little Jimmy showed up. He came in from Agua Fria Street, squeezed between a couple of cars and stood scanning the parking lot. He did not move for maybe five minutes. Then he eased off toward the back of Sanbusco where Stick sat waiting.

"Took your damned time," Stick said, trying to sound irritated.

Jimmy looked at the mangled cigar tube that Stick still held lightly in his fingers. "Thet ain't a White Owl."

"White owl? What's that?"

"Best damned see-gar ever made," Jimmy said, sliding onto the bench.

Stick looked at his friend. "White Owl. That's what you like to smoke—White Owl?"

"Nah, never did smoke 'em. My uncle used to bring 'em home now and again. Bite the end off. Chew it. Made good chewin'. Never did actually see him smoke one. Got so, he'd leave 'em layin' around and I'd chew me one, just like he did."

Stick held the tube out to Little Jimmy. "Here, take this one. It's not a White Owl, but it might do the job."

Jimmy carefully took the cigar tube. "You mean it? I kin have this?"

"Yeah. But you have to get it out of the tube. Might look like it's already been chewed. In fact, if you can get it out of there, you might try smoking it. Do you good."

"I'll think on it," Jimmy said. He put the tube in his pocket.

"One thing I keep forgetting to ask you," Stick said. "When we were down there on Cerrillos, with the Socket Set, you took off on me again, just disappeared, before I could talk to Pablo."

Jimmy sat quietly, not looking at Stick.

"Look, Jimmy, I think my talking to Pablo may have gotten him killed. And I don't know why."

"No. Thet ain't it," Jimmy said, almost under his breath. "Them boys, they thought . . . they thought Pablo was me. Didn't have nuthin' to do with yew."

Stick ran it through his mind. Nothing about it made any sense.

A large woman came out of the mall, heading toward them, her hips pushing out against her dress, a large silver cross dangling from her neck and resting prominently on her huge breasts. The woman passed closely but did not look at them. She got into a car, started the engine, and drove away.

"I reckon we ain't here," Jimmy said.

"What do you mean?"

"I mean sometimes I jist do things to make Citizens look at me, like I really am here. Elsewise, they don't look."

"Yeah," Stick said, "so I've noticed."

"Had me a cross like that, once't."

"Like what?"

"Like thet big 'un a-hangin' on her tits."

"Big silver cross?"

"Nah, mine was jist wood. Was big, though. Was so big I kept it on a big 'ol chain."

Stick looked directly at Jimmy. "What happened to it?"

Jimmy inhaled deeply. "C'mon," he said, "I promised the gallery lady that I'd bring you by. Do the windows, or some such."

They started across the parking lot. Stick heard the rumble of a heavy engine coming up behind them. He turned, and a dark-colored lowrider slid by, its exhaust pipes nearly dragging the pavement. Stick turned, grinning.

"It's not the car . . ."

But Jimmy was gone.

* * *

Stick walked casually from the far corner behind Sanbusco, across Sanbusco's parking lot and across Montezuma Street, looking straight ahead, his back erect and his hands in his pockets. He had perfected the speed and look of his walk after being stopped in the parking lot of a shopping mall on the south end of town. A security guard at the mall had thought he was casing cars. He had been walking across the lot, wondering what had been on the land before the mall paved it over, wondering what would be there when the mall was gone, wondering if he had ever walked on this ground before it was a mall. He was walking very slowly. He had no place in particular to go. Walking slowly was a mistake.

It surprised him that he never saw her, the security guard. For some reason he thought he should have, should have known she was there, should have been aware. But, suddenly, there she was, as though stepping out of another dimension, walking beside him, close enough to touch him before he even sensed her presence, the security guard, a small, compact blonde who seemed perfectly at ease matching his stride as they walked together past several cars.

"Looking for anything in particular?" She didn't look at him when she talked, but he knew she was watching.

He glanced at her name tag. Darci. "No. Just passing through. Left the Bently at home today."

She grinned. "Just passing through? On your way to another life?"

"Don't think so. Think maybe this is my other life. Be interesting to know for sure."

She stopped. He took another few steps and looked back at her.

"I wasn't checking out the cars," he said.

"I know that. Seems to me you have other things to check out." She paused. "Look, when you walk through parking lots, don't mope along, but don't run, either. Walk as though you know where you're going and need to get there. Walk in a straight line. Don't weave in and out of the rows, don't look in the car windows. Makes people like me nervous."

He nodded. "What's a nice girl like you doing in a place like this?"

"Just passing through," she said, "maybe on my way to another life."

"You should consider . . . philosophy."

"Maybe I will." She raised her hand to him, palm out. "Take care." And she was gone.

* * *

Now, when he was around Citizens he didn't walk too slowly anymore. And parking lots always had a few Citizens in them, watching him from the corners of their eyes. He walked exactly as she told him, kept himself straightened up, his shirttail tucked in, his hands out of action, ignoring the windows of the cars. Didn't want Citizens to think he was hurrying away from something. Didn't want Citizens to think anything about him at all.

Across Montezuma Street there was another parking lot. On the far side of the lot a low wall was topped by some metal railings. He crossed the lot, hopped on the wall and swung himself over the railings and was in the parking lot behind the Zia Diner. The lot was full, as it always was. At the far left of the lot a small patch of grass and a tree guarded a tiny plot of ancient Santa Fe soil from the onslaught of cars and pavement. Under the tree there was a plastic milk crate shoved far back into the corner. He had put it there a couple of weeks ago, the first time he and Jimmy had checked out the back of the Zia. No one had moved it. He went to the crate and sat down, leaning back against the wall. When he sat like that, absolutely still, he knew that most of the people going and coming from the restaurant didn't see him.

Looking between a couple of cars he could see the back of the Zia. The back door was open. Two large Dumpsters guarded the door and some crates and other restaurant overburden lay scattered about. Some trash had fallen from the Dumpsters.

Stick had no watch; he hadn't been wearing one when he woke up in the motel room in El Paso. But he never seemed to need one.

If he looked closely, he could tell the time within reasonable limits. Like now, for instance. A few of the cars in the parking lot were pulling out and Stick knew some of the early lunch crowd had already finished and were leaving. So it must be somewhere just before one o'clock. He was right on time.

The woman came out of the back of the Zia. She was taller than average, fully built, with liquid red hair that sprinkled hints of light when she stepped into the sun. She wore a white blouse, a crisp white apron tied around her waist. She stepped to the edge of the parking lot and faced into the sun. She spread her legs, arched her back, raised her arms and held them over her head, stretching every part of her body at once. He watched the prominence of her breasts as she rotated her full hips, her arms still in the air. She could have been thirty, could have been forty, could have been any age at all. He had no idea. When he looked at her he realized how much about women he didn't know, or had forgotten. But she was a full-grown woman and she was beautiful and he knew she was looking for him.

She didn't look directly at him. Never had, not since the first time she had seen him. But she knew he was there. He sat quietly on the crate, his hands folded in front of him, waiting. And when she was satisfied he was there, she went back inside the diner.

She was gone maybe two minutes. When she came out again she carried a bag of trash and a white foam carry-out container. She flung the trash carelessly into one of the Dumpsters and almost as an afterthought tossed the foam container on top of a pile of crates. She never looked at him, didn't even glance his way, and went back into the diner.

He waited. Then, watching to make sure he wouldn't run into anyone else coming out of the diner, he moved quickly past the crates, picking up the foam container as he went.

In less than a minute he was back at his sanctuary on the crate behind the tree. He settled himself and opened the box. Meatloaf. And mashed potatoes. And some green stuff that he didn't recognize but knew he should eat. And half a wedge of pie. A plastic fork. Stick knew the food was maybe food sent back to the kitchen by some guy trying to impress his girlfriend, food carefully selected and rescued by the redheaded woman. It was hot and it was good and when he sat there like that, in the shade, with a wall at his back, eating, no one watching him, no one even looking for him, he wondered how much better life could get.

When he finished the food he took the container to one of the Dumpsters and threw it in. Then he straightened the piles of crates and picked up all the trash. A hose was connected to the back of the diner and he uncoiled it, turned it on, washed down everything he could see.

He drank from the hose and then put it away. And then he was gone.

* * *

He stood inside the open door, looking back through the gallery, the first time he had seen the art except through the windows.

Elena Montoya was wearing a black silk blouse and a gray velvet skirt, a single strand of beaded silver around her neck. She held a delicate coffee cup and leaned against an antique jewelry counter, polished turquoise and silver gleaming on the shelves.

Just beyond her, a black woman was moving slowly along the wall, head back, hands clasped behind her. She was tall, rangy, staring intently at the art displayed along the wall. She did not look around. Farther back in the gallery, a middle-aged couple wearing new western boots walked stiffly in a loose circle, trying to see everything in the gallery in a single pass.

"I haven't seen you for a while." Elena's voice was low register, almost silky, no hint of aggression.

"I've been . . . hiking . . . sort of camping out. Looking at the river."

"River? The Rio Grande? You hiked all the way to the Rio Grande."

"Yes. My driver didn't want to take the limo down there."

She stood looking at him, waiting for some further explanation. Nothing came.

"Where's Jimmy?" Elena asked.

"Hard tellin', not knowin'," he said.

The woman felt her breath catch in her throat. She stared at him, looking for something in his face that she did not find. "Do you frequently use such old clichés?"

He thought about what he had just said, wondered where it came from. "Don't really know," he said. "Maybe if we talked more, you could help me figure it out." He smiled. She did not smile.

"You never told me how much you charge," she said.

"Charge?" And then he realized what she was talking about. "I charge . . . a single cup of coffee," he said, his eyes flicking to the cup in her hands. "That's for the windows. And I'll do the floor, if I can touch the sculpture and look at the art."

A broom was leaning on a counter to his left. Stick picked it up, looked at the heavy bristles. "You don't want to sweep a dry floor with a broom like this. Stirs up too much dust. I'll damp-mop it, then . . ." He stopped. He knew about cleaning floors . . .

Someone loafed through the door and Stick heard lazy steps behind him. He turned, seeing the man, and stepped to the side. The man was an Indian, somewhere in his late twenties, maybe early thirties, ruggedly handsome and well built, long black hair flowing down over the collar of his dress shirt. He wore suit pants and moccasins, carried the suit coat over his arm, a tie draped untied around his neck. He stopped directly in front of Stick.

"Elena has told me about you. What do you want here?" The Indian's voice was deep and firm, demanding.

The woman looked at the Indian, but said nothing.

Stick knew he should leave, but he did not.

That's an expensive suit, Stick thought. *He won't risk dirtying the coat. He'll lay it down somewhere, try to be casual about it, before he makes a move. That'll give me time.*

"I want to wash the windows and look at the art," Stick answered, trying to keep his voice in neutral.

"And to look at the *señorita.*"

Stick thought about lying, but he didn't. "That, too," he said quietly.

"I told you he was honest," she said.

The Indian stood looking at him. Stick held his ground.

"Where's the other one?" the Indian asked.

Stick said nothing.

"The other one," the Indian repeated. "The scrawny little guy."

"I don't know," Stick said, "and I was watching him so closely, too."

The flick of a smile caught at the corners of the Indian's mouth. And then was gone.

The middle-aged couple edged past them and went quickly out the door, their boots clopping on the wooden floor. Stick didn't see the black woman.

"I've got an office in the back," the Indian said.

"Don't go in there." He reached out slowly, deliberately, and took the broom from Stick. Stick did not resist. Without looking at the woman the Indian turned and walked toward the back of the gallery. In the far back corner was a door, partially hidden by a Navajo rug. The Indian turned, looking back at Stick. Softly, the Indian said something, the words rounded and musical. And disappeared through the door, still carrying the broom.

"When you find out who I really am, maybe you will let me know," Stick said.

The Indian reappeared in the doorway.

"You speak my language?"

"Damned if I know," Stick said. "But you said you were going to run me down, find out who I really am. Maybe I just *thought* that's what you said."

Stick hadn't expected a confrontation. To his surprise, it excited him. He could feel his heart beating.

"Matthew. Matthew Klah," the woman said, still staring hard at Stick. "Lawyer. He rents office space from me. Looks out for me."

Stick felt a slight tingling sensation in the back of his head. He raised his hand and raked it through his shaggy hair.

"I'd like to tell you to pay no attention to him, but people who pay no attention to Matt Klah are making a serious mistake."

"You don't seem to be a person who needs looking after."

"Maybe. Maybe not. But I've known Matt Klah since we were children. As far as I'm concerned, he can do anything he wants . . . and, no, I don't know what he said. In all the years I've known him, I've never learned a single word of Tewa."

"He said . . . I think he said . . . he was going to check me out." Stick looked at the closed office door at the far end of the gallery, still hearing the smooth, round sounds of the language rolling softly across his mind.

Elena stood silently, looking at the street guy, visions of her youth rolling across her in a wash of color that blurred all the images.

Matt stopped just inside the door to his office and carefully put the broom down. The room was formal, strictly business, a conservative law office with diplomas and law books plainly in sight. And other books, shelf after shelf of them. But Klah was not impressed by possessions. Other than the books, the small room was Spartan, the desk, chairs and filing cabinets wooden. There was no couch, no secretary or receptionist. There was a single telephone connected to an answering machine, his answering message first in Tewa, and then in English. The only touch of luxury was the Navajo rug that covered most of the spotless floor.

But there was another room. Klah opened an inner door and stepped through into another world. There were no chairs and the sitting rugs were placed carefully around a small copper fire pan in the middle of the thick tile floor, a copper flue running straight up and through the ceiling. Skins and paintings decorated the walls. Klah looked briefly at the room, inhaled the aroma of the skins and the ashes from the *piñon* fires.

He stepped back into the front room, closed the door, and sat at the desk. He picked up the phone. He knew the number.

"Cordova," the deep voice said on the other end of the line.

"Matt."

"Well, Mr. Klah," Cordova said, a hint of humor in his voice, "is this about somebody I've arrested, or somebody you know I'm *going* to arrest?"

Matt thought he heard a slight chuckle on the other end of the line.

"How many lunches do I owe you, Cord, for things that are, uh, off the books?"

Silence.

"Well?" Matt asked.

"I'm counting, I'm counting. I think it's up to six, but, you know, I'm a cop—anything over five is difficult for me to compute."

"I'm going to owe you another one."

"What now?"

"Run some fingerprints. There's a street guy who has been hanging around the gallery. Might be intending to bother your cousin."

"Tall, skinny guy?"

"Yeah."

"Can you get the prints?"

"Already got 'em. Broom handle. I'll drop it by your house later this evening."

"I'll trade you," Cord said. "I'll run the prints, you make me a copy of the photograph."

*

In the gallery, Stick had been mopping the wooden floor. He paused, at the back, resting, leaning on the mop handle.

Directly under the picture.

Elena noticed, her eyes flicking from Stick's face to the picture. And back again. And again. An ancient roaring grew in her ears and her breath seemed to lie like stone in the bottoms of her lungs.

It cannot be, she thought.

ItcannotbeItcannotbeItcannotbe.

TWENTY-SIX

Little Jimmy hadn't seen Stick for, what, three days? When he tried to keep track of time, it made his head hurt.

Jimmy walked slowly beside the Santa Fe River, now and then looking up at the edge of the little canyon, just to be sure no one was watching him from up there. The sun was dropping over the Jemez Mountains. Long, soft shadows darkened their way up the river, filling in the shallow watercourse with a softness that Little Jimmy always waited for. When the shadows came, he could walk along the tiny river as he used to walk along the creeks in West Virginia, easily, comfortably, alive with the feeling that the water flowing beside him would actually go somewhere, somewhere he would never see, could not name.

Just downstream from the old stone bridge Little Jimmy climbed out of the canyon and ghosted along the edge of the grass, one eye on the bridge, the other on the street in a constant search for the shiny car. He held the foam container out in front of him, careful not to tip it and cause the food inside to run together. He wanted the food to look nice, knew that Hale Mary liked it that way, sort of proper like. He had picked up the food on the street in front of the Zia diner. A couple had come out of the diner, the man carrying the foam box. He had put it on the roof of the car while he fumbled for his keys. "Watch out!" Jimmy had shouted. The man whirled, expecting to see a car coming his way. There was nothing. When he turned back around, the foam container was gone.

Little Jimmy was always amazed at how easy it was.

At the end of the bridge, he stopped, waiting. It was full dark but Hale Mary was not there. He could see vague shapes through the early night—cars parked along Alameda, trees growing by the river. But he could not see Hale Mary.

He had no idea why he liked her. But he did.

The People called her Hale Mary because she was nearly as tall as the average guy, nearly as strong, never seemed to get sick like the rest of the People did. Maybe that was because of her clothes, Jimmy thought. She wears all them clothes all the time. All them layers, maybe they keep the germs out.

They called her Hale Mary but that wasn't her name. She knew her name, had known it all her life, knew exactly who she was, but would tell no one. She would never speak her name, a name she hated. In fact, as far as the People knew, Hale Mary could speak no words at all, ever, not a single word.

She was one of the People, the street people, had been since anyone could remember, but she seemed to have no particular territory, no favorite place, no routine. She made no rounds like the rest of them. And yet, she was everywhere, but never anywhere you could count on, always carrying her gunny sack, a rope tied around it as a handle. She would disappear for days, only to show up in some unexpected location, in some unexpected way.

She walked with no one, hung out with no one, and no one knew her hide.

And she didn't take shit from anybody.

Hale Mary could bite the heads off nails.

She trusted only Little Jimmy.

And other than Stick, she was the only person Little Jimmy trusted. Ever.

But she wasn't there, at the bridge, like she was supposed to be.

Well, he thought, *maybe the old babe found something better somewhere. Not like her to be late, though . . .*

And then he saw her, her heavy shape coming slowly onto the bridge, the big shawl unmistakable.

He started toward her, being extra careful with the foam container in his hands, watching her odd, stiff gait and the way she was holding her arms across her stomach, as though she did not want the shawl to get away.

Both of her arms were folded across her stomach—and Little Jimmy realized he could not see her gunny sack. He had not seen Hale Mary without the sack, ever.

He hesitated. And Hale Mary charged toward him, her feet slapping on the hard surface of the bridge, arms reaching for him.

Little Jimmy spun, dumping the food container over the heavy railing as he whirled around and took a few quick steps toward the other end of the bridge. Barely outlined by a distant streetlight, another heavy figure blocked the end of the bridge. Jimmy slammed to a halt, looked quickly over his shoulder. Hale Mary had stopped. And then he realized . . . Hale Mary was big, but not that big.

He was trapped on the bridge. And Little Jimmy knew exactly who had trapped him.

The figure dropped the shawl onto the black street, stood up straight, something dangling from an outstretched arm. Angelo began to gently swing the heavy wooden cross back and forth, taking a couple of slow steps toward Little Jimmy.

"Been lookin' for you, you little shit. Wanted to give this back to you. Matter of fact, wanted to shove it up your ass 'til I can't see the chain no more." Angelo was having trouble talking, his voice a heavy whisper, sounds forced out of a bad throat, his throat still so painful, so swollen from the beating in the alley that the only thing Angelo could eat was milkshakes. Angelo liked milkshakes, he really did, but no one ever *gave* you a milkshake; you couldn't *steal* a milkshake. He had to buy the damned things. And then walk around like a kid, sucking it through a straw.

Jimmy's head swiveled back and forth. He knew the guy on the other end of the bridge was Beano. And he knew some terrible bad shit was going to happen.

"C'mon, Ange, quit fuckin' around." He heard Beano's whiny voice behind him. "Just git on with it," he grunted. "We still got that old bitch to take care of."

But Angelo was in charge, enjoying it now, wanting to make it last a little longer. He moved closer to Little Jimmy, and Jimmy could see the cross clearly now, and the pistol in Angelo's other hand.

"How'd you know where to find me, me out at night like this?" Jimmy didn't give a shit how Angelo had found him—he was just stalling for time.

"Didn't take no rocket science. Just followed the old broad. If we can't find you, we can sure find these other trash you hang out with." Angelo paused. Little Jimmy thought he got a better grip on the pistol, raising it slightly.

And then Jimmy realized . . . "You followed Mary? You got Mary somewhere?"

"You worrying about the wrong piece of trash, hillbilly. You need to be worrying about your ownself.

"Just stay where you are," Angelo said his voice soft now, almost friendly-like. "We just gonna tie you up a little, go for a ride in my car. You remember my car, don't you, you little shit? Same car you saw out there . . . ?"

And Angelo stopped in mid-sentence, watching Little Jimmy put his hand on the bridge rail and spring over it, out into black space, and then down into the dark little canyon below.

Angelo heard Little Jimmy's body hit, and then Beano was trying to yell something, the words rattling around, covering all the other sound.

"Shut up, goddammit, Beano, I can't hear where he went!"

Beano shut up. But it was too late. There was nothing but silence from below the bridge.

* * *

Little Jimmy didn't plan to do any of it, it just happened.

He thought he would break both his legs, but he didn't give a damn. He wasn't going to let Angelo or Beano touch him, and he knew if he ever got crammed into the shiny car, it would be the last ride he ever took. He did not hesitate. He flipped himself over the heavy railing, plunged into the heavy grass below the bridge, dug into the soft earth, rolled, and ended up in the water. He felt an odd and tingling jolt in his right ankle and he thought maybe he had broken something. He crawled quietly from the cold stream and then through the grass and weeds, heading upstream. In less than a minute he snaked himself out of the streambed and onto the far bank and into a small stand of trees. He lay on his side, trying to control his breathing, both hands wrapped around his ankle. He could see the dim outline of two figures on the bridge and heard a faint, gravelly voice . . .

"Hell no, I ain't goin' down there!"

Jimmy heard them arguing, their voices rising and falling.

"Git her out of the car," the gravely voice said.

There was silence for a moment, and then one of the shapes moved off the bridge, disappearing along the dirt road that ran along the south side of the river. The other figure stayed on the bridge.

What the hell, Jimmy wondered. *If that'n stays on the bridge, I ain't ever gonna git out'a here . . ."*

The other figure reappeared at the end of the bridge. But there were two of them now, one seeming to drag the other through the dark toward the center of the bridge. The three bulky figures stood in a tight group, some sort of argument going on, voices rising.

"I told you, she ain't gonna yell! The bitch ain't never yelled, never said a word, not about anything!"

Jimmy heard the rough words clearly. Angelo. He started to haul himself up to his knees.

* * *

On the bridge, the woman stood with her hands lashed behind her, some sort of a cloth bag over her head. Angelo lifted the bound hands hard, bringing her up onto her toes.

"Payback, bitch," Beano grunted. He whipped the bag from her head. "I want you to see what's comin'."

The woman turned her face to Angelo, her lips moving.

"Hey, she's tryin' to talk! Well I'll be damned!" Angelo turned his head, feeling Hale Mary's face almost against his.

Hale Mary's lips stopped moving. She was looking at Angelo's face.

Angelo's voice was nothing, compared to his face. Both eyes were black, there were cuts on his forehead that were not healing properly. Nothing was healing properly. His head ached constantly. Once, about an hour ago, he had sneezed, and the pain it caused in his head made him cry, tears streaming down his face, Beano watching him, saying nothing.

214

Hale Mary grinned, and then spit into Angelo's ear.

And Beano shoved Hale Mary over the railing.

* * *

Little Jimmy couldn't hear Angelo and Beano running—they always wore those fancy sneakers with the silly logo —but he knew they were gone when he heard the heavy engine of the shiny car start up, and then fade down Alameda.

He crawled out of the brush and waited by the side of the river. He couldn't see where Hale Mary had landed, couldn't see the dark lump of her body somewhere down there in the blackness of the river bottom. But he thought nothing was moving down there.

He started crawling, the pain beginning to glow in his leg. He got back to the bridge, underneath, and still he saw no movement.

And then he found her.

Hale Mary was lying on her back, her arms sticking straight out from her body like thick wings that did not work, her eyes open to the darkness, staring up into nothing.

She did not move.

Tears formed in Jimmy's eyes. He crawled slowly toward the form, finally touching her heavy shoulder, then putting his hand on her chest. He thought his hand was between her breasts but he couldn't be sure through all the clothing. And he couldn't tell if she were breathing. He gathered himself, raised just above her, and put his face down against her nose.

Hale Mary kissed him on the cheek.

Jimmy fell backward, lying on the grass beside Mary.

Mary rolled her head and looked at him, his face almost invisible in the darkness. They lay like that for a few minutes, the little man and the heavy woman, neither moving, both wondering what it was that had brought them to this time, this place.

Mary rolled over and got to her knees, moving the various parts of her body, checking for damage.

She stood up, looking down at Jimmy.

On the ground next to him was the white foam container that he had had on the bridge. Mary picked it up, hefted it in her hand to determine its weight, and then walked slowly away down the river.

* * *

She had been resting her arm on the door of the car to steady her aim.

She lowered the pistol and took off the night vision goggles. This wasn't the little .380 that she carried in her purse. This was a stainless .357 revolver with a seven-inch barrel and custom grips. She had owned the gun for ten years.

She sat quietly while her eyes adjusted to the darkness. The two fat guys ran past her—she could have stepped out and kicked them in the balls, both of them—and in the streetlight she saw the guy from the Plaza, the fat face she had stuck the pistol into. And then the heavy sound of the shiny car fading down the street.

She knew that the skinny little man was the one who hung out with the tall guy, the one they called Stick. But that wasn't the name she knew him by. She had learned his street name from a cop, a muscled guy on a bicycle whose downtown beat included the Plaza. She was as tall as the cop, maybe taller, and when she had walked up to him it had taken him a few seconds to adjust to her, her color, her height.

She had lost that guy, Stick. It worried her. She wasn't used to losing people, unless she wanted to. So she had followed the skinny little guy.

She sat in her car with the windows rolled down, a fine soft breeze floating through the night and drifting down to her. A fire of *pinon* wood was burning somewhere nearby and the perfume of the wood smoke colored the air. She had watched the skinny man carry his clumsily held bundle out onto the old concrete bridge, watched him stop in the middle, watched the others block off the bridge.

She needed the skinny guy alive, at least for now. And that's when she put on the night vision goggles and carefully rested her arm on the car door, the pistol feeling cool and good in her hand.

And then the skinny guy jumped off the bridge.

Shit! What if he's dead! She almost shouted it out into the darkness, catching herself before she opened her mouth.

And then the strange business of the other one—a woman?—being thrown off the bridge.

I hate this goddamn town, she thought.

She got out of the car.

Shit, she thought, *now I have to go look for bodies.*

* * *

He tried to rub the tears out of his eyes, but it didn't work.

He didn't know why he was crying. Could have been because of the pain in his leg. Maybe because Mary was alive, really wasn't even hurt. Maybe because *he* was alive.

He held his leg in his hands, trying to squeeze away the pain. And then he looked up, toward the street. There was a tall figure up there standing at the edge of the river wall, black outlined on black, arms hanging slightly out, a figure ready for flight. Or attack. And obviously staring down at him.

Jimmy couldn't hide and he couldn't run. Whatever was going to happen, he couldn't do anything about it. So he just stood up as straight as he could, stared up and the figure above him, and waited for what would come next.

A car drove by on Alameda, its lights briefly on the figure. A woman. A black woman. Maybe the tallest black woman Jimmy had ever seen.

The car passed and the light faded from her. She turned and walked regally away.

Jimmy could have sworn that a pistol dangled from one of her hands.

TWENTY-SEVEN

Stick took a step back, angled his head to the left and looked at the glass. It was spotless. He had missed nothing. The Alvarez Montoya Gallery now had the cleanest windows on the Plaza.

Not bad for a street guy, he thought.

He took another step backwards and continued to stare at the window glass. But he was not really looking at the quality of his work; he was looking at the Plaza, the whole of the tiny ancient park reflected in the window. He started at the left, his eyes sweeping the reflection, knowing that anything familiar would stop his gaze. He saw nothing that he recognized.

Where are you, little man?

He continued to work the reflection. But Little Jimmy was not there. He had not seen Jimmy in days.

At the far corner of the Plaza a long, low-slung sedan eased into view, pausing briefly before it continued around the corner. Stick turned quickly and stepped behind one of the posts that held the *portal*, easing out just far enough to get a good look at the car. It was not *the* car, not the one with the spider web on the trunk.

"Where are you, little man?" he said, almost to himself.

"He'll show up when he wants to. Always been that way. Elena always has him build crates, even if she doesn't need any," Klah said. "His work in the basement won't go away. He can come back at any time."

Stick turned slowly. Matt Klah stood directly behind him, Klah carrying his briefcase.

"How come you don't mind Jimmy hanging around here," Stick asked, "but you make it clear that I'm not welcome?"

Klah stared at the tall man for a moment, studying his face. "Because I can look at Jimmy and tell that he's harmless, that Elena has nothing to fear from him."

"And when you look at me?"

"I can tell nothing at all, Thin Man. Absolutely nothing. It's as though there's nothing behind your eyes. As though you don't exist. I don't trust you, pure and simple."

Klah reached into a side pocket of his briefcase and pulled out a photograph, held it up in the light, his eyes fixed on the image. Then, slowly, he raised his eyes to Stick's face. The two men stared at each other, each waiting to see what was on the other's mind.

"Cinco," Klah said softly, his eyes still on Stick's face.

"Five? Five what?" Stick said, tilting his head, waiting for more.

For a few more seconds Klah stared into Stick's eyes. He found no flicker, no light, nothing. He stuffed the photograph back into his briefcase.

"Five . . . it's just a word that came to me."

"Mind if I take a look?" Stick asked, nodding his head at the photograph.

"It's not important. Maybe some other time."

Klah turned and took a few steps down the sidewalk, his briefcase dangling from his fingers.

"What did you find out?" Stick asked softly.

Klah stopped, looked over his shoulder. "What? Find out about what?"

Stick stepped closer to the Indian. "About my fingerprints. From the broomstick."

Klah couldn't keep the surprise from his face.

"You need a little practice," Stick said. "Need to keep that expression off your face. Wouldn't do to look surprised in a courtroom." Stick smiled, waiting.

"You think you're pretty clever, don't you, Thin Man. You play at being a street guy, but there's something else going on. And as long as you hang around Elena, I'm going to be on your case."

Stick waited.

"You really want to know? About the broomstick? It's possible you won't like what you hear," Klah said.

Stick waited.

"I found out nothing," Klah said, a slight edge growing into his voice. "As far as any print records in America are concerned, you don't exist. You want me to try DNA?"

"DNA?"

Klah stared hard at the thin man but saw nothing in his face. Again, Klah started to walk away.

"One more thing," Stick said softly. Klah stopped, but did not look around. "Words that 'just come to you', don't just 'come' to you. You think them out. Like that word, 'Cinco'."

* * *

The traffic on St. Francis was light. Stick and Little Jimmy crossed over towards a park, Jimmy limping heavily, and stood by the edge of the huge grassy field. It was one of Jimmy's favorite places to spend an afternoon. "People don't come to parks when they feelin' bad," Little Jimmy had said. "Only come here feelin' good. Makes me feel good jist to be here."

That day, around noon, Stick had been dozing under the bridge when Little Jimmy had simply appeared in the canyon, hobbling through the heavy grass. Nearly a week without Little Jimmy, and suddenly there he was. Without a word of explanation.

"What's with the limp?"

Little Jimmy sat on the grass and leaned back, his head in the shade, his bad leg in the heat of the sun.

"I jumped offa sumthin' the other night."

"You jumped . . ." Stick looked at Jimmy, waiting.

"Kind'a hurt my leg," Jimmy said. "Just stayed in my new hide fer a while." He paused, waiting for a reaction from Stick, getting none. "Yew want to know where it is?"

Images of Pablo's mangled body were like ghosts in Stick's mind. "You tell me," Stick said, "but only when the time is right."

Jimmy thought about that, about telling Stick things he should know.

"And they's sumthin' else maybe yew should know," Jimmy said. He didn't rush into it, taking a deep breath, gathering in his mind what he wanted to say. "Yew know them big ol' boys in thet shiny piece-a-shit car? Well, they, they . . ." Jimmy swallowed, trying hard, but not making it. "Well, them boys is bad. Real bad. They . . ."

Stick waited for the rest of the story. But nothing came. Jimmy rolled fully out into the sun and went to sleep.

* * *

Out on the grass a soccer game was in full swing. Small boys with chubby legs ran and yelled and kicked at a ball that looked too big for them.

"Ever play soccer?" Jimmy asked.

"I . . . don't know."

"Yeah. I forgot. Sorry."

"Don't be sorry. Maybe one of these days you'll ask a question I can answer. I'd sure as hell like that."

Jimmy grinned.

"You ever play?" Stick asked, watching a skinny kid trip, plant his face in the grass and get up running, hardly missing a step.

"Naw. Never did even see one a them soccer balls 'til I got out here. Never did really git into high school, and they didn't play nothin' in junior high. Mostly, I jist set around and played with myself." He walked off toward the far corner of the park. "C'mon, lets go over there and set on one of them picnic benches, watch the game."

They walked slowly around the edge of the park, circling it on the north side to a children's playground. Some pre-schoolers were chasing each other around, a couple of moms sipping late afternoon coffee and talking. Picnic tables and benches were scattered along the edge of the playground and in the far corner of the park an enormous steam engine sat on a short set of rails inside a chain link fence.

Stick nodded at the engine. "What's that thing doing there?"

"Don't know. But it's good fer a laugh, now and then."

"What do you mean?"

"We ain't got nowhere to go. Let's jist set here and wait a while. You'll see."

Stick moved toward a bench.

"No, don't set there," Jimmy said. "Too close to the playground. Them nice little yuppie moms bring their kids down here don't like us no-accounts sittin' too close. Makes 'em nervous." He nodded at the women, who were looking toward them over the tops of their coffee cups. "Makes 'em walk around with them little cell phones in their hands, ready to make thet nine-one-one call."

"Nine-one-one?"

"Yeah, I fergot," Jimmy said. "It jist the one number yew don't want anybody to call."

Stick let it go.

They sat on a bench as far from the playground as they could get.

"I got some of that see-gar out'n thet tube," Jimmy said. "Smoked it. Didn't never know thet a see-gar could taste like that. Damndest, most wonderful thing I ever did taste. Like to made me pass out."

"Better than sex," Stick mumbled.

"Nah, not really. But iffen you ain't got no sex, thet see-gar might do."

* * *

He heard the heavy clanging sound through the cloak of his sleep and then he was fully awake but did not move or open his eyes, his body tense and waiting.

He could feel the late sun on his face. He and Little Jimmy had moved off the bench and were lying on the grass, napping, the soccer game over, all the kids gone.

The clanging sound again, and an angry voice shouting dark words he couldn't quite make out. He opened his eyes, raised his head cautiously and looked around. As far as he could tell, they were alone. He nudged Jimmy.

"Yeah, I hear him," Jimmy whispered. "He's on the other side of the engine. Work his way around this side, directly."

Stick didn't move.

Clang! "I hope that one hurt, you motherfucker!"

An old man came around the front of the steam engine, long gray hair flying, sweat running from his face. He wore bib overalls, a filthy red bandanna hanging from a back pocket. He seemed lean, almost skinny, and yet his belly pushed out against the front of the overalls, giving the impression that he had a pillow stuffed in there. The front pockets of the overalls bulged, and the man reached in and pulled out a rock. With every ounce of strength he could manage, he threw the rock at the steam engine, aiming high above the fence.

Clang!

The rock bounced off the engine. "There's another one, you big bastard!" the man growled.

He continued to move along the side of the train, throwing a rock every few steps. *Clang! Clang!* Muttering.

"Hey, you crazy son-of-a-bitch!" Jimmy yelled.

Stick tensed, waiting for the confrontation.

The man fished in his pocket and came out with one last rock. He turned and looked at Jimmy, cocked his arm back, then spun and fired the rock at the engine. *Clang!*

He turned back toward Jimmy and walked toward them, a smile on his face.

"You feel better, now?" Jimmy asked.

"Hell, boy, always feel better when it's all over. You know that." The man's voice was relaxed, almost as though he had just awakened.

"How many times a week, now?"

"Got 'er down to only three times. Monday, Wednesday and Friday. Mostly here at this big motherfucker.

"Seems yer gittin' better," Jimmy said, standing up and shaking the man's hand.

"Stick," Jimmy said, "this here's the Engineer. He's got this here . . . problem . . . with train engines. But he's a-workin' on it. Got his rock throwin' down to three days a week, now."

Stick nodded and stuck out his hand, the Engineer taking it with a firm grasp.

"Got to get going," the Engineer said cheerfully. "Time's a-was-tin'. Have to be down to the crossing for the train from Lamy." The old man walked quickly away across the park, never looking back.

Stick watched him go. "What's his problem with trains?"

"Don't nobody know. All I know is, he hates 'em. I first met him, he was down by the railroad yard, waiting for that little tourist train to come in. Stand there and scream at the thing, throw a rock or two. I knowed it wouldn't be long before they come and took him away, so I convinced him to come down here, throw at something that didn't move."

"Well, he seems happy enough, for now." Stick said.

"Always is, after one of his 'sessions' with that engine."

"It's not Friday," the Stick said.

"I know. Thank God yew didn't tell him. Would have really screwed up his ther-a-pee."

TWENTY-EIGHT

It was time to move on. The sun was gone, the hot scent of summer still hanging in the air, the park empty of soccer players, the mothers and kids long absent from the playground. The first edge of darkness had inched its way onto the park.

Little Jimmy didn't like it when the park was like this, no people, no shouting from the soccer players. No mothers. No kids. He got up from the grass and stretched. Stick was sitting on the bottom of a slicky-slide, scribbling in his notebook and now and then staring blankly across the park at the string of cars, headlights coming on and moving in glittering unison along St. Francis Drive.

Jimmy walked over and stood by Stick. "You fall asleep?"

"Yeah," Stick said softly. "Must have slept more than an hour."

"Me too." Jimmy paused, looking around the empty park. "We can't do thet again. Ain't good to fall asleep out here in the open like that, when there ain't no people in the park. Jist ain't good . . ." His voice trailed off.

Stick stood up and put his hand on Little Jimmy's shoulder. "Who you watching out for, pard? You or me?"

"Both of us, I reckon," Jimmy said, trying to sound easy about it. "See, there's somethin' I been thinkin' about tellin' you . . ." Jimmy's voice trailed off, his eyes staring away at nothing.

"Is it something I really need to know?"

"I think maybe so. I jist been tryin' to figure out how to say what it is."

Stick put his notebook in his ragged pack and they walked slowly past the park's empty playground and stepped into a dimly lit parking lot. There were a few cars in the lot but it was too early for Sunday evening's classes in the building across the way. Stick did not know what the classes were, but he wondered if he had ever done that, come to that building, or any place like it, maybe with a wife or girlfriend, sat in a room, taken a class in . . . something . . . maybe gone for a hamburger later. Maybe gone home, had some wine, made love.

"See, them two fat guys thet always show up when yew don't want 'em to . . ." Jimmy said.

They took a few more steps, Stick waiting for the rest of Jimmy's story.

He was still waiting when the chain whipped into the side of his head.

He went down, hitting the pavement in a ball, his arms over his head. He could already feel the blood coming.

He heard the singing rattle of the chain as it came down again, this time across his back. He felt his flesh tear, but somehow the pain seemed confined to his head. He rolled sideways and bumped into a car, watching through blurred vision as a pair of feet stepped in front of him, one of the feet moving back and then ramming forward into his stomach. He tried to flinch with the kick, tried to suck away the power of it, but he was backed against the car and it didn't work. He thought something inside of him broke. He heard some words and knew that they had been screamed but didn't know if they were his. Maybe Jimmy's. A pair of hands reached for his head. He pushed his feet against the pavement and shoved his head under the car. The hands moved down his body, grabbed his legs and pulled at him. He straightened his body, flattening, scrambling, reaching further under the car and groping for anything he could find. His hand landed on an exhaust pipe and he gripped it desperately, knowing, whatever the cost, he couldn't let himself be dragged out into the open.

The chain was snagged over a hook in the ceiling, the ends dangling down and wrapped around his wrists, cutting into them, hauling him upward. He tried to reach the floor with his toes, take some weight off his wrists, but all he could do was lightly touch the cold concrete, just enough to tell him it was there, not enough to save his wrists. A single bulb dangled from the ceiling on a wire, giving off the sort of light that illuminated only bad and painful things. He could see the thin clouds of his breath bursting out in front of his face, see out of the corners of his eyes the heavy fur-lined coats of the men. Even so, he was sweating.

He wondered about the men, dark, thick bodied, who stood always at the side, never in front of him. And only one of them talked.

"Where is it?" the man said, his English thick with accent.

He said nothing.

The man did not speak again.

And then he heard the thin singing of the chain. Another chain. Smaller. Sharper.

Little Jimmy heard the singing of the chain.

He spun around, saw Stick already down, the two guys on him, saw the kick.

Saw Angelo and Beano.

"Get the little fucker!" Angelo was pointing at Little Jimmy and shoving Beano off after him.

Jimmy thought Beano was carrying something, some kind of club, maybe a ball bat. He didn't wait around to make sure—he leaped on the trunk of a car and then on the top and then across the tops of two more cars, his injured leg instantly bursting with pain, but his fear pushing him. He dropped into an empty parking space, trying to land on his good leg but not quite making it, turned for the park and hobbled across the grass, his running a pathetic attempt at speed caught on a bad leg. He ran beside the steam engine's fence, cut hard to the left, circled the engine, slammed to a stop, flattened on the grass and poked his head out beyond the fence. Beano had not even made it to the other side of the engine yet, but Jimmy could see his bulky silhouette against the far lights and hear the thud of his heavy feet.

Beano stopped. "C'mon out, you little son-of-a-bitch!" He tucked the club down against the side of his leg.

Jimmy didn't move. He saw the outline of the club.

"You little bastard!" Beano screamed, his voice oddly whiney even when he yelled, "We got your asshole buddy! Come on out and we can talk!" He took a couple of steps, frustrated, not knowing where to go.

*　*　*

Angelo Marcuso had one end of the chain wrapped around his wrist and the chain made almost musical noises as it dangled against the pavement. He held Stick's legs, yanking as hard as he could. His hands slipped and he flinched backward, watching as Stick inched further under the car.

Angelo noticed his hands were sticky. He held them up in front of him, the blood on them almost black in the dim light.

"You motherfucker! You give me the AIDS! All you street fuckers got them AIDS!" There was an edge of panic in his voice.

Beano appeared at his side, the ball bat dangling from his hand.

"Shit, he's got blood all over him. You got it on you, too," Beano said, stepping back from Angelo.

"No shit, genius. Where's the little fucker?"

"Couldn't find him. Faster'n greased shit. Must'a got over there past that grocery store."

"You goddamn dummy! You know we got to get *both* of 'em!" Angelo's voice shook and he wanted to clench his fists, but thought that would somehow make the blood on his hands more dangerous.

"You ain't got to call me no dummy," Beano mumbled, fingers tightening on the ball bat. "'Sides, we got this one." Beano waited. Angelo didn't say anything. "Well, ain't we goin' to put him in the car?"

"Yeah, we'll put him in the fuckin' car. In the fuckin' trunk. Reach under there and grab his shoulders," Angelo said, stepping back away from Stick.

"Hell, no, I ain't grabbin' no bloody shoulders. You already got the blood on you, *you* take that end of him." Beano tossed the ball bat back on the grass, grabbed Stick's feet and started to pull. Stick didn't move.

"We got to get him to let go of whatever he's holding onto under there," Angelo said, his voice almost pleasant. "Maybe I can convince him if I break his fuckin' shin bones." He picked up the dangling end of the chain. "Stand back a little," he said, pulling back his arm.

"Why don't you just go git the gun? Stick it up his ass. Pull the trigger. Be easy to pull him out of there then."

"Nah," Angelo said, "fire a shot around this friggin' park and the cops'll . . . Besides" he said, enjoying himself now, "this here is for what the sumbitch did in the alley. This here is payback."

Dimly, through the fog of pain in his head, Stick heard the voice. He knew the voice. The fat guy, Angelo. And Stick knew the chain would be coming. Something inside of him firmed up and waited almost calmly, waited for the strike of the chain and the cracking of his bones.

The man worked the chain until his arm was tired. And then he stopped.

He hung there by his wrists, making no attempt, now, to support himself, feeling the blood oozing from his back, running down onto his oversized pants, covering the cheeks of his ass in dark-bright red.

"Beri,'" the man said.

And he knew another man had taken the chain. He waited, almost calmly.

He heard the crunching of chain against bone but felt nothing.

It will take a second, he thought, *before the pain kicks in.*

He heard a crunching sound again, a different sound this time, and then Angelo screaming in anger. And he heard Beano, wonder in his voice.

"Well if that don't fuckin' beat all," Beano said.

* * *

Little Jimmy crawled all the way across the grass on his belly, just like they did in those army movies he had seen. He snaked along the edge of the parking lot until he was only a couple of cars away from where Stick had clenched himself under the car.

He inched closer. When Beano had tossed the ball bat onto the grass, it had almost hit him. By the time Beano had grabbed Stick's legs, Little Jimmy had the bat and had worked himself around to the other side, behind the lowered sedan with the paint that seemed to glitter, even in the last thin twilight. It was the car, Little Jimmy knew. It was *the* car. *The* car. He drew back the bat, twisted his wiry little body, and whipped the bat down across the car's back window. There was a crunching sound, an explosion of glass, one of the most beautiful things Little Jimmy had ever heard. He raised the bat over his head, lurched toward the front of the car and took out the windshield with another of the whipping motions, another of the wonderful crunching sounds. And then he stood in front of the car, bouncing like a fighter—ignoring the bands of pain in his leg—wanting them to see him, wanting them to watch. He brought the bat whistling down across the hood of the car, down across the beautiful paint job, down and into the metal. He heard Angelo scream something but he didn't know what it was and he didn't care. He backed off a few steps, tense, still gripping the bat, saw Angelo coming, swinging the chain . . .

Jimmy took off into the darkness of the parking lot, his bad leg throbbing. He still carried the bat.

"Get in the fuckin' car!" Angelo yelled.

Angelo and Beano jumped into Angelo's car, his beautiful, damaged car, bits of glass grinding against Angelo's ass as he slid heavily behind the wheel. In an instant the car came alive and leaped forward, tires spinning, single headlight on, a monster searching for Little Jimmy. Jimmy ran straight down the parking lot as long as he dared, suckering the car into following him, then flashed across the grass onto the playground. But the car followed. It rammed across the parking barrier, bottoming out, sparks flying. It clipped the side of the slicky-slide and plowed through the sand, heading straight for Little Jimmy.

Shit, Jimmy thought, *I cain't dodge thet fuckin' car fer long, my leg like this.*

Jimmy cut back toward the soccer field. At the edge of the field he slanted toward the parking lot.

The hands came out of the darkness and locked onto his arm,

using his own momentum to spin him sharply into a car. He hit the car with his shoulder and the side of his face, tiny little lights beginning to flash in his brain, vision blurring. His body sagged.

"No you don't, you little prick," the voice said. A woman's voice. "I'm not carrying you a goddamn inch."

The hands pulled at him, forcing him upright, marching him. Jimmy's didn't think he was moving his legs, but they moved anyway.

He banged into another car, heard a metallic noise of some kind, and then felt himself being shoved forward. He fell heavily into some sort of box. And then the woman slammed the trunk lid shut on Little Jimmy.

*　*　*

The Engineer sat up on the steel deck of the cab of the old steam engine and raised his head over the edge of metal railing. Little Jimmy and that new skinny guy were asleep at the edge of the park. The Engineer was surprised; he knew Little Jimmy never slept in the open like that. And it wasn't even full dark, yet.

He massaged his sore arm. He had thrown more rocks than usual today, maybe strained a muscle or something. He had gone down to the railroad tracks and then cut south until a high fence shielded him from sight. When the train from Lamy had rumbled slowly through the gap he had thrown a couple of rocks at the engine, but somehow didn't feel satisfied. He grabbed some gravel and flung it at the passing cars, but nothing seemed to help.

He had decided to try his latest therapy. He had come back to the park and climbed the fence that surrounded the engine. He put his hands on the black steel, his body shaking so badly that he was afraid to try to make his legs move. Finally, he was able to claw his way up into the cab. He had been doing this lately—sleeping in the cab. When he awoke in the morning he felt better, as though sleeping with the demon, being close to it, somehow lessened the terror.

He watched as Little Jimmy and the skinny guy started across the parking lot, disappearing between the cars.

Sounds carried clearly through the night. The Engineer heard voices, and then some sort of metal sound.

Something was wrong.

The Engineer climbed down from the engine, climbed the fence and eased slowly toward the parking lot, peering into the gray light. He could see nothing.

And then the unmistakable sound of something hitting a windshield. And then again. And then screaming voices.

The Engineer eased around a car, keeping low. It was them, he knew them, the two fat guys, always hassling street people. But what were they doing here?

Jesus Christ, is that Little Jimmy haulin' his ass across that field?

And then a car started, engine revving, the car moving, jolting onto the grass, a single headlight lighting up the Engineer like a beacon.

The car jerked straight toward him.

The Engineer threw himself to the side, legs out behind him. The fender of the car nicked one of the Engineer's boots and spun him in mid-air. He hit the grass with a twisting motion and was up and running before he even knew what had happened. Before he thought about it.

The car slid to a halt on the grass—the Engineer kept running. And then the car swerved back toward the street and was gone.

The Engineer hunkered down at the edge of the parking lot. He wouldn't move until all this shit was over.

At the far end of the parking lot another car came to life, lights on, backing swiftly from a parking space, turning into the lot. The car sped through the lot then slid to a stop. The Engineer heard a car door open, saw the dim glow of the dome light, saw a tall figure get out, heard some scraping sounds, heard the door slam shut. The car surged out of the lot, tires burning on the black pavement.

Whatever had happened, it wasn't good. Whatever had happened, it was over.

There's too much shit going on here, the Engineer thought.

He ghosted back across the park, across the street and into a space between some buildings, back toward the railroad track.

TWENTY-NINE

She was bored out of her mind. She hated this kind of work. She craved action, anything to make her time in this little mud town seem worthwhile. She let her mind wander, thought of the old hotel in the center of town—not a bad hotel, all in all—on the corner of the Plaza. The hotel bar. She needed a drink. And then she thought about pulling the gun on the fat guy in the car, raking the gun down the side of the car, fucking up the paint job. She smiled to herself. She knew she shouldn't have done that, shouldn't have let him get a clear look at her face. But she couldn't help herself. After all, in a town full of pasty-faced Anglos and mustachioed Hispanics, she could hardly remain anonymous, all six feet of her, her lustrous black skin shining even in pale light.

Besides, how did she know she was going to run into the fat guys again? In fact, they were a real mystery in this whole thing—too openly mean to be competition, too stupid, really, to be much of anything. What the hell did they want?

Her smile faded. She was incredibly tired of watching this guy. All he ever did was wander around town, maybe spend a few hours in the gallery, hang out with that little creep that he was hanging out with now. But the money was just too good not to finish the job.

Twice, she had to move her car to keep them in sight.

The only thing that broke the boredom was watching the old

man in the overalls pound rocks off the side of the train engine. A train engine. In the middle of what appeared to be a soccer park. Made no sense. But then, in her time in Santa Fe, nothing else made much sense, either.

They were still there, the two of them lazy in the late sun, napping. That was a little strange—she had never seen them nap before, not in the light, not out in the open.

Maybe he's getting careless, she thought. *Maybe he's getting comfortable. Would that be good? Who the hell knows?* she thought.

As it got darker she sat up straighter, afraid she would fall asleep.

The big car was suddenly right in front of her, gliding slowly past, engine rumbling, lights out, heading for the far end of the parking lot, the two men inside not looking at her.

That's the car, she thought. *It had to be the car. Goddammit, what are those two idiots doing here?*

But of course, she knew.

The big car slid into a parking space. The engine went dead.

She waited. She would do nothing unless she had to.

And then she saw the man she knew as "Pyat" and the other little guy appear at the edge of the parking lot and the dark shapes of two others coming up behind them.

She had waited too long. If Pyat couldn't get out of this himself, she would have to kill the fat guys.

* * *

Little Jimmy felt the car moving. He felt around inside the trunk for something he could use to pry open the lid, but there was nothing. He had no idea there was a trunk release.

But I was outrunnin' them boys, he thought. *Had 'em beat. This ain't fair.*

The car stopped. A door opened and the car shook slightly.

"You look like shit."

Jimmy heard the voice, a woman's voice, up in the car. And then the door slammed and he felt the car lurch forward.

* * *

She opened the car door. He sat there, motionless, his head dropped forward, chin on his chest, blood everywhere.

Fuck! I'll have to ditch the goddamn car.

Not really a problem. She never rented a car under her real name, under her real anything. When they ran a check on the rental, they would find that she didn't exist.

She looked at the man bleeding in the front seat.

Might as well get it over with.

She started to close the door, then stopped. On the floor in front of his feet was a tattered day pack. She reached inside, took the pack, opened it and dumped it on the floor.

Street guy shit. Not a page of paper . . .

A small, crumpled notebook lay at the edge of a pool of blood. She opened the cover and thumbed through a few pages. Nothing but notes about living on the street in Santa Fe.

Still scribbling, eh Pyat?

She stuffed the bloody junk back into the pack and started for the back of the car.

She hesitated, looking at the pack, thinking about the notebook. She took a pencil from her own purse and probed the pack again, finding the notebook. She took it out and held it, the edges of the front cover worn soft and smooth from being carried in the pack, or a pocket. She slowly turned the notebook over and opened it from the back. There were entries made in the back of the notebook, as though hidden. And she read about the dreams—the memories.

THIRTY

It was a slow night, exactly as Evelyn Sena liked it. She leaned against the counter of the emergency room nurse's station and took a deep breath, glad for a peace and quiet not broken by the arrival of ambulances. Down the short hallway to her right, an orderly slowly mopped the already-glistening tile. Beyond the orderly, heavy doors led out onto the dock where ambulances off-loaded kids with gunshot wounds, boys with broken and cut bodies, young girls in the final stages of labor, old men whose hearts had finally stopped. All in a night's work for Evelyn Sena.

At her counter a buzzer went off. Someone was outside the doors at the dock, wanting in. Evelyn looked down the corridor and through the windows in the doors leading to the dock. She couldn't see an ambulance out there.

"Frankie, see who's outside, will you? And be careful before you open the doors . . ."

The orderly looked back at Nurse Evelyn. He liked working in the emergency room, mostly because he got to look at Nurse Evelyn, maybe the best looking nurse at St. Vincent. Maybe the best looking nurse in New Mexico. He stood the mop in its bucket, wandered down the hallway and peered through the glass. He paused, then hit the big steel button that opened the doors and went out onto the dock.

Through the doors, Evelyn could see a car parked outside, Frankie bent over, peering inside.

Frankie straightened, turning back to Evelyn. "You better come," he said, the words hardly more than a whisper. Frankie cleared his throat. "*You better come!*" he shouted back at Evelyn.

Evelyn ran down the corridor. Outside, the dock was empty except for a car sitting broadside to the doors, its motor running, lights on. Frankie stood frozen in place, eyes wide, his arms frozen at his side.

Evelyn opened the car's passenger door.

Stick sat rigidly, bent forward, fists clenched against the pain, dried blood covering the side of his face and the front of his shirt. His legs were splayed out in front of him, more dried blood gluing his pants to the wrecked flesh underneath.

There was no one else in the car.

"Jesus H. Christ," the orderly mumbled.

"Get a gurney, *now!*" the nurse said, reaching for Stick.

* * *

Jimmy felt the car jam to a stop. He lay in the darkness of the trunk trying to hear, trying to learn something, anything, that would save him, get him out of there. He thought no more than a minute passed.

"You better come!" Little Jimmy heard the words clearly. A guy's voice, but he didn't recognize it.

"You better come, *now!*"

Jimmy thought he heard someone running. Then heard the car's door opening.

"Jesus H. Christ!" The same guy.

"Get a gurney, *now!*" A woman. Jimmy didn't recognize her voice. It wasn't the woman who put him in the truck.

Oh, Christ, he thought, *they got a whole bunch helpin' now.*

Heard feet shuffling, felt the car shaking, and then silence.

He lay quietly, trying to control his breathing.

When are they gonna come back fer me?

And then there was the unmistakable sound of a key being inserted in the trunk lock. The trunk lid popped open. Stick's pack hit him in the face.

* * *

They cut away his clothes and found that he wore no underwear. A nurse covered his groin with a folded sheet and they began to scrub away the blood from his face, chest and legs, searching for wounds. They found them—the jagged gashes on his face, the discoloration on his rib cage, the heavy lacerations across his shins. And then they saw the old, pale scars.

* * *

He lay on a table in a cubicle, a huge white bandage taped to the side of his face, his lower legs wrapped heavily in gauze and tape, a sheet across his groin. He raised his head and tried to look down the length of his body. He thought he looked like a mummy in progress. He felt pretty good.

They must have given me something for the pain. But they never give me anything for pain . . .

One of them grabbed him around the waist and lifted. Another unsnagged the chain from the hook in the ceiling. They dropped him to the floor into a pool of his own blood. The blood was cold now, chilled by a floor that had not been heated in a decade. He heard the clump of heavy boots and then the heavy metallic sound of a steel door slamming shut. They left him alone there, in the dark and the cold, lying in the congealing blood.

Anthony Cordova got out of his car and walked quickly into the emergency room. He had known Evelyn for a long time; she wouldn't have the hospital cops call him unless there was some really strange shit happening.

He found her at the nurse's station. She didn't waste time in idle chatter.

"There's a guy over there," she said, nodding at a cubicle with a curtain drawn across the front. "Cut up, but not with a knife. Something thick, heavy. No broken bones, but he bled a lot. Some damage to the side of his head."

"So?"

"So, you maybe should take a look at him. There's a lot of old business on his chest and back, some on his legs. Might mean something. Might not. I've got him bandaged, but you can still see what I mean."

Cord moved toward the cubicle.

"I don't keep a journal. Never did . . ."

Cord heard the rumbling voice. He peeked around the end of the curtain, checked the cubicle, then stepped inside. A tall, skinny guy lay on the table. Even with all the bandages, he knew it was the guy they called Stick. Stick, the guy from the bus station; the guy from the alley, from the little dead guy they called Pablo.

"What journal?" Cord asked softly.

Stick lay quietly for a moment. There was something familiar about a journal, about writing, about the concept of a journal, but he couldn't make it clear. He lifted his head slightly, eyes sweeping the small space, seeing the cop, Cordova.

"Don't know, officer . . . detective. Must have been dreaming about my Pulitzer Prize speech."

"You don't change your act, do you. Still a smartass." Cord moved in more closely. "And I'm getting tired of looking at your ugly face." He saw the faded scar tissue on the man's chest and arms.

"How'd you end up in here, smartass?"

"Don't really know. Was just walking along, suddenly started bleeding. Seems like every time I see you, there's blood involved."

Cord almost smiled. "You can tell me now, or I can find out later. And I get really pissed when I have to find out later."

Stick said nothing, closed his eyes.

Cord shrugged. "Okay, pal, have it your way."

Cord pushed through the curtains and back out to the nurses' station.

"He say anything to you when he came in?"

"Not a word," Evelyn said. "Kept his jaw clenched so tightly I thought he would break his teeth. Like, maybe, he had been through this before."

Cord stared back at the cubicle for a moment. "This guy is always showing up in bad places." He paused, staring at the cubicle. "He have anything with him when he came in?"

"Just this." Evelyn pulled a plastic bag from behind the counter, held it open for Cord. Inside, a tattered Hawaiian shirt lay on top of bloody rags that once had been a pair of old pants.

Cord thought for a moment. "You're holding back, making me ask questions."

Evelyn smiled. "The better to keep you here, Detective Cordova." She touched the lapel of his coat. "See, this busted-up guy was dressed like a street guy. Except, he arrived here in a brand new Pontiac, parked out there by the dock, motor still running. A pile of stuff around his feet, a cup, a knife . . . like camping gear. He had bled all over the seat. We pulled him out, left the car sitting there. Thing is . . ." Evelyn paused, looking at the cubicle, "he was sitting in the passenger seat. Just before you arrived, I asked Frankie to go out and move the car. Guess what? It's gone." She playfully tugged Cord's lapel.

"I'm gonna cuff him to the bed. Might take him with me when you release him. I want to check on a few things." Cord took her hand from his lapel, holding it gently.

"Oh," Evelyn said softly, a smile behind her eyes, "he had this in his pocket." She held out a business card from the Alvarez Montoya Gallery.

Cord took the card, stared at it. "Yeah, Elena knows this guy, I think." He looked at Evelyn, wondering how much to say. "Matt asked me to run his prints. I did. I got nothing. Maybe DNA will tell me more." Cord waited, thinking. "Eve, you ever get the feeling that the past is about to screw up the present? Maybe a past you don't even remember?"

Cord picked up the bags. "Get this," he said, "I run into this guy a while back, he's covered with blood. I ask him if it's his blood. He wants to know if I'm going to take his blood type. *Type?* The only people I know concerned about blood *type* these days are hospital people." Cord paused. "But I will run his DNA."

He turned back toward the cubicle. "Can I cuff him now?"

"Any time you want. I don't think he cares."

Cord whipped back the curtain.

The cubicle was empty.

THIRTY-ONE

He walked slowly down the hallway, holding himself erect, trying not to stagger. There was a large bandage on the side of his face, more bandages on his legs, some sort of wrap around his stomach. He passed a couple of people who wore scrubs. They only glanced at him. A cart sat outside a swinging door, some plastic cups stacked on one end. He took one.

A man wearing scrubs, a stethoscope hanging from his neck, came around a corner.

"Restroom?" Stick asked. "They want a urine sample but didn't tell me where to go." He held up the cup.

"On down the hallway. On your left." The man kept walking, glancing over his shoulder at Stick.

* * *

The doctor pushed into the emergency room. "Damn, Evelyn, you sending ER patients down the hallway to pee? And how much pee do you need? Guy had a cup big enough to hold about a pint." The doctor grinned and kept going.

Evelyn Sena stared at Cord.

Cord turned quickly and ran through the door and down the

hallway, checking open doors as he went. At the restroom he pulled his pistol and barged through the door. The restroom was empty.

* * *

Stick leaned against the outer wall, breathing in night air that was so cool and sweet that he could actually taste it. It had taken him a long time to find his way out of the confusing hospital, walking down bright hallways, his bandages flashing like warning lights, his ass showing now and then through the gap in the back of the paper qown he was wearing.

But he found a door. He was out.

Now what?

His mind was active enough to ask the question, but not enough to answer it. He sank down on his heels and leaned back, the paper gown pulling farther apart, his bare back pressing against the cool stone of the building. Whatever energy he had left began to flow from his body, emptying him. His consciousness ghosted out into the safety of the night. His head fell forward. His eyes closed. It wouldn't be long, now. They would find him. But he didn't really care.

He sat in the mud and leaned back against the rock. He had nothing left. It was as far as he could go. His breath came out of his chest in metallic bursts, each heave of his ribs a reminder of their damage. It was midsummer but, still, he was cold. He wrapped his arms around his upper body.

He hadn't counted on the dogs, didn't know they were there. They had brought the dogs in secretly, knowing that he would try again, knowing that he would not plan against dogs that didn't exist. But they did exist, and he heard them coming. He would have to do something about the dogs, figure something out. But not now. His head fell forward. It wouldn't be long, now. They would find him.

Hands grabbed him roughly, lifting him . . .

Hands grabbed at his arms, tearing the paper gown. He felt himself being dragged, his feet being sandpapered by the concrete of the sidewalk.

"Goddamn, if'n yew gonna e-scape from a hospital like thet, least yew could do is git some clothes on!" The voice was a half-whisper, but there was no mistaking the sound of it, the cadence of words, the words themselves, cutting through the muddle of Stick's mind. Little Jimmy.

"We got to git out of here. I don't know what's goin' on, but we really got to *git.*" Jimmy's head kept turning, eyes sweeping the dark.

Stick tried to stand, but nothing seemed to work.

"Where . . . are . . . they?" Stick pushed the words out one breath at a time.

"Who? Where's who?" Little Jimmy had his ear next to Stick's mouth, trying to hear the mumbled words.

"Our friends . . . from the park . . ."

"Jeeesus, Stick, I don't know. But they ain't here."

"Thanks . . . for bringing . . ."

"Goddammit, Stick, I didn't bring yew anywhere. That's what I mean. There's somethin' else a-goin' on, man. Somebody else is . . ."

But Stick wasn't listening. He was lying on the sidewalk.

* * *

Elena Montoya unlocked the door of the gallery, the sun not yet fully into the Plaza. At the back of the store she put water on to boil and then picked up a plastic bag of trash, carried it down the back stairs into the basement. At the back of the basement she unlocked the heavy door that led directly to the alley and the Dumpster that the gallery used. She swung the bag up and into the bin. She turned back to the door. Stick lay behind the opened door, his bare feet and legs stretched out in front of him, his head in Little Jimmy's lap. The remnants of a hospital gown clung to his shoulders. Little Jimmy had torn off a piece of it and covered Stick's groin. Even in the dim early light in the alley, Elena could see the new wounds, and the old scars on Stick's chest.

"Jimmy, what happened?"

"Stick got hurt," Jimmy whined.

"I can see that. I mean, what . . . Never mind for now, let's just get him inside, keep him warm. I know someone I can call . . ."

"No, you cain't do thet! Stick said not to call nobody!" Jimmy looked away, wouldn't meet her eyes. "Least of all yer cousin," he mumbled. Elena heard.

Elena bent over Stick, her fingers trailing briefly over the old scars. She took his arm and lifted. She could feel Stick's body come alive, trying to help.

"He cain't walk too good." She could hear the tears behind Jimmy's voice.

Elena looked at the little man. "Jimmy, if he can't walk very well, how did you get here?"

Jimmy glanced down the alley, as though looking for something. He turned back to Elena.

"Thet's the part yew ain't gonna believe."

Matt Klah sauntered across the plaza, coat and tie over his arm. This morning, just for the hell of it, he was barefoot, his pricey shoes stuffed into the side of his briefcase.

Georgie Suina saw him coming. A smile played across her face— and then she saw his bare feet. *Oh, God, what now?* Knowing he was watching her, Georgie covered her face in her hands. But she couldn't help but giggle.

She waited.

When she took her hands down, he was gone.

Georgie felt a small nudge of disappointment. She always looked forward to her morning meetings—her morning contests—with Matt. She sat back . . .

The bare foot poked slowly out to her side.

Georgie jumped up. Matt was standing directly behind her.

"I still got it. Still got that Indian thing," he said, grinning, "just like the old days. Could'a taken you prisoner. Could'a hauled you off into the hills, made you my slave. Made you boil up my venison stew. Make babies."

Matt stepped across Georgie's jewelry blanket and strode off across the Plaza, not waiting for whatever Georgie was going to say.

"You still could," she said softly, too softly for Matt to hear.

* * *

Stick lay on the work table where Jimmy built crates. Jimmy had taken a small bag of packing foam and put it under his head. Stick raised his hand and Jimmy took it.

Stick turned his head slightly toward Jimmy. "Is this fun, or what," Stick mumbled.

"Goddammit, Stick, yew . . . yew . . . yew ain't gonna die on me."

"Nah. Too soon. Got a whole lot of remembering to do before I check out. Besides, I haven't finished my flamenco lessons."

Jimmy's head dropped to his chest. He did not know what flamenco was, but it could not be good if you had to take lessons.

Stick waited, his breathing coming hard. "Besides," he said, "can't die, until you tell me."

Jimmy's smile faded. "Now, goddammit, there yew go again. Sometimes I don't know what the hell yew talkin' about."

"Yes, you do," Stick said, his voice rasping. "This wasn't random, Jimmy. Some serious shit going on here. Those boys aren't professionals. They're worse. They're just fucking crazy. I know their names, but that's all I know." He waited. Jimmy didn't speak. "But you do, Jimmy. You know a story that I don't know."

Jimmy stood silently, looking away from Stick.

"You have to tell me, partner," Stick said, "so we can do something. Anything. Or this shit storm is just going to keep on happening."

Little Jimmy knew it was time. Way past time. He pulled a wooden stool next to the table and sat stiffly, his head still down. "Them boys . . . Angelo, he's jist plain evil. He ain't got no good things about him. Thet other'n, Beano, folks say he ain't all there, but I think he's just fakin' it."

Jimmy paused, took a deep breath. "I'm sorry, Stick, I truly am. I didn't mean for any of this stuff to happen. I should'a tole you sooner, 'cause them boys, they must think I tole you . . . stuff . . . jist because we hang out together." Jimmy stopped, his voice caught in his heart. "I didn't want to *know* any of it, didn't want to *see* any of it. I was jist sleepin' out there in the desert, south of town, waitin' fer enough light so I could check out that big gulch. I was jist sleepin' there, when this big ol' piece of shit car come slidin' by, it's lights off. And then it stopped . . ."

* * *

Matt pushed through the door of the gallery.

Elena was at the back, waiting, her arms folded across her breasts.

Matt walked up to her, kissed her on the cheek.

"Put your stuff in your office," she said. "Come downstairs with me. There's something you have to see."

THIRTY-TWO

The last couple of miles were always the hardest.

Matt Klah eased his middle-aged pickup truck along the rutted road to the abandoned ranch, trying to avoid the deepest ruts and sharpest rocks, the road wind-eroded, nearly washed out, clumps of chamisa growing at the edges, narrowing the track. He knew the stuff he had in the back was bouncing up off the bed. He tried not to let that happen, but, on the other had, he didn't really care.

The road was fine dirt, almost sand, and it snaked through rocks and along the bottoms of shallow *arroyos* and then over low rises, some places with *piñons* and rabbit brush growing in the tracks and he wondered how the hell anyone had ever made a ranch work in a place like this.

Maybe they hadn't.

There were some wind-worn tire tracks along the road, but they ended where the road broke over the rise and into the canyon, the tracks digging and turning as whatever local guy in his four-wheel-drive had come to the old wooden gate, saw the heavy chain and padlock, read the KEEP THE HELL OUT sign, and decided it wasn't worth it. Had turned his truck and gone away.

A front wheel bounced over a rock, and then a rear wheel, and he heard the stuff in the back bang down onto the bed. Matt winced, not because of the stuff in the back, but because he liked his pickup, was somehow attached to it in a way that he did not fully understand, did not want it damaged. It had been given to him by a father, a Santo Domingo, who was grateful that his son did not go to jail for something he didn't do. Matt had defended the son pro bono. But the father was a proud man and he insisted on paying. He had no money, so he gave Matt the pickup. Once the father had made up his mind, it was useless to resist. Matt kept the pickup, now and then lending it to the son. A year after the trial, the son hanged himself. Matt had not seen the father since the funeral.

In the back of the truck Matt had a little food, some old sleeping bags and a collection of odds and ends of first aid stuff, a battered daypack that Jimmy said belonged to Stick. But, mostly, the stuff he had in the back was Stick and Little Jimmy, Stick still mostly unconscious, Little Jimmy holding Stick's head in his lap.

Elena had talked him into it, talked him into taking the street guys out to the old ranch, the ranch she never visited, the ranch she had bought years ago.

Elena was a strange woman. He had never really known her until he graduated from law school, returned to Santa Fe, saw the Alvarez Montoya sign hanging in front of the gallery. Alvarez Montoya—the closest friend of his brother, Wendell. And then Matt had gone inside, met Elena, and had seen the photograph on the wall at the back of the gallery. Alvarez. And Wendell. And a guy called Cinco Becknell.

* * *

The lock was rusted shut. Matt squirted some oil into it, jiggled the key until it turned. He opened the gate and rolled the pickup through. They were almost at the house.

Stick woke in darkness. And in pain.

It was familiar to him—darkness and pain—so familiar that for a brief moment he felt oddly secure. There was pain, yes, but he was awake. And that meant he had survived another night.

He was lying on a pad on the floor, exactly as he remembered . . . before he passed out.

He slowly moved his arms and legs, his head and neck. There seemed to be pain everywhere. But he was not chained. He could move his arms fully. He could sit up.

And that's where the memories stopped. This was not the same room, he could feel that, somehow. He forced his body to turn, so he could crawl. He felt along the wall until he found a door, reached up for the doorknob and slowly turned it. He pulled open the door and felt the warm air flow over him.

He would escape while he could.

He crawled across what he thought to be a porch, down a couple of wooden steps and out onto the dirt. His knees and arms gave out and he crumpled, rolling over on his back, staring up at . . . stars.

Stars. He was outside, and alone. He rolled over on his stomach and pulled his knees up beneath him, slowly forcing himself to his feet. There was enough light for him to see that the land rose slightly to his left, and then the dim outline of a canyon wall. Not too far away. If he could make it to the top, he might be safe.

* * *

When he awoke, it was full light.

Off to his right the red ball of the sun sat exactly on the near horizon, heat pouring through a cloudless sky. He could feel an easy breeze across the back of his neck.

He was dressed, and warmly, a heavy cotton shirt hanging down over thick cotton pants, a knitted wool cap. Almost-new sneakers. He looked at the clothes, felt them, tried to remember putting them on. He felt in his pockets for the big folding knife. It was gone.

He sat under an ancient *pinon* tree, eons of dead needles prickling his ass through his pants, the caress of a desert morning familiar to him, here, in these clothes he did not remember owning.

He tried to focus his mind. The fight in the park. Then nothing until the hospital. The nurse, the cop. Walking down a hallway, looking for a door, a window that would open. Jimmy on the outside of the hospital. The black woman putting him in the car . . . and then nothing after that. Huge blank spaces.

A black woman put me in the car?

And then lying on the table in Elena's basement, and Little Jimmy telling him. Telling him everything.

Angelo and Beano, he thought. *Christ, why couldn't he be hunted by two guys named Dirk and Denali, or Hulk and Strangler? No, he had to be hunted by two guys out of a comic book. Two guys who would shoot you just so they could piss in the bullet holes.*

He crawled out from beneath the tree, new wounds and old wounds clanging together to make a sort of agonizing music in his mind. He was in a small stand of *piñons*. He came out through the trees, pulled the wool cap down low on his eyes and sat on the edge of a low west-running ridge. He was on the south side of a narrow, shallow canyon, another ridge on the far side cupping the canyon and cutting it off from the world. Rabbit brush and more squat *piñon* and juniper trees were scattered as far as he could see, some of the trees higher than his head. A tiny stream cut through the canyon floor. Huge billowing cottonwoods rose randomly along the water and patches of grass grew on the edges of washes and he knew the tiny stream ran year-round.

He had seen this before. At least part of it.

He put his hands up to the sides of his face, shading his eyes as he sat quietly and scanned the canyon. To the east the ridges seemed to rise and come together, boxing in the canyon. Down below he saw the remnants of old barbed wire fences scattered on the tops of rises and across the mouths of *arroyos*, the last vestiges of some long abandoned, miserable old ranch. His eyes followed the stream a quarter-mile to the west where it disappeared into the back of a particularly thick grove of cottonwoods that seemed to stand a dark and heavy guard over something in their interior. His eyes came back to where he was, finding his own footprints, eyes following the clumsy trail he had left from the cottonwoods. Whatever was inside the grove, that was where he had been.

Leave a trail like that . . . I'm losing my touch. Why haven't they caught me by now?

Farther west the ridges spread out more, but got steeper, rugged walls of rock and earth that formed a natural barrier all the way to the river that he knew was down there, somewhere. He saw what he thought was a narrow dirt road running along the canyon floor.

He rose and walked slowly west along the ridge, staying as high as he could, his legs radiating pain, his feet dragging in the dust. This canyon. He thought he was supposed to be feeling something, recognizing something, knew that his heart was supposed to beat faster. But nothing came except the sweat that ran down from beneath his cap and stung his eyes. He pulled the cap off and stuffed it into his back pocket.

As he drew even with the stand of cottonwoods he saw they were not as thick as he first thought. They were spread in a pattern, almost as though they had been planted that way. Among the trees he could see a scattering of buildings, each of them shaded by several trees.

On the eastern edge of the cottonwoods an enormous old *adobe* house sat brooding, its ancient face looking directly south. The house seemed to sag, withdrawn from structure, as though bearing the awful weight of history. From his place on the high ridge he could see that the flat roof of the house wandered and turned, chimneys poking through at odd places, and he realized the full size of the place, knew that rooms had been added over the years wherever they would fit as people came and children were born. And died. The rooms wandered in a loose square, enclosing what he thought was a central court. Plaster had washed from some of the walls, the *adobe* bricks showing through. Windows were open, or were gone. A *portal* ran across the front and along the near side, its roof sagging. Beneath it, he could see only one door, standing open. A plank lay on the porch by the door, as though it had been pulled from across the door and dropped there.

Twenty yards downstream, a barn twice the size of the house loomed above everything, its heavy timbers graying in the sunlight. Outbuildings in various stages of disintegration were scattered beyond and behind the barn, the whole place, even the house, surrounded by the skeletal remains of fences.

He sat on the ridge and kept scanning the old ranch. There was something not right about what he saw, but he was having difficulty getting it clear in his mind. He eased down off the ridge, moving in toward the side of the house. He kept looking, but saw nothing more. And then he realized what was wrong—he saw *nothing* more, saw only the buildings, saw no ancient equipment rusting in the sun, no junk beside the barn, no decrepit furniture propped under the *portal*, not a tin can, not a broken axe handle, not a scrap of cloth fluttering in a vacant window, not a single piece of anything that could be picked up and carried. Not a single breathing thing, not a person, not an animal, not a bird—nothing that lived wanted to be found on this long-dead *hacienda*. The place was a shell, an empty container, a vessel with no contents through which to explain its place in life, its history, nothing that gave a hint of the agony and joy that may once have been in the very air of the place.

He eased down the ridge and stood in front of the place, just off the *portal* in front of the door that had once been boarded-up. The *hacienda* was left only with the scars that could not be carried away: knife gouges in the doorframe, as though someone had marked the growth of a child; marks of wear in the planks; *portal* posts worn smooth from the constant rubbing of hands. The *hacienda* was something waiting for the revelation, something ready to be reoccupied, if only it stood long enough for that to happen.

Something waiting, thought Stick. *Exactly as I am.*

He looked at the *portal* and the two wooden steps, the marks in the dirt in front of them.

I was in there. I escaped from there last night.

He chose not to go back inside the house, afraid of what he might find. He wandered around the periphery of the homestead, inspecting the buildings from a short distance and waiting for some sign of life.

At the front of the house the dirt road he had seen ended in a rounded flat yard overgrown with *chamisa* and tumbleweeds, the shallow ruts of wagon wheels and tires still visible under the growth. The road itself had patches of scrub growing in its tracks. At one time the road had gone around behind the house, but was now blocked by limbs that had fallen from the giant cottonwoods.

He eased past the house and through the edge of the trees, moving slowly toward the barn that dominated everything around it, a barn that looked as though it had been built to stand a hundred years. Maybe it already had. Heavy timbers, cross ties and *vigas*, all looking as though they had been shaped by axes, were held together with bolts, spikes and thick metal strapping, a building created by the joining of anything too heavy and massive to fit anywhere else, as though a railroad trestle had been torn apart and was reborn as a barn.

A heavy chain looped across the barn's heavy doors, three large, rusted padlocks dangling from it.

He reached for the chain.

Something flopped over in his mind, and then in his stomach, a sensation, an image—*a memory*—trying to explode out into the crystal morning air.

He spun around and looked at the house. There was nothing.

When he felt his heart begin to beat heavily in his chest he backed quickly away from the barn, back through the trees to the tiny cool stream and across it and over a fallen fence and into a small field. He backed the whole way, afraid to turn away from the *hacienda*, afraid to take his eyes from it, his breath coming in hard surges, images flying through his mind as though from a fast-forwarding film, the projector being operated by a madman.

The doors of the massive barn hung open, sunlight streaming inside. A man stood in front of two high sawhorses that held a heavy wooden airplane propeller. With a large, soft rag the man rubbed wax on the propeller, its smooth curves and planed surfaces gleaming in the soft light, sweat running from the man's face.

A small boy stood watching.

"I want to go," the boy said.

"I'm sorry, niño," the man said gently, his voice deep and rich, "but

this is just for Harry and me. Tio Cecilio and Tia Maria will take good
care of you. Anyway, we won't be gone long."

"But I will not know what to do."

"Of course you will, niño. After all, there is only one thing to do," the
man said, "only one thing—lock the barn doors." Laughing, the man
tossed the rag onto a table and walked out into the hot summer air, head-
ing for a large house that seemed to grow out of the earth underneath
giant cottonwoods. "Now, let's go eat. Harry made posole," he said over
his shoulder.

The boy did not move. He watched the man enter the house, leaving
the door open.

The boy was young, but there was a weight on his heart that he didn't
understand. Too large a weight for such a young boy. He turned and
started toward the stream that flowed under the cottonwoods, his feet
scuffing the dry earth. At the edge of the water he looked at the line of
rocks that he had placed across the flow, a shallow pool built up in front
of them, the water glistening in the heat. He slowly took off his clothes
and waded into the stream. He sat in the pool and waited for the heavi-
ness to leave his chest. But it did not.

At the edge of the field an ancient cottonwood stump waited, de-
fying the passage of time. Stick sat on the stump and felt the sweat
running down his forehead and into his eyes and he didn't bother
wiping it out.

Harry? Harry? Who the hell was he, this "Harry"?

He was into something, onto something, at the edge of something, but he couldn't bring it into focus, couldn't slow the images.
He felt the nausea grow in his stomach and he wrapped his arms
across his belt, rocking slowly back and forth, the pain from the
beating thundering in every cell of his body.

He stared into the gently running stream. In some other, older time, someone had placed a line of rocks in an arc across the stream, just below the line of the house. Someone had once made a pool. The rocks were dislodged, some scattered, as though cattle had walked through them. Stick spent an hour rebuilding the tiny dam, watching the water gather behind it. A bathtub. At least as long as the weather was warm. Without thinking about what he was doing, he stripped off his sweaty clothes and lay in the shallow pool, moving his back against the bottom of the softly moving stream until he had nestled fully into the water, only his nose and eyes above the surface. His bandages began to come loose. He closed his eyes.

* * *

He opened his eyes and sat up.

He looked down-canyon. He could not quite see it, but he knew the river was down there. He raised his eyes to a cut in the wall across the river, another canyon that came down to the water, the rock walls a soft pink in the early sun, cottonwood trees clustered on the banks.

And then he heard a door open. Little Jimmy walked around the side of the house, his head swiveling up and down the canyon. He stood under one of the huge cottonwood trees, motionless but alert, as though waiting for some movement in the distance to tell him which way to run. Very slowly, and very carefully, Jimmy unzipped his fly, pissed on the ground, and then disappeared among the cottonwoods.

Stick got up from the pool and picked up his clothes, moving silently back to the house.

Little Jimmy was not there. Little Jimmy was not anywhere.

THiRTY-THREE

When he opened his eyes the room was gray with the dirty light that came through a small, grime covered window high in the wall. The window was too high for him to look through. He knew he could reach the window with his hands and had thought many times about trying to break it, but that would only allow more frigid air into a room already so cold that the air seemed to have solid weight against his body.

He had been sleeping in his clothes, the collar of his overcoat pulled up across his face, his hands drawn up into the sleeves like a turtle pulls back his head. A scrap of woolen cloth was wrapped across his scalp and tucked down into his coat. Only his eyes were exposed to the room.

Against the wall opposite the window was the room's only piece of furniture, a heavy wooden chest that looked as though it had been there for decades. Inside the chest was a metal pot—his toilet. He had urinated and defecated in the pot yesterday and he knew that, now, his urine and stool would be solidly frozen. That was good. It was what they wanted. They wouldn't let him take fresh stool out and bury it. It had to be frozen.

He felt the urge move inside his bowels and he concentrated on choking it back. If he shit in the metal pot they wouldn't let him take it outside until it froze, and he desperately wanted to go outside.

He pulled himself deeper into his clothes and closed his eyes.

Maybe they would come soon.

When he opened his eyes the room was almost bright, light streaming through a small, dusty window on the wall above him. Across the room was the only piece of furniture he had found in the house, an ancient *comoda*, a huge wooden upright chest with heavy doors scarred from use. The *comoda* loomed in the morning light, the doors shut tightly, a man-made presence in a house that otherwise seemed to have grown organically from the earth.

His pack lay on the floor beside the *comoda*. Inside it, he found the big folding knife.

He had picked the room because it had a door that opened into a small courtyard at the back of the house. All he had to do was open the door and walk outside. Walk outside. Into the warmth of sunlight in the canyon. And he walked out now, not looking at the *comoda*.

Yesterday, he had seen Little Jimmy pissing under the cottonwoods, but when he went back to the house Jimmy was gone.

He had put new dressings on his wounds and then had spent the day wandering around the old house. The place was big, rambling, with heavy plank doors and small windows, most of them covered with thick wooden shutters. At the back, he found what had been a tiled area, a patio, the tiles now mostly covered with dirt and spiny desert grass, the giant cottonwoods shading everything.

A man could sit out here, he thought, *soak his bones in the sunlight, smoke a cigar, drink some tequila, watch the water in the stream run to the river . . .*

He looked through cracks in the heavy timbers of the locked barn but saw only large lumps, maybe furniture, everything covered with old canvas; stood beneath the cottonwoods; stood in the sun; trudged down to the river, his cuts, aches and bruises marking his every step with pain. He didn't care.

He came back to the room with the *comoda*. *Comoda?* A strange word. He had never thought to open the huge doors.

Why not? he wondered. *Why wouldn't I just open the thing?*

The doors were stuck. He gently pried the doors open with his knife. A scrap of paper fluttered to the floor, sliding gently underneath the front of the *comoda*. There were no drawers inside, only thick wooden shelves, empty. Whatever the shelves had once held, there was nothing now. Nicked and cracked, the shelves seemed to be layers of time, vacant space, waiting. He knelt, to see into the lower shelves. A soft glimmer of light. A reflection? He reached in and brought out a glass jar, old, the sort of jar used for home canning, a screw cap of some sort of metal. Zinc?

A Mason jar, he thought. *I know what this is. A Mason jar.*

The jar was heavy, full of something. He moved to the door and held the jar into the light. It was . . . dirt? Loamy dirt, heavy with dark color. He stared at the jar, something fluttering in his memory. He had held the jar before. He knew it. He pressed his brain, concentrating, mentally straining, trying for anything that was there. There was nothing.

He forgot about the scrap of paper.

* * *

Just inside the front door of the house he had found some food, two well-used blankets and an old tarpaulin. He stuffed some food in his pockets and for the next three days he kept up his wanderings, going farther each day, always returning to the house. He moved slowly up the canyon, coming to the box end where the old road climbed steeply up and away. Then back down canyon, finding the tattered old fences, corral poles, shallow dry ditches that once must have carried water to gardens. His wounds hurt less as his body slowly recovered. As he explored he had vague memories of being moved, carried, dragged; a truck; some voices—he knew one of the voices was Jimmy's—that somehow kept up a stream of questions and answers. But he knew he had not answered anything. It was not his way. And he knew these were new memories, not old ones.

* * *

On the evening of the third day he took the last of the food, stuffed one of the blankets into an old burlap sack, and went down to the river, swatting away tiny flying bugs and finally nestling down among the roots of salt cedars. He lay there, staring across the river as night came into the canyon and the air thickened with coolness. Once, in the middle of the night, he sat up, startled, a black outline on the bank of the river across from him. He struggled to sit up, pulling at his pocket for the knife, the thorns of the spiny Russian Olives punching at his skin. He stepped into the water, rubbing his eyes. The outline across the river was gone.

* * *

He heard soft bird sounds carrying in the early morning air. He opened his eyes, trying not to make any other movement. He waited, listening. He heard nothing, saw nothing. He eased himself upright and stared across the river where he thought he had seen . . . what? For the first time he looked *carefully* across the river, trying to see what he had not seen before. But there was nothing, just the river, and the narrow, brush-filled canyon that ran away to the west, a sheer wall rising on the north side.

He stared at the wall. Midway up he saw a shelf. He knew he had been there. His eyes fell back to the canyon at the base of the wall.

The deer. That's where I hung the deer. When I looked back across the river, this is the place that I saw. I've come full circle.

His mind clamped around a singular thought . . .

I'm where I'm supposed to be.

Stick waded into the river, the water barely rising to his knees, soaking his leg bandages again. He eased across an exposed sandbar, checking for footprints, finding none. On the far bank he checked the mud and sand for any signs that someone, or some thing, had been there. There was nothing. He moved quietly through the brush, following the shallow channel of the small stream that ran there, now down to a trickle, barely enough flow to actually reach the river.

He stood under the tree where he had hung the deer.

The deer, the ashes of his fire—it was all gone, along with any sign that Stick, or anyone else, had ever been there.

* * *

In late morning, Stick sat on the ancient stump across the stream from the house. Something had changed. He played Little Jimmy's story—his confession—back across his mind; Angelo and Beano; the dead woman in the *arroyo* . . . Things had begun to make some sense. They were being watched, stalked, hunted. Little Jimmy was being hunted. And Stick was being hunted, just because he hung around with Little Jimmy. And what about the Montoya woman? Beano sometimes worked a scam on the Plaza, and Stick and Jimmy were in and out of the gallery in broad daylight. If Beano saw them with the Montoya woman . . .

Stick waded into the cool stream, stripped, and scrubbed his body, knowing he would have to, once again, replace his bandages.

Bandages. They were familiar things.

He would go back into town and find Jimmy. They had to have a plan.

He had been hunted before. Somehow, he knew that.

He was goddamn tired of being hunted.

THIRTY-FOUR

Angelo Marcuso and Beano Clapper sat on a metal bench, staring across the Plaza at the art store. They slouched, legs splayed out in front of them, trying to appear relaxed, just two local guys taking in the tourists on a hot afternoon. Two fat local guys.

Angelo wasn't talking. He sat with his jaw clenched, his fingers drumming on his thighs, his right foot now and then tapping the sidewalk, the newspaper jammed under his arm, the paper now so old it was becoming soft and tattered. It was a hot morning, but Angelo still wore a jeans jacket, mostly to cover the pistol jammed into the side of his pants.

Beano wasn't talking, either. He sat quietly, now and then letting his fingers wander to his face. Old scabs on his forehead itched and his nose ached constantly, the tape across it doing nothing to keep it open. Mostly, these days, Beano breathed through his mouth.

Tourists strolled by, ignoring Angelo, trying not to look at Beano's face.

"We shouldn't be sittin' out here like this. Little hillbilly shit ain't gonna show up, us sittin' here, right out in broad daylight.," Beano grunted, fingers still wandering lightly across his nose.

Minutes passed.

"Little hillbilly shit," Angelo muttered, the first words he had said in an hour.

Beano said nothing. For the past week, Angelo had had some moods. That's what Beano called them. Times when Angelo would not talk for a long time, and then talk straight on until Beano could not stand it anymore. Beano would finally leave, or hide, leaving Angelo talking, spittle bubbling at the corners of his mouth. Sometimes the spittle bubbled out of his mouth even when he wasn't talking. Moods.

They sat, watching the art store, waiting for Little Jimmy, hoping that, sooner or latter, the little man would return to the Montoya Gallery.

Beano's sullen gaze caught a movement at the far corner of the Plaza, something familiar. He tensed slightly. Coming across the grass on the far corner, Beano saw a slender figure wearing a duster and carrying what looked like a large cup of coffee in a foam cup. Beano knew it wasn't coffee. It was vodka. And Willie the Hook was going to walk right up to them.

Well, what the fuck, Beano thought, *maybe it's time Angelo found out he ain't my only friend.*

Willie stopped in front of the bench. Angelo didn't look up. "You boys got any spare change?" Willie asked, looking at Angelo.

Angelo said nothing, did not even look up, still staring at the art store.

"Well, no problem," Willie said, a slight lilt in his voice, "just thought I'd ask." He turned to walk away, glancing down at Beano. "You got to pick your friends a little better, pardner," Willie said. Beano thought he saw him wink.

"Get the fuck out'a here," Angelo grumbled, still not looking at Willie. Willie walked away. Quickly.

"Fuckin' street guy," Angelo said, his voice so low Beano almost didn't hear. "When we get that little hillbilly shit, maybe we do that one next." Angelo flicked his hand at Willie's back.

"Well, we got one street guy already," Beano said. "The wrong street guy."

Beano waited, but Angelo just sat there. "And we tried to get them two, both of 'em at once, like you had a plan or something."

"We did get the tall bastard. Beat him pretty good." Angelo almost grinned with the thought of whipping the chain across Stick's legs.

"Yeah, and all that got you was your car busted up more," Beano grunted. "And he still walking around, probably shooting off his mouth."

For once, Angelo didn't have anything smart to say. He pulled the newspaper, stained from his sweat, from under his arm and unfolded it. On the front page, Pablo's picture stared out at them, a thin, bony face, large eyes, lips that tried to smile but did not quite make it.

"I wonder where they got that picture?" Beano said.

"Says here, his 'friend' gave it to the newspaper. Wanted the paper to say nice things about him. One faggot trying to get nice things said about another faggot. Who gives a fuck. Faggot's still dead."

"How you know he's a faggot?" Beano asked. "We didn't even know him."

"We didn't know none of 'em," Angelo said. "Didn't have to know 'em. Just had to know they was whores or street trash."

"Yeah, but . . ."

Angelo held the newspaper higher, spreading it, his blacksnake eyes glittering over the top. He nodded in the direction of the gallery. "Stop whining, and look."

Across the Plaza, Beano saw a black woman walking casually along under the *portal*, stopping in front of the Montoya Gallery, looking in the window. But that wasn't who Angelo was looking at.

Scurrying along under the *portal* was Little Jimmy, shoes slapping the pavement, head swiveling back and forth like human radar, scanning everything. At the Montoya gallery he turned sharply and disappeared inside.

"Well, now, if that don't fuckin' beat all—little sumbitch goes in there just like he owns the place. I guess this is our lucky day. C'mon." Angelo started quickly across the Plaza.

"Wait a minute, Ange," Beano grunted, "that other one there, that woman. That's the woman pulled a gun . . ."

But Angelo was halfway across the Plaza.

THiRTy-FivE

She was checking the Plaza, casually strolling along San Francisco Street, now and then glancing around, just another tourist looking for another way to spend money. She knew if she went into the Montoya Gallery the Hispanic woman might remember her. But she didn't care. With each passing day, she was getting more and more bored with this game. She might go into the gallery; she might not.

Of course, she saw the two fat guys on the bench over near the Palace of the Governors. How could she *not* notice them, them just sitting there, staring at the gallery, like two fat toads on an iron lily pad.

The fat boys.

They had become a real problem. They had damned near killed both Pyat and the little guy. She was going to have to stick closer, pay more attention, keep them in her sights a little more.

Bored.

She would have to do something, maybe push Pyat a little, try to get him more tensed up. Jog his memory. She smiled to herself at the thought of jogging a memory that wasn't there.

She had thought she could just hang around until it all came back to him. She had steered him to some of the right places, put him into the stream of his own history, but nothing seemed to have any effect on him. The bony bastard just wandered around the streets with the little hillbilly, neither of them showing the slightest interest in much of anything, except staying alive.

All she wanted was the journal, the notes, the book, or whatever the hell it was. As far as she knew, no one had ever actually seen the damned thing, but everybody wanted it. That was all she was being paid to bring back—the book. Once they had the book, and she had a very nice payday, then she could get the hell out of Mudville. Of course, there was one additional item: after the journal was found, Pyat had to disappear. It would not do to have him hanging around; his memory might come back.

That was Plan A.

Plan B was different. In Plan B, Pyat's memory never came back. The journal would never be found, if, in fact, it really existed. In which case, she simply killed Pyat and left town. Make it look like an accident. They would pay her for that, too, only not as much. Not nearly as much.

Of course, in Plan B, if the fat boys killed Pyat that would not be all bad. They could take care of that part of the job for her. It wouldn't look like an accident, but, what the hell, it would still be a killing.

But she wasn't ready for Plan B and the smaller payday, not just yet. If the fat boys kept pressing, she might have to take them off the planet. Keep them from using up space. Keep them from breeding. The thought of Angelo's or Beano's kids running loose on the planet made her skin crawl. Angelo and Beano. She knew their names. And, actually, the thought of removing them didn't bother her at all. Hell, she would enjoy it. Except . . . this was strictly business. And Angelo and Beano weren't in the contract. No money for killing them.

But she was going to have to do something. She was going to have to find the key to this mess.

Christ, I've never been this uncertain before. I'm going to have to make up my mind about something, anything.

She walked slowly past the Montoya gallery, glancing casually inside. She was there, the Hispanic woman, the Latina, or whatever she was supposed to be called.

* * *

Elena Montoya stood at the front of the gallery and sipped dark coffee from a delicate China cup. A black woman walked slowly past the front windows, her eyes drifting over the paintings, pots and works of bronze displayed there. Her eyes never rose, never looked through the glass at Elena.

I've seen her somewhere.

The woman passed the windows and wandered out of view.

In the basement of her gallery a tall, gaunt man was building a shipping crate. He worked slowly and carefully. He had looked different when he had come in, healthier, somehow . . . but even more intense. It was the ranch, he had said. The work. And the pool in the stream that he bathed in every day. It focused him.

Focused him on what, she had wanted to know.

He did not answer.

She smiled, inviting more conversation, but he had kept his head down, concentrating on his work.

For a short while she had watched him, knowing that he did not know how to build the crate, knowing he was trying to remember how Jimmy had done it. All the time she had watched him, he did not look at her, so she had gone back upstairs.

It had been a slow day, one of those days in Santa Fe when time moved in the ancient manner, flowing quietly over the earth beneath the sunlight, hidden.

Thinking of the man in the basement.

Elena turned and looked at the photograph on the wall at the back of the gallery, then walked slowly toward it.

And that is when Little Jimmy scooted quickly through the front door, eyes wide, his breath coming in hard pumps, heading straight for the back of the gallery.

"'Scuse me, missus," he said, not even slowing down as he passed her. "Is Stick downstairs?"

But he was gone down the stairs before she could answer.

* * *

Little Jimmy wasn't going to show up.

Stick looked at the crate he had built. It wasn't as good as Jimmy's, but he thought it would do. He would have to ask the woman. He wanted to ask the woman, wanted to ask her anything, wanted to talk to her, wanted to breathe the same air she was breathing.

He ran his hands over the work table, the table where he had lain, beaten and bleeding, the table still stained with his blood.

He put the crate against the wall and opened the door that led to the alley. He swept up the wood chips and sawdust with a thick-handled push broom and dumped them in a trash bin outside. He looked around, wanting to find something else to do, something else to keep him from going upstairs. But there was nothing.

He started toward the stairs, carrying the broom. He knew she would not let him use the broom in the gallery—it raised too much dust—but he had to have something in his hands, something to hang onto when he talked with her.

The upstairs door opened and Little Jimmy came stumbling down the stairs.

"They's out there!"

"Who?" Stick said, but it really was not a question. He knew who was out there. "Where are they? Are they in the gallery?"

"Naw, they's acrost the Plaza. I got a good look at 'em. I was careful—I'm purty sure they didn't see me," Jimmy said, his breath still coming hard.

"Goddamn, Jimmy," Stick said sharply, his eyes squinting as he looked at the little man, "you can't be sure of that. They have no reason to be out there except to look for you or me. If they saw you come in here . . . Jesus, man, Elena's up there by herself!"

He ran for the stairs, still carrying the push broom.

"Yew know one of them boys got a gun!" Jimmy said in a loud whisper. But it was too late. Stick disappeared up the stairs.

Jimmy stared after him, not moving, hardly breathing now. The stairs. He should go up the stairs. Help Stick, if Stick needed help. The fat boys. They killed women. They killed Pablo. They would kill him.

Jimmy turned and stared at the back door, standing open to the alley.

* * *

Stick paused at the top of the stairs, checking the room. Elena was standing just to his left, staring up at the back wall. There was no one else in the gallery.

She glanced at him. "What in the world is the matter with Jimmy?" She said it lightly, a smile on her lips.

"It's just Jimmy. One of his many moods," he said, trying to keep it light, his eyes still sweeping the long gallery room, bright light pouring through the door from the street. He stood there with the push broom, feeling foolish, forcing himself to keep his breathing under control, feeling stranded, out of place.

Feeling her presence.

She held out her hand, beckoning him forward. He took a step toward her.

"Have you ever noticed that picture?" she asked, her voice in some deep register that he didn't know existed.

He turned and looked up at the black-and-white photograph. Three young guys, seemingly happy, in front of an ugly building, doing nothing in particular. Smiling. In the window a sign, "Eat At Joe's." In the background the ass-end of a bus. Stick stared at the picture, not at the young men, but at the sign.

"Eat at Joe's," he mumbled.

She looked at him. "Yes," she said. "Joe's. That was the name of the café. Wasn't much of a place, but the locals liked it. My brother played chess there."

Stick could hear a ringing in his brain, something hard and metallic, something trying to become real. Something trying to become a memory.

"Is that . . . a bus station?"

"Yes," the woman said. "Used to be right behind this block, on Water Street. Tiny place. The buses had to negotiate streets that originally were made for burro carts. They moved the station years ago, down to St. Mike's." She had not taken her eyes from his face.

"They look . . . happy," he said, trying to keep his eyes off her face, her body. He could smell the fragrant scent of her, her perfume, or maybe just her soap. He didn't care which, he only wanted to breathe it in until his eyes glazed over.

Goddamn, what the hell is happening to me?

"They were happy. They were going off on some great adventure they wouldn't tell anyone about." She paused, staring at the picture, remembering. "I took the picture. It was the last time I saw them."

"Who are they?" He wasn't sure he wanted the answer.

"I thought maybe you could tell me," she said softly.

* * *

She was a half block away when she saw the little hillbilly dart into the gallery. But she had seen him go in there before. Apparently, he did odd jobs for the Hispanic woman. Nothing unusual about him going in there, although he did seem a little more jittery than usual. Of course, with the hillbilly, it was hard to tell.

But then she saw the two bear-like shapes rumbling across the Plaza, trundling across sidewalks and grass, on a straight line for the Montoya Gallery. The fat boys.

Shit! They're out of their fucking minds! In spite of herself, she smiled. *Of course they're out of their minds!*

She started for the gallery, trying not to break into a run.

* * * *

Something came into the light at the front of the gallery, causing shadowsto shift along walls hung heavily with art.

Stick was still looking at the woman, but he knew who was in the long room. He turned, stepping in front of her. Angelo and Beano had stopped just inside the door. A pistol dangled from Angelo's right hand. He was not even pointing it, just let it hang there, pointed at the floor, almost as thought it were beneath him to use it.

"Didn't know you was here," Angelo said, his voice almost normal, no hint of fear.

Stick said nothing. He gripped the push broom, beginning to twist the thick handle very slowly.

"Where's that skinny little shit?" Angelo's eyes swept the gallery, the sculpture, the long counters. "They's too many things in here to hide behind. Get the hillbilly out here."

"He isn't here," Stick said, his voice even and controlled.

"Must be a basement in this place," Beano whispered to Angelo out of the side of his mouth.

"Beano here says there's a basement," Angelo said. Beano flinched. "Goddammit, you didn't have to use my name," he hissed.

"Fuck it. You think they don't know who we are? By this time tomorrow, the whole goddamn world will know who we are."

* * *

The black woman stopped at the edge of the gallery window, trying to look casually inside without exposing her whole body to any line of fire. The view was not perfect—there were reflections in the glass—but she could see the fat boys just inside the door, saw them take a couple of steps forward, saw the pistol hanging in Angelo's hand. She eased her hand into the slot at the end of her shoulder bag, her fingers wrapping firmly around the butt of a small automatic.

Whatever was going to happen was going to happen now. And so she made a decision: nothing else was working, so let it happen. Whatever it was.

A middle-aged couple walked up to the window, gazing at the display. Silently, they moved along the glass, then turned into the entryway.

The black woman stepped toward them and held up her hand. "I don't' think I would go in there," she said. "There are some folks in there who think this gallery ripped them off. Probably going to be a bad argument. And the woman who owns this place has a simply terrible temper. Why it wouldn't surprise me if . . ."

The couple backed out of the entryway, but stood on the sidewalk, trying to see inside the gallery.

* * *

Beano was thinking again. He was thinking that he didn't want to be Beano, but he was. He was thinking that he didn't want to be Angelo's sidekick, but he was. He was thinking that he didn't want to be here, but he was. And he was thinking that he knew what Angelo was going to do.

"Jesus Christ, Ange, you can't kill 'em all," Beano whispered again. At least, he thought he whispered. But he knew the tall man had heard him.

"Why not? Maybe it's time for us to be famous."

Elena stepped out to the left side of Stick, away from the broom. "Take whatever you want. There's nothing in here worth dying for."

"Bitch, there ain't nothing in here I want. What the hell would I do with this art junk?" Angelo was sneering now, in control, enjoying it, slowly bringing up the pistol, taking another step forward.

"Then why are you here?"

"I'm here to shut you up, the hillbilly talkin' to all of you, all of you maybe tellin' what we done. Make sure you don't ever tell."

Stick kept his eyes locked on Angelo, but he reached carefully out with his left hand and grabbed a handful of Elena's skirt, his fingers briefly squeezing the cheek of her ass as he dragged her back behind him. In spite of the fact that he was staring at a man who intended to shoot him, the feel of Elena's body under his hand made his mind start to wander. He let go of her ass.

"Think about it," Stick said. "You don't want us to tell the cops about the woman out there in the desert." He could hear Elena's breathing change. "We tell, you get the death penalty. But here you are, ready to kill some people in broad daylight, everybody knowing who did it, everybody knowing who you are." Stick paused, watching the confused expression spread across Angelo's face. "That make any sense to you?"

"Them women . . . that woman . . . I can . . . *don't you fuck with me!*" Angelo was yelling now, his face contorted.

Stick had been slowly twisting the handle of the broom, and he felt it come loose. It wasn't much, but it was all he had.

"Hey, Beano," Stick said, "you know how they execute people in this state? They hang them. Take them out in the desert; build one of those big wooden gallows like you see in the western movies. Hang your ass. Leave you out there for the buzzards to pick at. First thing those buzzards eat is your eyes. It's really something to see, your body hanging out there, swinging in the hot wind, shit running out of your eye sockets, those big birds circling. Your buddy there is going to get you hanged."

Beano's mouth was dry. "That ain't true. They don't hang people no more . . ."

Stick snapped a step forward, his right arm pulling fast across his body, whipping the heavy broom handle out in front of him, letting it go, the handle wind-milling horizontally through the air toward the fat boys, Stick close behind. The throw was clumsy, unpracticed, missing Angelo entirely and glancing off Beano's shoulder.

Stick knew he would not make it. Too much distance to cover. Too little time. He saw the sneering smile on Angelo's face, saw him point the pistol . . .

Angelo loved it. He watched Stick coming at him. Plenty of time. He was going to blow a hole right through the bony bastard's chest. He could actually feel his finger on the trigger, pulling, the hammer coming back. He was truly surprised when the beautiful, flint-pointed, highly decorated lance tore through his shirt, sliced through the thick layer of fat on his side and glanced off his ribs, ripping off shards of bone.

THIRTY-SIX

Little Jimmy could hear the voices as he sneaked up the stairs but couldn't tell what was being said. He could hear Stick talking, and somebody else, but he wasn't sure who it was. He eased his eyes just above the last step and tried to get a fix on what the hell was going on in the gallery. To his left, he could see Stick and the woman, both of them looking toward the front. Oddly, Stick had hold of the woman's ass. Looked like he was trying to pull her to him.

Jaysus, Stick, this ain't no time to be thinkin' 'bout poon . . .

And then he heard Stick talking about somebody killing somebody, and Jimmy knew who was at the front of the store.

He eased forward on his belly, sliding quietly along behind the long counter. He didn't know where he was going, or what he was going to do when he got there, but maybe he would figure that out when he came to it. He would go as far as he could go.

"Hey, Beano," Stick said, "you know how they execute people in this state?"

Jimmy's breath caught in his throat. *Goldamn it, Stickman, don't yew know better'n to stir them assholes up like that?*

And that's when he saw the lance, lying on top of a long shipping carton against the base of the wall. It was beautiful, lovingly made, graceful. Even Jimmy could see that it was a work of art. And even Jimmy could see that he could kill someone with it.

He picked up the lance.

*   *   *

Stick saw Little Jimmy rise above the counter, saw the shaft of something in his hand, saw Jimmy drive the thing forward as hard as he could.

Shit, he only nicked the bastard!

Stick would never get there in time. He knew the pistol was going to fire, and it did. He dove forward on the floor, sliding on his face on the polished wood. He heard screams—Angelo, and Elena.

He hit Elena! The bastard hit Elena!

Stick rolled on his side, glanced back at the woman, her fists clenched, face masked in anger. But he could see no blood. And she was still standing.

He whipped his body around, gathered his feet under him and came up in a crouch. Except for Elena, the gallery was empty.

*   *   *

She watched, fascinated.

From her angle outside the window, she saw Angelo, saw the pistol, saw Pyat lunge forward, saw the hillbilly suddenly pop up from behind the counter. She even saw the lance, although she wasn't sure what it was.

Heard the shot.

And she never took her pistol out of her bag.

She never moved as Beano charged out of the gallery, followed by Angelo, still holding the pistol, his left arm clamped to his side. And then the hillbilly, panic frozen on his face. In seconds, all three of them had disappeared.

There is no sound like the sound of gunfire. Those who have heard it do not mistake it for anything. It is not sharp thunder, not a car backfiring, not a firecracker. It is gunfire, and nothing else. Across the Plaza and along the street some people turned and stared toward the sound, watching as the three men exploded from the door and scattered along the street.

Gunfire. She loved it.

And then Pyat ghosted out of the gallery door, his eyes roving, a long stick in his hand.

The middle-aged couple was still standing there, fixed in place, faces carved into masks of disbelief.

"I tried to warn you," the black woman said. "I told you it might get ugly."

She started walking away. She had decided that she had business with the Hispanic woman, but she would come back later, after the cops had cleared out.

As she passed the couple, she noticed blood spatters across the front of the woman's blouse.

From Angelo, she thought. She had a new respect for the hillbilly.

* * *

Inside the gallery, Elena looked up at the back wall, at the photograph, at the shattered glass where the bullet had hit, at the hole dead in the center of Cinco Becknell.

And the man she knew as Stick was gone.

THIRTY-SEVEN

All the cops were gone except Anthony Cordova.

The front door of the gallery was closed and locked, a Navajo weaving hanging over the glass.

At the back of the gallery, Elena Montoya, Matt Klah and Cord sat at a small table, had been sitting there for several minutes, no one speaking, the bullet-punctured photograph lying on the table in front of them.

Klah got up, went to a cabinet behind the counter and returned with bottle and some glasses. He poured three drinks.

Cord picked up his glass. "What is this?"

"Cognac," Klah said.

"I thought Indians weren't supposed to drink," Cord muttered.

"We only drink to forget the Spaniards," Klah said softly. "Male Spaniards. We Indians like female Spaniards."

It was their usual routine, only now it seemed to fall flat.

Elena gently touched the frame of the photograph. "He said there was a woman, out in the desert."

"What?" Cord put down his glass. "Who said that?"

"Stick. He said it to the guy with the gun. I think he was trying to keep their focus on him. But he wouldn't have made that up, would he?"

"No, he didn't make it up. We found a woman. The fourth woman," Cord said.

"Four?" Klah asked.

"Yeah, four," Cord said. "Four that we know about. And we don't have a single lead." Cord thought for a moment. "How would Stick know about the women unless he was involved?"

"He said 'woman', not 'women', Elena said. "Whatever he knows, he was trying to stir them up, the fat men. It must have worked—the guy with the gun started yelling."

"So Stick just ran out? Before the cops got here?"

"They all ran out," Elena said. "First, the two fat guys and Little Jimmy. Just burst out through the door. Stick said something about finding Jimmy before 'they' did. I think he meant the fat guys. He ran out."

Cord took a long sip of the cognac, cleared his throat. "Okay—you know I've been keeping an eye on this 'Stick' guy, ever since I saw him at the hospital last week. And since you two have been hiding him in the basement, or out at the old Becknell ranch . . ."

Elena and Matt glanced at each other. Matt took a deep breath. "Okay, how the hell did you know that?'

"I'm a dee-tek-tive," Cord said, drawing out the word, "we know things like that."

"We thought . . ." Elena paused. "It just seemed like a good idea, get him way out of the way, someplace . . ."

"But why the Becknell ranch? You haven't let anyone on that place, except Matt, since you bought it years ago."

"I don't know. I just thought . . ."

"I know what you thought," Cord said softly. He pushed the photograph toward Elena. "You thought it might fire up his memory. Did it?"

"No . . . I don't think so . . . I don't know."

"But you think it's him?"

Elena said nothing.

Klah leaned toward the woman. "You want it to be him. And, I guess I want it to be him. I want all the questions answered."

"Well," Cord grunted, "other than the fact that he's out there, running around my streets, he doesn't legally exist. No prints, no DNA records." He looked at Elena. "There will be a warrant out for the fat guys. But, Cousin Elena, you know I have to find him, Stick. He's part of this, at least a witness, maybe to a bunch of stuff we don't even know about."

They sat in silence for long minutes.

"About the basement and the ranch," Klah said. "If you knew he was there, how come you didn't just pick him up?"

"Maybe . . . maybe I want what my cousin wants," Cord said. He stared into his glass. "Maybe, sometimes, rules have to be bent."

"About the ranch," Matt Klah finally said, "you think you might look for him out there?"

Cord swirled the cognac in his glass. "Well, it might take me a long time to get out there. Outside my jurisdiction." He let the statement sink in. "Maybe he needs a safe place from which to . . . operate. Maybe find the fat guys before we do."

Klah looked at Cord. "You condoning street justice?"

"Me? You know better than that," Cord said, his face serious, no hint of lightness in his voice. "Couldn't do that. Never." But he would not look at Klah.

"I'll keep that in mind," Klah said, glancing at Elena.

"He's looking for the same guys we are," Cord said. "Makes sense that we cut him a little slack."

"Of course," the woman said.

Cord sipped his cognac. "I sort of hope he finds them." He glanced at Klah, their eyes locking. "Who knows? Hell, there's a lot of things we don't know about that guy . . . may never know."

"I'll know," the woman said, staring into her glass.

* * *

She didn't know how long she was willing to wait. She fidgeted on the iron bench, her arm flung across the back, now and then crossing and uncrossing her long legs, just to see the expressions of the faces of male tourists.

She had walked calmly back to the bench and sat down, watched the cops arrive, watched them put up their yellow tape, shooing the crowd of tourists away from the gallery. Watched the good looking guy arrive, the detective.

But then someone had closed the gallery door and hung something over the window.

She could wait, she decided. Somewhere, sometime, the woman would be alone.

The bus ticket had not worked. The ranch had not worked. What the hell would it take to jog the memories out of the skinny bastard? The woman? Maybe the woman. Yes, it was time to talk with the woman.

So she waited.

* * *

Elena still sat at the small table, an empty glass in front of her. Matt Kalh and Anthony Cordova stood in front of her.

"I think you should keep the gallery closed for a few days. Let this stuff shake down a little," Cord said.

"I'll . . . maybe I'll do that," Elena said.

The men walked to the front door, Matt opening the lock. "Lock this behind us," he said.

Elena stared after them as they left, the gallery falling quickly into silence and darkness. She sat, controlling her breathing, waiting for something that did not come, wishing for something that would not happen.

She walked slowly to the front, noticing the push broom without its handle, the blood spatter on the floor, the busted lance. She reached for the heavy knob of the deadbolt on the door.

The door opened slightly, someone standing outside.

"I'm sorry, we're closed," Elena said.

"That's the way it should be," a woman's voice said, low, silky.

Elena tilted her head and tried to see through the narrow opening. The woman outside was the color of night, tall, taller than Elena, leaning almost casually against the door frame.

There could only be one such woman.

"What do you want?" Elena asked, her voice firm.

"Just a few minutes of your time, to talk about old friends."

"I'm not sure you know any of my old friends," Elena said, her voice taking on an edge.

"Oh, but I do," the woman said.

"No, you don't," Elena said. "You may have brought them to the gallery that night. You may have even saved Stick's life. But you don't know him."

The black woman was silent for a moment. "Saving his life means nothing to me. That's not why I'm here."

"Who the hell are you?"

"You can call me . . . Grace," the woman said.

She leaned harder on the door. Elena saw a movement in the narrow opening.

"And you can call this anything you want."

And then Elena saw the muzzle of the compact automatic pointed at her chest.

THIRTY-EIGHT

It was a time for disappearing.

Little Jimmy and all the People were gone.

Stick did not run, and he did not seem to walk. Instead, he ghosted soundlessly through the night, a specter in search of something he would not find. He passed under the bridges and behind the buildings, moved out to the edge of town and circled it, thinking maybe Little Jimmy would be sitting out there, waiting. But he was not. Stick followed Jimmy's routes, his rounds, hoping that the little man's habits would be hard to break, that he would find him sitting by the dripping standpipe in the grass by the side of the courthouse, his hands cupped under the cool water. But he was not.

Wherever he was, Little Jimmy would not be found. Not by Stick, not by anybody. Stick had to have help.

Stick waited in the shadows at the edge of the soccer park, the train engine hulking in the evening light. He sat for three nights, his head nodding against his chest, waiting to hear the clang of hard stones against the aging sides of the engine, but no sounds came. The Engineer was gone.

And there was no dead car at the All-Nighter, or at any other gas station that Stick could find. Without Pablo, the car scam was over. The Mechanic had vanished.

Hale Mary was not under any of the bridges.

And Mulligan was not at his corner; there was no soft jazz being played on San Francisco Street.

But Jimmy was not the only one Stick was looking for. He was looking for Angelo and Beano. And they, too, were gone.

And the cops were looking for everybody.

Jesus Christ, what the hell am I into?

Stick sat on a bag of trash behind an auto parts store and stared into the darkness.

Everybody is looking for somebody.

In spite of himself, he began to laugh.

* * *

Stick crouched on a rise in the land behind a hotel on the north side of town, his legs gathered under him, ready to run. But he saw nothing that worried him.

He looked south over the low rooftops, the early light beginning to touch the tops of trees standing motionless in the cool air. Daylight. As the light came forward, Stick knew he would have to retreat. He could only search in the dark, when it was easier to avoid the cops. The cops had not found him, but neither had he found Little Jimmy. Or anyone else. All the People gone. Angelo and Beano, gone. How the hell could anyone disappear in so small a town? He knew there was an answer. Somewhere, inside his head, there was an answer.

He had to take a break, to recover, to think this through.

He eased up from his crouch, turned, and began a slow walk north away from the hill, away from the hotel, away from the houses and the city. He began to walk faster, then broke into a jog, his long legs beginning to travel the soft earth effortlessly, gliding through the low brush and out into the desert.

He ran all the way to the ranch. It took him hours.

He meant to keep going, to stick to the top of the low canyon on the south side of the ranch, stay out of sight of the ranch house and drop off the steep rise near the river. The muddy water was even lower this late in the summer and he would wade across and go to the cave, sit on the ledge, watch the light fade into the Jemez and know that he was safe.

That's what he meant to do.

He ran through the low *piñons* on the top of the canyon, the sun high and hot, sweat streaming from his body, a vulture circling to the west, over the edge of the Jemez across the river. He was drawing even with the ranch house.

He slowed to a walk, then stopped. He had to see the house. He stepped through some low trees, dropped to his stomach and slid forward until he could see over the edge of the canyon. The house lay below him, silent, empty. But it was a different house, now. He knew the house, knew how the rooms lay, knew where the doors were. He knew the heavy chain and lock on the fort-like barn, knew what the rusting metal felt like under his hands . . .

The young man and the old man stood looking at the barn.

"You are the last one of them, niño, "the old man said softly "Los otros, they did not come back. When you go, I will not know what to do. What if you do not come back? I will not know where to go."

The old man turned and looked behind him at the house. An old woman stood in the doorway.

"You will go nowhere," the young man said. "This is your home."

"The world is a big place," the old man said, "and dangerous. If it is the will of God that you do not return to us . . ."

"Then you will stay until it is your time," the young man answered.

"And when it is your time, just make sure you lock the barn." He turned
toward the old man, laughing. "And before it is your time, vamos a
cenar.*"*

They walked toward the house, the young man careful to walk slowly,
for the sake of the old man.

The old woman waited.

Maria.

Stick stared at the barn.

Maria. Who was Maria? And who was the old man?

Behind the house, he could see tiny bits of the stream glittering
in the dappled light. And he thought about the shallow pond.

He stared at the road that led down toward the house, stared almost
foot-by-foot at the length of it leading from the far rise. From the top
of the canyon wall he could see no tracks, no sign of anyone having
come to the ranch, at least not by the road. But he would make sure.

He dropped off the ridge and worked his way to the road, staying
in the brush, pausing every few feet to listen. He didn't know why
he did that, but he knew it was a habit learned of experience. There
was nothing to hear but a few birds; there was nothing to see. The
dirt surface of the road was unmarked except for the tiny dimples
left by jackrabbits that had been there, and gone.

No one had been on the road.

* * *

He fell asleep in the stream behind the house, his body under the
cool water of the pool, head resting on his rolled-up pants and shirt.

It was after mid-day when he had gotten there, circling the house
looking for tracks, finding none, and sliding naked into the water.
He closed his eyes.

I'm going to have to stop napping in this pool, he thought.

The light was fading when he awoke.

The woman stood on the far side of the stream, across from the house, her back to the dying light, her legs spread, her arms hanging easily at her side. She stood as though she had been standing there for a long time, watching him, waiting.

Seeing her. Deep inside his mind there was a tiny electrical spark that he could feel running from his brain and down through his chest and then into his legs. He thought the spark made the water move.

He was awake, and he was naked. She looked away.

He tried not to look at her, fumbling for his ragged pants, his eyes flicking through the trees, at the house, at the road. In the cottonwoods at the far end of the house he could see an old pickup truck, the driver's door standing open. He could see no one at the truck. She was alone.

He struggled into the pants, trying to pay attention to covering his naked ass, but his eyes came back to her face, her profile, as she stared out and away from him, waiting. She was not there by accident. She was not anywhere by accident.

He took a deep breath and moved next to her.

Still, she did not look at him, did not even acknowledge that he was there, seemingly only interested in the way the colors faded into the growing evening.

And then she spoke. "A boy kissed me, once. Here, by this stream. It wasn't a real kiss. More like a brother. But he had never kissed me before, and I was too young to know he was being . . . brotherly.

"He used to go up there on the ridge, where he could see the river, watch the sun go down behind the Jemez, watch the night come out of the east. Chasing the sun, he said. He thought it was beautiful.

"And then one night, when he came down here, I was here. And he kissed me.

"And then he went away," she said, her voice so soft that he barely heard her.

They stood in silence, watching the outlines of trees against the blackening sky. She still had not looked at him.

"Was that a long time ago?" He didn't know why he asked the question.

"It was . . . another lifetime."

They stood in the warm, still air, listening. From somewhere near the river a coyote yipped and then the sound of dogs, giving chase, a melody of sounds as old as time.

"It is very inappropriate to make a woman ask you to kiss her. But if you insist, I will ask." Still, she did not turn to face him.

"You let me live on this ranch. And I know the cop, . . . your cousin . . . I know he knows I'm here. I'm grateful.

"But before this place, I lived on the street. You know that. I slept in the shade of bridges and under trees up in the mountains. I think that's where I still belong. I'm a bum. I don't even know my name. I don't have the right to touch you. And I sure as hell don't have the right to kiss you." He dropped his head. "Why are you doing this?"

"Because," she said softly, "I need to know." She turned and stepped in front of him.

He had been close to her before, touched her, had even put his hand on her ass, but that was different. This was personal, the two of them, maybe the most personal thing that had ever happened to him.

And then he noticed the swelling, the ugly little wound at the edge of her right eye. He reached out and touched it gently.

"Who?"

"It doesn't matter. Not right now."

He stood for a long moment, still touching her face, knowing her well enough to know he would get nothing more.

"I'm waiting," she said.

His mind intended to do nothing but his arms acted on their own. They moved around her and gently pulled her to him and she raised her face and he touched her lips. He thought his mind had left his body and entered hers. He could feel the race of her blood, feel the course of it through her heart, feel it pump in her breasts and through her neck and down through the inner parts of her thighs, feel the rush of it through her brain. His mind locked to hers and seemed on the smoky edge of being able to recover, to remember, to come alive with the history of his life. It was as though his mind were somehow a part of hers, the part that held the secrets that would tell him who he was, who he is, why he is.

He felt joined to her, as surely and as tightly as any two humans were ever joined. He could taste his life in her mouth.

And he felt his body come alive with the want of her.

He held the kiss for a long time and she made no move to break it and when he finally released her she stepped back away from him, turned, and stepped into the stream as though the water were not there. She crossed, and walked slowly toward the pickup.

The lights of the pickup came on.

She stopped and looked back at him, standing straight, one leg turned to the side, a model posing in backlight. She did not wave. Neither did he.

"Cinco," she said, barely loudly enough for him to hear.

"Cinco?" he asked?

"You," she said. "Cinco." And then the woman took a breath as deeply as any in her life. "Cinco. Becknell." And then she was gone.

"Cinco Becknell," he whispered to himself. An odd name, a very odd name, but he knew it was his.

* * *

He stood by the stream long after she was gone, staring after her, staring after the truck. She had gotten in the truck on the passenger side. There had been a driver.

In darkness he crossed the stream toward the house, but he did not want to go inside. He had to be in the air and the clear night and space. He had to be in some place where his heart could beat. He turned down-canyon and past the barn, his feet almost shuffling in the soft earth, his mind on the woman, his groin aching with the thought of her.

I want her. I want her. I want her.

He was halfway to the river when he heard the dogs again. Two of them, maybe three, yowling now, still chasing the coyote through the night, the coyote probably leading them on, enjoying the game.

And then the sounds of the dogs changed. He stopped, listening carefully. The dogs had found a new game. Him. And he realized it was a game he knew well.

They seemed to be circling. He thought they had not really located him yet. He eased off the path and to his right. A rock outcropping cluttered the canyon wall. He found a crevice wide enough to fit his body and he sat as far back into it as he could get, gathered some rocks that he piled at his feet, and waited. If the dogs found him, they could only come at him from one direction. He wasn't worried. His mind turned back to the woman. He saw her in his mind, standing straight in the backlight, one leg turned to the side. She did not wave.

Sooner or later, the dogs would figure it out. It was always the dogs, not the men. He thought the dogs were smarter. But before they figured it out this time, he thought he had a couple of extra hours, maybe more.

He had never headed back toward the camp before. Always, he had wanted to see how far away he could get before they caught up with him, each time getting just a little farther, a little deeper into a forest that seemed to have no beginning and no end. The forest was, and always would be. He thought maybe, one day, they would tire of the game and just stop chasing him, knowing that he would die in the forest as all the runners did, as they thought the Indian had done. But he had no intention of dying. If they ever stopped, he would not. Somewhere to the west there was an ocean. He thought he could get there, even if it took the rest of his life. It was a small price to pay. He had no life now. He wouldn't be paying anything.

But this time, as some sort of perverse joke, he curved around and turned back toward the camp. Yesterday he had smelled food cooking— some sort of meat, and the harder smells of vegetables and vinegar. If he could slip into the large building they used as a kitchen and dining hall, maybe he could eat, steal some food, hide it in his hut. The dogs would probably find it, but, what the hell, it was worth a try. He didn't have anything else to do.

It was late when he got there, long thick shadows flowing out from the buildings as though the buildings were moving, leaving the shadows behind. The low, squat dining hall sat at the edge of the camp, its slab sides faded and peeling. If they had eaten in the hall, they should be gone now, unless, of course, they were having one of their late dinners, their excuse for getting drunk.

There was no smoke rising from the metal flue, no trucks parked outside the kitchen. The windows of the dining hall showed dull yellow light from *bulbs that would never hold back a coming darkness that would seem thick enough to touch. He could see no shadows moving across the light.*

He knew the building would not be locked. This was a camp to be broken out of, not broken into. He opened a small door at the rear of the kitchen and slipped quietly inside, closed the door behind him and stepped silently to the side. He stood motionless, waiting for his eyes to adjust to the dim light coming through the doorway into the dining hall.

Nothing moved.

The kitchen was big and crude; heavy stoves and thick wooden tables; racks made of scrap metal dropping from the ceiling, large dented pots hanging from them like things dead and hard; a stack of clean rags piled on a table. The place smelled of a thousand meals cooked in the hard grip of winter and the thick heat of summer, the steam rising from the pots and infusing the smells into the very walls of the place. A heavy smell. Oppressive.

He eased across the cluttered kitchen to the doorway and squatted low against the frame. He stood up, a few inches at a time, changing his angle. The dining hall was empty.

He would not waste this opportunity.

He saw several large metal pans on the stoves. Inside one, he found some sort of meat roasted to a dryness that made it crisp. In another, potatoes boiled in their skins. He found a small wooden box on a shelf under a table. He lined it with a rag and filled it with the meat and potatoes. It did not take long to find bread, the heavy loaves lined up on a shelf above the stove.

And then he saw the knives. He handled several, feeling the weight of them, the balance, testing their sharpness. He put them all back. If they found him with food, they would beat him. If they found him with a knife, they would put him in the hole. And besides, he couldn't kill them all with one knife. He left the knives where he found them.

He thought he would take the box and run, go back to his hut, the last place they would look for him. At least this time. Each time he found a new way to confuse them, they never forgot it, always looked in that place the next time. With his own inventiveness, he was teaching them to find him.

Fuck them. They would beat him anyway. He would dine in their own goddamn kitchen.

He sat down at a heavy plank table and put the box in front of him, breaking off a piece of bread and stripping a handful of meat from a heavy bone. He was biting into the meat when she put the empty wine glass down beside him.

He dropped the food and rolled out of the chair, turning, coming up in a crouch. He knew it was useless. They always came in bunches and there was no way he could avoid whatever it was that they were going to do. But this time, maybe he could make a couple of them pay.

There was no one there but the woman, the slender blonde woman, the woman with the silky skin and the small breasts and the firm legs that he could still feel rubbing against him. She was wearing a thin dress, so black it seemed to make most of her body disappear. Her right hand was empty. In her left hand she held a wine bottle and another empty glass. She put the glass on the table and carefully poured wine into both glasses. She moved gracefully to the other side of the table and sat, reaching for her glass, delicately sipping. Waiting.

How the hell did I miss her? How the hell did I not know she was here?

He was being set up. He knew it. Somehow, they had anticipated him, had hidden the woman in the kitchen, were waiting, would come bursting into the kitchen any time now, laughing, swinging their rifle butts.

The woman sipped her wine, leaving the glass against her lips.

No one burst into the kitchen.

He straightened up, dropped his arms, breathed deeply. Again, he scanned the darkened kitchen, more carefully this time. In a far corner he saw a rickety cot and a chair, a cheap suitcase on the floor beside it, what appeared to be some sort of light jacket dropped across it. She was waiting to leave this place but they had not come for her. She wasn't important anymore.

He eased back into his chair, the wine glass and the food between them. He stared at the woman, the far-glow of the light from the dining hall making her sharp features softer. She stared back.

He picked up the bread and meat and took small bites, eating slowly, carefully, almost ritually. Amazingly, he could smell the wine.

They sat in silence so absolute he could hear her sip the wine.

He broke off small pieces of the bread, meat and potato and put them on a rag and carefully placed it in front of her. She took a small shred of the meat and put it into her mouth, chewing so gently that he could hardly see movement in her face.

* * *

He had no idea how much time had passed. Much of the food was gone, and all the wine, the windows of the kitchen black with heavy night.

He stared across the table at her, her large eyes, the shape of her shoulders. In a slow, deliberate motion, she pushed the empty wine glass to the center of the table and leaned back in her chair, her breasts rising high and prominent in the dim light.

He walked slowly around the table and stood behind her. She did not move. He put his hands on her shoulders, squeezing gently, feeling the total lack of tension in her, her shoulders compliant, her body relaxed. He closed his eyes. Any minute now they would come crashing in and beat him. But he did not care.

The woman stood up and turned to face him, his hands going to her *waist. She leaned back against the table and he saw, felt, her legs spread slightly. She unfastened something at the top of her dress and the dress slipped from her shoulders. She took his hands and placed them on her breasts and left them there. She leaned farther back, bracing herself with her arms, her legs coming farther apart.*

When would they come in? He didn't care.

He moved his hands to her legs, gathered the flimsy material of her dress in his hands and raised it to her waist. She was wearing nothing underneath. He untied the cord that held up his tattered pants. And then he was in her.

For brief moments she stayed at the edge of the table and he could feel her move, pressing against him. And then one of her legs came up and wrapped him, and then the other. She brought her body forward and laced her arms around his shoulders and then she was off the table and he was carrying her, walking slowly around the table, around the room, each step a movement inside her, each movement a connection with something he could hardly remember, and might never know again.

Any minute now they would come out of the darkness and beat him.

But they did not.

* * *

He came out of the door and was in the darkness. He moved down the short wooden steps to the ground and started walking slowly toward his hut at the other side of the camp. He heard the slight noise behind him. As he turned he could feel the woman next to him, in front of him, her arms coming up and moving firmly around his neck, her mouth on his sunken cheeks and then on his eyes and then on his own mouth, working, a hungry sort of searching, a connection to another human. A woman.

She slipped away from him and drifted across the short distance to the dining hall, silently climbing the wooden steps. The woman stood in the

*doorway of the kitchen and looked back at him, standing straight, one leg
turned to the side, a model posing in backlight.*

She did not wave. Neither did he.

"Pyat," she said.

It was the only word spoken.

He opened his eyes. There was early light in the world and he
could see the trail to the river and the stand of cottonwoods in the
distance.

He had been someplace. Another place.

And then he realized that tears were drifting softly down his face.

Pyat.

Cinco.

THIRTY-NINE

"He is Cinco."

She had not spoken until the old truck had cleared the end of the canyon, rolled onto the high desert and finally hit the hardpan that led to the narrow two-lane blacktop.

"You're sure?" Matt Klah asked.

"Yes."

Matt drove in silence for a while.

"Did you ask him about a journal?"

"No." Elena hesitated. "No one really knows anything about this sort of stuff, this 'condition', amnesia, or whatever you want to call it. What if I tell him something, ask him something, and it hurts him, forever?"

His forever is already gone, Matt thought.

He looked over at her. "Has he become that important to you?"

She changed the subject. "This whole thing is crazy. A black Amazon sticks a gun in my face—the second time in one afternoon that someone has stuck a gun in my face in my own gallery—and asks me about a journal, or a book, or something. I got the impression that she wasn't exactly sure what to call it."

"She said it was Stick's?"

"Stick's. Cinco's. Yes. But she called him . . ."

"And when did he write it?"

"Matt, I've told you all this. It was when he was 'away'. That's all she would say. But she said if I helped her get the journal that she would just disappear from my life. She seemed to think Cinco had given the thing to me."

"The man has no memory. How can he give you something that he doesn't even know exists?"

"I asked her about that. I could tell she had already thought about that. And that's when she told me."

"Told you she would kill him."

"She said, if I helped her get the journal, she wouldn't *have* to kill him. That he might even live a few more years and . . ."

"And what?"

Elena took a deep breath. "And be around so I could fuck him whenever I wanted."

Matt felt a small grin coming on. He suppressed it. "And that's what got you in trouble."

"I was already in trouble. The woman had a gun in my face, for God's sake."

"But you didn't have to . . ."

"All right! I told the bitch to stick the gun up her ass and fuck *herself*! And I took a swing at her."

"And that's when she hit you."

"Yes! She didn't even bother ducking my punch. She just threw her arm into it and then she hit me with the gun. Backhanded me, if you want to be specific! Now will you stop with the damn cross examination?!"

They drove in silence, the lights of the city coming up in the darkness in front of them.

"So she might kill him if she doesn't get this book she's looking for," Matt said, "and the fat boys are trying to kill him. Is there any-one who doesn't want this guy dead?"

Elena stared out the window. "She called him something else, some word I didn't understand."

Matt waited.

"She called him . . . . 'pyat' . . . or something like that."

Matt pushed the word through his memory, but got nothing. "I still think it's all bullshit. I think it's some woman living a fantasy life."

"I haven't told Cord, yet."

"You have to tell him, even if none of it is real."

"This is real," she said, touching her swollen eye.

They came into the city from the north, dropping into the lights.

There was the jangled ring of a cell phone. Matt jammed his hand into his jacket pocket, came out with the phone. He stared at the tiny, shiny screen.

"It's Cord," he said. He punched a button.

"Matt, where are you?"

"North side of town, passing through. Heading for Elena's place."

"Where's Elena?"

"With me."

"Meet me at the station. We've found Little Jimmy."

"Well, finally some good news," Klah said. "Maybe now we can get some answers."

"No, we won't," Cord said, and hung up.

* * *

Little Jimmy was running again, his big canvas shoes slapping the blacktop of the Solana Center parking lot. Even in the dark he knew he couldn't stay in the open, had to get to cover, had to keep the big headlight from finding him again. He angled to his left in front of an auto repair shop and saw the traffic light ahead. He rounded the corner and ran south with the traffic, his breath coming harder now, arms pumping, head jerking around in a constant attempt to spot the dark sedan.

He saw a break in the traffic and he bolted across St. Francis and through someone's backyard, scuttled across a porch and down a short driveway and then onto Alto Street, heading wildly east. He heard the car behind him, saw the glare of the headlight. He cut between two houses and across a cluttered backyard, tripped over a broken bicycle. A dog lay sleeping on a tiny back porch. The dog woke up but Jimmy was up and out of the yard and gone before the dog could bark even once.

He snaked along some sagging wire fences and across one narrow back street and then was on Alto Street again, wondering what had happened to the car.

He stopped. All he could hear was the booming of his own blood in his ears and the rush of his breath. There were few lights on in the houses and the single street light was out, the darkness as thick as tar. He edged along the street, keeping to the low walls and ragged fences of the neighborhood.

The outline of the car was barely visible against a front porch light a half block away, the car pointed away from him. He pressed himself tightly to a wall and stared at the outline. Probably a car that belongs here, he thought. Probably been there all night. Probably.

But he had to be sure. He edged forward, checking out some escape routes as he went. He got closer to the car. It was a lowered sedan, with the windshield and back window shattered.

How the hell did they find me? How did they know where to look?

Before he could decide what to do another car turned onto the street and the glare of headlights caught him against the wall, frozen there, in plain view of the lowered sedan in front of him. The big sedan's engine growled and the back-up lights came on and the big car shot backward, tires scraping against the low curb and then climbing it and then the car was rushing backwards at the low wall.

Jimmy timed his leap. At the last second he jumped the wall into the yard behind it and ran up and across a front porch, hearing the car slam into the wall behind him. He pounded down into some flowers and sailed over another fence and then was in another back yard. He knew he was near the river and he kept working through the houses until he burst out on the high bank and leaped into the small canyon and in two steps was in and out of the water and scrambling up the other bank, spray flying from his shoes.

He was on Alameda, not far from the Salvation Army. Familiar ground. It was where he wanted to go. The dark car would have to go on to Montezuma Street in order to cross. He had a minute to think, to plan. He thought he could get there before they did. And then they would never find him.

He had no where else to go.

He ran east along Alameda, cutting across to the north side. The light was better on Alameda and the running was easier and in less than a minute he was at the Salvation Army. As he turned into the parking lot he heard the squealing of tires. He ducked behind a low wall, looked east and saw the sedan come hard across the Montezuma Street Bridge and slew into a tight left turn, heard the engine gunning as the car struggled to straighten out. He rolled over backward behind the wall, then ran, bent over, until he was sure he was out of sight. The drop box was straight ahead.

He grabbed the handle of the bin and swung hard, pulling up with his little body. The bin swung open and he flipped himself up on the shelf, curling into a fetal position. The heavy bin hinged back-ward inside the drop box. As Jimmy rolled off the shelf and dropped into the total darkness, plunging toward the pile of clothing on the floor, he knew it was one of his best pieces of running, ever.

The drop box was empty. Little Jimmy slammed into the metal floor, his right arm twisting awkwardly. He heard the bone snap before he felt it.

A small scream, not a scream, really, something less than that. Whatever it was, it slipped out of Little Jimmy's throat.

* * *

Beano thought he saw the runty little shit hop over the wall. He jammed the accelerator to the floor and the sedan shot forward, odd noises coming from the damaged right rear fender, cool night air wind flowing through the windshield—where the windshield used to be, chunks of broken window glass still scattered on the floor and seats.

In the passenger's seat, Angelo hunched against the door, his left arm bound to his side by strips of bed sheet that he had torn from his own bed. The strips were caked with dried blood, his blood, blood that had dripped out of his body because of that little hillbilly shit. Since they had spotted the hillbilly, Angelo had said nothing, had just sat there, gritting his teeth, tiny lances of pain stabbing up into his brain. How come he didn't see it coming? How come he just forgot that the little hillbilly would be there, in the gallery? How come? Sometimes Angelo could not answer his own questions.

But Angelo wasn't pissed about the busted windshield. Not any more. And he wasn't pissed about the fender, about the dent in the top, about all the other damage, some of it caused by Angelo.

Angelo had wanted to crush the little street punk behind the Dumpster and had forgotten all about what that might do to his car. He did things like that, now and then. He knew he did, knew he lost his temper and did . . . things. He was usually sorry afterward, but if he admitted he was sorry then people might think he didn't *mean* to do those . . . things. And if he didn't *mean* to do them, then why did he do them? Angelo sometimes tried to figure out the answer, but the effort always made his head hurt.

Angelo was not even pissed that they had killed the street guy behind the Dumpster. He was pissed because they had killed the *wrong* street guy.

Before they got to the Salvation Army parking lot Beano turned out the headlight and killed the engine, drifting the big car up to the driveway and into the lot. The noise from the fender was louder with the engine off, but it wasn't exactly a car noise and Beano thought no one would notice.

Jesus Christ, Angelo thought, *I can drive better than Beano, just one arm working.*

The lot was empty.

Beano used the parking brake, bringing the car to a stop without brake lights flaring.

Thin light from a couple of weak overheads gave the lot an almost-dark, washed-out look, the lights not really holding back all the darkness. All Angelo could see was the outline of a small shed next to the main building, some sort of storage place.

That's all he needed to see.

He got out quietly and leaned against the front fender, holding his arm tightly against his aching side, the pistol jammed inside his belt. Tiny beads of sweat gathered above his eyes and he could feel the heat under his skin. Probably a fever from the jagged tear in his side. He would have to do something about that. Maybe take some aspirin. He pressed his arm more tightly into his side and stared into the silence and the darkness. And he heard the tiny noise, the human agony noise, from the box. The little street shit was in there, just like Beano had said. In there, in that goddamn metal box.

Inside the car, Beano Clapper stuck his head out the window. "See? See? I told you that's where he would be. Couldn't be no where's else."

"Yeah," Angelo muttered, "but I still want to know how you found out." *But not right now*, Angelo thought. He could wait. More tiny pains jumped up his side.

Beano Clapper got out of the car and stood beside Angelo, staring off into the darkness. He was not going to tell Angelo that it was Willie who had told him. There were some things Angelo did not need to know.

"Gimme the keys."

Beano handed the keys to Angelo. Angelo went to the back of the car and opened the trunk.

"It's time for our rich-u-all," he muttered.

*   *   *

He thought he was going to cry. A little mewling noise slipped out of his throat. With his teeth, Little Jimmy tore a piece of cloth from the bottom of his shirt an then lapped it into his mouth, making a ball he could bite on, anything to help him not make a noise. With his good arm he pressed the broken one to his stomach.

He stood up and leaned against the tiny door in the back of the drop box, shoved against it, knowing it was padlocked from the outside. He went back to the shelf and pressed his face against the wall. The shelf did not fit tightly and through a crack he could see part of the rear end of a car out there. His ears rang and the pain from his arm seemed to shoot into his brain and he couldn't identify what he was seeing or hearing. The rag he was chewing tasted sour and he thought it was mostly from his own bile boiling up from his stomach. He spit out the rag and the slight movement caused another flash of pain and without him knowing it was happening his brain closed down and he slumped to the floor.

* * *

He heard the metallic scraping sound and he knew his brain had come on again. He was lying on his back. He opened his eyes and saw the sliver of weak light coming through the crack beside the shelf, saw dark movement and realized the shelf was being pulled open from the outside. He struggled to sit up, got dizzy and slipped down to his back again.

He was still on his back when the shelf slammed back inside again, something smashing down onto the floor, water splashing over him, covering his face, shooting out against the walls.

Goddamn asshole, Jimmy thought, *think he can flush me out'a here . . ."*

Gasoline. He knew it was gasoline, only his mind wouldn't let him think that. He was still refusing to think that when the drawer opened again and a lighted match flicked through the darkness, a tiny flare falling in slow motion down into the wetness. It took a long time for the match to fall, and in its bright light Little Jimmy could see the end of the universe, such a long way away, and so close.

* * *

Angelo hadn't known the metal walls of the drop box would get so hot so fast. He was standing too close and the heat flashed against his face. He stumbled slowly backward, unable to take his eyes from the flames shooting out of every crack, every tiny opening in the box. Jesus, he had never seen anything like this. This was different. Way different. He wanted to remember this, do it even better next time. He squeezed his arm against his side and felt the wetness begin to seep down into his pants. Damned thing was bleeding again. But Angelo did not really care. All he cared about was watching the burning box. It was the best thing he had ever seen.

Beano was already at the car. He jumped into the driver's seat and started the engine, revved it, waiting for Angelo to turn and run toward the car. But Angelo didn't turn. Beano glanced around the neighborhood, noticed a light come on in a window down the street, knew that people would be getting out of bed, telephones in their hands.

He stuck his head out the window. "Ange! Goddammit, get in the fuckin' car!" But Angelo still did not move.

Beano jammed the transmission into Reverse and punched the gas. The tires chirped and the car moved backward a few feet. Beano hit the brakes. Angelo still stared at the flames shooting from the box, his back to the car, standing like a statue planted in the middle of the parking lot.

I got him. I fuckin' got him, was all Angelo could think, over and over. *And I'll get the rest of 'em.*

It was time. It was *the* time. Beano had been thinking about it, wondering when it would happen, and now it was. The time was now. It was right there in his hands, under his right foot.

He would be his own man.

Fuck you, Angelo.

Beano slowly let up on the brakes. The big car rolled grudgingly backward, out of the parking lot and into the street, Beano cranking the wheel. He stopped the car. Beano looked toward the parking lot, saw Angelo still standing there, still not moving, a fat, black outline against the glow of the fire.

He would be his own man. He rammed the shift lever down into Drive, revving, the tires screaming against the pavement, the heavy machine jerking forward into the darkness. The damaged rear fender was pressing against the tire and before the car reached St. Francis the metal cut into the rubber and the tire blew and disintegrated, shreds of rubber flapping darkly out into the street. Beano ran the traffic light at St. Francis, the car's rear wheel running on the naked rim, sparks dancing out behind it.

Beano drove stone-like, staring straight ahead, thinking about the fire, about Little Jimmy, about the sounds that came from the Salvation Army drop box. It was not like anything he had done before It was not like doing the women.

It was better.

✗ ✗ ✗

Hale Mary sat on the ground across the street from the Salvation Army. She leaned back against a tree, dozing, her sock-and-soap weapon twisted around her right hand. That afternoon, she had seen a *rico* stuff some bags into the drop box. She knew Little Jimmy sometimes worked the box in the early morning and she would wait until full daylight to see if he showed up. Sometimes the Salvation Army people emptied the drop box before they closed up for the day. If they had done that, then the *rico's* clothes would be gone. But it didn't matter. Hale Mary didn't have anywhere else to go. She had been hiding for days.

She was not surprised to hear the sounds of running feet. She often heard the sounds of running in the dark, feet slapping the pavement, skidding, changing. But she was surprised that the sounds turned into the Salvation Army. There was nothing in there but the drop box.

Hale Mary sat up—and in the dim streetlights saw a small figure grab the metal drawer of the drop box and whip it open . . . *Jimmy* . . . climb on the shelf and disappear into the box. Heard the drawer clang shut.

What the hell was he doing?

She got clumsily to her feet. She would go across the street . . .

A car with no lights drifted past her. She knew the car.

Hale Mary backed away and tried to shield her thick body behind the tree. Dimly, she saw the car slow to a halt, saw it sit there, a huge metal thing that seemed to smell of evil. She could see the two shapes in the front seat.

And then they got out. She knew who they were, could even tell them apart; knew their names. It was them, the creeps from the bridge. The creeps who had tried to kill her.

They just stood there. And stood there.

She saw Angelo whirl and go to the back of the car. She heard the clink of keys as he popped the trunk, some other clinking sounds and some sounds she did not understand. He closed the trunk lid, as silently as he could. But Mary heard it. The men stood together for a few moments, and then she saw the one named Beano walking toward the drop box, holding something in his hand out away from his body.

And then the sound of the bin of the drop box opening; the sound of breaking glass.

Beano stood motionless, looking back at Angelo. "I don't know if we ought to . . ."

Peeking around the tree, Hale Mary saw Angelo move quickly, rushing toward Beano, his heavy body seeming to float across the blacktop. He shoved Beano out of the way, grabbed the handle on the metal drawer.

"Hold the goddamn door open!" She heard that. And she heard the door clang open, saw a tiny flame dance briefly in the darkness and then disappear.

There is a sound a fire makes that is like no other. Even those who have never heard a fire can recognize it, a sound caught in the evolutionary corners of our brains and wrapped tightly around our survival, a sound that was, and is, both life and death. For thousands of years we feared it, and we needed it.

And Mary heard it now.

Firelight bloomed around the bin in the drop box, probing out into night through the cracks, the entire box taking on a new character, a new purpose. A funeral box.

Mary dropped to the ground and covered her face.

The car sped away.

Mary raised her head. The box glowed red now, the crackle of the fire the only sounds jerking across the blackness of the street.

One of them was still there. She saw the fat, black outline against the glare of the fire. She thought she heard a dull groan but could not be sure. The fat man turned and looked at the space where the car had been, the void left by the disappearance of security.

Angelo.

He looked around, then staggered off into the darkness, one arm pressed tightly against his side.

Mary forced her feet to carry her across the street. She got as far as the sidewalk on the other side before her legs gave way and she dropped to her knees.

On the sidewalk next to her sat a whiskey bottle.

They had a drink!

She opened her mouth and tried to scream out of her mind and into the night. But she was Hale Mary. Her mouth open, her breath storming out of her throat, she tried to remember how it was to make sound, to bring anguish out of her body. But nothing came.

It did not matter. From inside the fire-blasted box came screams that would stay with Hale Mary for the rest of her life.

FORTY

Cinco Becknell.

He rolled the words, the name, around in his mind, banging them against the inside of his skull, waiting for the reaction, waiting for the memories. There were none.

He sat up, pushing the old blanket from him, feeling the crisp morning air against his warm body. He had been sleeping under one of the old cottonwoods across the stream and he got up, took off his clothes, and waded into the pool, sitting, then lying back, letting the chilled water cover his body, then lay in the sun until he was dry.

He had no food but it didn't matter. He had to go into town. He had to find Jimmy, had to find him before the fat guys got hold of him.

*

He was not far from the house, maybe half a mile, when he saw the glint of something through the brush, a flash of metal.

He stepped off the dirt track and eased behind a clump of brush, his eyes sweeping the area, looking for anything that did not belong. There was nothing.

He eased forward, changed angles, and could see the outline of a pickup truck jammed back into the trees, the front pointed toward the road.

Watching the road, he thought.

He moved again, farther to the side, could see the rusty color of the truck, the missing tailgate, the driver's door hanging open.

Angelo! That has to be Angelo. The son-of-a-bitch is laying for me.

Cinco eased farther to his left, keeping low, moving just out of sight of the truck. He took off his pack. Out of his pocket he took the big folding knife and locked it open. He moved toward the truck.

Cinco Becknell had become the hunter.

He thought about Angelo's pistol. He crawled up on the truck from the right rear, putting as much truck between him and the driver as possible, trying to get to the passenger door before Angelo saw him. He thought about the door, maybe locked, maybe rusted shut, but it was too late to change his plan. He would try to whip open the door, dive inside, do anything to close on the fat man before he could get the gun into play.

He jerked the door open easily, slamming it back against its hinges, plunging into the passenger seat, his left hand bracing down against the seat, the big knife in his right hand out in front of him.

Kill him!

The truck was empty. Cinco rebounded, dropped backward out of the door, rolled quickly and came up in a crouch, head swiveling. He saw no one. He waited, posed, arms out, trying to let his senses work, listening.

He was alone.

His body stiff with tension, he moved slowly around the back of the truck and then out to his left where he could see past the open driver's door. He saw no one.

He squatted at the side of the truck, waiting, listening, until he thought it was safe to relax, just a little, and take a closer look.

The driver's seat was covered with blood, old blood, but not that old. Blood from last night, or earlier this morning.

How do I know about old blood?

On the ground next to the truck heavy grooves, like drag marks, led away from the truck and into the brush, down canyon, toward the river. He followed the marks. After no more than fifty yards the drag marks stopped, replaced by foot prints that pressed heavily into the soft soil. He started to follow the tracks, then stopped. There was only one place the tracks could go—to the river. And to get there, whoever had carried Angelo had carried him right past the ranch house.

Cinco went back to the truck, wondering how he would explain the truck and the blood to Cordova, to anybody.

He saw the pistol lying on the hood of the truck. He stepped around the open door, the knife still in his hand. He stuck the tip of the blade into the trigger guard and lifted the pistol, looking into the cylinder, seeing the noses of bullets resting in the chambers. The pistol was fully loaded, old blood drying on the grips. Cinco took a plastic bag of beef jerky from his pack, emptied the bag, stuck the pistol into it and put it in his pack.

He moved away from the truck and sat at the edge of the road. Nothing moved, the air so still he could hear the sounds of flying insects. He stared at the truck and tried to figure out some obvious situation that he was missing. But the only obvious thing was that Angelo had been there, waiting in ambush. Angelo. It had been Angelo.

But nothing else, none of the rest of it, made any sense at all. Angelo died, and Cinco had no idea why. Unless . . . it was to keep Cinco alive.

He sat, doing nothing, until the sun was almost directly overhead. He would have to tell Elena about the truck, the blood, the pistol. If she wanted to tell Cord, that was her business.

Cinco got up and put on his pack, looking at the truck. Something about the driver's side was not quite right, some line in his vision that did not quite even out, something out of place. He moved to the door and looked inside, seeing the same thing he had seen before. And then he noticed, stuck to the back of the seat, at the top, covered in blood and almost invisible among the gore, a small hank of hair that seemed attached to some sort of pad. He looked more closely. The pad was skin.

Cinco was looking at a scalp.

FORTY-ONE

Cinco Becknell sat at one of the picnic tables beside the river and watched the tourists. It was almost noon and he would not sit there long. He knew some of the locals in nearby businesses liked to eat lunch at the tables and wouldn't come to that table if he were there. If he stayed at the table too long, disturbing their lunch, sooner or later they would report him to the street cops.

Today, he held his ground. Today, he didn't give a damn. Today, he sat at the table, looking down into the Santa Fe River, at the grass beginning to crisp up from early autumn nights, at the grass he and Jimmy had walked through, slept in.

The gray sedan pulled to the curb and stopped. Detective Anthony Cordova got out, stood looking at Cinco for a moment, then walked slowly to the table. He sat beside Cinco, neither looking at the other, Cordova taking off his sunglasses and cleaning them.

"Elena said you might be here."

Cinco said nothing.

"I understand you have a new name," Cord said.

"I had a new name. Jimmy gave it to me. Now, I've got my old name back."

At the sound of Jimmy's name, the men fell silent for long moments.

"I never liked him much. Always seemed afraid of cops. Never would hold still for any sort of conversation. I could have arrested him, but what would have been the point of that?"

"He wasn't afraid of cops. He was terrified of cops. Especially big ugly ones."

A tiny smile flicked at the edge of Cord's mouth.

"I need you to do something for me," Cord said quietly.

"Somebody else can do it," Cinco said, his voice heavy.

Cordova looked at him. "You knew him."

"I didn't know him. Nobody knew him. He wasn't a man who let you get too close."

Cord turned to look at him. "If you didn't know him, then what did you know? What do you know now?"

"I don't know anything. I don't even know why I'm here. I don't know why I stay. Like I said, get somebody else."

"Somebody else. That would be Elena," Cord said.

Cinco tried to keep his breathing steady.

"You really want Elena to ID Jimmy?" Cord said. "To look at what's left of him? To see how his clothes are melted to his body?"

"Leave Elena out of this. Leave me out of this. Get somebody else."

"There isn't anybody else. Maybe you haven't noticed, but that bunch you hang out with—all gone. That thick, ugly broad, no one's seen her since the fat guy shot up the gallery. Hell, even Mulligan is gone, and he hasn't left that corner for as long as I can remember."

"You knew Mulligan?"

"I'm a jazz fan," Cord said sarcastically. "So, other than Elena, you're the only one."

"You want me to identify a body. That must mean you think it's Jimmy. How the hell do you know it's him?"

326

"That's why we need you."

"How can I identify a body when I didn't even know his real name?"

"It's more than that. I want you to see how he died. What they did. If you think you're mad now, you haven't seen anything."

"You want me to do something about it."

"Me? Nah," Cord said, "that would be against the law. Was just thinking maybe you could tell us why, or who."

"You know 'who'. There isn't any doubt about 'who'."

"Yeah, I know. But those guys are just one step up from street guys." He glanced at Cinco. "No offense, but if they don't want to be found . . . I mean, think about it."

They sat silently at the table, neither seeming in any hurry to end it.

"You had lunch yet?" Cordova asked.

"I don't have lunch," Cinco said. "If there's food, I eat it. The time of day doesn't make much difference."

Cordova got up and started back toward his car.

"Wait," Cinco said.

Cordova stopped, turned.

"You only have to find one of them. The other one, the shooter, is . . . missing. For good, I think."

"Where?"

"Where?" Cinco's voice got darker. "Look, if I knew 'where', then he wouldn't be missing. But it started at the ranch. Don't know where it ended. You'll need to take a look."

"Why are you telling me? You don't tell me anything."

"It's Elena's ranch. But I don't want her involved. She doesn't even know about this. I want to be the one to tell her. I need some time."

"The ranch." Cord paused. "Out of my jurisdiction. I'll tell the county boys about it. They're short-handed. May take a while to look into it."

"You giving me enough rope to hang myself?"

"Yeah, oh yeah, Stickman. You may already have done that. Isn't that what you want?"

*

Beano Clapper stood in the late afternoon sun outside his trailer-house and looked at the car; at the front grill; the bumper, crumpled from smashing into the Dumpster and shoved almost back into the radiator; the busted headlight; smashed windshield; the rear window broken out and missing; long deep dents in the hood and trunk, all done by that little hillbilly son-of-a-bitch; the dented top where the rock had hit; the deep scratch on the driver's door. He measured the scratch with his hands—a very long scratch. Beano remembered the scratch, remembered how pissed off Angelo was when the black woman had dug her pistol into the door. Beano grinned. The scratch was hardly noticeable now, compared to the other shit that had come down on the car.

But none of that mattered. It was his car, now. Beano's car. Besides, Angelo had another car. No, it was a truck, another piece of shit that he kept parked by his house, an old pickup, body rusted out, no tailgate. But that was okay, Angelo said. A real pickup is supposed to look like shit, at least here in New Mexico. An old pickup parked . . . somewhere. Beano had never seen where Angelo lived.

Sometimes Beano had flashes of . . . thinking. Like now. He knew he would have to be careful with the car—knew the cops were probably looking for it, and Angelo was damn sure looking for it.

Beano thought of losing the car, taking it out into the *arroyos* and just losing it, just like they would lose the women. But the car was useful, especially now that it was Beano's, Beano driving it, Beano hanging his elbow out the window, Beano leering at the women.

The mirror on the driver's side of the car was still intact and Beano stared into it, his fingers softly touching his nose, running gently over his cheeks.

Maybe I should wash my face. He rubbed his chin. *Aw, fuck it. There ain't no water in the trailer-house, anyway.*

Beano looked over his shoulder at his trailer-house, the metal steps that didn't quite come up to the front door, the front door that didn't quite close, the heavy wire that Beano used as a door latch, hooking it over the railing on the metal steps. The mangled corner at the end of the trailer where something heavy had fallen, beating a hole through to the inside, somewhere, sometime, before Beano owned the trailer. Beano didn't care about the hole. He had covered it with duct tape two years ago, and the tape was still there. Beano grinned. The car, the trailer-house and his own face were now matched—beaten to shit. Even Beano could see the humor in that.

The trailer-house was the only home Beano could remember. Well, every now and then he had a thought about a farm, somewhere. He didn't know where.

Beano had to piss. The toilet in the trailer house did not work, had never worked. When Beano needed to piss or take a shit, he just walked out into the desert, dropped his pants, and let fly. Just like he did now. Beano thought the desert around the trailer house was beginning to take on a bad smell.

He went back to the car.

Angelo had taught him how to drive, taking him out into the

mesas and letting Beano steer the car down narrow dirt roads. Might come in handy, Angelo had said, in case you have to drive one of them women out in the boonies. Beano didn't drive very well and he had no license. Didn't matter, Angelo had said. Only time you drive is when we got a dump problem. Otherwise, you ain't drivin' my bitchin' ride.

Now, the car sat outside Beano's trailer-house, waiting. It was a piece of shit, but it was Beano's piece of shit. And Beano could drive it whenever he wanted.

Fuck you, Angelo.

They had split up right after the shooting in the gallery, agreeing to meet at the bridge where they had thrown over the ugly old broad. When they met, Angelo had his side and arm wrapped in strips of a filthy bed sheet. To make him feel better, Beano had told him where the little hillbilly was. But it didn't seem to make him feel better. It only made him foam at the mouth.

Beano had not been out of his trailer house since they set fire to the little hillbilly bastard. He drove away, left Angelo standing there—the dumb son-of-a-bitch—drove home to the trailer-house and parked the car around back, covered it with some cardboard. The wind had blown the cardboard off, but Beano didn't really care—no one ever came out here in the desert beyond the town. But Beano knew Angelo wouldn't be able to sit still for long. He would want to find Beano, find his car. Maybe look for the tall guy, maybe have another go at the Spanish chick that worked in the art store. Have a go at *somebody*. And he would need the car. But he would never find the car here, at the trailer, where no one ever came.

But what good is the car just sitting there? Bitchin' car like this.

Beano got into the driver's seat. It was time to take his car for a ride. He reached for the key, then noticed the big wooden cross on its heavy chain still hanging from the rearview mirror. Beano stared at it for a moment, watching it swing gently in the sunlight, its shadow crossing Beano's face. He reached out and gripped the cross, pulling.

Fuck it, he thought, *leave it there. Better'n them fuckin' fuzzy dice.*

He let go of the cross.

Beano started the car, gripped the greasy steering wheel, and drove very slowly down the narrow dirt lane, his eyes flicking constantly to the wooden cross.

FORTY-TWO

Cinco Becknell sat on a bench on the north side of the Plaza, the woman beside him. They looked south toward the Montoya Gallery, the gallery closed, the door locked. They had been sitting there for an hour, neither speaking, the woman holding a small plastic bag in her lap, the bloody pistol inside. She had not asked him about the pistol. But she would.

"He saw them dump a body," Cinco said, his voice tired.

"The woman in the desert?"

"Yeah. Jimmy was there. They damn near ran over him, coasting the car down a dirt road, no lights."

"They saw him?" Elena asked.

"Yeah. And then they wanted him dead."

"She was not the only one," Elena said.

"How many more?"

"Three. That Cord knows of. He thinks they will find others, sooner or later." Elena paused, the sun against her skin, the smell of her brushing his face. "We can't play games anymore. We have to work with Cord. Those bastards have to be stopped."

"Cord and I had a talk, down by the river, a couple of days ago."

"I know. He told Matt, and Matt told me. He said you identified Little Jimmy . . ."

"One of them. He's stopped."

"What do you mean?"

He nodded toward the pistol. "That's Angelo's pistol. I think that's his blood."

For a moment, she did not breathe. "Did you . . ."

"No."

The woman shuddered. "Cord will think you did. But if you didn't, who . . ."

"I don't know. We may never know. And whoever did it took away the body. I never actually saw it. Just the blood, and the gun." He was breathing deeply now, the images of the blood coming quickly. "And there was only one reason to take the body. So it would never be found."

Elena slowly stuffed the gun into her purse. "How did you get the gun?"

"It was just lying there, on the hood of his truck. Had to have been left there intentionally."

Elena thought about it. "The killer hides the body, but leaves the gun in plain sight. Doesn't make any sense.

"Nothing about any of this makes any sense. It's almost as though we're living in two different worlds and we didn't create either of them."

"Why didn't you give the gun to Cord?"

"I don't know why. Maybe I just don't like him. You can do it." He paused. "The truck is still there, half mile from the ranch house."

Elena felt her body stiffen. "They know about the ranch? I thought you would be . . . I thought it would be safe out there."

Cinco remembered the first time he had seen Angelo's truck at the ranch.

"They've known about the ranch for a long time. Maybe as long as I have."

He turned, facing her directly. "You need to listen carefully to what I'm saying." He did not know if he could make himself say the words. "You need to know who I am, how I think, what I have become. You say I'm Cinco, someone you knew. But I'm not sure if you know me now." He paused again. "If I had found him first, Angelo, I would have killed him, without hesitation, without blinking. I would have looked him dead in the face while I snuffed him out. I would have watched the light go out of his eyes while I had my hands around his throat and I would have been glad. And I would never have made him disappear. I would have left him lying there, bloating in the sun."

She slowly took his hand, held it softly, waiting for him to go on.

"When I first woke up, in El Paso, I thought maybe I couldn't do it, couldn't kill anybody. I was wrong."

He sat, breathing deeply, the late air carrying soft sounds of a piano somewhere. "Jesus," he said, "I'm sorry. I don't know how I got to be this way. I don't know where this stuff comes from . . ."

She wondered if this were the time. "Cinco . . ."

He turned at the sound of his name. He was trying to get used to it.

". . . do you know a tall, black woman? Maybe six feet. Good looking."

He thought about it. There was an image there, but he could not place it. "I don't think so. Why?"

Before he could answer, Anthony Cordova appeared in front of them.

"Don't you have a funeral to arrange?" Cord asked.

"Only if I'm not in jail," Cinco answered.

"Maybe later," Cord said, glancing at Elena. "And it's looking more and more likely."

Cord took out his cell phone and flipped it open, punched a few buttons. He looked at the phone, seemed satisfied. "There's something I want you to see." He handed the phone to Cinco. "Is this why you needed more time?"

Cinco did not bother pretending he had held such a thing before. He turned the phone in his hand, looking at the edges, the ends.

Cord took the phone, held the tiny screen toward Cinco's face, and handed it back to him.

Cinco stared into the screen, not understanding, or not believing, what he saw.

"It's not the shooter," Cord said. "It's the other one."

Cinco stared at the picture. "How did you find him?"

"Anonymous phone call," Cord said. "You do know how to use a phone, don't you?"

* * *

Hale Mary stood under the rusting windmill in the hot mid-day light, her hand resting lightly on the rim of the metal stock tank. She stood motionless for long minutes, listening, her eyes scanning the rolling hills, the low-growing brush, the earth around the tank. There was not a single sign of another human in any direction, no tracks, not even cattle. Nothing had visited the stock tank in days, maybe weeks.

The windmill was not turning, not pumping, but the water in the tank was almost to the rim, a few random bits of leaves floating quietly on the clear surface. She dipped her fingers gently into the water. It was warm. It was perfect.

A few sun-grayed planks were piled next to the tank, left over from a lost dream of building something on the land. Hale Mary put down her gunny sack on the planks and carefully opened it. She took out soap, shampoo, a hair brush, a towel.

And then Hale Mary began to undress.

She pulled off her fingerless gloves, flipped her hat away and let her thick, brown hair fall to her shoulders, dropped the long shawl, sat on the planks and took off her high-topped shoes and heavy socks. Her feet seemed small, not the sort of feet that would support Mary's thick body. She stood again, unbuttoned her heavy shirt, and then another shirt, and then another, shucking them from her body like layers of skin.

Skirts dropped to the wooden planks. More skirts. And a pair of pants.

And then Hale Mary stood in the sunshine, wearing only an expensive bra and silk panties, her full breasts and slender waist accentuating her round, taut hips.

And, finally, she was naked.

Hale Mary slipped over the edge of the stock tank and lowered herself gently into the warm water. She turned, lazed, soaked. She climbed out of the water and stood on the planks, soaping herself, shampooing her hair. She took a small plastic milk jug from the gunny sack, filled it with water and poured it over herself, again and again. When she was sure there was no more soap on her, she lifted her leg and scissored back into the tank, feeling the hard metal up against her crotch. The feeling aroused nothing in her. For a long time, she soaked in the tank, keeping an eye on the sun.

It was time.

They knew, sooner or later, he would come down the only road there was. They knew he couldn't resist.

Mary got out of the tank, dried herself carefully, and once again reached into the gunny sack.

* * *

Beano Clapper jammed the battered car down the dirt track, the track so narrow that low-growing *piñons* and alligator junipers brushed the fenders. Just around the turn the track entered a slightly wider dirt road, but there was a rutted patch just ahead and Angelo's car had bottomed out there. But Beano wouldn't take it slowly. He liked it when the car bottomed out, bouncing, the busted bumper rattling. Didn't make any difference now, he reasoned, damn car was already trashed. He drove the nose of the car out through the brush toward the road.

Beano couldn't believe what he saw. Directly across the narrow road a woman stood in the shade of a large *piñon*.

Beano stopped the car, eyes fixed on the woman. The woman stood quietly, watching the car.

She was tall, slender, long shiny brown hair flowing to her shoulders. She wore a thin dress with a deep neckline, the slight breeze molding the filmy dress to her long legs. She seemed posed, one leg pointed out to the side, a milky white arm resting lightly on a tree limb.

Beano could see her cleavage all the way across the road. Beano could see that she was a real looker.

Slowly, the woman raised her hand, a sort of wave, but not really. To Beano, it was an invitation. He couldn't believe his luck. A good looking woman, out here in the boonies, probably stranded. There can't be nobody else around, Beano reasoned, else they would be with her. She's alone. She's just all fuckin' by herself. Alone.

Beano shoved at the car door, forcing it open against some small tree limbs. He got out of the car, leaving the engine running.

"Hey, there, lady," Beano said, trying to keep the excitement out of his voice. "You need some help?"

The woman said nothing. Beano stepped through the limbs and out into the road. "I got a car here. Take you anywhere you want."

The woman said nothing, her hand still in the air.

Beano knew the woman had nowhere to go. He could chase her down if he had to. "Now look, I ain't got all day. If you . . . just get in the car and . . ."

The woman turned her hand and pointed past Beano's shoulder, her long, slender finger steady, no expression on her face.

Beano turned his head to look over his shoulder. "What the hell you pointing . . ."

The enormous crescent wrench, long and clean, gleaming in the sun, whipped down across the bridge of Beano's nose. The nose flattened, blood shooting down across Beano's mouth. But Beano didn't know that. His brain had already turned off.

＊ ＊ ＊

His face hurt. Jesus H. Christ, his face hurt worse than he could ever remember. And his head. His head hurt, too, right in the dark center of it, but not like his face. He started to open his eyes, only they wouldn't open. Not all the way, anyway. Wouldn't open more than thin slits. And what he could see through the slits was blurred. He tried to raise his arm to rub his eyes but his arm wouldn't move. It was fixed against his body somehow, tightly. Just like the other arm. Just like his legs. Beano was duct-taped in place.

He felt the panic come from his stomach and up through his brain, so big, so quickly, that it covered even the pain that was already there. He twisted hard, pulling against whatever was holding him; tried to ram his body forward; tried to swing his legs out to the side. His feet were taped together. He could move his legs up and down a little. Other than that, nothing worked. Through his almost-open eyes, through his blurred vision, through the shattered windshield—he was in the car, they had him in the car—he could see figures. People. They just stood out there, looking in at him.

But Beano's mouth worked. He had to breathe through it. "What the fuck . . . ?"

"See if you can fix his eyes," a man's voice said. "He needs to see. He needs to know."

Beano felt a wet cloth across his face, gently rubbing his eyes. Beano's eyes began to sting.

"His eyes is almost swole shut," another man said. "You done a good job with that wrench. Dang near killed him."

"Could'a killed him if I wanted. Didn't want to. Wanted him to be alive. Wanted him to see this."

The wet cloth moved gently across his eyes a few more times. He could feel the fingers inside the cloth, probing carefully at the corners of his eyes, wiping away the blood and mucous that had dried there, his eyes stinging more.

"Where'd she get the water to put on that rag?" one of the men asked.

"That ain't water," the other man said, laughing.

The cloth was taken away. It was still daylight, enough late sun for Beano to see faces. He blinked hard, trying to clear the stinging. Two men and a woman stood outside the car, looking in at him. The woman was the bitch he had tried to pick up. Beano was thinking again—he knew the woman had set him up. She was closer now, holding the wet cloth, her head next to the open driver's window, looking directly at him, her face expressionless. Behind her, the men, one older and dumpy, bib overalls. The other tall, hard boned, rangy. He didn't know them; had never seen them before.

Beano realized that he could turn his head. He tried to see where he was, where the car was, but everything looked the same, scrub trees, puffy soil stretching away from the car, late sun turning everything to a gold that would eventually deepen into a blood color. Somewhere out there in front of the car the land seemed to fall away. In the distance he could see trees on a far ridge. None of it made any sense to him.

He turned back to the woman. "What the fuck you people think you're doin'? I don't know you goddamn people! You goddamn well better untie me right now. I got friends. We don't forget shit like this."

The woman whipped the wet rag across Beano's face, turning on her toes as she did it, a smooth, practiced turn, dancing.

Beano screamed, blood coming again from his mangled nose. "All right, all right! Just tell me what you want. It can't be money! I ain't got no money to speak of!"

The woman held up her hand. Beano shut up.

The Mechanic stepped up next to the woman. "No, you don't know me," he said, "and you didn't know Pablo, either."

"Pablo? Well, now, that's right. I don't know no Pablo. See, you got the wrong guy here." Beano tried to keep his voice softer, more polite.

"No, you didn't know him, but you killed him, you motherfucking son-of-a-bitch shit-eating maggot. You crushed his bones behind a trash bin. A bunch of his bones was sticking out though his skin. His head was cracked. And through all that crushing he was still alive, right up until all his blood run out."

Beano had another flash of his . . . thinking. And he knew, right then and there, that whatever had happened to him before, in all his life, was nothing compared to what was going to happen to him now.

"It was a mistake," Beano said, his voice whining, his whole body quivering. "It wasn't supposed to be him. Was supposed to be some other guy. It was all a mistake. You can't kill somebody because they made a mistake!"

"Yeah, it was a mistake," the Mechanic said, "and you went and killed Pablo just because he knew where Jimmy's hide was."

"Oh, shit," Beano whined, "it was . . ."

"Yeah, but you corrected the mistake, didn't you?" the Mechanic said reaching through the window and grabbing the front of Beano's shirt. "Turn your head, maggot." Beano turned his head. "See this woman here? Do you know her?"

Beano tried to focus. It was the woman he had seen back there on the road, but he didn't know her, had never seen her before.

The Engineer stepped up next to the woman. He had Hale Mary's big floppy hat. He put it on the woman, helping her stuff her hair up inside. "You think hard, now. You think about a night on a bridge there on the Santa Fe River. You think about you and your fat friend throwing a woman over the rail, no hesitation, just throwing her over, like garbage, leaving her down there, maybe to die. You think about that."

Beano was thinking again. It couldn't be her. It couldn't be. But it was.

The woman reached inside the car, leaning across Beano, her breasts rubbing against him. Carefully, she took the big wooden cross from the mirror and pulled it to her as she backed out of the car. She looked at Beano, held the cross in front of his face, and then pressed the cross to her chest, covering it with her hands, her body rocking slowly back and forth, tears starting from her eyes.

"Yeah, Little Jimmy," the Engineer said. "The woman don't talk. But then you know that. If she could, that's what she would say— Little Jimmy. Her friend."

Oh Jesus oh Jesus oh Jesus. It was all Beano could allow to run through his mind.

Beano heard a metallic sound. He twisted his head as far as he could. The Mechanic was opening the trunk. Beano thought there was something heavy in his hand.

The Mechanic reached into the trunk and rummaged through the trash that Angelo had collected—food wrappers, old towels, empty plastic oil bottles. None of that interested him. He kept searching . . . then saw what he was looking for. He reached toward the back, wrapping his long fingers around an unopened bottle of cheap whiskey. The Mechanic handed the bottle to the Engineer.

"For later," the Mechanic said.

There was no ceremony. No hesitation. No second thoughts. The Mechanic raised the gas can he was holding and emptied it into the trunk of the car.

Beano's life caught in his throat.

The Engineer opened the passenger's door, reached inside and turned the key. The car started.

"Put your feet on the brake."

Beano did.

The Engineer pulled the gear shift into Drive. Beano could feel the transmission thunk into gear—and then he noticed that the steering wheel was lashed into place.

"You been eating and making shit on this planet way too long, dog boy. It's time for it to end. So, here's where you get to choose. See out there about 30 yards?" The Engineer pointed out in front of the car. "That's the edge of the Baca Cliffs. Off them cliffs is the river, the good old Rio Grande, about a hundred feet or so straight down. You got a choice, dog boy—burn in the car, or drive off the cliff."

The Mechanic threw a burning match into the trunk of the car.

Flames blew up from the open trunk, whirling above the car, bright orange clouds of unbearable heat reaching into the sky. In the car, Beano could hear the fire, begin to feel the heat claw its way through the back seat. In minutes—no, in seconds—the fire would be inside the car, searching for Beano. He could not die in the fire. He couldn't. He couldn't die like the hillbilly. He had to take a chance.

He had to make a choice.

The woman leaned forward and put her face next to Beano's, oblivious to the heat. Beano could see the tear streaks on her cheeks, feel her breath on his face. Her mouth opened, muscles in her throat seemed to writhe, her jaw worked slightly up and down. And then Beano heard two simple words, words formed by a voice long unused and raspy, the sounds made by the opening of a tiny, ancient door.

"Fuck you," the woman said.

She stepped back.

For long seconds, no one moved, the two men and the woman standing back from the fire, Beano sitting, his eyes wide from fear.

Only the fire moved, growing, making that fire sound, the sound that anyone would recognize.

And then Beano smelled his own hair burning.

Beano lifted his feet from the brake and stomped on the accelerator.

The Mechanic, the Engineer and Hale Mary watched as the car's rear wheels dig into the loam, gathering traction, the car fishtailing slightly as it gathered speed, engine blasting in some sort of odd death rale, flames bursting and trailing, the car a crude rocket heading for its own version of space.

As the car neared the edge of the cliff the engine blew, a cloud of black smoke pouring from underneath, curling up, adding another dimension of color to the flames.

The car shot over the edge of the cliff. At the last moment, the brake lights came on.

FORTY-THREE

People were dying. Some of them should have died, some not.

His mind flashed to the picture on Cord's phone, the piece of shit car nose down in the river, only the rear doors and trunk showing, the car slightly buckled, everything not covered by water charred to a blackness that fit perfectly with what, Cord said, had been in the front seat.

Beano was dead, and Cord thought Cinco had done it. But there was no real connection between Cinco and the killing and Cord did not arrest Cinco. Or maybe Cord was just giving him "more rope."

Angelo was probably dead, but Cinco thought no one would ever know for sure.

And Jimmy.

And the women in the desert.

Cinco Becknell made his rounds, Jimmy's rounds. He made them slowly, thinking the little man with the grating voice would be just around the corner, waiting, irritated that Cinco was taking too long. But Jimmy had disappeared for the last time.

After a few days he admitted to himself that the rounds were useless, that he was making them only in some perverse attempt at grieving.

Now and then he went by the gallery, sometimes watching Elena through the windows, sometimes going inside for the comfort of being there, with her. The floor had been scrubbed and bleached; the photograph restored, the glass replaced, the frame repaired, hanging again on the back wall over the bullet hole.

The picture. *His* picture, she said. Cinco, with two guys he did not remember, did not recognize.

Cord and the sheriff had been to the ranch. They had checked the old truck, taken evidence from the crime scene—if it was a crime scene. The truck was still there.

Cinco left the city and went up into the mountains, drinking from small streams, sleeping when he needed to and in places where he felt safe, constantly marveling at his security there, the comfort he felt in the mountains, in the woods.

But he ran out of things to do. Whatever life he was living in Santa Fe or at the ranch, he had to get on with it.

Angelo and Beano were gone. He was safe.

* * *

He came down out of the mountains and kept to the east, intersecting the Santa Fe River at the far edge of town. He walked downstream, knowing he would pass under the bridge, Jimmy's bridge, the place where Jimmy sat in the shade, napped, told his stories of swiping food from tourists. Cinco would sit in the same shade. It would not be, he promised himself, the last time he would ever sit there.

He saw the bulk of her in the shade, the heavy body, the large hat, the layers of clothing. She was watching him come. He could see that she was not nervous, not ready to run. She seemed calm, waiting. Hale Mary.

She was on one side of the stream, he on the other. He wondered if she knew about Jimmy.

He slowed his walk, moving carefully toward the bridge, not changing his posture, giving no outward sign that he intended anything except to walk past her. As he drew even he glanced at her, nodded, and kept going.

She held up her hand.

He stopped, turning to face her.

"Mary," he said, knowing she would not answer.

The woman leaned over and reached down into her shopping bag. She came up with something in her hand, something that dangled.

The wooden cross. Jimmy's cross.

He stared at it, feeling his eyes start to sting slightly.

"Mary, where did you get that?"

Hale Mary held the cross out to him and flicked her hand. *Take it.*

"Are you sure?'

She flicked her hand again.

He stepped into the stream in front of her. Slowly, carefully, he took the cross.

"I have a pad and pencil," he said. "Will you write it down, where you got this?"

The woman gave a sharp shake of her head, the brim of her hat flapping slightly.

"Mary, the last time I saw this, it was in Angelo's car . . ."

The woman's eyes seemed to light up, her chin came up, she stood straighter, taller.

And then he understood.

FORTY-FOUR

It was to be a funeral.

Elena had suggested it. Closure, she said, although he was not sure there was ever closure on anything in a human life.

It was Elena who had paid for everything, Elena who was with him, every step of the way. He thought Jimmy would approve.

It was Elena who had been telling him of the mountain, of his friends, telling him easily, in bits and pieces, of the first part of his life, his life with Alvarez and Wendell, and her. There are things we can do, she had said, things we can look at, libraries, high school yearbooks, university records. We can reconstruct a life, she said, one piece at a time.

But he was not interested. Not yet. There would be time for that.

She had not yet told him about Grace, about Grace's so-called search for a journal that probably did not exist. She wanted to be careful; she almost had him back, and she did not want to lose him again.

* * *

Cinco Becknell left the heavy stand of trees long before daylight and was high on the mountain, climbing steadily above tree line with no hint of light showing in the east. The cold night air kept him energized and it was a long time before he began to sweat. When

347

the sweat did come he got more comfortable, his muscles looser, his breathing deeper, his feet feeling every step of the trail through the thin tennis shoes.

The climbing was long but the going was easy and he worked at it gently in the dark, his body in low gear and pulling steadily toward the summit high and above him in the darkness.

The black sky pressed down against his skull and the stars glittered against his face. When he looked up the stars seemed flat against him and he thought he could taste the stars but he could not and in the end he shifted his small pack, drank some water and strapped the dark sky down over his head and kept going.

He reached the silent summit of the mountain before the light was anywhere and it pleased him to sit there in chilled isolation, breathing the thin black air and waiting for the light. He found a cleft between some boulders and settled himself in there, feeling the stones, a stone cradle that held him, and facing east.

He sat at 12,200 feet, 1,500 feet above tree line, and he knew, at that moment, he probably was higher than anyone else in the county. Maybe the state. It was important to him.

He had been here before. He was sure of it. Because she had told him.

Somewhere below him lay Santa Fe. He could see some of its lights, like a cluster of inverted stars, down far and away. He was alone in the wilderness, but less than 20 miles from sixty thousand people.

He fished his water bottle out of the pack and drank. To sit on a summit waiting on the sun and drinking good water . . . Maybe there was no way to improve on that, but he would try.

The black at the edge of the world began to roll slowly back and then faster and then it was first light, one of his two favorite times of day. Stars faded and were sucked, powerless, into the quickening sky. Somewhere out there sunlight was racing across prairie grass and he knew it would be on him soon.

He got up from the boulders and found the highest point on the mountain, a bare knob that sloped down and rolled away to the north. Over the years climbers had added stones to the point of the summit and now there was a wide cairn almost as tall as he was. He climbed on top of the cairn. There was no wind and in the ringing stillness he thought he could hear the day thundering down on him from behind the flare of crystal light to the east.

* * *

They had come up the evening before, Cinco hearing the woman following steadily behind him. He had asked her to come and she had not hesitated, seeming to feel, as she always did, what he felt. Before he felt it.

They hiked the Windsor Trail until they came to the hard rise that gained the last stand of trees. In the early afternoon they had met a few hikers but later in the softer light near the trees they had met no one. The hikers in their expensive shoes and designer jackets had spoken politely to Elena but had barely nodded to him, moved aside for him to pass, tried not to stare at his over-sized pants, rolled up blanket and meager little pack. They seemed puzzled—what was he doing with such a woman, a woman dressed as they were? Not a single person spoke to him.

He sat on a deadfall, the trunk so old and weathered it was almost soft, and the woman sat beside him. He heard her breath come in strong pulls, the sort of breathing she might have toward the end of love making—not at the very end, but just before. The thought reached down deep inside him. He put his arm around the woman, felt her warmth, felt the history in her. His history.

349

The woman had said little since they had started up the mountain. She seemed to speak only to answer his brief questions. What was his father's name? His mother's? What happened to them?

She was there, and that was enough. But he knew she was holding something back.

They camped alone in the edge of the high trees, making no fire. They ate some hard cheese and harder jerky and drank some water and then slept, Elena in her sleeping bag, he rolled in his thin blanket, a foot-thick layer of pine needles cushioning him. Once he was awakened by an owl making its flat noise and he sat up and waited and tried to see it, but he never did.

The woman was already awake, sitting motionless. He moved beside her, put his arm around her, kissed her.

"What is it that you need to tell me?"

She said nothing. He kissed her again.

"Cinco," she said, her voice no more than a whisper in the night, "the black woman that I asked you about, the woman you said you did not know. She said . . . she said there was a journal . . ."

What was it that Cord had asked him as he lay there on the gurney?

"What journal?" Cord wanted to know.

"Journal?"

And she told him about the black woman, and the journal, and the gun.

He found the stump, lay down in front of it and reached inside, working his arm upward. Jammed up inside the stump was a heavy glass jar, the kind Maria used for canning. Except this jar was heavier, the crude glass almost too thick to see through, the screw-on top made of some metal that he couldn't identify. He pulled out the jar. It was empty. It was always empty when he found it, no matter what he had put into it the last time. He rolled over and dug down inside the front of his pants to the tiny pocket he had sewn inside. He pulled some small scraps of paper—pages ripped from some sort of manual—from the pocket. Around the edges of the pages he had written in tiny script a segment of his life, what was happening to him, what he saw, what he felt, and what they were doing there in the town next to the camp. And who they killed. He put the scrap of paper inside the jar . . .

A journal. The key to the middle part of his life. The key to life itself.

They want it. Where is it? Who the hell are "they?" Do "they" exist? Is the black woman a nut case?

"There may have been a journal, maybe in another time and place. But I came here with nothing. Whatever the woman was looking for, it isn't here.

"It's over." He hoped Elena would believe him.

He kissed her. She took his hand and pressed it against her breast. He knew it was not an invitation, but a promise. Later, when things were right. When all of this was over. He kissed her again.

✳ ✳ ✳

In the middle of the night he had started up the mountain. She had stayed in the high camp, knowing this was something he had to do alone.

She had told him about the mountain, that it was always one of the things he loved most, looking toward a horizon he could not see and watching the light paint its way up and over and flow toward him wherever he was.

She had told him that, back then, in the first part of his life, she was not there with him on the mountain, never allowed to go with him and Alvarez. And Wendell.

And she had told him and told him and told him, everything she remembered about the first part of his life, told him how he loved it.

Wendell and Alvarez. He didn't remember any of it. But he believed her. And now he had some sort of a past.

And he loved it now, in this third part of his life, seeing the light come, no matter where he was. Each time he saw the light come he knew he had another day, or at least a piece of it, and he was grateful. If the light could come again then anything was possible.

The light came now.

He took some things from his pack, his breakfast, hard cheese and heavy bread. He ate slowly, in time with the light, watching the light grow.

He waited, sitting on the highest point of the mountain, facing east. He drank more water.

The light kept coming.

Some time passed; he didn't know how much and he didn't care.

And then the sun came, pushing the light in front of it. The sun lit his face before it lit his chest and then flowed golden and slowly down him lighting each inch of him until he was alive with the light and the heat and for some short minutes he was the only thing west of the Pecos River that was in the sunlight. He owned it. As he warmed, he took off his ragged jacket and then his shirt and then he was sitting half naked on the cairn in the sunlight.

He fished a short tube of thin plastic pipe out of the pack. The tube was only an inch in diameter and six inches long, capped at both ends with discarded crutch tips he had picked up behind a fire station. He took off one of the caps and tipped the tube into his hand and a single cigar slid out, short, thick, dark brown. He lit the cigar with a wooden match, drawing in smoke so rich that it could kill hunger, spin the brain, cause eyelids to fall gently.

He sat warming in the sun, cigar smoke rising almost directly above him in the still air, the light washing down the mountain now and he knew that somewhere down there people were beginning to stir around. He would not stir around. He would smoke the cigar at 12,200 feet and maybe he would pass out and maybe he would not. Either way, he did not care. He would sit there until it was time for him to leave, and only he would decide that.

He would smoke the cigar for Jimmy.

The cigar went out, but he did not relight it.

He brought the ragged day pack in front of him and opened it, gently taking out a plain, squat clay pot with a lid and something wrapped in a rag. Out of the rag he took Little Jimmy's wooden cross. He held it for a while, up into the sun, gripping it, letting the rising sun warm his face and his hands and the worn wood of the cross. He opened the clay pot and carefully placed the cross down into the center of it, resting it gently on the ashes of Little Jimmy.

"Welcome to the mountain, *mi compadre major amigo.*"

He got to his knees and in the center of the cairn he began to carefully remove stones, placing each stone to the side in the exact order that they came out of the cairn. The stones came out easily, as though they were meant to be removed. Lying on his stomach, his arm dangling into the hole, he kept taking out stones until he had a hole in the center of the cairn almost as deep as his arm and as wide as his body. He came to a large, flat stone at the bottom of the hole and he thought the hole was deep enough. The flat stone was slightly tilted and he reached into the hole and straightened it, lifting it slightly. And that is when he found the eagle feather.

He held the feather in his hand. It was firm and full and perfect. He did not know how he knew it was an eagle feather, but he did know. He could not tell how old it was, but it did not seem damaged by water that might have seeped down into the cairn.

He had stumbled onto something that he should not disturb. He carefully put the feather back as he had found it and replaced the flat stone. He thought for a moment about Little Jimmy sharing the sacredness of the eagle feather and he decided it was good. He put the clay pot—he put Little Jimmy—into the center of the hole. Beside it, he placed the last of the cigar. And then he put the rocks back, as carefully as he could, fitting them into a sort of structure so as not to break the pot.

He did not sit back down on the cairn. Instead, he moved down and off to the side, sat on some flat stones and watched the sun heat the stones of the cairn. He wondered if he should say anything over Little Jimmy, waiting for something to come to him. Nothing did.

Will it still be a funeral if I say nothing? He grinned. Jimmy would think that was funny.

He stared at the cairn. He wondered, when he took the stones out to make room for Jimmy, did he touch any of the stones that he had put there when he and Wendell and Alvarez had climbed the mountain to celebrate his and Wendell's birthdays? Stones they all had touched, as she had described it to him?

He and Wendell sipped cognac all the way up the mountain. Alvarez, a year younger than both of them, being the band leader, pushing them along, singing, calling them old men.

He sang in Spanish, Alvarez sang in English, and Wendell sang in . . . well, he said it was Tewa, but they were never really sure.

Birthday on the mountain, three friends celebrating by doing absolutely nothing, but doing it extremely well.

And before they left, each of them placed a single stone on the cairn, Wendell putting down an eagle feather and carefully, gently, placing his stone on top of it.

He stared at the cairn baking in the morning sun, but he was not really seeing the stones, he was seeing a memory. A memory. He had had a memory. And this time he knew it was a memory, not just a fragment, but a true memory.

And then something else glittered in his mind and he was back in the ancient cave across the river from the ranch . . .

There were some rounded scratches, one leading into the other, like a climbing thunderstorm of clouds. Maybe a mountain. Next to the clouds there was some sort of short, square tower. Lines crossed the tower, each line precise and never running off the square. Maybe a garden plot. Clouds over a garden. Rain. Food. A time of plenty. Survival.

Or maybe stones. In a pile. He took out his notebook and looked at his sketches of the petroglyphs. His breath caught in his throat.

How many goddamn signs do I need?

He got up and stood beside the cairn, reached out, put his hands on the warm stones. For a moment he closed his eyes. It could not be true, but he knew it was.

He climbed slowly to the top of the cairn and once again, carefully, reverently, began removing stones. He was, after all, digging up Little Jimmy's grave. But he thought Jimmy would not mind.

Sweat poured from his body, but it was not from exertion. It was from fear of finding what he thought was in the cairn. It was from fear of *not* finding it.

He came to the pot, and the cigar, and he took them out of the hole.

Sorry, Jimmy.

And then the eagle feather. And the flat rock. Under the flat rock the stones were small, almost gravel, and he knew no climber would have used such small stones to mark the cairn. He brushed the stones aside.

Or maybe not a garden plot. A page from a book.

He felt the thing before he actually saw it, his hand brushing the smooth top, knowing that whatever it was, it was not stone. He cleared the gravel from the lid of a five-gallon plastic bucket.

Before he pulled the bucket from the hole he stood up and scanned the mountain, the ridge, and the open mountainside down to the trees. He lay on his stomach and scanned the mountain again, slowly, staring intently at each patch of dark shade down below him. Long minutes passed. There was no one. He was alone against the sky.

He pulled the bucket from the hole and climbed down from the cairn. He set the bucket beside the cairn and carefully pried open the lid.

The bucket was stuffed with paper, bits and pieces, scrap, tissue, cardboard, fragments, full sheets, pages from books. He carefully lifted a handful and held it up into the light. On each piece, each scrap, words, handwritten in tiny script, filled every blank space of both sides.

His words.

This is what they want from me. This what keeps me alive.

We were wrong about the black woman.

He forced himself not to start reading the words. It was not the time, or the place, not here on the mountain of his youth, not here at Little Jimmy's grave. If he lived, if "they" did not kill him, there would be plenty of time. Time was all he had.

He put the scraps back, and then noticed, tucked into the side of the bucket, carefully cushioned by all the paper, a jar of thick glass, a sort of Mason jar, its heavy metal top screwed firmly in place, more scraps of paper inside.

In front of him, in a cheap plastic bucket, he had the middle part of his life. He had the journal of Cinco Becknell. For that was his name.

Cinco sat, staring at the collection of paper scraps.

Now, he thought, *now I will remember.*

But he did not.

* * *

It took almost an hour for him to replace the stones, this time putting Little Jimmy deeper into the cairn, deeper into his place at the top of the world. When he was done, he inspected the cairn from all sides. No one, he thought, would be able to tell the stones had been moved, rearranged. It looked like any other cairn.

He started down the mountain, carrying the bucket. He hoped he met no one. He did not want to explain the bucket to anyone but Elena.

As he moved down the mountain he kept an eye on the cairn, receding in the distance. Just before he lost sight of it he stopped and put down the bucket. From his pack he took a tiny bottle of cognac, sealed with wax. He opened the bottle and held it in front of his face, looking over the top at the cairn glowing in the high distance. He stood facing the light, held the cognac up into the rising sun, then brought the bottle to his lips.

"Wendell", he said.

"Alvarez."

He paused, took a heavy breath deeply into his lungs.

"Jimmy", he said softly.

And he drank.

FORTY-FIVE

He hitched a ride in an ancient pickup truck driven by an equally ancient Hispanic.

"*Señor, como se llama usted?*" the old man asked, his voice formal.

The tall man hesitated. The word "Stick" flashed across his mind.

"Cinco," he said. "Cinco." He paused. "Becknell."

The old man looked at him oddly and did not speak another word until he let Cinco out.

"*Bienvenido,*" the old man said.

"*Gracias, Maestro.*"

He had to walk the last two miles, his pack on his back, a heavy box of paperback books in his arms. His legs ached, sweat ran down his face, but he kept his feet moving on the dirt track that was the road to the ranch. Autumn was coming on, the air cooler now, somehow richer, comfortable.

The gate was closed and locked, but Cinco could see marks in the dirt where it had been pulled open in the past few days. Cinco put down his books. He leaned on the gate and stared down along the road, seeing it grow fainter until it could barely be called a road when it ended at the cottonwood grove, and the house. There was nothing for him to do but keep going. He had promised her he would.

He had promised. She owned the ranch, but did not live on it. She lived somewhere else; he did not know where. But she seemed eager for him to be on the ranch, to spend time there, to walk under the cottonwoods, to wander through the old house. An empty house. Her deal was simple—he could live at the ranch as long as he worked, took care of the place, cleaned it up, re-strung some of the fences, maybe fixed up the house a little.

He pushed his box of books under the rusting wire and climbed over the wooden gate. He left the KEEP THE HELL OUT sign where it was.

He never liked walking down the last half-mile of road to the house. He thought the road was too exposed, remembering Angelo's old truck.

It was still there.

It had been pulled out of the trees and sat in a small clearing. Tatters of old crime scene tape fluttered in the brush like little yellow flags advertising the scene of old death. He walked a short way down the road and put down the box of books and his pack. He went back to the truck and walked around it, looking at every part of it. The scalp, or whatever it was, was gone.

Well, she said to clean the place up a bit.

He took some matches from his pocket and set the truck on fire.

* * *

He left the books under the corner of the *portal* and walked softly around the old house, kicking back the dry brush that in some places came up against the adobe walls. As he circled the house he thought he could smell a sweet smoke, but he knew the smell of smoke carried for long distances and he thought nothing of it.

For some reason, he didn't want to make noise, getting the same feeling he always got when he went inside a church, some need for silence. He supposed some would call it reverence, but

359

he thought had never felt very reverent inside a church. He tried to concentrate on it, that feeling of having been inside a church. But nothing came. He thought maybe it was the silence, the need for silence, as though he were afraid God would discover him there, inside the church, where he didn't want to be found. And then he would have to deal with God, and he didn't know how to do that.

He felt that way now, coming back to the *portal*, climbing the low steps and standing in front of the wooden door worn slick by the touch of countless hands. He hesitated, his breath coming slowly in his throat. His eyes rose slowly, following the door upward, to the heavy lintel above the door, the lintel covered with a thick layer of dust, spider webs, and the detritus of countless bird nests built above it over the years.

Something was carved under the dust.

He reached up and slowly dragged his hand across the ancient wood, dust and bits of twigs raining down on him, uncovering the carved letters.

Becknell.

It said *Becknell.*

"Bienvenida a hogar," the old man had said. Welcome home.

He felt as though he had been hit, feeling the strength run out of his legs . . . and the thick wooden front door whipped open and snapped back inside the house.

Cinco jerked himself backward a couple of steps, his arms coming up in front of him. The Indian stood in the doorway, stripped to the waist, sweat running in streams down his chest, raven hair hanging loosely to his shoulders, old cotton pants and worn moccasins, a burning smudge stick still in his hand.

"I'd advise you to wait a minute," Matt Klah said. "Place is full of smoke."

Cinco said nothing, arms still up in front of him. Klah was the last person he expected, or wanted, to see here.

Klah looked pointedly at Cinco's arms, the stance, the readiness.

"You've been wanting to do something like that since the first time we met," Klah said, his voice deep and direct, without a hint of concern. "Go ahead. You can punch around on an Indian and a lawyer at the same time. At least you can try. Average white boy redneck would think that was pure heaven."

"I'm not a white boy," Cinco said. He didn't know why he said it.

Klah seemed to be thinking something over. "Okay," he said, "let's start again. She sent me out here to purify the place. The house. Said it would be better for you, even if you didn't know it."

Cinco's arms came down slightly.

"The place is clean now. No bad spirits." Klah stepped through the door and moved slightly to the side, not wanting to move directly at Cinco. "Oh, yeah, I guess I should tell you that I cleaned out all the good spirits, too. You want good spirits in there, you'll have to call 'em yourself."

A tiny smile bent the corners of Cinco's mouth.

"One more thing," Klah said, his voice slightly softer. "Looks as though we're going to have to start your education. Don't know what you know, or what you don't know." He turned and reached inside the house, came out with a book. "So you can start with this. Written by a white woman. Looks like a white woman, acts like a white woman, but no one is really sure. Thinks more like an Indian. Doesn't matter. Good stuff in here."

He tossed the book toward Cinco. Cinco caught it in both hands.

"There, see? You must be relaxing a bit. Any other time, you would have stepped aside, let the book fall on the ground, afraid I'd be right behind it." He paused. "Am I right?"

Cinco never looked at the book, kept his eyes on Klah. The two men stared at each other for long seconds, but each knew their stares were not challenges. They were questions.

"I put some food in there. Some things to cook with. Elena sent it. Wouldn't want you to think I was helping too much."

Cinco stood silent.

Klah stepped off the old porch and laid the smoking smudge stick on a flat rock.

"Leave it there 'til it dies," he said, not looking at Cinco.

Klah turned and looked toward the narrow stream flowing through the edge of the cottonwoods.

Cinco raised his head, pointed with his chin toward the door. "Up there. It says 'Becknell'."

"Yeah, it does. This is the old Becknell ranch." Klah paused. "Cinco," Klah said, almost to himself. "Cinco. I remember that name, but I don't remember you."

"Becknell had a ranch?"

Klah ignored the question. "Just like you don't remember my brother. Look," the Indian said, "you have your name back, but I don't have my brother back. Somewhere in that black box you call a memory, my brother is waiting. So I'm going to wait until you find him. You and me, we are truly going to become blood brothers until that happens."

Klah paused, took a deep breath. "No one seems to know what happened to the fat guy, Angelo. Maybe you know, maybe you don't. Considering what happened to the other one, Beano, maybe we don't want to know. Either way, he seems to be gone, and I'm thinking he's gone for good. Won't ever lay hands, or eyes, on Elena. And I'm grateful for that."

Cinco stood silently, his blank face admitting nothing, the book still in his hands.

"Okay, if that's the way you want it," Klah said. "Keep your mouth shut. Admit nothing. Don't say anything until you talk with your lawyer. Just remember this, white boy . . . I *am* your lawyer."

"I'm not a . . ." Cinco did not bother finishing the sentence. He slowly dropped his head, looking down at the book, then raised his head and looked into Klah's face, his right hand coming up, extending. Klah took a step forward and took Cinco's hand.

"My brother always had to take care of you. Is that my job, now?" Klah asked softly.

Klah walked away toward the stream, stepped across the water and stopped. He stood for a few seconds, his back to Cinco. Then he turned his head.

"About the spirits. You *will* call some, whether you want to or not. Just be sure you call the right kind."

Klah moved quickly away from the stream, off through the scrub and then smoothly up the far side of the canyon, seeming to float over the rough earth and rocks. Cinco watched him until he got to the top of the canyon wall, waiting for the Indian to turn back for a last look. But he did not. The Indian turned west, toward the river, and began to lope along the rim, his stride covering distance in a flow of motion. And then the Indian disappeared over the wall. As far as Cinco knew, there were no roads in that direction for miles.

* * *

He lay on his blanket inside the small room at the back of the house, the room with the old *comoda*, his head even with the open door. Outside, the last of the light faded from the canyon, the shadows of the cottonwoods growing longer across the old patio.

An odd sensation began to flow through him, something that was a surprise to him. But he recognized it immediately. He knew that he had sought it for a long time, even from that time he could not remember.

It was comfort. It was safety.

He took a candle from his pack and fixed it to the low wall beside his head with a forked stick. He pulled Klah's book up in front of his face. It was *The Book of Elders* by some woman named Sandy Johnson. He opened it at random, came to a section about an Indian named Pete Catches.

"*I love this life, with all of its misery,*" Catches had said, "*with all of its pain . . .*"

The candle burned out and he slept.

* * *

At first light the next morning he heard the coyotes howling and the owls hooting in the canyon. The sounds were familiar.

He went into the kitchen, a long, wide room at the back of the house. A *kiva* fireplace and an elevated shepherd's bunk anchored one corner of the room, the sleeping poles and supports still in place. In the ceiling above the back wall a piece of metal flue stuck down a few inches, the end of it covered with a piece of gunny sack held in place with baling wire. But whatever else had been in the kitchen, all of it was gone.

The box of supplies was in the center of the room. He rummaged through it, found some clothing and other things he was looking for and went outside to the old patio. He built a small fire in a long-unused fire pit and made himself a cup of coffee in a heavy enameled cup.

He sat on a thick piece of cottonwood trunk that must have been cut to make a table. He sipped the hot, black coffee and looked at the old house, the barn, the tiny stream, the cottonwoods, and across the stream at the field that ran up against the canyon wall. And at the canyon wall where Klah had disappeared. *Klah. Klah.* He rolled the name around in his mind. Maybe he would just whack that arrogant Indian across the mouth, see what happened, just for the hell of it.

Or maybe he would run up there, along that far ridge, as Klah had. Just to see what happened. But not today. Today, he had nothing to do. And all day to do it.

He finished his coffee, lay in the shade of the cottonwoods, and took a nap.

* * *

He found some tools leaning against the barn—axe, huge bow saw, shovel, pick, rake. They hadn't been there when he was last at the ranch. Klah must have put them there. A hint.

He looked at the old house, the sagging *portal*, adobe crumbling from the walls, dead cottonwood limbs on the roof. Okay, he would go to work, clean the place up a little. Maybe make it a little easier to live in. If he were going to stay here—and he was not sure about that —he owed the woman at least that much.

He thought about Little Jimmy. Jimmy, so good with his hammer and saw. He would have found another cigar for Jimmy to smoke, built a real bed for him, left the door open so Jimmy could leave—or come back—any time he wanted.

Jimmy.

Cinco spent the rest of the day clearing brush from around the house, gathering deadfall and bucking it up into fireplace lengths, pulling tumbleweed from the fragments of fence that seemed to hang and lean in every open space.

An honest day's work.

And then he lay in the pool.

FORTY-SIX

He sorted through the collection of clothing in the kitchen, put on some thin cotton pants with a drawstring—peasant pants, and he knew Klah had picked them out—*huaraches*, a t-shirt.

He ate some of the food in the kitchen and made himself another cup of coffee.

He sat on the corner of the porch at the front of the house, sipping his coffee, concentrating on the coyote that was loping across the far end of the canyon, down near the river. He could barely see the coyote through the soft, early fringes of darkness. He knew the coyote would probably not make a sound, not out in the open like that, but he would listen, anyway, for the sound of the coyote.

But that wasn't the sound that he heard.

What he heard was the sound of a gunshot. He thought he heard both sounds at once—the shot, and the sound of the bullet cracking off the post at the corner of the *portal*. The bullet didn't seem to ricochet, maybe dying deep inside the old post.

The gunshot was a flat sound, heavy, a sound booming from a short barrel.

Handgunheavycaliber. He thought this as he was falling backward, down off the porch and onto the dirt, rolling over and clawing his way around the corner of the house. There was a sharp stinging sensation in his right shoulder but he could not take the time to inspect it. He got to his feet and ran to the back corner of the house, hesitated. He looked across the stream to the open field, decided against it. Too much exposure. Even with a handgun, a good shooter could hit him. He moved quickly along the back wall of the house, across the old patio, heading for the door to the room where he slept. If he could get inside the house, at least the shooter would have to come inside to get him. Come inside, where Cinco could reach him.

He was less than 10 feet from the door when the next bullet dug into the *adobe* by the door frame, *adobe* and surface plaster spraying into him like tiny shrapnel. Seemingly without losing speed, Cinco turned and ran back toward the corner of the house, across the short distance to the barn, and around the wall near the stream.

There had been a shot at the front of the house, and then a shot at the back. Either the shooter was one smart *hombre*, knew that he would head for the back of the house, or there was more than one shooter.

He had never unlocked the barn; he had never had the keys. There was no way in.

Cinco ran along the wall, reached the corner, turned it, and stopped. He stood, his back against the heavy timbers of barn, heart beating heavily, eyes trying to focus in the dim light. Down-canyon, there was the river. And across the river, wilderness. If he could get across the river, he might have a chance.

He grabbed the corner of the barn and eased himself out, ready to run. His arm gave way and he fell out into full exposure and instantly he heard another shot, another bullet going by. He dropped to the ground and crawled back behind the barn, dirt sticking to the blood on his right hand.

Blood. It ran all the way down his arm from the jagged hole high and on the outside of his shoulder, the wound neatly taking away most of the use of his right arm, the wound an announcement of worse things to come.

It was too late in the autumn, almost winter. He knew that. But if he didn't get across now, he might never. It had started freezing at night and when the river froze the dogs could track him if he tried to cross. They had done it before. It had become a game. They knew he would run. He knew he would run. And then they turned the dogs loose. The last time, they had only used one dog, the big wolf hybrid, the dog they made him feed, the wolf-dog lunging at the fence every time he walked by. One dog. They knew the dog would catch him easily. They let the dog range out ahead, let the dog get to him long before they did, let the dog tear at him for long minutes. The last time, the dog had nearly chewed off his arm.

This time, he waited at the edge of the water. If he could get across now, before the dog . . .

He heard the dog coming, running free.

He plowed into the freezing water, then turned downstream for a few staggering steps, then out of the water again.

He got down on his knees and eased his head around the corner of the barn, his face only a foot off the ground.

The bullet hit the corner of the barn just above his head, an angled shot, maybe coming from across the stream, splinters digging into his scalp.

Instantly, Cinco rolled over, gathered himself, got up, ran a few steps, and dived behind a rotting cottonwood trunk that lay only a few yards from the barn. But he knew it was a wrong move. Now, there was no place for him to go and no room to go there. If he stayed where he was, he was dead.

Before he had a chance to change his own mind, Cinco was on his feet, running for the river, zigging, dodging behind every bush, tree, fence post that he could find, his feet digging into the soil, his mind waiting for the next shot, his body waiting for the ripping entry of the bullet. But he heard no more shots.

He made it to the river, driving his legs into the water—shallow, very shallow. And then, abruptly, he turned downstream, crashing through the muddy water.

The wolf-dog stopped at the edge of the water, yowling its anger into night air. It sniffed at the mud, breathing in his scent, knowing that he had gone into the water. The wolf-dog bounced on its front feet, rising, standing on his hind legs, frustration oozing from its hide, front feet coming down and splashing in the edge of the river. Again and again the wolf-dog bounced, howling now, its prey gone. At the height of a bounce, the wolf-dog extending upright as tall as a man, front paws in the air, mouth open in a prolonged howl, the man launched himself from the top of the rock and stuck the wolf-dog in the center of his back, long, skinny arms circling the animal. The man and the wolf-dog disappeared into the dark, muddy water.

Only the man waded to shore.

A lone, dark figure loped down the canyon, running effortlessly, the pace of a long distance runner out for a relaxing jog. A few yards from the water the figure slowed to a walk, then stopped, arms out in front, both hands holding the pistol. He stood there for long moments, silently, in a slight crouch, moving only his head and arms. His head turned to one side and then the other, eyes and ears sweeping the thin darkness, searching. And wherever the head turned, the pistol was already pointed there.

He moved slowly, the pistol still sweeping back and forth. He squatted at the edge of the river, examining the footprints that entered the water. The shooter knew that the tall man had not hesitated, knowing exactly where he was going. He had simply plunged into the water.

He had given the target too much room to run.

He rose slowly from the squat, relaxing, pistol dangling at his side, staring across the river into the dark patches of wilderness. He was still staring when Cinco launched his body through the air and tore into him from behind.

* * *

Cinco curled into rough spaces in the low jumble of rocks and tried to control his breathing and the shaking of his body, clasping his hand across bleeding shoulder. He had to control himself. If he made even the slightest sound, made the slightest motion, he knew the shooter would spot him. The guy was good. The guy was a pro.

But even pros relax now and then, Cinco thought. He didn't know why he thought that, but he had given up trying to figure out why he thought things. He would just think them and let the shit fall where it would.

The guy came loping down the canyon, then slowed, and then stopped, the pistol racking back and forth. Long, slender barrel.

Revolver, Cinco thought. *Better for pointing, better for shooting in bad light.*

Once, the guy pointed the pistol directly at Cinco's face. Cinco's body clenched. But the pistol swept on.

The guy must have been wearing black from head to toe—no hint of color, no flash of light. He stood silhouetted against the river, black framed against brown. He squatted. He stood up. He lowered the pistol to his side.

And Cinco moved.

He drove himself into the center of the guy's back. They flew forward, Cinco wrapping his good arm around a body that he knew was strong, sinewy. They hit the water, not very deep, but deep enough if Cinco could stay on top, hold on, keep the guy under, make him let go of the gun.

Cinco grabbed for clothing, feeling strangely slick material under his fingers. He pulled hard, something ripped and the guy twisted violently, trying to get his arms into play, to bring the pistol around. Cinco tried to squeeze harder, to use the clothing for control, but nothing worked.

Cinco felt his fingers being bent backward, painfully levering his arm away from the guy's body. His arm loosened slightly and the guy was easily out of his grasp, rising, his other arm coming up. Cinco shot to his feet, his hand full of river mud, flinging it at the guy's face as he made a grab for the gun.

Too late. The gun whipped down across his forehead.

Goddamn, not the lights again, Cinco thought. *It's always the goddamn lights . . .*

Tiny sparks of pain—tiny lights—burst in his head. He fell backward, the guy on him now, fingers wrapping on his throat, both of them rolling in the muddy water, only half submerged, both of them choking, sputtering.

There was only one move he could think of. He rammed his hand up into the guy's crotch, his fingers curling, searching for the guy's balls, ripping at the odd, slick material.

Again, too late.

He felt the pistol jam hard into the side of his face. He could smell it, taste it, knew it was the pistol that would end his life. Fuck it. He didn't care. He waited for the bullet, relaxing in surrender, his arm still around the guy, his hand still grabbing between his legs.

"What was it they used to say in high school . . . ?" the low, silky voice of a woman said as she spread her legs slightly and moved her crotch hard against his hand, ". . . I'll give you an hour to stop that."

FORTY-SEVEN

It was a blood moon coming, red-gold light slipping in wisps between the rocks and over the rim of the canyon. Not full moonlight yet, not daylight, not dark, but a time when the light is so heavy it seems not to illuminate, but to paint. A light that you can hold in your hands.

They were still in the edge of the river. He could feel the water under him. She had moved above him, sat on him, straddling his hips, the pistol punched firmly against his chest, at his heart, a black woman in black clothing in a near-black night, an almost invisible apparition until the heavy gold light began to fill in the curves of her, the secret places. Her blouse was ripped down the front, a piece of it hanging from a button. She made slight splashing movements with her legs as she settled herself.

"I should shoot you just for ruining my ninja outfit. Real silk. Bought it in Hong Kong. One of my favorite outfits."

She reached into the river and scooped some water onto the bleeding lump on his forehead, her fingers moving across his eyes, almost gently. Almost.

She sniffed at her fingers. "If I don't kill you, this water surely will."

He said nothing, waiting.

"Look at the pistol," she said.

Cinco did not move.

"I said, look at the pistol." She dug the long barrel harder into his chest.

He raised his head slightly, looking across his chest, trying to see the gun. It was a long-barreled revolver, heavy caliber. Nothing more, nothing less. Except that the woman was holding it oddly, her thumb wrapped around the hammer. He dropped his head back.

"You don't get it, do you? Look again." She punched the pistol into him again. He looked.

"You think I'm going to let this pistol get within your reach without some insurance? I've already pulled the trigger. Only thing between you and your other two buddies is my thumb, holding back the hammer. You make a move, you twitch, you even blink too hard, my thumb comes off this hammer and your lungs end up straining river water."

He dropped his head back. "Who the hell are you?"

"I'm either your executioner or your executioner. It's not much of a choice, don't you agree?"

"What the fuck are you talking about? And why do I get the feeling you could have killed me with the very first shot, back there at the house . . . and why didn't you?"

She tilted her head, seemed to be thinking about something. The pistol never moved.

"The first round was just to take a little of the fight out of you. Apparently, that didn't work. I kept shooting at you because it was gunfire that took away your memory. Just wanted to see if it would bring it back."

Gunfire took away my memory? What gunfire? Where? He started to ask her . . .

"Besides, I have a certain amount of professional admiration for how you took out the fat boy."

"Fat boy? Which fat boy?"

"Cut the shit. The guy back up canyon, in the truck."

"Angelo? You mean that wasn't your work?"

"*My* work? For Christ's sake, I would *never* do anything that messy. Anyway, messy or not, nice piece of work. Imaginative. Show-biz, almost. I liked it. The scalp was a nice touch."

She had been there, maybe at the same time he was there. But something was not adding up. He thought about Angelo, about drag marks, about the footprints. "I'm not sure I could have carried him to the river," he said, "and I don't think you could have, either."

The woman seemed to think about what he said. *Jesus, this isn't the time to figure this shit out.*

"Sure, she said. "Whatever. At this point, it doesn't matter."

She shrugged her shoulders, did not get it quite right, then with an exaggerated motion shrugged again. Her tattered blouse fell open, her breasts firm and golden-black in the heavy light. He thought maybe he had seen breasts like those—Christ, he *hoped* he had seen such breasts—but he didn't know, didn't know if he had seen them, touched them, tasted them.

He knew what was happening, tried to hold it off. Too late. He felt her raise her hips slightly, placing herself more carefully, searching for greater contact, greater sensation. He felt himself getting hard.

She felt it, too.

"Seems as though you've recovered some of your strength. That whore in El Paso couldn't get a rise out of you. Cost me twenty bucks to have her try. Wanted to see how sick you really were."

El Paso. He stored the words in his mind. Wouldn't try to sort it out now. But . . . El Paso. If she knew he was in El Paso, then she had put him there.

"The bus ticket cost me another twenty. Christ, I had to tell the whore to leave it in your pocket. Otherwise, she would have cashed it in."

She sent me here, to Santa Fe.

"You paid the whore? To give me an erection? What the hell would that tell you?"

"Jesus," she said, "I didn't pay her to give you a hard-on, I paid her to *fuck* you. Think about it. You're a *male*." She said "male" as though the word might die in her mouth. She shifted her hips slightly, feeling him grow. "I knew you were alive, but I didn't know how worn down you were. Males have some basic drives, right? First you want to stay alive. Then you want to fuck—even before you want to eat. I thought that if you fucked her, you were farther along on your comeback than I had hoped. Maybe even remember some things. But, nope, she couldn't get a rise out of you." She shifted her hips again, hunching against him now. "But I can."

She reached under her and pulled his penis from the old cotton pants, gripping him firmly.

His breath got jumbled in his throat.

"Pyat," she said. "Does that word mean anything to you?"

"Pyat." He rolled the word around in his mind, trying not to feel the movement of her hand. He knew the word. "Five," he said. "It means five." And he knew it was Russian.

"Now we're getting somewhere."

"I thought we already were somewhere."

"Not really. But here's the best part." She gently placed him inside her under the water, settling him deeply, moving her hips, the pistol still punched into his chest.

"You're the one who ripped the crotch out of my ninja outfit. Is this what you had in mind?"

Cinco tried not to move, tried not to participate, but his resolve lasted only seconds. He drove himself up against her, deeper inside her.

"Dnevnik." How about that one? That word mean anything?"

Journal. He said it in his mind. But he did not say it aloud. If he admitted there was a journal—*if* there were a journal—he was probably dead.

His breath was coming harder now, short bursts in time with the movements of her hips.

"Here's the deal," she said, "I don't mind fucking you. But I didn't come here to fuck. I came here to get the journal, or to kill you, whichever happens first."

Or to kill me anyway.

With a quick movement she pulled away from him, moving her leg across his body and kneeling in the mud beside him, the pistol never leaving his chest.

He felt the sound gather in his chest, some primeval grunt, some guttural rasp that rose into his mouth.

She was smiling. "Tough, isn't it. You lying there, hard as a rock. Can't even remember the last time you had an orgasm. Can't even finish yourself off, afraid I'll shoot you just for trying.

"Oh, hell, enough of this high school bullshit." She stood up and moved quickly out of his reach, her blouse still hanging in shreds from her shoulders, her breasts seeming to glow in the pale light.

"Stand up." She flicked the gun barrel at him.

He gathered his legs under him, wondering if he could get to her before . . .

"I don't want to kill you before we've had a chance to talk about the journal, but I can, if that's what you want."

He stood up, water dripping from his body, his pants hanging on his hips, blood running from his shoulder.

She laughed. "Didn't take you long to go soft, did it?" She laughed again. "Looking into the bore of a gun will do that to you.

"Now, back up—move out into the river."

Cinco could feel the thin mud under his feet, like heavy silk, the kind of feeling a man might yearn for before he dies. He moved backward, carefully. The water rose to his hips.

"That's far enough. That's enough water to keep you from doing anything quickly. Besides, my thumb's getting tired." She let the trigger move forward, cocking the hammer back.

"Now I want you to listen to me," she said, her voice losing any softness, a hard edge creeping in. "I'm tired of this job, I'm tired of this town, I got tired of following those two fat guys and the hillbilly, tired of waiting to see if the fat guys would kill you. And, come to think of it, I'm tired of you.

"This is over. This whole thing. One way or another, I'm going to get paid. Like I said, I came for the journal. I know you have it. You had a page from it back at the house. I read the page. Interesting stuff, what there was of it. Now I want the rest of it."

A scrap of paper, fluttering to the floor in front of the old comoda. And then the question hit him. *How did it get there?*

And worse, *She's been in the house.*

"Give me the journal," the woman said, "the whole thing, and I'll let you live. I'll even split my payday with you. Even better, I'll fuck you again, really fuck you, for days if you want. Unbridled sex. Anything you want." She paused, her voice dropping to a lower register, her face hardening. "Or, you can tell me you don't have the journal, don't know where it is, and I'll just twitch my finger and turn your heart into dog food. Your choice. Either way, this is over."

He did not believe her, of course. Nothing she said was real. No matter what, he was dead.

Other two buddies? Is that what she said?

"You knew the others?"

"What?"

"The others. The other two buddies."

"Goddammit, you're a few pages behind in the script, Pyat"

He stood in the center of the river, his life divided between the sides, an ancient ranch on the east, a wilderness on the west. Water flowed around his hips and he thought he should piss in it, but then he wondered why he thought such a thing at a time like this. At a time when he was going to die. He was tired. There had been nothing but death around him since he came to this place, to this river. Maybe the woman was right. Maybe this was a good time for it to be over. No regrets.

How the hell can I regret a life I don't even remember? He laughed softly.

The black woman stood in the edge of the river, the water barely covering her feet. She sighed deeply, the breath of her rushing softly out of her body. Maybe he really didn't know, didn't know about the journal, didn't know about anything. He was standing there, laughing. He was useless. He was crazy. She could feel the weight of the pistol pulling at her hand.

Cinco did not look at the gun the woman held on him, unwavering, the brushed stainless surface trying to catch the moonlight, the sweat and river water running in small lines from her face and arms, down across her breasts. But none of it on the gun. She was so close, and yet he knew he could never drive himself through the water fast enough to get to her before she brought the big gun to life.

She raised the gun slightly, the muzzle directly at his chest. She was close enough for an easy offhand shot, but she would not do that. She would aim. She would skillfully blow out his heart.

He did not look at the gun. He did not have to. His nerves were on the surface of his skin. He knew where the gun was and he thought when the time came he would be able to see the bullet blow from the barrel and hit him, see the gun smoke, hear the dull thunder. But knew he would not. He would already be dead.

He did not look at the gun. He looked into the woman's face.

He waited.

The woman did not move. She stood on higher, firmer ground, her legs spread, looking down at him. "Twenty years, Pyat," she said softly, "twenty years of hardship

that would have killed the average man, and you come to this." She centered the pistol on his chest.

Pyat. Russian. He would try one last gamble.

"Fuck you," he muttered. "If I didn't tell the fucking Russians, I'll never tell you."

The woman hesitated, a stunned look on her face.

"The Russians!? You remember the Russians!? You son-of-a-bitch, how long have you . . ."

There was a flicker of movement before his eyes, something passing that he did not see but knew was there, the batting of some cosmic eye, a movement so subtle that it might have not been a movement at all. But he knew what it was, because he heard the noise of the movement. The noise, a heavy whisper that followed the flicker, the sound of a bird's wing being ripped through the air.

The black woman slowly lowered her head to look at her chest. Exactly between her breasts a long blossom of feathers had appeared, their edges ragged, their colors the somber hues of birds of prey. Except for one. Bright red. She studied the feathers, not touching them, not believing they were there. But they were.

The woman's gun arm began to lower slowly, until it hung straight down, her hand relaxing, the heavy gun slipping gently from her fingers and falling into the water with hardly any noise at all.

She stared at the feathers.

Her legs began to lose their purpose, buckling slightly at the knees. She did not try to stop them. She did not try to stop anything. Her eyes could see and her brain could display the sight but the woman was already dead.

Her legs bent more and then she was in the river on her knees, her softly relaxing upper body leaning slightly forward, then more, and then she fell face-down into muddy water so shallow that it barely reached her back, the current so slow that it did not move her body, as though the river had stopped in order to accept this new offering, another death in a line of deaths that reached a thousand years into the past.

Her body did not move. The arrow, thick and bloody, rose from her back, the heavy arrowhead pointing straight at the sky.

An arrow? He bent forward, squinting in the weak light of the moon, staring at the arrowhead that pointed at the sky. He cupped his hands in the river and let the water run over the arrowhead and down the shaft, rinsing off most of the blood. He leaned closer. He saw the black, obsidian arrowhead. He saw the thin red stripe that ran down the shaft and into the woman's body. A bloodline.

His legs weakened and he crumpled into the water, sitting beside the woman, staring at the arrow.

And then he saw into his own mind.

He felt a flash of light inside his head—no, not light, something else . . .

a glass jar full of rust-colored dirt

. . . something with weight, heavy, falling on his entire being and yet totally within his body . . .

an ancient leather belt, dry and cracked from the years, a silver coin falling from a tiny slot in the back

posole in heavy bowls on a the thick surface of hand-planed table

. . . and things awful and strange and terrible . . .

a rude shack, a stovepipe sticking at an odd angle through the roofa man coming, with a knifeforests and running dogsrunning, always running, images of running a man in a heavy, dark coat, handing him a cigara room full of people, eating, drinking, laughing, laughing at hima clumsy truck with a crude wooden coffin frozen to the worn planking of the bedthe sear of quick leather on naked skin gunfire, more than he had ever heardgunfiregunfire

. . . something he wanted so desperately that he began to go light-headed, something that filled him with enormous dread . . .

the Russians, the goddamned Russians

He stared at the arrowhead.

He rose, stood straight, his face raised to the blood moon, the heavy light filling him. He turned carefully, facing west, staring into the wilderness.

"Wendell," he said, much too softly.

"*Wendell!*"

The weight of his history, his life, filled him.

And he was terrified.

"WEN-DELL!! WHERE THE HELL ARE YOU?!" he screamed into the black wilderness.

There was no answer.

EPILOGUE

from the journal of Cinco Becknell

The birds awaken me and I lie quietly. I hear a coyote, somewhere far down canyon. The woman and I lie on the bed in a large room of the old house, the door to the outside fully open, the early winter air crisp and hard, thick woolen blankets covering us. In my mind I hear the words of Pete Catches, an Oglala already gone to meet his grandfathers, words I have read in the Johnson book, words I have memorized . . .

> At first light showing in the east,
> I lie listening to the coyotes howling
> and the owls in the canyon hooting,
> and I do nothing but listen.
> Pretty soon, on the eaves of my house,
> little birds begin to sing their morning song,
> the waking song . . .

I have been repeating the words every morning for weeks, mouthing them in half-whisper, trying not to awaken her. But, although she does not move, I know that she is awake, always listening to the words.

Time seems to have calmed things down.

Cord and some local deputies pulled Grace from the river. It was ruled self defense. I said that she had been shooting at me for some unknown reason—Elena said that the woman was crazy—and that I grabbed the only weapon I could find to defend myself. An arrow. And that was the end of it.

Lots of arrows lying around the ranch, Elena had said.

She never questioned where the arrow really came from. And I never told her what I thought.

Elena gave the pistol to Cordova. It was the same pistol used to fire at Elena, that was fired when they killed Pablo, that fired a bullet into the brain of the girl in the arroyo. Angelo's pistol. A lot of cases got closed because of that pistol, or so Cord said.

Elena brought an old farm tractor out to the ranch and I used it to drag the blackened hulk of Angelo's truck out to the main road, where some scrap-yard guys picked it up. They didn't ask any questions and I didn't offer any answers.

They have stopped looking for Angelo. Deputies made one short foray across the river and then came back, sure that no one could survive over there, not for long.

Things have a way of disappearing in the Rio Grande. Always have.

There was never enough evidence to point the finger toward anyone in Beano's death. Cord is sure I did it, but I am not sure he really cares. Cord is not an enemy, but he is not a friend. He is Cord. I think if Elena snapped her fingers, Cord would snap my neck. I'll have to keep her fingers otherwise occupied.

I never saw Hale Mary, or the Mechanic, or the Engineer again. They simply disappeared from Santa Fe. About a month after the death of Little Jimmy, Mulligan appeared once again at his place on the corner. For an entire day he stood at his spot and played

"Amazing Grace" on his sax. Only that song. Nothing else. The next day he did not show up, and no one has seen him since.

I jog up and down the canyon every day, then strip and lie in the bathing pool behind the house. Sometimes Elena joins me. She hangs towels and thick cotton robes on the stumps of tree limbs sticking out from the ancient cottonwoods. Sometimes we get all the way back to the bed before we are dry.

Now and then Matt Klah comes out and we run the canyon rim, always ending up overlooking the river and into the Jemez beyond. I do not know if we are actually racing, but if we are, Matt always wins. Sometimes we stand looking over into the wilderness until we are too cooled to run and have to start walking back to the ranch. I know what Matt is looking for. He never, not for a moment, bought the story about my finding an arrow to use as a weapon. But neither of us know what to do next. Except wait.

Alvarez is dead. I know that, and I know that he has been dead for a long time. I know how he died, and I know how much I loved him. It took me more than a week to get it all out, to explain it all to Elena. I cried, just like I cried for Jimmy. It seems the only time I cry is when someone dies.

I ease out of bed and go into the kitchen and build a fire in the fireplace. The kitchen is soon warm and I make some coffee, knowing that the aroma will bring the woman from the bedroom.

And it does. Elena stands in the doorway. She is wearing a robe that hangs open in the front. She glides across the room, takes a sip of the coffee, takes my hand, and leads me back to the bedroom.

And that just leaves the journal, and the middle part of my life.

I have slowly started telling Elena about Siberia. I have to do it a small bit at a time. I am still not sure whether I am dreaming, that I will wake up and find that I am not in New Mexico. I am pretty sure

I would not want to live over that. She will hear the whole story, in time.

In a small cave up on the canyon wall to the north of the ranch house, there is a five-gallon bucket wrapped in plastic and buried under some rocks. In the bucket are countless scraps of paper detailing more than 20 years of my life in a prison camp. I was a soldier, a spy, and I got caught. And no one cared. Specifically, not my government.

Except, no one wanted the journal to go public.

Someone hired Grace to find it. She did not. And I am still alive. And Grace did not live to explain.

That probably means that someone else will come looking for it.

If someone comes, Elena says, we will deal with it. And I will not be alone next time.

I plan to read the journal, to organize it, to write it fully. But not until I know I am safe. And that day may never come.

There is snow on Baldy now, but a good cigar can keep a man warm.

This evening, as I do most evenings, I will go down to the river and sit on a rock and wait. I will sit there until I see some movement, some flicker from the thick brush on the other side of the river. The movement could be an animal, a bird. But I do not think so.

ABOUT THE AUTHOR

Lee Maynard was born and raised deep in the mountains of West Virginia, a location that drives the emotion and grit of most of his writing. He says he had never had a "career." Rather, he sought out "day jobs" while doing his real job—writing. Among several other things, he has been a criminal investigator, college president, and COO of a national experiential education organization. He now lives and writes at the edge of an Indian reservation in the high desert of New Mexico. He is the author of *The Pale Light of Sunset: Scattershots and Hallucinations in an Imagined Life* and the Crum trilogy: *Crum, Screaming with the Cannibals,* and *The Scummers.*

CPSIA information can be obtained
at www.ICGtesting.com
Printed in the USA
FFOW01n1243090415
12512FF